Scandal's Daughter

By Emma V. Leech

****

Published by: Emma V. Leech.

Cover Art: Victoria Cooper
ASIN: B06ZY9PMNW
ISBN-13: 978-1545392409
ISBN-10: 1545392404

Table of Contents

Where true Love burns Desire is Love's pure flame;
It is the reflex of our earthly frame,
That takes its meaning from the nobler part,
And but translates the language of the heart.

Desire by Samuel Coleridge

Prologue

Eton. Windsor. England. September 1798.

To Sebastian Grenville, newly The Duke of Sindalton, this year had been the most miserable and painful of his short life. A life that had now been subject to further upheaval by getting sent away from his home to school at Eton. At twelve years old he had lost his charismatic father in a scandal that had rocked the *ton* to their foundations; and now everything he knew, everything that was dear to him and familiar, was gone.

That was bad enough, but coming from a home where he was cherished and feted as the heir to the dukedom to a cold and unwelcoming place, was almost more than he could bear. He was regarded with a mixture of appalled awe and disgust in the light of his father's actions.

A previously loquacious and confident boy, in a matter of months he had turned inward, lost a vast amount of weight - making him gangly and awkward - and most mortifying of all, developed a stutter.

The bullying had been as inevitable as it was terrifying and it was with a resigned and fateful air that he watched Lord Robert

'Boko' Bexley's fat fist swing back to *'draw his cork'* with a fateful punch.

The hand trembled in mid air for a brief moment before losing its momentum, but this was curious rather than relieving to one who had lost any interest in life or the effort of living it. It was also strange to see the dawning look of anxiety on Boko Bexley's face, as a bored and cut-glass voice drawled behind him, "I really shouldn't do that if I were you."

Boko was a ruddy faced, square-jawed boy who naturally excelled at sports but could barely add two and two without the help of his blunt, stubby digits. That being the case, coming face to face with the deadliest tongue in the entire school was not something the little Lord entered into lightly. The Marquis of Beaumont was also in his first year but his fame had already been established long before he set foot on Eton's hallowed grounds. His reputation was that of having a fast pair of fists and a way with words that could shred a boy many years older to devastating effect.

Sebastian turned his head, which was not as easy as it sounded with Boko's meaty left hand wrapped around his throat, while his face awaited the attentions of his right. Although he'd heard of the Marquis, as had the whole damn school, this was the first time Sebastian had laid eyes on him. His own dark brown eyes met those of a startling, if rather icy, blue. A mop of thick blond hair crowned the most angelic face that had ever graced the visage of a twelve year old boy.

"This is none of your affair, Beau," Boko said, his voice full of righteous indignation and just the hint of a whine.

"Not so," Beau replied, his demeanour one of someone bearing bad news. "You see, I've decided it is, and so ... there you have it." The angelic countenance confronted Boko's scowling, mulish expression as Beau gave an apologetic shrug, apologetic because the only way for Boko to now save face was to fight Beau.

Ten minutes later and Boko was being supported by his cronies as he stemmed the tide of a very bloody nose.

"M-much obliged to you," stammered Sebastian, looking at his strange angel-faced saviour with something close to awe. "Though I don't understand w-why you s-should help me."

A slight frown creased the saintly mien and the Marquis gave a shrug. "Neither do I," he replied. "I tend to act on a whim now and then, devil knows why." He grinned suddenly and Sebastian could see a lot more of the devil in his laughing eyes than the angel that innocent face might imply. "Besides," he added. "I was interested to meet someone whose father was as much a black-hearted scoundrel as mine still is."

Sebastian gaped at him, unsure whether to be furious at the insult to his late father or shocked and impressed that he should speak of his own in such an insulting manner. He was saved from the trouble of figuring it out as Beau spoke again, amused by his dumbfounded expression. "Oh, come on. You're not going to tell me that if your father appeared to you from beyond the veil you wouldn't have a few choice words for him?"

"W-well ... no," Sebastian replied somewhat doubtfully. Further discussion was halted, however, as the bell intoned sonorously over the quad.

"Good God!" Beau exclaimed. "We're going to miss breakfast. Come on, I'm starving." And grasping Sebastian firmly by the hand he towed his new friend behind him, back into the school.

Chapter 1

"Wherein lifelong friends discuss the idiocy of the past and plan for the future."

London. August 1816

Sebastian remembered that fateful day, some seventeen years earlier, with a wry smile. He hadn't seen his closest friend for almost six months and was chagrined to find he'd missed the insolent fool. Beau could push his temper to the limit like no one else, never mincing his words or curbing his sharp tongue. But for Sebastian, who was at the receiving end of constant toadying and flattery in most every other quarter, it was as refreshing as it was brutal.

A slight scratching on the door made him aware of the presence of his butler, the redoubtable Biddle, who announced the Marquis as the man himself walked into the room.

"Well, well," Sebastian drawled, lounging back in his chair and regarding Beau with amusement. "The return of the prodigal son."

Beau lifted an eyebrow, his cool blue eyes amused. He turned to Sebastian, raising his hands in a beatific manner. "Father, I have sinned against heaven and before you. I am no longer worthy to be called your son."

"Well that I do believe," Sebastian replied, snorting with amusement. "I'm only amazed you could remember the quote, you heathen."

"Don't talk to me of heathens," Beau said in disgust, taking a seat and waving his hand to indicate Sebastian should get him a drink. "Six months! Six whole months in that God forsaken place. I was almost ready to cast myself in the river, I can tell you. And *I'd* have been damn sure to find myself one that was good and deep."

"Ah yes," Sebastian said, grinning as he got to his feet to pour them both a drink. "And how is the estimable Lady Worth?"

Beau scowled at him and took his proffered drink with a huff of annoyance. "Bearing in mind I've been in Scotland for the sole reason of *not* knowing how Lady Worth is, I can't help but feel you are trying to annoy me."

"As if I would," Sebastian murmured, returning to his seat. "Still, she lives at least, that much I do know. No more the worse for her plunge into the river Cam," he added, chuckling.

Beau gave him a dark look. "It may seem amusing to you but I have suffered on account of that idiotic creature. I'm almost sorry the fool didn't realise the Cam is rarely more than three feet deep and tried the Thames instead. Though if she really intended to put a period to her life it's a wonder she didn't think to try it without a dozen of her admirers there to pull her out again."

"Well, perhaps that will teach you to trifle with married ladies," Sebastian said, his tone chastising, though his eyes still danced with laughter. "So tell me," he continued, ignoring the look of disgust on his friend's face. "Are you getting the cut direct or do people still acknowledge you in the street?"

Beau snorted and stretched his long legs out in front of him. "Oh it seems as if I may have come through it well enough, though I've not seen my father yet," he added with a casual tone that didn't fool Sebastian for a moment. Beau's father was a cruel and malicious man who delighted in tormenting his only son and heir.

"Are you going to?" Sebastian watched the shadow flit over Beau's face before he looked up, seeing Sebastian watching him.

"Not if I can help it," he replied, the glimmer of a smile appearing. "Actually I was going to go down to Cornwall. Gower invited me, said you could come too by the way."

"To Carn Brea?"

Beau nodded. "He's promised entertainment," he added, grinning and downing the last of his drink in one large swallow

Sebastian pursed his lips. He had a fair notion of their friend Lord Gower's entertainments and was discouraged to discover the idea bored him. In fact he had been aware for some time of a creeping sense of disquiet and dissatisfaction. Since his father's scandalous exploits he had become hardened to gossip but, besides a shocking and well-deserved reputation with the ladies, he rarely did anything to set tongues wagging too hard. He gambled moderately and rarely drank to excess. Unfortunately his friendship with Beau was such that he didn't need to. Beau was a scandal looking for a place to happen and Sebastian was tarnished by association.

"Oh come on, Sin," Beau wheedled. "Don't say you won't. I've been devilish bored and it won't be the same if you don't come."

Letting out a breath, Sebastian frowned and stared at Beau. "Oh very well, I could do with getting out of London, truth be told. Not that the weather looks very promising."

"God no, it's bloody freezing, more like March than August though it was worse in the North I can tell you," Beau grumbled. "I was surprised to find you here actually. Thought I'd have to head out to that crumbling pile of yours to ferret you out."

"It is not crumbling," Sebastian retorted, though he well knew Beau was baiting him. His interest and the amount of time he devoted to his estate was something that had always bewildered Beau who had begun referring to him as Farmer Grenville. "And I'm hiding from Mother," he admitted.

"Ah," Beau nodded his understanding. "On about you getting riveted again I don't doubt."

Sebastian acknowledged this with a grimace. He was well aware of what was due to his rank and his obligation to provide an heir. He had agreed over eighteen months ago that he should take a wife and soon. Agreeing to do the right thing and actually going through with it, however, were entirely different things. Now, though, everyone knew he was in the market for a wife and he was heartily sick of having every eligible young woman thrust in his face at every turn.

The sight of another simpering miss batting her eyelashes at him in the hope of becoming his duchess was enough to turn his stomach and have him running for the hills. He had even gone so far as to compile a list of all the attributes necessary in his future spouse in the hope of making a sensible decision - something Beau had thought hilarious in the extreme. In Beau's absence, however, he had met the Comtesse de Lavelle and thrown the list away.

What a beauty she had been, and not at all in the ordinary way. There had been an intelligence and a weight of experience in her eyes that belied her youth. But Celeste Lavelle was missing. He didn't believe for a moment the story that Lady Seymour had spread that she had gone to stay with family in France and guilt twisted in his stomach. There was something between her and Falmouth, he was sure of it. The foolish child was in love with him but a rake like the earl would never marry her. Sebastian had been struck with the chivalrous longing to save her, to protect her from her own folly, and all of his plans and lists had gone out of the window.

In a move he now shuddered to remember he had sent Mrs Morris, Falmouth's glamorous mistress, to the man's London home to make a scene. A scene that Celeste would be unable to ignore. She would see just the kind of man Falmouth was and when Sebastian came the next day to make his offer of marriage, she would be moved to accept.

But Mrs Morris had gone too far. She'd had her own score to settle with Falmouth and settle it she had. When Sebastian had arrived the next day he had been greeted with frigid politeness by Falmouth's sister in law and given the news that Celeste was not at home. When she continued not to be at home for another ten days and rumours began to circulate he had forced Mrs Morris to tell him everything. His anger had been something to behold.

"Penny for them," Beau demanded, forcing him out of his reverie.

He shook his head.

"Still no news of your French fancy then?" he asked, one eyebrow cocked.

Sebastian scowled. Beau had an uncanny habit of knowing what he was thinking. He should never have told him about Celeste but the guilt of his actions had been eating away at him and he'd needed to unburden himself. Beau, as ever, was a good sounding board.

"What about Mrs Morris?" his friend asked, curiosity glittering in those cold blue eyes. "Are you still her protector?"

"After what she did?" Sebastian replied in disgust. He shook his head and traced the pattern on the crystal glass he held with one long finger. "I think not. Why?" he asked, looking up. "Are you interested?"

"Good God no." Beau grimaced and flicked a piece of lint from the sleeve of his perfectly tailored jacket. "A ready buttered bun has never been to my taste," he murmured, a flash of malice in his eyes.

"Vulgar, Beau," Sebastian said, his tone reproving. "Vulgar."

Beau laughed, perfectly unrepentant.

"So, as we speak exactly how many lonely Scottish ladies are languishing with broken hearts or throwing themselves off bridges now you have left them alone, pray tell?" Sebastian asked, turning the conversation back to Beau.

His friend raised one haughty eyebrow. "A quite respectable number I'm sure," he replied with utter seriousness.

For a moment Sebastian was appalled by Beau's apparent lack of regard for the women he dallied with. It was something he had always had a problem with, how Beau, who was such a loyal friend and capable of quite humbling, if capricious, acts of kindness, could be such a cold-hearted brute where women were concerned. "She's ruined, you know," he said, watching Beau's face for any trace of regret or guilt. He found none.

"Well that's what you get for throwing yourself off a bridge in front of a dozen or more spectators," he said in disgust. "When I think of the pains I took to be discreet ... and it's not the slightest bit of use looking at me with such reproach. It's not like I seduced an innocent. Idiotic woman, she well knew there was nothing serious in it."

"You don't always choose who you fall in love with, Beau."

"Love?" Beau replied, his face incredulous. "She didn't love me. You know as well as I do a woman like that doesn't love anything more than your title and your purse."

Sebastian was shocked by the vitriol of his words, not that he could contradict him. He'd learnt at a very young age the truth of it and shut his true feelings far away, though perhaps not quite as far as Beau had managed. Celeste had reminded him that it was possible for him to feel, though he had no illusions about being in love with the girl. They had only met a handful of times, but it had reminded him that he was flesh and blood and that his feelings were still there, dormant, but not dead.

"Well then, it's agreed," Beau said, returning to the earlier point of their conversation. "We'll head down to Gower's in the morning, yes?"

Sebastian nodded his agreement. "I'll pick you up at eight. Do *not* keep me waiting," he warned, giving him a fierce look from under thick dark brows.

Beau rolled his eyes. "Why do we have to leave at such an ungodly hour of the morning?"

"Because I say so."

"Yes, your Grace," Beau replied, giving a rather impressive imitation of Biddle.

Sebastian grinned. "Quite so. But mind we keep off Falmouth's estate. It borders Gower's if I remember rightly, and I doubt he'll be glad to see me."

"Really?" Beau said, his expression thoughtful. "I wonder if I could arrange it. Now that *would* be entertaining."

Chapter 2

"Wherein we meet our heroine, as yet blissfully unaware of the future."

Georgiana strode into the house, flinging her bonnet onto a chair in the hallway and calling for her uncle. An excitable black dog of indeterminate parentage followed her, tongue lolling after a morning of great exertion. Making her way down a slightly shabby corridor with a worn carpet and a draft coiling around the window that made her shiver, she gave a peremptory rap on the study door. Entering a moment later, she found her uncle with his head bent over an enormous medical text.

With a sigh her relative glanced up and gave her a look of reproach as she flung herself down in the chair in front of his desk. She blinked up at him, wondering what she'd done now and raised an enquiring hand to her hair to find it had, as usual, escaped all of her pins and was in a tangled mess of fiery locks about her shoulders.

She gave him a sheepish grin and shrugged. "I took the medicine to the Farley's. They say the boy's fever broke last night like you said and he's sitting up and complaining fiercely about being an invalid."

Her uncle, Doctor Joseph Bomford, a small but stocky man was blessed with a mild manner and a pleasant face with neatly trimmed white hair and sideburns. He nodded and removed his spectacles, placing them carefully on the pages of the massive text book.

"I thought as much. Well thank you for running the errand. Did you tell them I'd call in tomorrow to see how he goes on?"

"I did." Georgiana nodded, grimacing as she tried to pin her hair back into something Aunt Jane wouldn't scold her for. She looked up to see Uncle Jo watching her with affection. He gestured to her right shoulder, one eyebrow raised.

"You missed a bit."

"Oh, thank you." She grinned, tucking the errant strand back up with the rest. Getting to her feet she went to stand beside the fire, which was lit even in August due to the terrible lack of any real summer, and commenced absently picking horse hair off the fine merino wool of her riding habit. Though more than two seasons old and a little frayed, the olive green sat well with the shocking blaze of her red hair, and unlike most of her clothing, she tried her best to keep it in good order.

"I've been wanting to speak with you," her uncle said, making her look up. "You're not to go riding out alone towards the Gower estate for the next few weeks."

Georgiana frowned with annoyance. Some of her favourite places were along the land that bordered the neighbouring estate. "Why ever not?" she demanded. "Old Gower said I could go where I liked, you know he did."

"Old Gower may well have done," he said, a stern look on his usually mild face. "But old Gower is not in residence, young Gower is, and from what I've heard of the goings on up there you'll keep well clear and that is my final word on the matter."

Georgiana opened her mouth and closed it again. Her uncle and guardian was the sweetest and kindest of men and she had never felt the lack of a father for he filled the role in every way that anyone could hope for. But she well recognised the set of his jaw and doubted she could change his mind. Indeed she considered herself more than fortunate that he and his wife, her Aunt Jane, had been kind enough to take on their orphaned niece. They'd had no children of their own and doted on Georgiana as though she was their own daughter. Nonetheless, she was sorely disappointed that some of her favourite riding country was now out of bounds.

She huffed in annoyance and folded her arms. "So what dark doings are going on up there then? Orgies I've no doubt," she muttered, wondering why on earth that should stop her from going where she pleased.

"Georgiana!"

She looked up to see her uncle staring at her in shock and bit her tongue.

"Sorry, Pops," she said, using the pet name for him that never failed but to soften his eyes. He had refused to let her call him father when she was a child, deeming that it wasn't his right, but he had allowed the affectionate nickname and she knew it pleased him. She grinned and he rolled his eyes at her.

"I'm going to take every one of those wretched novels away from you if you don't have a care and curb that tongue of yours," he scolded, tutting at her. "Orgies indeed. As if you have the slightest idea ..."

"Oh of course I do!" she replied, choking with laughter. "It's like a great party where ..."

"Georgiana!"

She smacked her hand over her mouth, trying and failing to hold back her laughter while her scandalised uncle looked at her in horror. He picked up his spectacles and waved them at her.

"You will stay away from the Gower estate and if the word *orgy* escapes your lips in your Aunt's hearing you'll get everything that's coming to you. I give you a great deal too much freedom, miss. Allowing you to go racketing about the countryside with none but that idiotic dog for company." He tutted and Georgiana looked down at the far from idiotic dog who had raised his head and thumped a happy tail on hearing himself referred to.

"I know, Conrad," she said as the mongrel scurried to his feet, tail wagging with enthusiasm and gazing up at her with adoration. "You are a very fine guard dog, aren't you? Why just this morning he saved me from an attack by a very vicious hare, didn't you, love. Yes, I know," she crooned, stroking the ecstatic hound as she pulled his soft ears in just the way he like.

Her uncle heaved a sigh. "Conrad," he repeated, not for the first time. "If ever there was a more ridiculous name for a dog I've yet to hear it." He shook his head and waved his hands at her. "Now run along, foolish girl, and find your aunt. I've no doubt she can find something more productive for you to do than ride about the countryside like a hoyden or sit here and annoy me," he said, though the warmth in his words dispelled any possible notion of a real scolding. "Off you go now, and mind what I told you about the Gower estate. You stay away. And no more talk of orgies!"

"Yes, Pops," she replied, casting an impish grin over her shoulder and calling Conrad to follow her as she closed the door and left her uncle to his studies.

Her uncle, Doctor Bomford, was a very respected man in the area, in fact the Earl of Falmouth himself had sought a second opinion from him before now when a wound had gone bad, having had no great opinion of the doctor who had historically treated him and his family since he was in short trousers.

The doctor's wife, Jane - Georgiana's aunt - was from an old and very wealthy family and when she disobliged them by marrying beneath her they had cut her off without a penny. Happily it was a love match and while Georgiana might see her aunt sighing with longing over the fashion plates in the latest copy of *La Belle Assemblée,* and wondering how she was going to remake an old dress to look like a new one, she never believed she had for a moment regretted her decision. Georgiana only hoped that she might one day find a man as agreeable as her uncle, and as happy to turn a blind eye to her habit of *racketing about the countryside alone.*

She found Aunt Jane in the scullery, tutting sadly over the state of the linens, for it was wash day and the scullery was heaped with dripping fabrics in various states of the process. With a sinking heart Georgiana knew that what was about to come her way was hours of sitting and helping her aunt mend and repair.

The scullery was thick with the heavy, damp fog of hot water and wet linen. Georgiana stepped across the duckboards by the sink to give the young housemaid a grimace of sympathy as the girl stirred the great copper. Water ran in thick rivulets down the clouded window behind the copper and Mary looked up at her, grinning and wiping the sweat from her face on her plump arm before poking another armful of linens into the bubbling water with the laundry stick.

"Oh there you are, Georgiana," Aunt Jane said with obvious relief. "Do tell me your uncle has no other errands for you today for I am at my wit's end.

"No, indeed, Aunt," Georgiana replied, though her reply was so despondent that Aunt Jane couldn't help but chuckle.

"Oh come now, we'll sit in the back parlour. The fire's been lit, and I shall get a tray of tea brought while we make the best of this heap of tatters," she replied, looking at the mountain of linen with just as much dismay as Georgiana had. "We can enjoy a comfortable prose and you can tell me all the gossip you've no doubt gleaned on your jaunt to the Farley's this morning."

Georgiana nodded and tried her best to look as though it didn't sound like a terrible waste of an afternoon. "I'll go and change and be with you in a trice, Aunt."

An hour later, changed into a much worn and mended spotted dimity gown, Georgiana looked up from her mending as Mary came in bearing a tea tray.

"Just pop it on the table, Mary," her aunt said, smiling at the girl. "We'll serve ourselves."

The maid did as she was bid but Georgiana exclaimed as the girl put the tray down.

"Why, Mary, look at your hands! They're all red and chapped. Do go and get the pot of cream by my bed and put some on, you poor thing."

Mary blushed and stammered about it being nothing at all but Georgiana was adamant. "Nonsense, go and use it this instant or I shall go and fetch it for you."

Bobbing a curtsy, Mary left the room with a devout promise to do just as she was bid.

Georgiana looked up to see Aunt Jane chuckling at her. "What?"

"Nothing, my dear. You have the kindest heart and it does you credit but ... well you are very *determined* in your advice on occasion, love."

Snorting with amusement, Georgiana looked back down at her row of uneven stitches with a frown. "Bossy is the word you are searching for, Aunt," she replied, wondering whether she should unpick the lot and start over.

"Oh, no, dear," her aunt replied with a placid tone. "Just a little ..."

"Overbearing?" she added helpfully, at which her aunt laid down her needlework and glared at her niece.

"Do stop putting words in my mouth, dear. It's just that a young lady ought not to be so ... well, sure of herself."

"Oh, fiddle," Georgiana replied, deciding against starting the work over again and picking up another sadly frayed piece of work. "I refuse to act like those empty-headed ninnyhammers who go around blushing and stammering like the feather brains they are. I *do* have a brain in my head and if I can see something needs doing I don't see why I oughtn't say so."

"Well, because gentlemen don't like a girl to have opinions, that's why. Particularly not strong ones!" her Aunt replied, sounding flustered now as she put her needlework to one side and turned her attention to the tea tray. "And you don't want to get a reputation for being ... *fast,"* she mouthed, as though the word was too offensive to say out loud.

Georgiana yelped with laughter. "Fast?" she crowed, stabbing her thumb with the needle in the disarray caused by her amusement. "Ow! Oh dear, Aunt Jane, where pray do you think I could get a reputation for *that ... around here?"* She stuck her injured thumb in her mouth in an attempt to curb her laughter as her aunt was looking really rather cross.

Huffing, the older lady put a cup of tea in her hand and admonished her not to bleed on the linens. "And from what I hear you'd need not go far at all. Not safe for decent folk," she muttered, with a sad shake of her head.

"Whatever do you mean?" Georgiana demanded, and then remembered her Uncle's warning. "Oh do you mean up at the castle. Oh, Aunt! What have you heard?"

Her aunt sniffed and shook her head. "As if I would tell you!" she said in disgust, stirring sugar into her tea.

Georgiana pouted and her aunt set down her cup and saucer with a sniff. "Well ..." she said with reluctance. "They do say that the Marquis of Beaumont is there."

"No!" Georgiana exclaimed. "He's shown his face again at last. I was beginning to think he didn't have the pluck I believed he did."

"Georgiana!" Her aunt said, clutching at her bosom and returning a pained expression. "I should never have let you start reading those dreadful scandal rags. May I remind you that his *lady friend* tried to drown herself."

"Oh stuff," she replied, quite disregarding her aunt's cry of disquiet over her less than genteel observations. "By all accounts the woman had lived in Cambridge all her life so how she couldn't know the Cam is barely deep enough to wet her feet is beyond me. The only thing likely to kill her was catching a chill from going home in wet skirts. Oh and I think you'll find a fellow's mistress is called a Cytherean."

"Oh good God, Georgiana, you'll be the death of me, I do swear!" cried her appalled aunt.

Chuckling mischievously, Georgiana returned to her botched mending attempt.

"Well, just you stay away from the Gower estate, young lady. For all your reading and knowing talk you've no understanding of how these men carry on and I won't have you putting yourself in danger. If you don't promise me I'll have to make old Lambert your chaperone and you know how well you'd like that."

"Lambert!" Georgiana cried in horror. The crotchety old man who passed for their groom would suck the joy from any walk or ride through the countryside like blotting paper on wet ink.

Her aunt gave a sage nod, pleased that she'd been so well understood. "We'll be needing a quantity of dandelion as I'm set on making a good batch of dandelion and burdock. Your uncle looks a touch liverish to me and I think it would do him the world of good. So if I send you out to gather dandelions, be good and sure you don't head over that way."

"Oh but, Aunt! You know the four acre field has the best dandelions, it will take ..."

She stopped in her tracks as a forbidding look entered her aunt's usually placid blue eyes. "Yes, Aunt Jane," she said meekly, and returned her attention to the linens.

Chapter 3

"In which the beau monde is too rich for his grace's appetite."

Sebastian looked out of the window as the rain lashed the surrounding countryside and he wondered what in the name of God had induced him to come here. He raised a slightly unsteady hand to his head and winced as he applied it tenderly to his aching temple. Never again. It was a phrase that occurred to him all too often in the aftermath of one of Beau's nights of debauchery and had never seemed more apt.

He had a vague memory of the room he was standing in filled with revelry and half naked women and suppressed a groan. How the devil was he supposed to extricate himself now? Gower had professed to have given extensive thought to the following week or so's entertainments, no doubt with Beau egging him on, and last night, he'd said with relish, was only the start of it.

Easing himself with care into a tapestry covered wingback chair with a groan, he massaged his pulsing temples. The vast stone fireplace beside him belched forth a disagreeable plume of grey smoke every time the wind howled past the chimney and Sebastian frowned at it, putting some careful thought into the idea of going home. As soon as possible.

He was getting old, he decided with a melancholy sigh. Once upon a time he would have been just as happy to spend a debauched week or three in the country while his commitments and obligations could go to the devil. Now he couldn't help but look upon those commitments with a rather fonder eye and wish to go back to them. Marlburgh House was an ancient and sprawling pile full of draughts and leaks, and the land had been growing steadily sicker due to neglect during his own youth and mismanagement by those who should have been keeping the place in order. But after a great deal of investment and a lot of coaxing the surrounding lands were beginning to repay that investment. It was therefore with a wry smile that Sebastian realised he'd rather be walking his fields and talking to his estate manager about the terrible summer and how it would impact on all their future plans, than lounging about with a scantily clad female in his arms. He resolved to keep such thoughts to himself. If Beau ever discovered his thoughts he'd never hear the end of it.

Speaking of the devil, he thought in amusement as the man himself came and sat opposite him. Moving just as carefully as Sebastian had, Beau lowered himself into the chair with a soft groan and sat back with his eyes closed.

"I take it the brunette was every bit as energetic as you imagined she would be?" Sebastian said, smirking as Beau cracked open one bleary eye.

Beau shook his head and then winced, clearly deciding the movement was a bad idea. "She was a blonde," he murmured, pinching the bridge of his nose with long, elegant fingers.

Frowning, Sebastian cast his mind back to the admittedly foggy events of the previous evening. "No, she was definitely a brunette when she left."

Beau opened his eyes, frowning and then giving a little shrug. "Well I woke up with a blonde."

Sebastian snorted and shook his head. "I need to get out of here, get some air."

"In this? Are you mad?"

Casting an eye back towards the window and the rain that lashed against the window, Sebastian stretched out his legs. "This will be gone by midday. Will you come?"

"No," Beau replied. "I will not."

"Suit yourself."

"I always do."

Sebastian regarded his friend with a frown. There was something troubling Beau, he was sure of it. But Beau was not one to share his troubles as a rule. Though Sebastian knew Beau would never begrudge him his wealth he was prickly about his own lack of it. His father, the Duke of Ware, gave him a pittance of an allowance and it was only Beau's own skill and the devil's own luck with cards and dice that kept him afloat. Most of the time Beau was paying off one creditor just as another began to pound at the door. His extravagant lifestyle was not something he would in any way curtail. It was a situation that Sebastian rarely referred to. He'd tried, once, to speak to Beau and to lend him money to see him through a particularly awkward time, but it had led to the worst and most violent argument they'd ever had and he would never dare broach the subject again.

To his surprise he didn't have to, as Beau brought the subject up later the same day as they ate lunch together. Lord Gower still hadn't appeared, which surprised neither of them, having seen the state of him last night.

"I have to marry," Beau said, staring with a gloomy expression into a mug of ale.

"Ah," Sebastian replied. "I did wonder what was amiss."

"I can't see any other way. It's that or debtor's prison."

"Good Lord, are things as bad as that?" Sebastian demanded, cutting into a thick piece of sirloin and beyond relieved that his stomach had decided to forgive him.

Beau shrugged and sat back in his chair. "Not yet, but give it a month or two and it may well be."

Sebastian chewed slowly and debated what tack to take first, knowing only too well how carefully Beau needed handling in this kind of mood and predicament. "Have you spoken to your father?" he asked, taking the safer option first.

Snorting with a combination of amusement and disgust, Beau's bright blue eyes met his. "Aye, and my worthy father told me he would walk me to the gates of The Marshalsea himself before he handed over a groat to save me." Beau glowered and shook his head. "The miserable old bastard. What right he has to be so self-righteous over me when I know damn well he's every bit the spendthrift ... and worse. God alone knows what I'll inherit, if I ever do," he said with a dark expression glittering in his eyes. "Reckon the whoremongering old bastard made a pact with the devil. He's too damn wicked to die if you ask me."

"Charles!" Sebastian exclaimed, startled into giving his real name instead of the habitual *Beau,* that everyone knew him by.

Beau raised one elegant eyebrow. "Oh, Charles is it? Good Lord I must have shocked you."

Sebastian sighed and shook his head. Even at his worst, Sebastian laid a great deal of Beau's bad behaviour squarely at his father's feet. He rarely spoke of his family at all but Sebastian knew his mother had died when he was born, and his father had never cared a jot for his increasingly wild son, ignoring him for the most part and abusing him for the rest. It was no wonder he'd run amok.

"Beau, I hesitate to offer ... after last time ..."

"Then don't," he replied, the blue eyes looking squarely at Sebastian. "I'd rather rot in gaol than take a penny from you and you know it."

Sebastian smacked a frustrated hand down on the table. "Yes, I know it, damn you. What I don't understand is why. Why won't you let me help you?"

Beau got to his feet, as languid and graceful as ever, stretching and yawning and grinning at Sebastian. "Sindalton, I have many faults my friend but I won't hang on your sleeve and that's a fact. So you may take your kind offer and go to the devil. I shall find myself a sweet little heiress, no doubt with a stammer and six toes, and we'll go along quite merrily after I'm sure." He executed an elegant bow and turned to leave the room.

"Where are you going, damn you?" Sebastian demanded. "I haven't finished with you."

"No," called Beau over his shoulder. "I don't doubt, but I've finished with you and I'm going back to bed to gather my strength for this evening."

Sebastian huffed with annoyance as the door closed on him and then cast his eye over to the window. The slightest haze of blue sky was visible beneath a fast moving froth of thick white cloud. It looked like the rain would hold off for a few hours at least, and with that happy thought, Sebastian headed out to the stables.

As he'd expected, John Jeffries, his head coachman, was found in the stables. Jeffries had started life as a groom at Marlburgh House and when Sebastian's father had died and his mother succumbed to hysterics for what seemed like the next ten years, Jeffries had been the one solid, dependable person in Sebastian's life. A gruff middle aged man, with salt and pepper hair and an air of unshakeable calm, he was undeniably fond of the duke but would stand none of his nonsense if he felt the young duke was getting too high in the instep. It had been Jeffries who taught Sebastian to ride his first pony and told him of the birds and the bees. Sebastian never went anywhere without him.

"Thought I might be seeing you this afternoon, your Grace," Jeffries observed with a grin, leading Sebastian's horse out into the yard.

"It seems I need to add mind reading to your never ending list of skills, John," Sebastian replied, more than pleased to see the horse tacked and ready and that he wasn't to be kept waiting. His head ached and he needed to get away from the thick air of dissipation that seemed to hang over the castle and cling to him like cobwebs.

"Aye, well, your Grace. I keep telling you, you don't value my worth like you ought," John quipped, just enough sparkle in his eyes to be clear that he was teasing as his manner was perfectly bland.

"Of course I don't," Sebastian said, raising an eyebrow at him and adopting a haughty expression. "I'm a duke. It is my duty to look down my nose at you even if you are in every way my superior."

John's mouth twitched just a fraction as he handed the reins over to Sebastian. "Just as long as that's clear, your Grace," he replied, utterly serious.

Sebastian vaulted elegantly onto the horse and grinned at him. "Oh, always, John. As if you'd ever let me forget it."

He clattered out of the yard and on down a narrow, winding path out into open countryside. The castle, more of a folly in truth, was built on a high outcrop of stone and the views across the countryside were spectacular. A chill wind howled across the open ground but Sebastian relished it, sucking in great lungfuls of clean, cold air as though they could purify him from the inside out. It seemed to work on some level at least and his head felt clearer, the future a little less tangled than it had after his conversation with Beau.

He wouldn't let his friend rot in gaol, that was for sure. If it came to it he'd pay the fool's debts off, even if it meant he never spoke to him again, though he hoped it wouldn't come to that. Sebastian had never made friends easily. It was too difficult to figure out who truly liked him for himself, and who just wanted to ingratiate themselves with a wealthy and powerful man for their own reasons.

He tended to adopt his haughtiest and most disobliging demeanour in company in an effort to keep the toad-eaters and flatterers at bay. It worked, to an extent, though it also alienated most everyone else. Not that it affected his success with the ladies. An accomplished flirt, he had a dangerous reputation and it was a gamble for any mother to place their daughter in his path. The stakes were high though, when you were playing for a duke.

The circus, as he referred to it, appalled him. Almack's, or as most people called it - the marriage mart, was worst of all. He felt the young women were paraded in front of him like cattle, waiting for him to bid on one that took his fancy. In turn their eyes on him were avaricious and it made him hate them all and hold them in contempt, though he knew at heart that this was as unfair on them as it was on him.

For a moment he envied Beau, and not just for his looks. Women wanted Beau because he was beautiful and charming and fun to be with. Oh he came from an ancient and dignified line, one of the oldest families in the country in fact. And that he was a Marquis and would one day be a Duke didn't hurt, obviously, but his father was still a virile and active man and showed no signs of relinquishing his title any time soon, and everyone knew Beau had pockets to let. Any woman who wanted Beau wasn't after his money at least.

With a sigh he reined in and took a moment to survey the countryside. It was beautiful, harsh and rugged and windswept, quite unlike the lush green, fertile lands around his own estate. Looking up at the sky and the clouds that scudded fast overhead he judged that he had time enough yet before he needed to head back, and carried on to farther explore the countryside.

Chapter 4

"Wherein mischief is made."

Georgiana looked down at her measly haul and huffed with annoyance. What on earth was Aunt Jane thinking, making Dandelion and Burdock so late in the year? The leaves were bound to be bitter and so late in the season the dandelions were hard to see, covered as they were by so many other taller grasses and flowers. Grumbling to herself she picked up her basket and called Conrad to heel. The big black mongrel came running back to her, tail wagging merrily and with every manner of burrs and seeds stuck to his coat.

"Oh really! Look at the state of you." Georgiana tutted with disapproval. "Aunt will give us both a scold if you go home looking like that, you wretch." She looked up at the sky and frowned. "But we'll both be wet through too if we don't hurry; I don't like the look of that sky."

Looking around her Georgiana made a quick decision. It would take hours searching out enough dandelions here, but if she was to head over to the Gower estate's four acre field where she usually gathered, she could be done within an hour at most, and no one any the wiser.

"Come on, Conrad," she called, stepping out. It would take her at least an hour to walk over there but better that than breaking her back in the meadow at Longbarrow.

Her instincts proved to be right on reaching the Gower estate and her basket was almost full when the heavens opened.

"Oh blast!" she cursed, squealing as a freezing drop of rain made its way down the back of her neck and made her shiver. Picking up her basket in one hand and her skirts in another she ran down the hill to the smuggler's cave. It was no longer used by smugglers of course, or at least rarely, as it was too well known by all to be a safe hiding place.

But it was a good place to sit out the rain storm. She sat on a ledge just inside the shelter of the cave and looked out as a storm boiled overhead. Heavy bruised-looking, indigo clouds tumbled together, blocking out the daylight and casting an eerie and melancholy light over the countryside.

"Oh dear, now we're in for it," she muttered, pulling Conrad's silky ears distractedly as the first fork of lightening crazed the skies and ended with a sharp crack before thunder rumbled through the landscape. Conrad whined and fidgeted beside her and she hushed him, thankful for his companionship. She was in no way a fanciful creature, despite her love of lurid Gothic novels and unsuitable romances, but the storm was unsettling and she would be glad to be safe back at home beside a warm fire. The wind turned and rain lashed into the opening of the cave, driving her farther back into the darkness where she lingered with unease whilst the storm raged.

She was just beginning to think the worst of it had passed when there was a commotion at the mouth of the cave and she stifled a scream of alarm as the shriek of a horse could be heard and she saw the great creature rear up, the black shape highlighted against a luminous white strike of lightening. A moment later and she saw a man leap down, pulling the terrified animal into the shelter of the cave and murmuring soothing words to it.

With her heart beating in alarm she took stock of the man, not a local man that was for certain, for she would have been well aware of having seen those broad shoulders and powerful legs before, had she but glanced at them in passing. The man stripped off his soaking wet jacket and waistcoat and laid them down over a rock to dry.

Very much alive to the impropriety of her situation, alone with a man in the middle of the countryside in a thunderstorm, Georgiana kept well back in the dark and prayed she wouldn't be noticed. But she had of course forgotten her recalcitrant hound.

At first slightly cowed by the spectacle of man and beast fighting each other and the elements, Conrad had hidden, quaking, behind his mistress's skirts. Now that everything had calmed down, however, he was feeling rather braver. Stepping boldly forward, he offered a sharp yip of disapproval to the newcomer before Georgiana had the wit or the time to stop him.

The man swung around and she was obliged with a view of thick brown hair, rather fierce dark eyes under thick eyebrows and a strong, square jaw.

“Who’s there?” he demanded.

Quite unable to do anything else, Georgiana stepped forward, out of the darkness into the purplish shadows cast by the storm that was finally showing signs of abating, much to her relief.

“Good God,” the man breathed, as she emerged from the gloom of the cave. It seemed to take him a moment to remember his manners, or at least, Georgiana assumed the next time he opened his mouth he would introduce himself and put her mind at rest that he meant her no harm. He did not. “Are you a witch?” he demanded, amusement glittering in his eyes as he looked her over, an openly appraising look that made her blood boil.

“Indeed I am not, Sir,” she replied, with as much froideur as she could muster. “For if I were I would conjure myself at home by the fire, instead of sheltering from a storm in a damp cave.”

The man gave a bark of laughter, apparently delighted. “Well, I’ll be damned. If you aren’t just the thing to brighten a tedious afternoon.”

She looked back at him in appalled silence while he continued to look her up and down in approval.

She gave him a disgusted sniff and glared back at him. “I’m sure I find myself relieved to have afforded you some entertainment,” she replied with cool dignity. “For you amuse me, not at all.”

"Mercy!" he replied, laughing, holding his hands up in mock surrender. "Come little witch, I think we have set off on the wrong foot. Will you not come and introduce yourself to me?"

"As you seem to have a lack of manners that is beyond anything I have had the misfortune to encounter until now, no. I shall not."

"Ah," he replied, the glittering amusement in his eyes darkening as he took a step forward. "Then perhaps I should introduce myself?" he said, his voice soft now.

"Please do not trouble yourself," she snapped in response. "If you will only stand aside I will bid you good day. It appears the storm is over and I can continue on my way."

"Alone?" he asked, quirking one eyebrow.

"Yes, alone!" she replied, any last vestige of patience long since vanished as this odious creature seemed determined to torment her. "I was born and raised here and everyone knows me. It is no great scandal for me to walk alone."

"On your own lands perhaps?" he acknowledged with no little scepticism. "But this isn't your land."

"Nor yours!" she retorted, trying to push past him and gasping in shock as he caught her by the arms. "Let me go!" she shouted, trying and failing to pull out of his grasp.

"Easy, love," he said, grinning at her. "If you want to pass you'll have to pay the toll."

She didn't have a moment to utter the bewildered question that came to mind as he answered it for her very neatly by pulling her into his arms and kissing her.

By now far more angry than frightened, she struggled to pull away but found his grip on her more than she could counter. He released her mouth and looked down at her, his eyes darker still and somewhat devilish in the dim light of the cave.

Belatedly, aware that perhaps his mistress was not enjoying the stranger's attentions, Conrad began to bark, leaping forward and back between the entrance of the cave and the stranger.

"Oh, thank you, Conrad!" Georgiana exclaimed in exasperation. "Just a little too late, you idiotic creature."

"Perhaps not," the man whispered, his breath hot and damp against her neck. He looked up, those devilish eyes sparkling with mischief. "Perhaps I have further nefarious plans for you?" he suggested, waggling his eyebrows in imitation of a theatrical villain.

"I will thank you to take your hands off me *this instant!"* Georgiana demanded, wriggling once more in the brute's ridiculously strong arms. The man looked down at Conrad, whose barking was becoming ever more alarmed as the stranger did not do as he was bid and release his mistress.

"Be silent!"

Conrad jerked in surprise, clearly recognising the voice of authority and lying down with meek obedience at the sound of a man's voice.

"Oh you faithless creature!" wailed Georgiana. "Of all the idiotic, disloyal ..."

"Hush yourself, little witch," the brute said, though his voice was soft as he returned his attention to her. "Now then, tell me your name and where you come from and I swear I'll let you go. I'm not going to hurt you, you have my word."

"Oh yes," she replied with asperity. "The word of a *gentleman,"* she infused that last part with all the scorn she was currently feeling, adding with venom. "How terribly reassuring."

"Oh, ho, little cat," he laughed. "Now, now, show me your claws and I may change my mind and keep you here."

"Of all the odious, vile, detestable ..."

"Loathsome?" he added helpfully.

"Yes, loathsome!" she repeated, stamping her foot. "And abhorrent, repulsive ..."

"Oh no!" he interrupted her stream of adjectives. "Repulsive I won't have." he shook his head, his eyes holding a faintly mocking gleam. "I have it on very good authority that I am not in the least bit repulsive."

"Whose authority?" she demanded. "Not mine I collect. Oh, and now we can add disgustingly arrogant and prideful!"

"Tell me your name, witch!"

"Oh!" In utter fury she bit back a very unladylike curse and replied. "My name is Georgiana Bomford and I wish you joy of it for you will never have cause to speak it again. Now. Let. Me. Go!"

"Oh but I have yet to introduce myself to you," the stranger replied, all mocking politeness.

"Then get on with it so I can make haste to forget it," she muttered furiously.

The man seemed to hesitate for just a second, his dark eyes full of something she could not decipher. "Charles Stafford, the Marquis of Beaumont, at your service, madame."

Georgiana froze and blinked up at him, disbelieving. She had long wanted to see for herself the dangerously beautiful *Beau* Beaumont, and while this man was very handsome indeed, and certainly a danger to her - or any other woman who had the misfortune to cross his path - he wasn't what she expected. She frowned at him.

"You're Beau Beaumont?"

She thought he looked faintly annoyed by the question which pleased her.

"I am," he replied, sounding a little defiant. "What of it?"

She pursed her lips and shrugged before replying, "Nothing."

"What?" he demanded. "What do you mean *nothing?"* She was intrigued to find he looked really rather ruffled, which tickled her enormously and decided her to fluff his upset feathers a little further - for his own good; for the devil was clearly in dire need of a set down.

"Well, my Lord," she murmured. "I suppose I'm a little ... disappointed."

"Oh?"

There was a dangerous note to that single utterance that didn't escape her, but she was too angry to deviate now.

With another eloquent shrug she simply added. "Yes. Well, I have read much about the dangerous Beau Beaumont, that he is devastatingly handsome and charming and that women melt into puddles at his feet and ..." She paused and looked up at him from under her thick lashes for effect.

"And?" The dangerous tone had grown and intensified and she experienced a moment's qualm before plunging the knife home.

"Well it is just a grave disappointment to find your technique relies more on the brute force of a caveman than the clever and sophisticated flirt I had supposed you to be."

For a moment she watched the emotions chase across his face. She was fairly certain that no woman had ever spoken to him so in his life before. Though she was only too glad to fill the gap in his education, she did admit to holding her breath as she awaited his response. It wasn't what she'd expected, as he tipped his head back and gave a hearty bark of laughter.

"Why you little wretch!" he exclaimed, grinning at her. "Well, well, Georgiana Bomford. I'm more delighted to have met you than you know."

To her astonishment he released her and stepped away, pausing for a moment to bestow a stroke to the traitorous Conrad, who wagged his tail happily in response.

To further her astonishment he looked back at her, smiling broadly and looking for all the world like a naughty schoolboy rather than the villain who had just manhandled her so outrageously. "I'll be here again tomorrow afternoon, Miss Bomford, do say that you'll come and meet me?"

Her mouth fell unwillingly open in a manner which would have had her aunt scolding her soundly and for a moment she felt quite incapable of giving an answer. It didn't last.

"Are you quite mad or simply foxed?" she demanded, for drink or an unsound mind could be the only explanation for believing she would willingly meet him again.

"Neither," he replied, sounding far too cheerful. "I'm stone cold sober and not at all unhinged I promise."

"Spoken like a true madman," she replied with a sniff, as she made to turn her back on him, adjusting her bonnet as she went.

"Wait!" he cried, grasping hold of her hand and disarranging the ribbons of her bonnet all over again.

"Oh! Will you stop manhandling me," she exclaimed.

"I beg your pardon," he replied, the dark eyes suddenly full of warmth though he didn't look the least bit remorseful. "But please, I meant what I said. I'm so pleased to have met you. Won't you come and talk to me again. I promise you, I will behave like a gentleman if you do."

"Certainly not!" she replied with some heat, though she was aware of a growing desire to do as he asked in response to the soft look in those dark eyes. Happily it was a desire she thoroughly mistrusted and would certainly not be foolish enough to act on.

"Oh, but you are cruel, little witch."

"Stuff!" she replied succinctly, taking up her basket and heading out of the cave.

"I'll find you again, Georgiana," he called, laughter in his voice as she strode away from him. "Just see if I don't!"

Chapter 5

"Wherein the fates toy with the future."

It was five days before he saw her again. The day after meeting his little firebrand in the cave the weather closed in and no one in their right mind would have set foot outside the door. Ruefully, Sebastian had to wonder if the witch had been right and he was unhinged, for it was all he could do not to make the attempt no matter what the vagaries of this strange summer's weather could throw at him. The day after that was stormy and threatening but he went out nonetheless, returning to the cave, though he'd have been almost disappointed if she had been there, and then spending hours scouring every inch of the countryside.

He repeated the exercise every following day and had to bite his tongue to stop himself asking for her by name in case he caused her trouble. He well knew his own, or rather Beau's reputation, and he wouldn't have her ruined for nothing but an enquiry. But the vision of the stunning red head with her sharp tongue and pretty brown eyes plagued him every moment that followed that stormy afternoon. So it was with an inward crow of triumph that he caught a flash of fox-coloured hair out of the corner of his eye as he rode out, uncharacteristically early, on a sunny autumn morning.

He paused for a moment, admiring the bucolic scene before him. She sat on a picnic blanket on a high ledge of rock at the edge of a meadow, with a sketch book and pencil in hand. Her bonnet had been laid aside and her hair was all askew, tumbling in glorious red swathes down her back. Dismounting and leaving his mount to crop grass, he stole quietly closer to see more. The indomitable Conrad lay dozing beside her and Sebastian could see an endearing frown of concentration on her face as she struggled with the scenery laid out before her. He crept closer behind her, noticing the hopeless dog didn't so much as blink, looked over her shoulder and tried to smother his laughter. Taking a breath once he'd righted himself, he asked gravely, "Is that a cow or a horse?"

"Oh!" Squealing in shock she dropped her pad and looked up at him in horror, while Conrad awoke and began to jump up at him with excitement. "You!" she uttered, managing to infuse the word with such fury that he couldn't help but grin.

"I told you I would find you, Miss Bomford."

"How dare you?" she hissed, looking around her in alarm.

"Oh don't worry, we are quite alone," he added, grinning at her. "No one for miles, as I'm sure you know. Oh and how dare I? Well as I kissed you last time we met I don't see why you should think me incapable of a little excitement."

"Abominable creature!"

He laughed and sat down beside her, shaking his head.

"Pax, Miss Bomford. Please, I beg you, let us at least try to be civil. I swear I will if you do. Surely we can speak a few words without insulting each other at every turn?"

"I sincerely doubt it," she remarked, those brown, no they were *green* eyes, flashing. She reached to pick up her pad again but he was too fast for her and snatched it up. Frowning he looked out at the scenery and back at the pad and then at Georgiana, one eyebrow raised. She huffed, her pale skin flushing in the most becoming manner.

"I know I can't draw," she replied, sounding miffed and intensely embarrassed. "I never have been able to, only ..."

He smiled at her, hoping his expression was as warm and friendly as he wanted it to be. He didn't want her to run away again. "Only?" he repeated.

She huffed and tried to snatch the pad back. "Only I enjoy trying. It never looks how it should but ... but I find it absorbing."

He tugged the pad from her reluctant grasp once again, a smile tugging at the corners of his mouth? "Is that a cow?" he asked, unable to keep the laughter from his voice.

"You know very well that it's a horse, my Lord," she replied with dignity, though he held onto a suspicion that there was mirth in her eyes, lurking just out of sight.

"What else do you enjoy?" he asked, genuinely curious now, allowing her to tug the pad from his grasp.

Frowning at him he watched as she warred with herself, wondering whether she would be as brave as he suspected she was.

"I-I like to read," she said, and her eyes drifted, he suspected unwillingly, to the wicker basket.

"What do you like to read?" he asked, wondering if she would admit to a love of novels or imply she read something far worthier and dull. It was frowned upon by most for young ladies of quality to rot their mind with such nonsense, though he himself could never fathom why, having been just as diverted himself. He had been accustomed to being given a list of far more serious titles while strongly suspecting the lady in question was more inclined to read a sensational romance, though none would ever admit it to him. He was surprised then when she reached into the basket and withdrew a tattered copy of *A Sicilian Romance.*

"Mrs Radcliffe," he said, his tone approving.

"You've read her?" She looked so astonished that he had to chuckle.

"Did you think I would scold you and tell you to apply yourself to something more serious?" He turned the well-loved copy in his hands, smiling. "I suppose I've been cast as the Duke de Luovo?"

He saw the corner of her mouth twitch though she managed to repress the smile that threatened. He determined he would make her smile yet.

"Perhaps," she admitted, her green ... no they *were* brown eyes glimmering. "I'm not sure yet."

"You mean I still have a chance at being the heroic Hippolitus?" he demanded.

"Certainly not!" she replied, holding out her hand in an imperious manner. He handed the book back to her and was charmed when she cast him a shy look, adding, "Though I have to say, I think Hippolitus is the most ridiculous name for a hero."

He nodded, picking a strand of grass that was bobbing in the breeze beside him. "Quite unsuitable," he agreed with all seriousness.

Silence stretched between them while he found himself lost in deciding exactly what colour her eyes were. She coughed, and looked discomforted by his scrutiny and he pulled himself up, startled to discover he'd been staring like a fool. "It's nice to finally have a little sun, isn't it?" he said, hurrying to fill the gap.

One, delicate, red tinted eyebrow quirked upward. "Oh dear. Really? The weather?" She tutted at him and began to pack her pencils and pad back into the basket.

"I'm sorry, that *was* shocking wasn't it?" he said, his expression rueful. "But I suspect if I'd told you the truth you'd be even more disgusted."

"Oh?" He was delighted to see curiosity in her expression, a slight frown over her eyes, and she paused with Mrs Radcliff's novel suspended over the basket.

"I can't stop looking at your eyes," he admitted, quite truthfully this time. "I can't decide if they're green or brown."

She snorted in amusement and dropped her novel into the basket. "Neither," she said, a prosaic tone to her voice. "They're hazel, and please, I beg of you. Don't go writing an ode or some such nonsense."

"Why ever not?" he retorted, taking the basket from her hands and placing it behind him so she couldn't reach it. "No don't go, not yet," he begged, giving her his most charming smile. "Tell me why I shouldn't write you a poem. You deserve a poem, I think."

She flushed and shook her head. "I will go if you keep speaking in such a ridiculous manner. You have no business flirting with me and well you know it, so please stop."

He sighed and stretched out on his side, looking up at her. "Very well. If I promise not to flirt will you stay and talk to me?"

She hesitated, but for such a short time he was relieved of the idea that she still found him as obnoxious as she'd first thought. "For just a little while then," she said, and he saw the first real glimmer of the smile he had been hoping for. His breath caught and he let out a huff of laughter.

"My God," he whispered, staring at her. Frowning, she began to get to her feet. "No!" he exclaimed. "That was involuntary, I swear. I didn't mean to," he said, half laughing, half pleading as he discovered he would be bitterly disappointed if she ran now.

"Last chance," she said, her tone fierce as she wagged a finger at him.

"Cross my heart and hope to die," he replied, making the cross over his heart as he spoke.

Apparently satisfied, she sat down again and he began to draw her out. He didn't ask her all the usual inane questions about her family and where she was born, but they spoke about books and poetry and music and horses - she loved to ride, he discovered, and had ambitions to drive a phaeton, which he secretly hoped to help her with. They talked through lunch and the remainder of the afternoon. She insisted on sharing her picnic with him, and made encouraging noises as he climbed an apple tree in the hedgerow after she discovered the biggest and shiniest red one was right at the top. So, it was with an exclamation of alarm that she looked up some hours later to discover the sky was growing dim.

"Oh my word!" she said, gathering up her belongings as she got to her feet. "It's so late, wherever has the afternoon gone?"

"It has been spent in the most delightful fashion," he said, with complete sincerity, finding himself truly disappointed that it had come to an end. He reached out and took her hand, enclosing it within his much larger ones. "Say you'll come back again tomorrow." She opened her mouth and began to shake her head. "Please?" he said, quite alarmed to hear the pleading note in his voice.

"I-I shouldn't. You know I shouldn't," she said, avoiding his eyes and trying to pull her hand free.

"I'll be here," he said, smiling at her. "I'll wait all day, and all day the next and the day after ..."

"Oh stop, you absurd creature!" she said, laughing, though her expression was troubled. "I-I don't know if ... if ..."

"Yes you can, I know you can, if you try." He gave her fingers a gentle squeeze. "I'll be here," he repeated. "Until tomorrow, Miss Bomford."

She gave a little huff of exasperation and curtsied to him. "Count Luovo," she said, with a smirk.

He dashed his hand to his heart with a wounded cry. "Oh, infamy! After all we have been to each other."

He watched as she scurried away, her cheeks flushed and her red hair escaping her bonnet as she ran, laughing at him with the dog gambolling at her feet.

He let out a breath, feeling that he had been holding it all afternoon in case she decided to change her mind and run away from him. But she hadn't run, she had stayed, and he had never been more glad of anything in all his life.

He made his way back to the castle, quite unable to shake the ridiculous smile from his face, a fact that was remarked on by Jeffries as he handed his horse back into his care.

"A good day, I take it, your Grace?" he asked, a quizzical expression fixed on his master from under his thick, grizzled eyebrows.

"I should say so," Sebastian replied, grinning at him. His smile dimmed a little as he remembered that Lord Gower's entertainments awaited him for the night. He wondered if he could find a way to excuse himself without being thought inexcusably dull. He had a reasonable idea that the truth, that he had a pressing urge to go to bed early with a copy of Mrs Radcliffe's - *A Sicilian Romance,* would not be met with approval. The idea amused him so much that he couldn't help but grin and it was with a contented air that he entered the castle, whistling as he went.

Chapter 6

"Wherein our heroine steps upon a perilous path."

To Georgiana's dismay, she awoke the next morning with a sore throat so severe that she couldn't speak and was ordered immediately back to bed by her aunt, despite her protests that she was really quite well. In point of fact she wasn't well at all, but the idea that Beau might believe she had stood him up without so much as a message of apology made her feel even more wretched.

The next moment had her scolding herself. Whatever was she thinking! Even to be considering the idea of going and meeting the most notorious rake in England, *alone.* It was beyond anything. Her chances of finding a suitable husband were dim enough in such rural parts but at least she would come out this year. There were the assemblies at Truro to look forward to and perhaps that wasn't as glamorous and exciting as a come out in London but plain old Miss Georgiana Bomford wasn't due such distinction and well she knew it.

It was perfectly clear to her that Lord Beaumont was just enjoying a flirtation to while away a pleasant day or two. She wasn't such a ninnyhammer to believe that there was anything more to it than that. Neither was she foolish enough to believe that any time spent in his company wasn't dangerous to her ... in more ways than she could count. In point of fact the idea of being discovered was the least of her concerns. She knew the area like the back of her hand. She knew where she could spend the day and never see a soul and she thought, if she put her mind to it, it would not prove difficult to meet him without arousing suspicion or being found out. What was less likely seemed to be the idea that she could spend more time in the man's presence without becoming ... interested in him.

Although he was not at all what she had expected, he was undoubtedly interesting. He was well read and engaging, charming in fact. He made her laugh, often at his own expense but also liked to tease her. His mind was quick and lively and he enjoyed her sense of the ridiculous ... which she had discovered was a rare thing indeed. And all that was without ever even considering those deep brown eyes and that astonishing smile that seemed to entirely change his rather severe countenance into something far more approachable and appealing.

He was also, she reminded herself as she brought to mind their first encounter in the caves, ill-mannered, rude, provoking and perfectly outrageous. To her chagrin those particular deficiencies only made her smile.

It was another three days before Aunt Jane agreed to let her out of the house. It was a fine autumn day, an astonishingly rare event after the past months of cold and rain. Georgiana had never known a summer like it, nor apparently had anyone else and there was much talk of trouble in the towns as crops failed and those less fortunate scratched about, struggling for survival.

But for today at least it was mild, with a teasing wind that skittered the leaves that had begun to fall around her feet and tugged at the ribbons of her bonnet. Conrad bounded ahead, turning every so often to bark at her, admonishing her to make haste. Indeed she needed no such urging, though she told herself over and again it was the height of folly. In the first instance, the very idea that Beau should actually be waiting for her still was ridiculous. A man like that did not return day after day for some silly country girl with neither title nor fortune.

Although she was well aware of her own worth she wasn't one to view the world in any way other than that of reality. She knew in this tiny corner of England she was considered a beauty, but she never doubted for a moment that if put against all the lovely young women at Almack's or some other elegant London affair, her own charms would be eclipsed.

Georgiana had no doubt in her mind that she would end up marrying some local squire who she met at the assembly rooms. She expected the courtship and subsequent marriage would be dull and comfortable and that was as much as she could hope for. She came from a good family, very respectable except ... she was aware that there was some shadow over her own parents' death.

Her aunt and uncle never spoke of it and had always become so agitated if she broached the subject that she had never tried. She knew how much she was in their debt for taking on a child that wasn't theirs and would do anything to save them from distress. It would no doubt affect her chances of marrying well and put that with the modest sum that she imagined her uncle might be so generous as to provide for her ... well it was hardly likely to turn the head of the Marques of Beaumont.

So what on earth she was doing retracing her steps to the secluded spot he had discovered her in four days earlier was beyond her. Her only comfort was the fact that he wouldn't be there and she would have enjoyed a pleasant walk and have been brought back down to earth. For no good would come of yielding to the temptation of dreaming about the enticing Beau Beaumont.

It was, therefore, with a start of surprise that she noticed a handsome chestnut horse grazing at the edge of the meadow, just as it had been the day she'd bid the Marquis goodbye. As she took a hesitant step closer she noticed a figure on the rock. He had cast his jacket aside and was sitting with one leg outstretched and his arms resting on his bent knee. Her heart seemed to do a little leap in her chest at the sight of him, though whether that was because of the sheer folly she was indulging in or for any other reason she had no idea. Taking another step closer she saw the wind ruffling the thick waves of his dark hair and as if drawn by some invisible force he turned his head and stared directly at her.

She was quite certain her heart stopped for just a moment. For in that brief second she was not quite sure of her reception. There seemed to be a flicker of hurt, or perhaps that was anger in those dark eyes. But then he spoke and there was a mocking amusement in his voice, and perhaps a little reproach.

"In secret we met, in silence I grieve, that thy heart could forget, thy spirit deceive," he said softly.

"Well really!" she replied, recognising the scandalous poem about a deceitful lover only too well. "If you feel that way I shall turn around and leave again." She went to do just that but he sprang to his feet and jumped down from the rock, running after her and grasping hold of her hand.

"No! Forgive me ..." he laughed, looking a little wild as the wind tugged at his hair. "Only you are very cruel to me, love, leaving me waiting for so long."

She swallowed, her heart thudding while a little voice in her head was screaming at her to turn around and leave ... *now!*

"I didn't mean to," she murmured, too stunned by the dreadfully inappropriate endearment he'd uttered to form a sterner reply. Her eyes drifted down to her hand where he held it clasped in his. "I--I was unwell."

"Oh!" he replied, clearly not having considered this as a possibility. "Oh, Miss Bomford please *do* forgive me." He laughed at the expression on her face. "I know what a shabby fellow I am. How many times have I begged forgiveness already in our short acquaintance?"

"Too many for propriety I think, my Lord," she replied, moving her hand as though she would take it from his grasp. His fingers tightened though, refusing to release her.

"Are you quite well now?" he asked and she didn't dare look up and meet his eyes while that soft voice enquired after her with such tenderness.

"Quite well," she repeated, feeling flustered. She should leave, now. This was the worst idea in the world. Oh her poor aunt would die of shame if she could see her now, dallying with Beau Beaumont of all people! "But I must go now. I only came to say that I was sorry ... I--I never dreamed you would actually be here ..."

"Then why did you come?" he asked again in that same caressing voice.

She couldn't answer, too aware that she was in danger and that she needed to go, but too driven to stay just another moment in his company to actually force herself to move.

"I don't know," she admitted. "I shouldn't have ..."

"Did you want to see me?" he asked, and the seductive tone lingering over the enquiry was only too apparent, and though she didn't reply her cheeks flushed, betraying her as eloquently as if she'd admitted aloud how very much she'd wanted to.

She felt his fingers beneath her chin and he tilted her head up so she was forced to look at him. "I wanted to see you. Very, very much. I came every day," he said, and she noticed for the first time that there were little flecks of amber and gold in the dark brown of his eyes. "I waited from morning until dusk each day, and I would have come again tomorrow and the day after ..."

"Oh stop!" she cried tugging her hand free and walking away from him. "This ... this is beyond foolish, it's ... it's ..."

"Madness?" he demanded, his voice rough. "Yes, perhaps," he said, shadowing her movements, not allowing her to move more than a foot or so away from him. "I have been considering all the ways in which I could discover more about you. Where you live, where I might find you ... some of my ideas were *quite* mad, I'm sure."

"Please, my Lord," she said, imploring him to be a gentleman and do the right thing because she was fast becoming aware that she would not be able to. "You must go. We both know there is no future for you here. I am far beneath your notice and ..."

She didn't get to finish the sentence as he closed the distance between them and took her face between his hands before pressing his mouth against hers.

His lips were soft and warm, and this time he was a little less violent in his attentions than that first kiss in the shadowy, dark of the cave. But there was fierceness enough in his manner as he pulled her closer, his arms enfolding her so tightly against him that she found herself shocked and stunned and beguiled all at once. Her hands were pressed against his chest and she could feel the heat of his body blazing through the fine white linen. Only too aware of the disparity between them as he towered over her, his much broader, harder body easily subdued her softer, smaller frame. She seemed suddenly fragile against all that coiled power, his muscular body so much heavier than hers.

He released her mouth and she dared to look up at him, feeling his breath fluttering warm against her cheek.

"Damn, I'm going to have to ask you to forgive me again," he said, with a rueful expression.

Against everything she had ever been taught about the appropriate behaviour for young ladies, Georgiana gasped at him in outrage ... and then laughed.

He grinned at her then and that smile was her undoing, and when he bent his head once more she didn't struggle but tilted her head to allow it, encouraging him to explore and to show her how a kiss should progress. His lips were soft and teasing now, feathering light butterfly kisses over her mouth that made her breathless. He nipped at her lower lip in a teasing gesture that made her gasp with surprise that was compounded as he traced the opening she'd made with his tongue.

Tentatively she copied him and allowed him to deepen the kiss, feeling her body suddenly languorous and boneless as she relaxed into his arms. He pulled her tighter still and she reached her arms up, coiling them around his neck to steady herself, finding that she had raised up on tiptoes to meet him, pulling his head down.

"Oh God," he moaned, as he drew back, his breathing heavy. She looked up at him feeling suddenly shy, which seemed strange in the circumstances. And yet she hardly dared meet his eyes, but when she did they were darker than ever, heavy with desire. She drew in a breath, alarmed by the intensity of his expression and he seemed to remember himself. He relaxed his hold on her, kissing her lightly and then taking her hand and leading her back to the place they had sat and talked before.

"Come and talk to me, Miss Bomford," he said, his tone light and charming, no doubt trying to settle her nerves which were indeed skittering about like a day old foal, trembling and uncertain.

"I think perhaps you may call me Georgiana," she said, relieved that at least her voice didn't waver as she felt everything else was quaking, that she herself was quavering on the edge of a precipice.

He paused and looked back at her, his smile warm. "Georgiana," he repeated, with such reverence it made her skin heat all over again.

Sitting down on the rock he held out his hand and she took it, settling herself beside him and demurely arranging her skirts to give herself a moment to take a breath. What *are* you doing, Georgiana? The voice in her head called out to her and she had no answer for it, instead she turned her face towards the man beside her and smiled and he traced the line of her jaw with his fingertip.

"So beautiful," he whispered.

She gave a little self-deprecating huff of amusement. "Come now, my Lord," she replied, with obvious scepticism. "Pretty enough for Truro perhaps, but hardly a diamond of the first water. Why just imagine me beside all those glamorous heiresses, I would fade away as if I'd never been. It's only here among the rocks and the fields that you find favour in an oddity."

"Is that what you think?" he demanded, and she startled a little as there had been a thread of real anger in his voice.

Her smile faltered but she knew it was the truth and she didn't want to hear pretty lies from him. She'd have no promises of love and devotion. He would dally with her a little while and she would have to work hard to keep her honour and her heart intact until the day he grew bored. "I think perhaps you are fatigued by the lavish entertainments provided by your friends, that the sophisticated entertainments you seek have begun to pall, and so you find diversion in other avenues ..." She looked away then, not liking to see the way anger lit his eyes at her words. "Like a naive little country girl who is foolish enough to meet you and let you kiss her."

She gasped as his hand grasped the back of her neck, pulling her closer to him and finding those dark eyes lit with much more than just anger. "I have thought of nothing else but you since the day we met," he said, his voice harsh. "This is not like anything else I have ever felt."

She stared at him, trying to smile but finding it impossible under the weight of his gaze. "I'm simply a novelty," she whispered, not for one minute believing it was anything more than that, no matter what he said.

"No." His voice was a growl and she thought - hoped, he would kiss her again but he released her suddenly and stared out across the fields. The silence was taut and uncomfortable.

"Perhaps I should go," she said, aware that she had annoyed him.

His hand shot out and clasped her wrist. "No ... don't, please. I ..." He gave a soft laugh and she knew he'd been going to ask forgiveness for his behaviour.

"I think perhaps I have reached my limit for forgiveness for one day," she replied, ensuring that he heard the teasing note in her voice.

He nodded. “I don’t doubt it. I can’t imagine what you must think of me,” he glanced sideways at her and smiled, and that sweet, boyish smile that seemed to be terribly rare stole her breath.

She didn’t move but returned her gaze to look out across the meadow. She felt his hand slide from her wrist to her hand as his fingers laced through hers. They sat like that for a little while, silently watching leaves as they fell, fluttering to the ground, only to be swept up again and set upon a different path.

“You like Byron?” she asked in the end, as it appeared she didn’t have the will to walk away from him and searched for something to break the silence that seemed to grow more intense with every passing moment. He turned to her, a slight frown over his eyes. “The quote, from *When We Two Parted* ... it’s Byron,” she added.

Smiling, he shrugged. “I like some of them, the ones that feel real to me.”

“Oh?” she asked, curious as to what he meant.

“The ones where I feel he’s speaking of himself,” he said, his eyes searching hers. “And you, I take it you are an admirer ...” He groaned and rolled his eyes. “Conrad,” he said, snorting with amusement.

Georgiana flushed a little as her dog, hearing his name called, ran back to them to see if his presence was required. She patted the squirming hound, making a fuss of him before she dared to look back at the man beside her. As expected, he was obviously amused.

“You are laughing at me,” she replied with a huff.

“No, no,” he replied, choking a little before giving up and laughing out loud.

Giving an offended sniff she looked away from him. “I take it *The Corsair* isn’t one of your favourites.”

He didn’t bother to hide his obvious disgust. “It is undoubtedly his most ridiculous poem.”

"It is not!" she returned, looking at him in astonishment. "It is ... it's all adventure and romance and ...'

'Piffle," he interjected with a sad shake of his head. He grinned at her, obviously unmoved by her pouting. "Before you even begin the title is all wrong. Conrad doesn't work for any government, he has no letter of marque, therefore he's a pirate, not a corsair. You'd think he could have at least done his homework."

"Oh!" she fumed. "That is so like a man. You clearly have no soul, or at least no heart or the slightest idea about romance ..." She realised her mistake before she'd reached the end of the sentence and felt perhaps she should pick up her skirts and run. Only knowing what she ought to do and actually doing it, seemed to be something she was entirely unable to accomplish. So she looked up into a pair of darkening eyes and awaited her fate.

Chapter 7

"Wherein safer waters are left far behind."

His dark brows drew together, the eyes beneath full of challenge. "Is that so?" he said, the tone of his voice sending shivers running over her skin.

Georgiana cleared her throat, the nerves which had dispersed a little during their heated discourse suddenly returning tenfold. Before she could open her mouth to consider a safer topic of conversation he had moved. He tugged at the ribbons of her bonnet and cast it aside before pushing her backwards and taking hold of her wrists. He held them captive above her head, pressed against the rock they lay on.

His body half covered hers and she was overwhelmed once more by the sheer size of him. Surely the nobility were supposed to be pale-skinned, bespectacled creatures, not this virile force of nature, all coiled power and heat. In turn she thought any decent young lady ought to be screaming and hysterical by this point, whereas she was held spellbound, captivated by the sheer masculinity of the body pressed so intimately against hers. She stared up at him, her eyes drawn to the curve of a generous mouth. She knew now that mouth was soft and giving, quite at odds with the harsh contours of his face.

"Look at you," he said, his eyes growing darker still as he did just that. "With your hair spilling out like molten fire. You look like a wild creature, something untamed and trembling, caught in a hunter's trap."

"I-I'm not trembling," she objected, though she felt perhaps she ought to be, her heart was certainly hammering against the cage of her ribs like fury.

"No?" he murmured, lowering his head until she felt those soft lips trailing across her throat. "You will be." She sighed and never doubted the sincerity of his words as he kissed a heated trail up her neck and over her jaw until he found her mouth again and claimed it for his own. She pulled against the restraint of his hands, wanting to sink her fingers into his hair and feel if it was as soft as it looked but he held her fast as he took her mouth. She opened for him willingly, feeling wanton and just like the untamed creature he had described. Her mind had been banished by the overriding sensations in her body as it came to life under his touch. She felt strangely like she had been sleepwalking her whole life and now, suddenly, he had awakened her.

He kissed her like there was nothing else in life, like her mouth was a whole new landscape to be explored and he intended to map it with exquisite attention to detail. She followed the path he laid out for her, a serious student as he taught her the moves of this new and sensuous game as their tongues parried and retreated before coming together again.

He released one wrist and his hand slid down over her arm and then lower. With deft fingers he undid the buttons of her pelisse and slid his hand under the fabric until it grazed her breast. She gasped, shocked by the intimate touch and heard a low rumble of amusement through his chest. He spread his fingers and his thumb rubbed over the sensitive peak of her nipple.

"Oh!"

He looked down at her, his gaze heated and full of delight at the sound of her pleasure.

"Yes, you like that, don't you, my sweet little vixen." He tweaked her nipple gently through the fine muslin of her dress and she found the sound was drawn from her again. "I want to kiss you here," he said, his voice rough as he lowered his mouth and pressed it against the thin fabric covering her breast.

“N-no,” she said, torn between desperately wanting to know how his mouth would feel against her skin if she allowed it and wondering just how far she would let this man go to ruining her. Good God, he was dangerous. She’d been in his company only three times and here she was, spread out for him like some cheap petticoat who earned her living on her back. She moaned as the moist heat of his mouth penetrated the muslin, heating her body all over as the sensation spiralled out. “No,” she said again, her voice breathy and quite unlike her own. “Y-you mustn’t.”

“Oh but I must,” he insisted, releasing her other wrist and pushing her pelisse aside, tugged at the shoulders of her dress, easing the fitted material down until one pink tipped breast peeked enticingly free.

“Oh, my God,” she murmured, quite lost as he grinned at her. He held her eyes as he lowered his mouth, watching as she turned crimson before giving his full attention to her uncovered flesh. He drew her nipple into the damp heat of his mouth as she hauled in a breath, arching beneath him and groaning. Desperate now she sank her hands into his hair as she’d wanted to from the beginning and far from pushing him away, held him in place as he suckled and tormented her. Hot and writhing now, her body seemed to be crying out, making demands of her which she was not totally sure she understood. Further than that she knew he could ease the ache that was growing beneath her skin and driving her to distraction.

He gave her breast one last lingering kiss before raising his head again and staring down at her. A frown appeared over his eyes as she smiled up at him, flushed and breathing hard, she didn’t know what he saw but he drew back suddenly, tugging her dress back into place.

“Come,” he said, a little gruff now. “It’s time you went home before you catch another chill.”

Unsure whether she was relieved or disappointed she got to her feet, picking up her bonnet and arranging her pelisse. Georgiana watched as he shrugged into his fitted jacket, easing the beautifully tailored fabric over the muscular arms that he'd put around her only moments ago. Wondering what came next she called to Conrad for something to keep her occupied, watching as he bounded back across the meadow after a happy afternoon chasing rabbits. She turned and found he was watching her and didn't hesitate to put her hands in his as he reached out. He raised each one in turn, kissing the fingers lightly.

"Tell me you'll be here again tomorrow," he said, stepping closer to her as he placed her hands against his chest. She looked up at him and nodded before she could even consider the answer. She ought to run. She knew she should. She could throw away her whole life if anyone discovered her here with him. She would be ruined beyond saving. He smiled, obviously pleased that she would come, and why shouldn't he be. He was risking nothing, just enjoying a dalliance with a sweet country girl before he left and went back to London and the glamorous life he lived there. He ducked his head and pressed one last sweet kiss against her mouth and then whispered to her.

"Maid of Athens, ere we part, give, oh give me back my heart. Or, since that has left my breast, keep it now, and take the rest."

She threw back her head, laughing and he gave her an offended look. "Well I see there is no pleasing you! You accuse me of having no heart and an unromantic soul and when I spout poetry as every fair maiden would desire, you laugh in my face!"

She covered her mouth with her hand, by now quite unable to stop herself as he looked increasingly torn between amusement and vexation.

"Oh, do forgive me," she managed, wiping her eyes. "That was unforgivable, and after you said it so prettily too."

"Well now you're just patronising me!" he said with a huff. He gave a dispirited shake of his head, though she could still see the laughter in his eyes. "I shall never declare myself again."

"No," she said, still smiling, though for her at least the humour of the situation had vanished as she had no such illusions about the validity of his words.

He frowned, sensing the change in her demeanour.

"What is it? You think I play you false I suppose?"

She shook her head and then reached up and kissed his cheek. "I think there is much you would give me, my Lord," she said, her voice quiet. "But I am not fool enough to believe your heart is among them." She cast him one last smile before turning her back and walking away.

"I will see you tomorrow," he called out to her, though she offered him no reply, just walked back the way she had come with her own heart full of apprehension and turmoil.

***

Sebastian watched her walk away from him and wondered what in the name of God he was playing at. He had never taken his own position lightly or used it to abuse others. Seducing a well bred young lady who was clearly intent on landing herself a duke was not beyond him, but taking the innocence of a sweet girl who knew well he had no intentions of ever offering her marriage, that was quite another.

He should have never begun this dangerous game. Yes she had more to lose than he did, of course, but he couldn't pretend that he was in no danger. He had never been so captivated by a woman before and he couldn't precisely say what it was about her that appealed so strongly to him. Perhaps the way she laughed and teased him and refused to be flattered. Maybe it was her forthright way of putting him in his place and showing she was unimpressed with his romantic declarations, believing them to be nothing more than part of the scenery set for her own seduction. He wondered what she would say if she knew he had meant those words?

***

The next three days followed much the same pattern, though Sebastian tried his hardest to be a gentleman and take things no further than he had before. But damn it was a hard thing to do. They talked of course, they spoke about so many things. In fact he couldn't ever remember finding anyone so easy to converse with. And yet in the end words couldn't be enough and he found himself lost in her kiss. It was after one such afternoon that he returned to find Jeffries waiting for him in the stables as usual.

He had already grown used to the ragging from his friends who gathered he had found some lusty wench nearby who had attracted his interest. He just grinned at them and let them believe it, better that than tell the truth - whatever the truth might be. Instinctively he shied away from it, not wanting to look too close. But Jeffries had known him since he was a baby and there was something in those shrewd eyes that told him he was found out.

He tossed his jacket over the side of the stall in a manner that would make his valet weep, before rolling up his sleeves and getting to work rubbing down his horse, Azor. Although he could easily have left the work as being far beneath him, and indeed he didn't always volunteer, Jeffries had instilled a work ethic in him from his earliest days. If he wanted to know about horses, to really know, then he needed to know everything, not just toss his reins to a waiting groom the moment he was done.

If he had hoped to distract his old mentor from his purpose, however, by pleasing him in such a way, it was soon clear he'd fallen short of the mark. The man's stony silence was a sure indicator that there was something on his mind, but Sebastian knew him well enough to know he'd say nothing unless he was invited to. Jeffries would never speak out of turn to his master, oh no. He'd just bludgeon him into submission with his silent scowl until Sebastian was begging him to tell him what the problem was.

"Alright, out with it," he said, dropping the curry comb and reaching for a soft brush. He glanced up to see real concern in the older man's eyes and hesitated. "Really, Jeffries, what is it?"

Jeffries ran one large, calloused hand through his hair and scratched at the stubble on his chin. "I don't know, your Grace. It's ... well it's not my place to say is it?"

Sebastian snorted and began to brush Azor with long, firm strokes. The horse whickered and twitched appreciatively, turning his head to nudge Sebastian with his silky muzzle. "Well it's never stopped you before to my knowledge."

To his surprise Jeffries stepped closer to him and Sebastian watched as he reached out and plucked something from his linen shirt. It was a long, fine hair.

"Red," Jeffries said, looking at it and shaking his head with a troubled expression.

Sebastian laughed, wondering what on earth had got into the man. "You have something against red heads?"

"Aye," he said, his tone bitter. "As it was a red-headed bitch who ruined your father, that I do."

Sebastian stilled. He knew well enough the story of his father's demise. Knew the name of the woman who had seduced him away from his wife and only son, and ultimately led him to his death. He hadn't known what she looked like though, other than that she was a beauty of course.

"I see the look in your eyes," Jeffries said, as foreboding prickled over Sebastian's skin. "He looked like that when it began. Like he needed her to breathe, like he couldn't sit easy in his own skin unless he was with her."

"Don't be foolish, man," Sebastian replied, returning to his job and trying hard to consign Jeffries' words to some distant place where he needn't consider them. "Just because the girl has red hair it doesn't mean I'm about to fight a duel over her. Neither of us is married, for one." *Damn.* He hadn't meant that information to escape him. He sighed and looked up, meeting Jeffries' eyes. "I appreciate your concern, truly. But I will be gone from here soon enough. It is simply ... a pleasant dalliance, nothing more." The lie tasted bitter on his tongue but he hadn't quite realised how untrue it was until the words had been forced from him. How in God's name was he going to leave her? The idea made his gut clench.

"I was there that night, your Grace. I was there the night he killed Baron Dalton and had to flee with that woman. He made me swear to protect you, to always look out for you and dammit I've tried my best and I'm trying now. Let's us leave this place today. Go back to London," he urged. "Or home to Marlburgh, wherever you like, only get away from her because I have a bad feeling about this."

Sebastian turned and looked at him, laughing and forcing a smile, both of which felt utterly fake. "Superstitious nonsense, man," he said, clapping Jeffries on the back. "I have no intention of following in my father's scandalous footsteps, I assure you. Now do stop fretting like an old woman and help me rub this fellow down as I'm half-starved and I need a drink."

"Aye, your Grace, whatever you say," Jeffries said, frowning. "But you mark my words, lad, nothing good will come of it."

Chapter 8

"Wherein hearts, minds and the future become tangled."

Sebastian ignored Jeffries' dark look as he left the stables the next day, but the warning was harder to dispel. He'd considered not going to meet Georgiana today, and dismissed the idea a bare second later. He couldn't. He would have to say goodbye to her very soon in any case. He wouldn't hasten the day. The very idea of leaving and never seeing her again made an ache bloom in his chest that he was having trouble identifying. He'd never had a problem ending love affairs before. Why it should suddenly become a problem now, he couldn't fathom.

He drew Azor up and looked over the rugged view spread out before him. He liked the landscape here, as uncompromising as it was. It had a harsh beauty that appealed to him, and now, all dressed in autumn colours, it was the perfect backdrop for his fiery Georgiana.

He felt that strange ache in his chest again and rubbed at it with the heel of his hand. If only she was from a better family. He could have overlooked her lack of fortune, he had wealth enough after all. But he couldn't ignore the responsibility he bore the family name. In any case his mother would have one of her spasms and probably never recover if he had the temerity to bring home a mere doctor's daughter. The dowager duchess had already given him a list of eligible women. It was what had driven him to try and make a list of his own. In the end, however, he had been forced to concede that the next duchess would likely be as plain and dull as she was well bred. Their kind didn't marry for love though, for power and land and money, but never for love. It was his duty, a duty that had been driven home to him since he had been old enough to understand the concept, and he wouldn't shirk it. No matter if it made him sick to the stomach.

But anticipation stirred in his blood as he arrived at their meeting place and he leapt down, loosening Azor's girth and leaving him to crop the grass while he paced, waiting impatiently for Georgiana to arrive. Looking up at the soft sound of footsteps he watched as she appeared out of the tree line. With red tinted leaves tumbling around her and the countryside glowing copper and gold, she looked like the goddess of autumn with her Titian curls framing her face. He felt his breath catch, and as she walked closer with Conrad bounding around her feet and barking with joy, he felt he would forever remember this moment, a memory caught in amber that he would carry with him for the rest of his days.

He held out his hands and she ran to meet him, holding out her own, but when she drew close he swept her up, laughing and spinning her around. When he put her down she stumbled, dizzy and delighted as he pulled her close. Staring at those hazel eyes so full of laughter, and her cheeks prettily flushed and with the faintest scattering of freckles, he knew leaving her would be the hardest thing he'd ever done.

"What is it?" she asked, reaching a hand up to his cheek. He leaned into it, turning his head to kiss her palm and shaking his head.

"Nothing."

"It's not nothing," she said, her voice quiet. "You were thinking that you must leave soon."

Her quiet acceptance of it made his heart clench. "I don't want to talk about it," he said, surprised at how gruff he sounded.

"I don't want to think about it either," she said, and he could hear the sorrow in her voice. "But you will go, and ... and I won't see you again. I know that ..."

"Don't!" he cried out and turned away from her, running a hand through his hair.

He felt her hand on his shoulder, felt it slide down his arm, until her soft fingers wrapped around his.

"Come, Beau. I will weep for a long time after you've gone I promise you. But there is no point in pretending it will be otherwise. We knew it from the start after all. A Marquis has no business marrying a girl with no name and no fortune. You must go and find yourself a wealthy heiress, and I will content myself with the idea that she will be dull and ugly."

He heard the catch in her voice, heard the effort she was making to be light hearted, no doubt thinking that he would be disgusted if she wept over him and pleaded for him to stay. Indeed, if she had been any other of his lovers she would have been perfectly correct. But now he wanted her to cry and beg him to stay, because he wanted to do it, foolish as it was. He wanted to stay so badly that it frightened him and Jeffries' words came back to haunt him all over again. He wished, apart from anything else, to hear her say his name.

How foolish he had been to want to be Beau, to want her to know from the outset that he wouldn't care for her, that he would likely ruin her and move on. Not that he was doing anything other than that. He was toying with her life, her future. If he truly cared for her he would go away now, before he did any more damage. But he was far too selfish after all.

He turned around and saw sadness glimmering in the pretty hazel eyes that stared up at him.

"I will never, never forget you," he whispered. "I swear it."

She smiled and stepped closer to him, one hand pressed against his chest. "I'm glad, for I could never forget you either. I ..." She stopped with a blush staining her cheeks and looked down.

"What?" he demanded, tilting her head back to look at him, wanting her to say it, even though it was selfish and cruel to take any more from her.

She shook her head and smiled at him, though it was forlorn. "No," she said, and the teasing look he loved so well gleamed in her eyes now. "You are quite conceited enough I think, without giving you another victory." She gave him a coquettish look before walking away a little, glancing at him over her shoulder. "It's not as if you don't know it."

He ran after her and tumbled her down into the grass as she laughed and pretended to fight him off.

"Release me, you fiend," she huffed, pretending to be cross with him as he pinned her down and desire rose through him like a tide. She stilled, seeing the truth of it in his eyes.

"No," she whispered, reading him with ease. "You know I cannot."

He didn't pretend to misunderstand her, or to argue the fact. He simply ducked his head and kissed her, relishing the way she responded to him, knowing that she kissed like she did because he had taught her well. The idea that she would one day practise such skills on another man made fury and jealousy ignite in his blood and he held her tighter. Forcing her knees apart with his own he settled between them, letting her feel the weight of him as he kissed her with rising need, as though he would cease to be if he stopped now. He moved his lips from her mouth and trailed a path down her jaw, down her neck, hearing her breathing coming fast and hot against his skin. His mouth moved on, restless, seeking, as he found the soft swell of her breasts and trailed his tongue over the silky mounds.

Dropping one hand he gathered up the soft muslin of her dress in his fingers and tugged it higher, exposing her skin until her skirts revealed one shapely thigh. His hand slid over her knee, moving over her skin and slipping under the fabric as she caught her breath.

"No," she murmured, sounding troubled and restive as she writhed beneath him, pushing his hand away. "Please, Beau."

Sebastian, he raged inwardly, *my name is Sebastian.* Though he didn't stop but shook off her grasp and allowed his questing fingers to explore beneath her skirts, shifting his position until he sought out the little thatch of curls between her thighs as she gasped in shock.

“Please don’t,” she whispered, clutching at his arm as he looked down at her, seeing desire in her eyes just as fierce as his own. If he was any kind of gentleman he would stop now.

“Please, love,” he begged, kissing the corner of her mouth. “Let me touch you.”

She swallowed and stilled, and though he hated himself he was driven to continue, seeking out the tiny nub of flesh that would bring her pleasure. Caressing, touching her so, so gently, he felt her breathing hitch as he returned his lips to hers, kissing her again. Tenderly this time, he explored the silky warmth of her mouth as her breathing grew more ragged, as her body twitched and shifted beneath him.

“Do you like that?” he whispered against her mouth as he slid one finger inside her, caressing still with small, careful movements.

“I ...” she began and stopped, staring up at him, fear and desire tangled together in her eyes. He watched her as the pleasure began to build, as her eyes grew hazy and she moaned, small, urgent sounds that made his own body tighten further.

“Let go,” he urged, desperate to see her pleasure. He would have this much from her at least, before he left. “Let it take you over.” He spoke the words against her skin as he slid another finger inside her and felt her body respond. She was slick and hot and he was so desperate to sink inside of her and find his own release, but he continued to stroke and caress as her body sang with tension. She clutched at him, one hand pulling at his hair as her head tilted back and she arched beneath him. Her body clenched around his fingers as she bucked and gasped and cried out and desire sang through him as he watched her come apart in his arms.

***

Georgiana fought for breath, gasping as pleasure and panic rolled over her in equal measure. She no longer knew what kind of creature she was. She felt betrayed somehow by her own skin. She had known he was going too far, taking too much and yet her flesh had demanded that he continue as he invaded her most intimate places.

She knew now, how it was he had gained such a reputation. For even as every argument for good sense had been put forth by her poor, desperate mind her body had rejected them with no more than a feeble protest passing her lips. Even now, with the traces of pleasure still fizzing in her veins and her body languid and sated, it wasn't enough.

There was a strange, dull ache inside her, a hollow feeling that hungered for more, for him. Instinctively she knew this was ground she could not set foot upon if she didn't want to end her days alone. If she gave herself to him she would be ruined and no matter that the desire to do just that burned like a brand inside her. That she couldn't do.

She tried to sit up, to push him away but he was too heavy and she stilled, suddenly afraid. Not afraid of him, but afraid of what she would allow him if he continued to persuade her in such a fashion, for she had no defence, no argument to pit against such voluptuous enticements.

He was staring down at her, such need in his dark eyes that her heart began to thunder as it just had when he had mastered her own flesh.

"Please, Beau," she begged, feeling tears spring to her eyes. "No more, please."

She looked up at him and saw the desperation, the raw desire to take her, fighting with whatever care he may have for her. In the end he rolled away and lay on his back with a curse and she let out a shaky breath.

"I want you," he said, his voice heavy with all of the same sensations that rolled over her skin at his words.

"I want you too," she whispered. "But we cannot be together, and I must be a virgin when I wed. I can't ..."

"I know!" he shouted. She jumped, shocked by the anger in his words. Without another word she sat up, intending to leave now, while she still could but he reached out and grasped her hand, yanking her to him so that she fell across his chest. "Would you leave me now?" he demanded. "Leave and not come back? Is that what you intend?"

She gasped at the fury in his eyes and shook her head, even though she had thought just that. This was too dangerous, *he* was too dangerous. "N-no ..." she stammered.

"Liar!" The accusation made her jolt with alarm but she had no time to react as he rolled her onto her back once more, finding his place between her legs. Grasping her thigh he pulled it around his hip and pressed himself against her, rocking against her tormented flesh. She could feel the hardness of him sliding over her as he moved and desire blazed to life beneath her skin like a spark hitting kindling, devouring it all in a fierce burn that left nothing behind but ashes.

"You want this," he said, his dark eyes treacherous with passion. "You want me."

"Yes," she whispered. "Yes, I do." She blinked up at him, willing him not to take it any further. For even as she knew she would struggle to deny him, it would break her heart to know he held her so cheap.

She saw the moment he realised it in his own eyes. With regret he moved away, though he pulled her with him and held her close in his arms.

"It's like a kind of madness," he said, his voice rough. "I've never known it feel this way before."

"Truly?" she looked down at him, wanting to believe she wasn't like all the others. But wasn't that what all the women before her had thought, that they were different, *special*. But he would leave her the same way he had left each of them. Moving onto the next challenge, the next conquest.

He grasped her face in one large hand and she saw desperation in his eyes. "I feel like I will lose my mind when I leave you."

She tried to smile at him but her heart was too numb to make it work as it should. "I'd settle for your heart," she replied, tracing a finger over his lips.

"You have it," he said, and the words were angry and urgent. "You have it all."

Chapter 9

"Wherein the truth is hard to hear, and harder still to act upon."

If Jeffries was troubled further by his demeanour when he returned he didn't remark on it as Sebastian flung Azor's reins at him and stalked into the castle without a word. He was less lucky with Beau.

Entering the book room, he'd hoped at this hour his friend would be dressing for dinner and he could help himself to a drink and try to calm his temper. His nerves seemed all too close to his skin, the slightest drag of fabric over his flesh tormenting him with memories of repressed desire. He was wound too tight, his body aching with the need for Georgiana, her body and heart both, and his own heart was raw at the idea neither could ever be his.

He had to get away. He knew it. For both their sakes before he dragged them into disaster. For while he could walk away from a scandal with no outward sign of hurt if he ruined her, he knew he would never forgive himself. The stain of it would taint his heart and soul for the rest of his days.

So finding Beau's speculative gaze weighing him up the moment he stepped through the door was not something to make him feel any easier in his skin.

"Well, well, the wanderer returns," he drawled, raising a crystal glass to his lips and sipping, his eyes never leaving his friend.

"Beau," Sebastian nodded a greeting and went to pour a large measure of his own. He downed it in one large swallow, savouring the burn for a moment before pouring another.

"You look like you needed that," Beau said. Sebastian threw him a warning glance and found he was being watched intently, those cool blue eyes assessing. "She must be quite something to have you in such a lather," he added, swirling the amber liquid in his glass with a bored air.

"I'm going to dress," Sebastian said, turning, drink in hand. He didn't reply to his friend's observations. There was nothing to be gained by it.

"Not so fast, Sindalton."

He paused, Beau rarely used his title, and though he wanted to avoid the coming discussion he could hardly slam the door in his face when he clearly had something to say.

"What?" he demanded, not bothering to hide the annoyance.

"What the devil are you playing at, man?" Beau gave him a hard look as he got to his feet and went to stand beside the vast stone fireplace. "You've got enough ladybirds here to satisfy any man ... even me for God's sake! And yet you're careering all over the countryside from morning till night like some lovesick mooncalf. What the blazes has gotten into you?"

"Don't be ridiculous, Beau," he snapped, turning away and taking a large swallow of his drink. He walked to the window and stared outside, the night was drawing in and the room seemed cold despite the fire that blazed in the hearth.

"Don't you *Beau* me," his friend continued, clearly unimpressed by his denial. "I know you too well, my friend. And I know that I've never seen that look of desperation in your eyes before. You've gone and fallen for some unsuitable piece haven't you? Haven't you?" he demanded.

Sebastian swung back around, fighting the desire to clench his fists. "Mind your own damned business!"

"Good God I knew it!" Beau ran a hand through his thick blond hair and looked at him in exasperation. "Tell me she's a widow or some such?" he said, and Sebastian was jolted by the real concern in his eyes. "Tell me she's not going to cause you trouble because if you think I'm accompanying you to Scotland for the duration you've got another thing coming I assure you!" Despite his acid tongue Sebastian heard the agitation behind his friend's words.

Sebastian snorted in disgust and shook his head. "She'll cause me no trouble I promise you, and there is no scandal," he said, hoping this at least would reassure him. Though he'd come close enough to playing the fool today. "We leave next week in any case," he added, wishing those words hadn't sounded quite so dejected.

"No." Beau shook his head, a determined gleam in the blue. "We leave Friday. That gives you one day to say your broken-hearted goodbyes and consign her to the past where she belongs."

"Dammit, Beau!" he exploded in fury, grasping the glass in his hand so tight it was a wonder it didn't shatter. "You are not my father. I don't need or want your help in this."

Beau stalked towards him and poked him in the chest with one elegant, manicured finger. "Well that's a pity because you have it. I'll not see you tangle yourself in a dreadful scandal because some chit has discovered she's snared a duke."

"She's not like that!" Sebastian roared, truly furious by now and realising he'd said too much, but Beau merely snorted.

"They never are, until they are," he replied with a cynical sneer twisting his handsome face.

"She's not, Beau. I swear it. She's sweet and innocent and ... I'm a damned bastard." Sebastian shook his head, suddenly exhausted. He didn't want to fight, he wanted to talk about her. He wanted to explain to Beau just how wonderful she was, how she didn't look at him and see money or a title but teased him and put him in his place. He wanted to tell him that he'd never felt like this before but he didn't dare. He swallowed the rest of his drink and headed back to the decanter to pour another.

Despite his reputation he didn't like to drink until he felt out of control, and liked the aftermath even less. But tonight he wanted to lose himself in it, so that he might drown the ache of desire and sorrow that had taken root in his bones. He turned back to Beau and shook his head in despair. "I'd marry her if I could."

Beau gaped at him. "You bloody fool. What have you been playing at?"

He laughed and flung himself down in the chair Beau had recently vacated. "Damned if I know," he replied, his tone bitter.

"Is she married?"

He looked up and met Beau's eyes, knowing he must indeed think him a fool. Cold hearted and sophisticated, no one had ever touched his friend's cynical heart, nor would they. Sebastian would think he didn't have one if not for his rather arbitrary acts of selfless generosity that would come out of the blue from time to time. He'd been a good friend to Sebastian, if one he still didn't fully understand.

"No," he said, his voice weary. "Not married, but her parents are dead and her uncle is her guardian. He's the local doctor," he added with a wry smile. "And of course she has no fortune to compensate for her lack of breeding."

"Oh, Sebastian." This was said on a groan of despair as Beau sought the chair next to him and stared at him with a pitying expression.

"I'm sorry, old friend. Are you terribly disillusioned in me?" he said, mockery in his eyes.

"I should be," Beau replied, shaking his head in disgust. "After the pains I have taken with your education. But I knew at heart you would not attain the heights of villainy I have gained. Your heart is still intact despite everything, and it's this troublesome organ that will lead you into far more misery than any other part of your anatomy I assure you."

Sebastian chuckled, acknowledging the truth of it, though he turned his gaze on Beau with a grin. "Then you'd best have a care, for I'm not quite certain you are as heartless as you make out."

"Oh do be quiet," Beau replied with a tut and a wave of his hand. "You've never seen me weep over a woman and you never will.

"I don't remember weeping yet," Sebastian said, his tone droll, though if he hoped to fool Beau he was far from the mark.

"No, but you've not endured your tender farewell yet have you?"

Sebastian scowled at him.

"For God's sake get it over with," Beau urged him, leaning forward in his chair. "We'll go back to London and busy ourselves in something sordid until you've forgotten all about her. You can't marry her. If you want to have her before you leave then so be it, but get on with it and then turn away. There is nothing else to be done."

His hand clenched around the crystal glass once more, his jaw clenched so tight it hurt. Forcing himself to relax he stared back at Beau. "How do you know I haven't had her already?" he said with a sneer.

Beau got to his feet and bestowed him with a shrewd glance. "Because I know you and your principles probably better than you do. Seducing a girl set on seducing you for your title is fair game, but this one ... She's got under your skin, and you care for her. No," he said, with a mocking laugh. "If you'd had her there would be guilt in your eyes rather than the self-righteous gleam of a broken-hearted lover." He turned and walked away, pausing at the door. "Do what you will, Sebastian, it's all one to me. But say goodbye to her. No matter if I advise it or not, you know you must."

Sebastian watched as the door closed behind him and had to hold back on the urge to fling his glass at the shut door in a fit of temper. He wanted to rage and sulk like some sullen young man in the clutches of his first love affair. *It's not fair.* The words raged in his mind with just as much impotence as they had when he'd been told his father was dead, drowned at sea when his ship went down. Both him and his beautiful lover lost in a raging ocean as they ran from the duel during which he'd shot her husband dead. Now *there* was a scandal to set tongues wagging. Nothing he could ever do could surpass that at least.

But now he had to try and restore some of the tainted gilt to the family honour. He had to marry a bride whose lineage was impeccable. A woman whose manners and breeding would return the shine to their sullied name. Perhaps then, by the time his heir was of age, the name Sindalton would stand for something other than murder and adultery.

He got to his feet and poured another drink. Dammit if he wasn't the biggest fool alive. But tomorrow he would do as he must. Not because Beau had told him to, far from it. Only because it was the right thing to do. If he stayed any longer he would take from her more than he already had and perhaps leave her with an illegitimate child to compound his villainy. And Beau was right in that at least, he wasn't bastard enough to scale those heights.

He tried to think of something he could do for her, something that would leave her with a tender place in her heart for him, no matter how the years passed for them both. In the end he decided to head into Truro in the morning. He would find something, small and discreet, something that wouldn't give her away and make her blush. And then he would walk away, and he'd leave her behind.

Chapter 10

"Wherein two lovers part."

Georgiana sat on her bed and wondered at the way love could change a person. She had always thought love a gentle and sweet emotion, something to be sought out and cherished once found. In her aunt and uncle she had only seen the best of it. Theirs was the happiest of unions, between two people of like minds. But what had it been like for them in the early days, she wondered now? When Aunt Jane's parents had issued their warnings, that if she chose Joseph Bomford she would be dead to them cut from their history as if she'd never been. It had never crossed her mind to wonder before, what kind of love could have made her give everything up that she'd ever known for a man her family deemed was beneath their association.

But this wasn't her choice to make. Only Beau could choose to ignore his family's wishes and she knew he could not. No matter if he wanted to. He needed money, she knew it, and even if he had it, she was so far below him in status that it would be talked about. People would stare at her and gossip, and wonder how she trapped him into it. She wondered if love could survive such trials. Hers could have. She had always considered herself a sensible woman, not the kind to swoon and fall into hysterics. No Cheltenham tragedies were acted in this house, her uncle would say with pride. The idea of what he would say if he ever discovered ... the look in Aunt Jane's eyes if she knew the liberties she had allowed him to take ...

Her face burned and she buried her head in her hands in shame. Perhaps there was bad blood in her. For what kind of nice young lady would writhe and moan and allow a man who had no intention of marrying her to touch her in such an intimate fashion? What nature of innocent young woman would spend all night lying awake, her skin burning with desire and with the desperate need for him to touch her that way again.

She took a breath and forced herself to her feet. It was time to go and meet him. She prayed that he would tell her he was leaving and in the same breath prayed that he would not. Though if he didn't end it, she knew somehow she must. She must find the strength to say goodbye. She was enmeshed, but she must find her way clear so that nothing could hurt her family. For she would not repay every kindness bestowed upon her by her aunt and uncle by bringing scandal to their door. Even if it broke her heart to do it.

She took a moment to check her hair, and pinch her cheeks, aware that she was looking dreadfully pale. She had felt guilt squeeze her heart just that morning as Mary had enquired if she was feeling quite well and offered to make her a posset to bring some brightness back to her eyes. Putting such uncomfortable thoughts aside, she tied on her bonnet, and smoothed out the pale green sarsnet of her walking dress before doing up her pelisse. With the lie coming all too easily to her tongue she told Aunt Jane she was taking Conrad for his afternoon walk, and headed out of the house.

It took little more than half an hour to reach their secluded little corner of the world. A place where impossible dreams had tried to make her believe in an unlikely future. Though at least she was not quite so foolish and green as to have fallen for them.

As ever he was waiting for her and she took a moment to admire the width of those impressive shoulders, the sheer size of him in that impeccably tailored superfine jacket. If ever she had been able to stand beside him in company, with her head up, instead of snatching clandestine meetings, she would have been so very proud. That was not her affair, she reminded herself, though the pain welled in her throat. That was for his future, and she ... She was merely a small chapter in his past.

Taking a deep breath she tried to put a smile on her face, and walked forward.

She was rewarded at least by the look in his eyes, by the way he jumped down from the rock he'd been sitting on and ran to her. Folding her in his arms and kissing her like he would never let her go, even though they both knew it was a lie.

"I was afraid you wouldn't come," he said, his big hands cradling her face.

She laughed and shook her head. "Don't be foolish, Beau," she said with that teasing note he seemed to enjoy. "You never doubted it for a moment. You know I really shouldn't have done, I can't help but think the set down would do you good."

He shook his head and her heart was gratified to see the misery in his eyes matched hers. At least it wasn't her alone who felt the pain of his leaving. That would have been hard indeed.

"A set down," he repeated, his dark eyes reproachful. "Is that all you think it would be for me?"

"Beau," she began, wishing he wouldn't make it so hard for them both. If perhaps they played their parts, if perhaps they teased and smiled and put on a brave face they would survive this. At least then she might be able walk away without breaking down and begging him not to leave her.

"Don't you understand how this hurts?" he demanded, grasping hold of her shoulders, his fingers bruising he held her so hard. "Don't you feel it too?"

Anger flared then, anger at the injustice of it. "Do you think I don't?" she flung back at him, tears pricking at her eyes. "Do you think I don't want to beg you to stay and marry me? To forget the fortune you need, to forget your duty to your title and your family and whatever other obligations would come before my happiness, of which I don't doubt there are many!" She paused, staring at him with her heart full of pain and holding hard to her dignity. "It's you who are leaving me, Beau. Not the other way around. But there is nothing I can do to make you stay. Nothing I can offer you of enough value besides my heart and you have that. So do *not* stand there and accuse me of being cold or indifferent to your feelings when I try to make it easier for you to leave me."

She saw her words register and his eyes closed as he acknowledged the truth of them.

"Forgive me," he said, his voice bleak.

Georgiana smiled at that despite herself. "Again? Well why not once more, to add to all the forgiveness you have had already." She hadn't meant the words to have such a bitter edge. Stepping closer she put her hands on his chest to show she wasn't angry with him, not really. He looked down at her, his dark eyes full of pain and any anger she might have had fled in the light of that unhappiness. "There is nothing you can do, nothing I can do," she whispered. "I knew you would leave me today. I--I half hoped you would, even though it breaks my heart because ... because there is too much at risk now. We both know it."

He nodded and pulled her closer, enfolding her in his arms and pushing her bonnet back to bury his face in her hair. "I know," he said, his voice desperate. "If I stay I will not be able to leave you be. You tempt me in ways I have no strength to fight against and I dare not allow it. I am too weak to be close to you and not have you and I cannot use you so ill as that, despite everything I have done already. I care for you too much for that at least." He gave a snort of derision. "Hark at me and my noble sentiments. I would have taken you yesterday if you had given an inch and we both know it."

She reached up a finger to his lips and shook her head. "Don't. Please don't. For there is a part of me that will always regret not giving myself to you and damn the consequences, but it is not just myself I must think of. I have been given so much by my family, I cannot repay them by courting such disgrace as this, no matter if my heart would do so willingly."

"Oh, God, Georgiana."

He kissed her then, a kiss that seared her soul and left her dizzy with longing, delirious with the need for more. As though he taunted her with everything she could never have, he kissed her like she was everything he had ever wanted and needed, until she wanted to cry out with the pain the loss of him would bring her. He released her mouth but held her tightly still as she trembled with desire and emotion, enclosed in his arms.

They stood together, neither of them willing or able to say a word for a moment. “I have something for you,” he said in the end, and she looked up as he reached into a pocket and withdrew a small box. “It ... it isn’t much,” he added, sounding apologetic. “You must believe me when I tell you I wanted to buy you diamonds and sapphires but ... but they would only have brought you trouble if they’d been discovered.”

She smiled at him, knowing he spoke the truth and beyond touched that he had thought so carefully about a gift for her. He opened the box to reveal a delicate gold chain, and suspended on it, a small gold heart.

“Just to remind you, if you should ever be in any doubt ... that you have my heart, Georgiana.”

She touched her finger to the heart and blinked away tears. “Thank you,” she managed, though her voice was thick. “I will keep it always.” She took the chain from the box and slipped it into her reticule. “I will have to invent a kindly old lady who will bequeath it to me, won’t I?” she said, trying to joke though it seemed very far from funny.

“I would ask something in return,” he said, reaching out and curling a lock of her hair around his fingers.

“Of course!” she said, wishing she had thought of it herself. “B-but I have no scissors, nothing to ...”

“I came prepared,” he said, smiling at her as he brushed her lips with his own and snipped off one thick curl. He held it to his mouth and kissed it, before putting it carefully in the box her necklace had come in. “I will carry it with me always.”

"Oh, don't promise that," she pleaded, shaking her head. "For your wife will discover it one day and then how should she feel? No, it is too cruel."

"And you are too good!" he shouted, pulling her close again. "Dammit, why should you care for her, whoever she may be. I know damned well that I shan't."

"Don't, Beau, don't please," she pleaded. "Kiss me again and then let me go, for if you don't I have the strangest feeling that everything will turn sour. Please, my love."

"And what will you do?" he demanded, his tone once again cruel and desperate with pain. "When I am gone what will you do then?"

She looked up at him and this time she was powerless to stop the tears that ran down her face with abandon. "Today?" she asked, her voice choking on a sob. "Today I will go home and tell them I am unwell as they all believed this morning, when I was so quiet and drab. And they will put me to bed and the moment they close the door I will cry and cry until there are no tears left in the world that I haven't shed." She laughed then, feeling really quite beyond her own sanity, as though she would run mad in her desperate sorrow. "You see I have the advantage of you in this at least," she said, smoothing her hands over his lapels with care. "I am only a woman after all, a weak creature governed by her emotions and fanciful whims. So if I take to my bed and cry no one will think too very much of it, other than perhaps that I am a little low in spirit. But you, darling Beau, you must be brave and swallow it down and pretend that there is nothing that you care for, that nothing has ever touched your heart, nor ever will. And I promise not to embarrass you by throwing myself into the sea on your account or something equally sordid." She tried to smile at him at that but could do nothing now but cry, and buried her face in his neck, sobbing and clinging to him as hard as she could.

It took a great effort to stop herself, and it was only the thought that his last memory of her shouldn't be of a red eyed, desperate creature that made her take a breath and steady herself again.

He was silent, but his hold on her was enough to speak for him, as was the aching sadness in his eyes. "Kiss me goodbye then, my own handsome scoundrel."

For a moment she thought he wouldn't but then his lips found hers in a tender kiss, full of longing and desire, and everything they both knew they could never have.

He caught her face in his hands, his expression fierce. "I will never forget you, Georgiana. I promise you."

"Nor I, Beau," she promised in return, kissing his cheek and somehow finding the strength to move out of his arms. She was so numb she didn't even call to Conrad who caught up with her farther down the lane with a bark of reproach. There was nothing that seemed real now, nothing that seemed to exist outside of this fresh, exquisite pain that tore at her from the inside and promised that she would never be happy again. So it was that she found her way home, and did just as she'd told him she would. And while Aunt Jane instructed the maids to bring a hot brick for her feet and hartshorn and water, Georgiana cried and cried until there were no tears left at all.

Chapter 11

"Wherein a villain brings past and future scandals to darken our heroine's life."

Georgiana sat on the rock, her arms wrapped around her knees, staring into the distance. She'd come back to their meeting place every day for the past fortnight though she knew it was foolish. He was never coming back again. Soon enough she would read the notice of his betrothal in the Gazette and even the faintest hope that her idiotic heart still clung to would be gone. She scolded herself every morning that passed, telling herself severely that it wasn't the least bit of good pining for something you knew you could never have and promising to put him out of her mind. And yet every afternoon she would call Conrad and retrace their footsteps to the exact same place. She just felt closer to him here than anywhere else, even though he was now miles away and perhaps already dallying with another pretty girl to chase the memory of her from his mind.

She swallowed hard as Conrad came bounding up to her and pushed his cold, wet nose under her arm, seeking attention.

"Yes, I think you miss him too, don't you, love? He always made a fuss of you and was very obliging at throwing sticks." She ruffled his chest with affection. "Yes, and I know he threw them a good deal farther than I did. I'm sorry for it, truly, but I do my best you know." She prattled on in this fashion for a while until even Conrad grew bored and took himself off to dig out a rabbit hole.

With care she took out the necklace Beau had left her, letting the fine gold slide between her fingers as the little heart sat in her palm, glinting in the feeble sunlight of the afternoon. The weather was closing in, the trees almost bare now and all the autumn colour stripped from the countryside. She felt like every trace of her short-lived affair was being taken from her as the season died and the cold hand of winter passed over the landscape. For such a short time everything had been golden, but now it was dead and cold and lonely, and she didn't know how she would endure it.

She tucked the heart back away and got to her feet, calling Conrad and walking back down towards the woods. She had the distance between here and the house to force a smile to her lips and drape the persona of Georgiana Bomford about her like a mantle, hiding the person she'd become since that fateful day in the cave. Because she wasn't the same anymore. No matter that she tried to be. Her world seemed small and confined and she chafed at the restrictions of her circumstances as she never had before. That was perhaps the worst of all, she thought. That he had made her so dissatisfied with her lot, when she knew that she was most fortunate in every way.

With a sigh and a final scold she turned the corner into the garden of her aunt and uncle's house and paused as she noticed a fine carriage in the driveway. Her heart picked up speed. It was impossible surely? But her heart did not consider it impossible or unlikely and she burst through the front door at a run, straight into the anxious bosom of the grey haired housekeeper, Mrs Gurney.

"Oh thank goodness, child! Wherever have you been? I've been looking high and low, and the house is all at sixes and sevens. Now go on upstairs, Clara is waiting for you. She's got out your best cambric, the pale rose, oh do hurry, Georgiana!"

"B-but who is here, Gurney?" she stammered, her heart thudding too hard to allow her fevered brain to make sense of it.

"Your uncle, Baron Dalton is here!" she hissed, flapping her hands to hurry Georgiana up the stairs.

For a moment the disappointment was so acute that she could do nothing but stare at Mrs Gurney and try to breathe through the pain in her chest.

"Well don't just stand there like a gudgeon, love," pleaded the older woman, flapping her apron at her in agitation. "You must go and make yourself presentable."

"I have an uncle?" Georgiana said, as Gurney put a hand in the small of her back and physically pushed her up the stairs.

"That you do," Gurney replied, sounding as though she'd found a weevil in the flour bin.

"Who is he and what's he doing here?" Georgiana demanded, still too shaken to put enough effort into wondering why she hadn't known she had another uncle.

Gurney hustled her through the door of her bedroom where Clara pounced on her and the two women wrestled her out of her walking dress between them.

"He's your Aunt Jane's elder brother, and my ma always told me if you can't say no good about a body, best keep your tongue between your teeth."

This rather bold statement from Gurney made it clear to Georgiana that not only did Mrs Gurney not like her new uncle, but neither did Aunt Jane and Uncle Joseph. Gurney would never have ventured such an opinion of one of her relations if she didn't know full well that her mistress's sentiments were of like mind, and this was no doubt why he'd never been mentioned before. She assumed that this was one of the heartless relations who had cast off her Aunt Jane when she had chosen to marry for love.

So once she was primped and tidied to Gurney's satisfaction, it was with no small measure of trepidation that she went to meet her new relation. Knowing what she did about how coldly her aunt's family had treated her when she married Uncle Joseph it was with no expectation of liking the man she found in the drawing room that she opened the door. It didn't take her long to realise that she'd misjudged the situation.

Her uncle, the baron, was a tall, severe man, with an autocratic manner. His dress was obviously of the best quality and he bore himself like a duke, looking around the room with distaste and like there was a bad smell lingering somewhere close by. He had perhaps been a handsome man in his youth as he was well made with a fine straight nose and a strong jaw. But every line of a cruel and avaricious nature seemed to Georgiana to be etched clearly on a face she found devoid of any of the kinder human emotions.

Indeed when her poor aunt, who was clearly in a state of great agitation, jumped to her feet as Georgiana entered the room and made to introduce them, the way he looked her over made her blood boil.

"As I feared," he said with a sniff. "You are the image of your mother."

Georgiana glanced at her aunt who had clearly been crying and was clutching a handkerchief in one clenched hand and her vinaigrette in the other.

"It's true, you are," Aunt Jane said smiling at her, before shooting a look of intense dislike at her brother. "She was such a beauty, you see."

"A pity she was also a whore."

Both Georgiana and Aunt Jane jumped in shock at the cruel vulgarity of his words.

"No, Lionel," Aunt Jane replied, with unusual force. "That is the outside of enough. I will not allow you to come here, to *my* house, and speak in such an abominable manner. If you cannot keep a civil tongue in your head you can leave now."

"I will do no such thing, madam," her brother replied with froideur. "I have come here, to your *house,"* he said, announcing the word with derision as though he stood in a hovel. "To speak to Miss Dalton and make things clear to her. You may leave while I do so."

"I will do no such thing as to leave her alone with you!"

Georgiana, quite stunned by this, went and sat beside Aunt Jane who was clearly on the edge of hysteria. Taking her hand, she held it in hers and squeezed to try and comfort her. Aunt Jane covered her hand with her own and clung on tight.

"Aunt Jane, what on earth is this about?" Georgiana asked, turning her back on a man she had quickly decided forced her emotions well past mere dislike into the uncharted territories of revulsion and abhorrence. "Why does this ill-mannered creature refer to me as Miss Dalton. I have been and will always be Georgiana Bomford."

"You will keep a civil tongue in your head, young woman!" the man purporting to be her uncle raged at her.

Georgiana turned and stared at him with disgust. "Sir, you have been in my company for barely a few minutes, reduced my aunt to tears, called my mother a whore and generally behaved in a crass and loutish manner ill befitting a gentleman. Therefore, I can only deduce that you are not a gentleman."

Her uncle seemed torn between his obvious desire to cross the room and deliver her a blow to the head and whatever his purpose had been in coming here in the first place. In the end his objective seemed to win out as he reined in his temper but looked at her with undisguised hostility.

"What do you know of your parents, Miss Dalton?" he asked, his voice harsh.

"Very little," she replied, meeting his eyes and refusing to be cowed by his high-handed manner. "Only that they both died when I was but less than a year old."

"And do you know *how* they died?" he demanded, and from the obvious relish he took from asking the question, Georgiana knew that here, at last was the shadow that covered her name.

"I do not." She spoke with dignity and clung to her aunt's hand as she began to sob, leaning against Georgiana's shoulder.

He gave her a cold, serpentine smile that made unease slither over her flesh. "Your mother was conducting an affair with another man, a duke of all people, though how she managed that is beyond me," he added with a sneer. "Your father, the previous Baron Dalton discovered the two of them together and challenged the duke to a duel."

Georgiana drew in a breath as her aunt began to cry harder beside her. She had constructed many stories about her parents when she was very small, inventing tales of lost princesses and bad fairies. As she had grown older she had come to believe that something had happened that would not cast her in a good light, and had instinctively shied away from asking too many questions. But never, in her wildest imaginings, had she considered anything so dreadful as this.

"Your father was killed outright by the duke," her uncle continued, unheeding of his sister's misery or of the obvious hurt he was inflicting upon his niece. "The duke in turn was forced to flee, taking your mother with him." He paused to give her such a callous smile that real fear bloomed in her chest. "Of course she abandoned you and left you without a second glance to run off with her lover."

"No, Lionel!" her aunt pleaded, sobbing. "You cannot be so cruel as that. She had no time to fetch Georgiana. She would have I'm sure!" She turned to Georgiana, her eyes full of compassion as she clung to her hand. "She loved you, sweet child. I'm sure she did. She would never have left you if she'd had a choice. I'm certain she intended to send for you once she was settled."

"You know nothing of the sort." The baron strode across the room to look out the window at the pretty garden that lay behind the house, though his eyes seemed to find nothing to please him. "The whore ran away and left her child and it was the only favour she ever did you, Miss Dalton, as she drowned with the duke when their ship went down in a storm."

Georgiana clutched at her aunt's hand and tried to keep calm. They couldn't both succumb to hysterics and she determined that this vile man would not see that he'd hurt her or discomforted her in any way.

"I see," she said, with the strangest feeling she was living in some kind of bizarre nightmare. Her emotions were already so raw and close to the surface with Beau leaving, that to add this melodrama to the misery of the past weeks was almost more than she could bear. She could only be glad that the shock of it had numbed her for the moment so that her voice did not tremble when she spoke. "I thank you for taking the time to come and divulge such unpleasant tidings to me, sir. I hope that you have taken enough satisfaction from the delivery of them and pray we do not keep you a moment longer from your affairs."

He laughed, a cold and unaffected sound that quite chilled her.

"Oh, but that isn't why I'm here, child," he said and when she looked up she discovered that her uncle had taken on the persona of every villain she had ever read of in all the Gothic novels she loved most. All she needed to complete the picture was that it be night time in a castle instead of afternoon in their cramped drawing room, that the candles should be guttering in their sockets and a thunderstorm raging outside.

To her relief this ridiculous notion made her smile as it cast her as the heroine, who must outwit her wicked relative, no doubt bent on murdering her or something equally nefarious. She thought perhaps her sensibilities must have suffered enough for one day and she was overwrought, as she began to laugh. Her uncle looked at her in astonishment.

"What the devil is wrong with you now?" He paced back across the room to stand beside the fireplace, and with such a furious look on his face that she was put strongly in mind of the wicked Marchese de Montferra, in *The Orphan of the Rhine*. The idea quite overset her and she had to bite her lip rather hard to restore her equilibrium. It did however remove some of her fear of both the situation and her uncle, and gave him a rather ridiculous character in the light of all his airs and graces.

"Why nothing, Sir. Pray do continue," she said, staring at him in quite a new light.

He stared at her with a cool expression for a moment before he spoke again. “I will speak with you alone, Miss Dalton.”

“That you will not!” her aunt shrieked, though she trembled visibly now and Georgiana was alarmed by the high colour on her cheeks.

“There, there, Aunt Jane, please don’t worry. You go and have a lay down. I will speak with my uncle and show him out as soon as he has said his piece. I’m sure it won’t take but a moment,” she added, glaring at the man.

With difficulty Georgiana calmed her a little and sent for Mrs Gurney who took one look at Baron Dalton, gave a sniff of outrage as she summed the man up with one disparaging glance and went to her mistress. Supported by Gurney, Aunt Jane was persuaded out of the room, leaving Georgiana alone with her uncle.

Chapter 12

"Wherein truths are uncovered."

Once alone Georgiana stood and faced her uncle. She did not know what it was he wanted from her but the sooner she discovered his purpose the sooner they could be rid of him and that, currently, was her only objective.

"Well then," her uncle said, clearly as eager to conclude his business as she was for him to be gone. "I'll make things nice and simple for you. Your father and my own wife's brother were very dear friends and it was his wish that you marry my brother-in-law's son, Swithin Rufford. You were, in fact, betrothed at birth. Personally I think the fellow is getting a bad bargain. But it was my brother's dearest wish and I mean to see that it is carried out now that, thanks to your mother's wickedness, he is no longer here to do so."

Georgiana grasped the back of the chair she stood beside and prayed she didn't do something as lowering as falling into a swoon. Though she felt that if anyone was due a swoon after everything that she had endured over the past weeks it was her.

"But I am only nineteen. I am not yet of age," she replied, astonished that she spoke the words without stammering, and grasping at whatever straw she could bring to mind.

"No. But I am your legal guardian and I consent to the match."

"But I do not!" she replied, staring at this already hated figure of a man and vowing to never do anything that he desired her to do. "I have not the least intention of marrying a man I have never even heard of before this day, just because my long dead father wished it!"

She was bestowed with a look of such frigid disdain that her nerve quailed for a moment, but she held his icy gaze, though her fingers were white where they held tight to the chair.

"No," he said, every nuance of that one word dripping with scorn. "I never imagined you would do anything to oblige your father. Indeed I find myself correct in supposing that you would be every bit as capricious and flighty as your mother was. Bad blood will out," he added.

"If you have quite finished insulting myself and my family, I would request that you leave now, sir. For I certainly have nothing further to say to you."

"Oh, but I have not yet concluded my business with you, Miss Dalton." He took a step closer to her and she could see the implacable nature of the man burning in his eyes. This was not a man used to being thwarted and he didn't expect to come away from this meeting without getting what he wanted. "I will make myself plain."

"Upon my word, Sir. If you haven't already been doing that I wonder if my poor feminine sensibilities can bear the strain," she retorted, narrowing her eyes at him.

He gave a snort, looking ever more disgusted. "You will never lead me to believe there is anything approaching feminine morals or sensibility about you, Miss Dalton. You are the daughter of a woman who was known to be a common flirt."

Fury brought colour burning to her cheeks as she raged at him in return. "Then I wonder that you would be so eager to pursue a match between one such as me and a man you apparently hold in some regard."

"Aye, and I wonder at it too!" he shouted. "But Rufford wants to wed you and I gave my word and the marriage *will* go ahead. I have arranged for you to meet Mr Rufford on Sunday next, at which time he will make his proposal, and you will accept him."

Georgiana gathered her strength and held on to the towering rage which seemed to be the only thing keeping her on her feet.

"You have spoken plain, sir, and now I will repay you in kind. There is nothing on this earth that would induce me to do anything of the sort. If and when I marry it will not be someone who has been chosen by either a dead man or someone I hold in utter contempt."

For a moment she wondered if she had gone too far as she saw his fists clench and he took a step towards her. He froze at the last moment, but she was left in no doubt at all that if she ever allowed herself to come under this man's power she would be in very grave danger.

"Miss Dalton," he said, the words full of cold rage. "Your mother was a whore and the scandal she wrought is talked about to this day. I have only to utter one word about your true parentage and you will be ruined. And you may rest assured that I will not utter just one word, I will destroy you. No man will ever touch you unless they paid coin for your services, no polite society will ever welcome you. You will be a pariah, belonging nowhere and to no one."

"So be it," she flung back at him, barely holding back her tears but determined not to crumble before this hateful man. "I'd rather die an old maid than oblige a despicable and vicious man like you!"

"Then it seems there is no more left to say. I will be here on Sunday with Mr Rufford. I trust after you have taken the time to look at your circumstances you will have a change of heart, for in a very short matter of time you will find those people here who were your friends will no longer wish to receive you. Good day, Miss Dalton."

She waited until she heard the front door close until her trembling knees gave out and she sank to the floor, crying and shaking, and wishing with all her heart that Beau could save her from such an ignominious fate. But Beau had gone and was never going to be able to save her, and if he ever discovered the truth, perhaps he would no longer wish he could. She would simply have to manage and find a way to survive that wouldn't bring disgrace to her aunt and uncle.

For a moment visions of nunneries and of fleeing abroad filled her head until she could scold herself away from such fanciful notions and get a firm grip on the real world. The first thing she must do was check on Aunt Jane, and then she must find her uncle. Between them, they would find a way. Between them they had to.

***

The next morning Georgiana sat at the breakfast table turning an untouched piece of toast in her hands and awaiting her uncle's return. Her aunt was still abed, too traumatised by the previous day's events to be able to face getting up. Georgiana didn't blame her. She had wanted nothing more than to bury her head under the covers and pretend it all away. But that was never going to happen.

On returning late yesterday afternoon and finding the household in hysterics, it had taken her uncle some considerable time to calm her aunt and get the facts of the matter from Georgiana. He had not denied any of the events involving her parents, as some childish part of her had hoped he may, but he'd been furious at her uncle Dalton's behaviour. Indeed she had never seen her kindly Uncle Joseph in such a towering rage once he'd vented his spleen.

But the only way to fight fire, her uncle said, was with fire. And to that end he had gone to pay a call upon the Earl of Falmouth. What Falmouth could do for her, Georgiana could not for one moment imagine. As far as she knew the man had a very black character and was a confirmed rake. Though she had seen notice of his marriage in the papers some weeks earlier so perhaps he had reformed.

Any speculation on the matter had to wait until late in the afternoon when her uncle returned and ushered her into his study.

"Well, child, I hope you are not too low in spirits after such a dreadful day as you suffered yesterday."

"No, sir," she said, offering him a smile to reassure him as she settled in the chair opposite his desk. "But I confess I am in desperation to know what it is you have been discussing with Lord Falmouth."

"Ah," her uncle said with satisfaction, rubbing his hands together. "As to that, I believe we have a plan."

"We do?"

She watched as her uncle rang the bell to summon one of the maids and waited in anticipation as Mary opened the door and her uncle ordered tea be brought forthwith.

Once Mary had gone to fulfil his command he returned his attention to his niece.

"Now, Georgiana. I know that everything that has happened must have been the most appalling shock to you and I feel I ought to offer you our apologies for not having given you any idea of your circumstances before this."

"Whatever for?" Georgiana exclaimed. "Of course you didn't wish to discuss such a dreadful scandal, and how could you? It is hardly the kind of thing you can easily discuss with your niece."

Her uncle smiled at her and gave a sigh. "Georgiana, I hope you know this already, but your aunt and I, we always have and always will love you as our own daughter. It was a terrible sadness to us that we never had a child of our own, and when you came into our lives, despite the circumstances, we were so grateful and happy to have you. You have been nothing but a joy and a delight and to see you forced into such ... such ..." His voice broke and Georgiana reached across the desk and clasped his hand in hers. She could not speak any further than he could manage as her throat was tight with emotion and her vision blurred with tears.

"Well now," her uncle began again, offering her a rueful smile as Mary brought them in a tea tray and then hurried away. "To the facts, lest we become prey to our emotions again. First of all,

Georgiana, I utterly forbid you to marry Swithin Rufford, is that perfectly clear?"

Georgiana choked on her tea and had to put her cup down on the desk before she spilt it down her dress as laughter shook her. "Oh, Uncle, yes indeed, it is quite clear and I've never been so happy to have a suitor rejected."

"Oh? Have you rejected many?" he asked with a twinkle glittering behind his spectacles.

For a moment Georgiana blushed, though it was nonsensical as Beau had never proposed. Obviously imagining it was just her maidenly modesty that caused her cheeks to glow, her uncle continued.

"So as for the rest of it. Your father, as you now know, was the Baron Dalton, and whilst his title went to your uncle when he died, he was in fact a very wealthy man and the majority of all of his estates and monies ... belong to you."

Georgiana gaped at him. "B-but ..."

He held out a hand to her. "Perhaps we should have told you sooner, my dear. But we could only feel that if you'd known about the vast sum settled upon you that it ... well it might be a burden to you or ..."

"Or it might turn me into the most shockingly spoilt creature imaginable," she offered and let out a breath as she tried to absorb the information. She was an heiress! Her heart gave a leap in her throat and unconsciously her hand covered that sorely bruised organ as she thought of Beau. "Uncle, I thank you with my whole heart," she replied, her voice shaking as she was torn between crying and laughing. All of her wildest dreams seemed to be coming true on the heels of the worst nightmare. "Indeed it seems incredible. Surely you know I could never reproach you for anything and in this I think you were undoubtedly quite correct. I would have been beyond bearing, I'm certain. But surely there is some mistake? Are you perfectly sure that such wealth is mine?"

Uncle Joseph sipped his tea and nodded. "Your father had a steward. A very fine man indeed and it is to him that we owe a great debt. It was he who brought you to us. He always felt your aunt had been harshly treated when she chose to marry me, but your father was a cold man, much in the style of your uncle Dalton I'm afraid. However, it was he who acted so swiftly in putting all of the papers that left everything to you into our hands. For your father and your uncle despised each other, that much I will say, and your father wouldn't have settled so much as a groat on him if he didn't have to. So everything was tied up in trust, and while your uncle is officially your guardian until you come of age, there was and still is no way for him to touch anything that belonged to you in any way other than as a caretaker."

She frowned at him as her uncle's plan fell into place. "So you believe he wants me to marry this Rufford so that he can control me and my inheritance through him?"

Her uncle grimaced. "Quite so," he said, shaking his head. "Indeed, whilst he had no power to touch your money, your uncle Dalton took no time in installing himself in your father's house and taking charge of the estates. To be fair I believe he has managed them well enough, but now of course he faces the prospect of being evicted when you come of age."

"Good God!" Try as she might to take it all in, Georgiana would have easier believed that she was trapped in some bizarre dream than accept everything she'd just heard. "But if he was so determined to control me through my inheritance, why did my uncle not make greater efforts to be conciliatory?" she asked, more perplexed than ever.

"Because your uncle is a bully just as, I'm sad to say, was your father. And I promise you this, Georgiana, I have every sympathy with your poor mother for I cannot imagine what she must have endured as his wife." He took a breath and set down his tea cup, pushing it away. "I am sorry to speak of your father so, my child. I cannot imagine that it is anything but distressing."

Georgiana shrugged. “They seem like minor characters I have read about in a book,” she admitted, smiling at him. “They have never been a part of my life and I knew so little of them that now they just don’t seem real. There is not enough of them left to hurt me I think.” She looked up and reached over, patting his hand. “And how could I possibly miss them when I have you and Aunt Jane? I am more than blessed in that I assure you.”

Her uncle returned her smile with just as much affection. “It’s an ill wind, I suppose, and your uncle didn’t know you any more than your father understood your mother. He thought he could come here and force you to bend to his will but he didn’t reckon with your spirit, Georgiana. He didn’t realise that you would not be so easily manipulated or cowed by such ruthless behaviour.” He grew serious then and his face was grave as he spoke again. “And you are going to need that spirit, child and all the courage you possess to face what comes next.”

Chapter 13

"Wherein our heroine meets the countess and finds an ally."

It occurred to Georgiana, in the light of these forbidding words, that she still didn't know the outcome of his meeting with Lord Falmouth.

"As I see it we have two choices," her uncle explained with rushed words. "The first is to do as your uncle wishes and marry Rufford." He grinned, looking over the top of his spectacles at her. "I feel we are of a like mind on this particular subject."

"Indeed we are, sir," she replied, smiling in return, though her nerves were once more all of a jitter.

"Then that leaves us but one course of action. We must face the scandal head on and in such a way that it dies away and no one has any further interest in speaking of it."

Georgiana felt her heart plummet and her stomach appeared to somersault, accompanied with a quite nauseating wave of heat that washed over her. "Oh dear," she murmured.

"Now then, love. You won't be alone in this by any means and that was why I contacted the earl. You see the man owes me a debt after his fool physician nearly killed him last year. A wound got infected and he was running a fever. If he hadn't called me in for a second opinion it could have been quite nasty indeed. Anyway, he told me he was in my debt and if I ever needed anything ... Well I do need something, and I didn't hesitate to tell him so."

"Uncle!" Georgiana exclaimed in growing horror. "Whatever have you asked him for?"

She watched as he sat back in his chair and stroked his thick white sideburns with the back of one hand. "Now don't panic, child.

The whole idea is that you must avoid any scandal attaching to you. You must act with the utmost propriety and good sense, of which I have no doubt at all you will be able to do quite admirably."

For a moment Georgiana's mind flitted back to an afternoon with Beau and the way she had cried out when his hand slid under the skirts of her dress. Her cheeks flamed but her uncle just chuckled, thankfully perfectly ignorant of the path her thoughts had taken.

"So I believe you know that the earl has recently married. In fact, I met his wife this afternoon and a more delightful creature you never did meet. I think you'll be enchanted by her. She's very young, mind, but nonetheless as a married woman she can bring you out in society and indeed she has very graciously agreed to do just that. And damn me, but with the Earl of Falmouth giving his name to your cause, you just let the bloody baron do his worst! We'll face them all down, Georgiana, and come out of this the winners. You mark my words!"

This impassioned speech did much to restore Georgiana's spirits, though she felt very close to fainting once more when her uncle gave her the quite stunning information that he believed she was worth close to fifty thousand pounds. The staggering amount of money made her head spin and her uncle's next words, about bewaring fortune hunters for they'd be on her like bees on honey, quite went over her head. The rejuvenating effect of this plan on Aunt Jane, though, was something close to miraculous.

She was swept away to Truro where several new gowns were purchased so that she wouldn't be put to the blush when she was presented to the countess the next day.

"But, Aunt Jane," she whispered, out of hearing of the shopkeeper. "I don't inherit until I'm twenty-one. That's a year and a half away. How on earth ..."

"Hush, love!" her aunt scolded her, pausing a moment to throw a smile at the shop keeper who had glanced in their direction. "Lord Falmouth has advanced you a sum to cover all of your expenses, which of course you will repay him when you come into your inheritance."

Georgiana looked at her aunt, quite aghast. "B--but he's never set eyes on me, I mean ... how ... why?" she stammered, becoming so flustered that her aunt held her vinaigrette close under her nose until Georgiana squealed with disgust. It did, however, bring her back to earth.

"That will be quite enough fretting, Georgiana," her aunt said, with quite astonishing severity from one who was usually so mild. "It just so happens that the earl holds the baron in as much contempt as you would wish and is more than happy to help you thwart his plans." She lowered her voice a little more, whispering to Georgiana. "According to Joseph he has some other, *private* reasons for his involvement that he didn't wish to discuss, but suffice to say your success would please him very much. Now your uncle and the earl have arranged it all for you and all you need do is enjoy the nicer parts of it, like the shopping and making new friends with ladies like the countess." Her aunt came closer and touched her face with empathy. "Of course facing the *haut ton* is going to wear on your nerves I know, child. But there is nothing like being properly attired to be able to stare down those who would say wicked things about you, take it from me!"

Seeing as her aunt must have run the gauntlet of just such kinds of ill-natured gossip when her family disowned her, Georgiana could readily believe the truth of it. Either way, there was little she could do. Everything was apparently arranged to everyone's satisfaction. All she had to do was play her part, do and say nothing scandalous, and hopefully her mother's infamy would not continue to taint her own future.

***

Both her aunt and uncle were right about one thing. The Countess of Falmouth was an absolute darling.

Setting foot inside the vast doors of Tregothnan was by far the most terrifying thing Georgiana had ever done. She was greeted by an elderly butler of such grave dignity that she might have been of a mind to turn around and flee had it not been for Aunt Jane's iron grip on her arm. They were led into a lavish drawing room, painted in the palest duck egg blue and with massive gilt-framed pictures lining the panelled walls. It was exquisitely furnished, and in every direction her eyes alighted on some beautiful piece to delight the eye. Nothing in the room, however, could compare to the vision that rose to greet them.

With the widest, bluest eyes Georgiana had ever seen, surrounded by an artless arrangement of guinea gold curls - that she could well believe had taken hours to achieve - the countess rushed over to greet them. She wore a dress of amber silk with a rich lace trim around the bust, and was quite the most dazzling creature Georgiana had ever seen. Holding her hands outstretched she drew Georgiana to her and kissed both of her cheeks.

"Oh, Miss Dalton," she said, with a pretty French accent that Georgiana thought utterly charming. "I am so 'appy you are coming to London with us. I 'ave the most wonderful things planned for us both. Oh, where are my manners, do please sit down and I will ring for some tea."

The niceties of any afternoon call were observed as the three ladies exchanged pleasantries. But then, to Georgiana's amusement, the countess changed the subject.

"Well now all the pretty nothings are done, we can talk properly, *hein?"* She said, giving an irrepressible grin, mischief glittering in those lovely blue eyes. It gave Georgiana no problem at all to imagine how this engaging creature had brought a confirmed bachelor and notorious rake like the earl to propose to her. She strongly doubted he'd had any choice, for surely no one could resist a smile like that.

"I want you to know that I do not care this much," the countess said, snapping her pretty fingers, much to the shock of Aunt Jane, "for what anyone says about your mama. And you just see if they dare in front of Alex, ha!" She winked at Georgiana and then glanced at Aunt Jane with an apologetic expression.

"Oh dear, I 'ave shocked you, yes? Aunt Seymour will scold me, and I 'ave been trying very *h*ard to be a good English lady."

"What the devil would you want to do a thing like that for?" said a cultured male voice from the corner of the room.

"Oh, Alex!"

Céleste, as the countess had insisted they call her, leapt to her feet as her husband strode into the room. For a moment Georgiana was struck with a dreadful case of jealousy as she saw the way the two of them looked at each other, as if neither her nor Aunt Jane even existed. The earl looked down at her with obvious adoration before planting a light kiss on her mouth to the delighted amusement of Aunt Jane. In that moment Georgiana found her longing for Beau a physical thing, a weight that hung about her heart and never allowed her to fully enjoy anything that might pass. If only she could be with him in such an easy, open manner.

The countess returned to her guests looking a little flushed and obviously believing Aunt Jane would be shocked by such behaviour. But her aunt, being so happily married herself, was only too pleased to see two people so well matched.

Once the formalities were over, Georgiana allowed herself to look the earl over while he spoke to Aunt Jane. He was a tall and forbidding looking man, broad and well made, with thick black hair and a stern, uncompromising face. There was a cruel edge to his mouth that made her believe he was not someone who you should make an enemy of. But every trace of that harsh cynicism vanished whenever he laid eyes on his lovely wife.

"Well then, Miss Dalton," he said at last, turning his attention to her. "I understand we are to have the pleasure of escorting you to London with us to make your come out?"

"Yes, my Lord," she said, smiling at him with real gratitude. "And I can only imagine that my uncle must have done you the greatest of favours, for I am well aware of the singular honour you do me in the circumstances, and I will be forever in your debt."

"Circumstances be dam ... dashed," he amended at a nudge from the countess. "Baron Dalton is ..." He glanced at his wife who was biting her lip in amusement. "Well," he said with a sigh. "I suppose I shouldn't disparage your uncle in front of you but safe to say I don't like the man, and his treatment of you is beyond anything. It would give me the greatest satisfaction to thwart any plans he may have and so I tell you, you owe me nothing. I shall enjoy putting his nose out of joint beyond anything."

Aunt Jane nodded and looked at him with great satisfaction. "I know I shouldn't say it, the baron being my brother and all, but you need have no compunction about cutting up his character before us. After the way he treated us ..."

At this point her voice broke and she was forced to hunt for her handkerchief and press it to her lips while Georgiana hunted through her reticule for her aunt's vinaigrette. This had the effect of unsettling the earl to the point that he made his excuses.

"I shall look forward to seeing you in London, Miss Dalton," he said before he took his leave of them. "I confess I am relieved that the countess will have someone young and amusing to bear her company in case she tires of her ancient husband." This was said with a very grave face, forcing his wife to exclaim,

"Bah! What a rapper! Indeed, Alex, you are looking for me to compliment you, and now I shan't, so run along and leave us ladies to talk in peace."

The earl looked at her in amusement, one eyebrow raised. "I shall do just that, but I will also be speaking to my cousin Aubrey, as I have no doubt that is where you learned such a vulgar expression. Good day, ladies."

Once divested of her husband, the countess turned to Georgiana and grasped her hands.

"Indeed, I am so looking forward to this season. The last season I was there ..." She paused and looked a little uncomfortable before smiling and carrying on. "Well, it was my first and it all went in rather a blur. I think I will enjoy it much more this year, especially now I 'ave a friend to accompany me."

Georgiana, tried to smile in return and then imagined the scorn of the *ton* when they discovered she was the daughter of the scandalous Lady Dalton.

Apparently well aware of her train of thought, the countess gave her hands a squeeze. "I know what it is to face scandal," she said in a whisper. "Alex is the dearest man but ... well I am sure you are aware of his reputation?"

Georgiana opened and closed her mouth, glancing to her aunt for help as she didn't really know how to reply to that question, but Céleste just laughed.

"Oh, don't worry, I know all of it, and most of it is quite true after all," she added with an irrepressible chortle of delight that made Georgiana chuckle in reply. "In fact, we are having to apply to his Aunt Seymour to try and get you vouchers for Almack's because poor Alex is banned! Can you imagine? Not that he cares a rush of course, but we will need to go for your sake and I admit I should love to see the marriage mart at first hand."

This last put Georgiana quite at ease and she felt sure that in the countess ... *Céleste,* she had found a friend with whom she could face the trial before her - if not with equanimity, then at least with courage.

Chapter 14

"Wherein Lady Russell weighs in and a grim winter passes."

As parliament didn't sit until February this season, and as most men were out of town to enjoy the hunting season, they found London in November practically devoid of company. As it happened this suited Georgiana down to the ground, meaning she could find her feet a little and indulge in some serious shopping without having to endure stares and whispers as word got about as to who she really was. Céleste was as good as her word and introduced her to a small circle of friends who were in town early for various reasons and who, in Céleste's words, didn't care a fig about her scandalous parent.

Their trips were hampered somewhat by the weather which was remarkably bad at times, to the point they often had to light candles during the day as the cloud cover was so very thick. On the nineteenth there was much excitement at the prospect of a solar eclipse, but during the event it was so cloudy that little could be seen of it.

Georgiana's enjoyment was not dimmed, though, as Lord Falmouth's home was luxurious in the extreme and Céleste's company a delight. She was further indulged by them allowing her to bring Conrad with her, which had been something that had been on her mind. She was afraid her faithful dog would have pined for her if she left him too long. As it was he and Céleste's naughty scrap of a spaniel, Bandit, became firm friends and caused mischief wherever they went, much to Falmouth's consternation.

Aware that Lord Falmouth and his wife were in fact newlyweds, Georgiana often retired early of an evening to leave them alone. Seeing as she had the run of his lordship's vast and well stocked library, however, she found no hardship in repairing to her lavish bedroom, with a fire that burned all day and night, and indulging in her favourite past time.

Indeed, the only note of sorrow in a very pleasant visit was that she had been unable to discover any news about the Marquis of Beaumont. She had heard in passing that he was staying with friends until the season began, but further than that, even the scandal rags had fallen silent. Her thoughts were rarely far from him, and despite knowing he wasn't in town, she found herself searching the faces of the people they passed as his lordship's carriage bore them around the freezing streets, hoping for a glimpse of him.

And so it was that November turned to December in a very pleasant fashion with intimate dinner and rout parties and a great deal of shopping. Never before having had money to spend, and being used to being thrifty, mending tears and turning cuffs, this was a revelation. To find herself suddenly with a vast fortune - if not at her fingertips, then certainly on the horizon, the amount of clothes that she was able to invest in, and which Céleste had encouraged her to buy, was quite staggering.

Céleste had in fact divulged a little of her own background, which was beyond any penny pinching that Georgiana had been forced to contend with, and indeed made her feel quite shamefaced for considering she had been in any way hard up. But it meant that for the two of them, shopping was a new and delightful treat which was beyond anything they had enjoyed before.

Céleste's favourite haunt was a modiste on Conduit Street. A charming French *émigrés* by the name of Madame Lisabeth. When the two women got together Georgiana would be lost in a flurry of rapid fire French until they remembered their manners and switched back to English. Madame Lisabeth had exceptional taste, however, with a great eye for colour and line, and Georgiana never failed to walk away without her purse a great deal lighter. Her favourite purchase was a gown of green sarsnet finished with a border of deeper green ribband *appliqué*. As Madame Lisabeth had predicted, it looked glorious against the red of her hair and she indulged herself with a little daydream of walking into a ball and finding Beau staring up at her with wonder and admiration.

The week before Christmas she awaited with impatience a visit from her aunt and uncle, whom Lord Falmouth had graciously invited to stay. Before that happy time however, she had to face a visit from Lady Seymour Russell.

"You'll be quite terrified of 'er of course," Céleste explained at breakfast with a mischievous grin. "And quite right too."

She gave a gurgle of laughter at the obvious panic in Georgiana's eyes.

"Oh, she's a sweetheart really, I promise," she said, waving a morsel of plum cake at her between elegant fingers. "And don't worry," she added. "I will protect you!"

"But why is she coming?" Georgiana asked, terrified that Lord Falmouth's aunt, the daunting Lady Russell who was known as the scourge of the *ton* would take one look at her and advise her nephew to cast her off. Though she doubted anyone but his wife, who could clearly wrap him around his finger, could get the earl to do anything he didn't wish to.

"Why because she's having the most terrible trouble getting us vouchers for Almack's and she wants to meet you before she goes to the trouble of blackmailing Lady Jersey."

Georgiana almost choked on her hot chocolate. "Blackmail!"

Céleste grinned at her and nodded. "It appears Aunt 'as the dirt on most of the *ton* and doesn't scruple to use it if she feels it necessary. Seymour and Lady Jersey - that's one of the patronesses of Almack's - 'ave been at daggers drawn for years according to Alex." She paused to cut off another slice of plum cake and deposit it on the pretty gold-edged Sevres plate. "Anyway, her mother-in-law, of course you know, was the Prince Regent's mistress, and I'm sure you've heard *all* the scandals ..." She winked at Georgiana and raised an elegant eyebrow. "Except you haven't. Apparently Seymour has proof of some dreadful misdemeanour that Lady Jersey would much rather keep away from the gossips. So she's coming to see if you are worthy of deploying 'er most lethal weapon."

"Good God," Georgiana replied, blinking at her. But Céleste just continued her breakfast, apparently unconcerned.

Dressed demurely in a soft sprig muslin with a pale green fichu and green silk slippers, Georgiana sat by the fire in the drawing room and tried to apply herself to some embroidery. Céleste said Seymour had a lot of rather old fashioned notions about how young ladies should behave and to find them thus employed would please her. Georgiana looked down at the little circle of crooked stitching on her own sewing frame and sighed. It was supposed to be a daisy chain but looked rather like a row of rather odd shaped splodges. She didn't have long to fret over it though as the butler announced Lady Seymour Russell, and the two young women put aside their sewing and got to their feet.

Georgiana bit back a nervous giggle as a tall, elegant older woman, dressed all in dove grey and lilac looked them over with clear scepticism in her cool grey eyes.

"Very pretty, I'm sure, child. Did you arrange this pleasing little scene for my benefit?" She looked at Céleste with the slightest twitch of her lips as the countess ran to greet her and kiss both her cheeks. "Oh, Aunt! As if you could believe such a thing of two such nice, English ladies."

Lady Russell gave a snort but allowed Céleste to fuss around her and get her settled before ringing for tea.

Shortly everyone was supplied with tea and biscuits to fortify their nerves, not that Lady Russell looked in anyway that she needed them as she raised her quizzing glass to survey Georgiana in a way that made her blush to the roots of her hair.

"So, you're the Siren's daughter," she said, her tone considering. Georgiana bristled. She had heard from her uncle that this had become her mother's nickname when she made her come out. She had been a huge success, not only because of her beauty but because of her vivacity and lively nature. Many men had vied for her attention, but it had been the cold and cruel Baron Dalton that had finally won her, though no one knew why she had chosen a mere baron over some of the far worthier offers she'd had. But sparks had flown, to all accounts, when they were together and they had married against everyone's advice. It soon became clear to all that the marriage was a disaster. The baron was jealous and despotic but Lady Dalton refused to be cowed by him, becoming ever more extreme in her behaviour and her affairs. Until she caught the eye of the Duke of Sindalton. It had apparently been love at first sight and their scandalous affair and the bloody end it came to had rocked the *ton* and kept the gossips talking for years after.

"Goodness yes," Seymour said, tutting and shaking her head. "It's a pity but you are the image of your mother."

"Oh, Aunt," Céleste reproached her. "But she is a great beauty! How can you say it is a pity?"

"Because it is!" the old lady replied with a huff. "Much better for the child if she'd been unexceptional. Then people wouldn't be so quick to judge and compare. But looking like that ... well, they'll all say the Siren's been born again." She pointed her quizzing glass at Georgiana, punctuating her words as she waved it at her. "You'll need to be beyond reproach, girl, do you understand? They'll be watching your every move, waiting to see if you show the slightest sign of following in your mother's footsteps."

Georgiana nodded, knowing she was right. "Yes, Lady Russell, I do perfectly understand. I promise I will do everything I can not to bring embarrassment to you or your family."

To her surprise the old lady gave a bark of laughter. "As to that! I assure you my nephews have blackened the family name enough to withstand anything you might bring down on us."

Georgiana smiled, as terrifying as she was you couldn't help but warm to the earl's outspoken aunt. "Well, I cannot tell you how grateful I am for your support, and that of the earl and Lady Falmouth. I feel blessed indeed to have such champions at my side."

Lady Russell gave her an approving nod. "Yes, you'll do. And you're welcome. I'd like to say you won't need us but you will. You'll have to be brave, brazen it out, you understand."

Georgiana felt her stomach twist but she nodded. "Yes," she said, hearing the tremble in her own voice. "I understand and I will do my very best."

***

The weather continued to be bleak and unpleasant and worsened as a thick fog descended on the capital. Some days it was so completely dark even in daylight, that coachmen were obliged to get down and lead their horses by lantern light. Reports of the Spa Field riots in Islington in early December seemed to echo the air of discontent that hung over the country as a whole as grey skies and freezing temperatures kept England feeling grim and grey.

Christmas came and went far too quickly and it was with a heavy heart that Georgiana bid goodbye to her aunt and uncle. Despite everything going on outside of Lord Falmouth's home, they had enjoyed a wonderful holiday. Lord and Lady Falmouth were gracious and generous hosts, and Georgiana and her aunt and uncle only too ready to be pleased by everything.

Little by little, however, the time passed and the weather improved, and the ton began to return to the capital. Georgiana knew that soon she would have to face them and this pleasant little interlude would be over. In a way she welcomed it. The fear of her come out had seemed to glower on the horizon for the last months and now she just wanted it over with. Of course what she wanted more than anything was to find Beau and let him know everything that had happened to her. That she was now an heiress. That she was not so very low born after all ... that they could be together, if it was still what he wanted. The thought of course crossed her mind that he would want nothing to do with her when he discovered who she was.

She was sure she had often read his name linked to the current Duke of Sindalton. They were close friends if the scandal rags were to be believed, and that might make things more than a little awkward but ... if he truly loved her, as he'd said he did, surely, nothing could keep them apart?

Chapter 15

"Wherein the fates cause trouble and our heroine sets a dog among the pigeons."

Sebastian ran up the stairs to find his mother's companion white-faced and agitated, waiting for him outside her rooms.

"What's happened?" he demanded. He was well used to his mother's bouts of ill health and her nervous dispositions but the summons today had seemed rather more urgent than usual.

"Oh, oh dear," the idiotic woman said. "Oh goodness me!" A distant and impoverished cousin, Lady Rush was as hopeless as she was bird-witted and never ceased to annoy Sebastian with her dithering and predictions of doom.

"Never mind," he said, striding past her and giving a brief knock before entering his mother's rooms.

He found his mother laying prostrate on a fainting couch, attended by her dresser who was applying a cool cloth to her forehead that smelled strongly of vinegar.

"Mother?"

She looked up with a small cry and reached out her hands to him as her maid snatched up the cloth before it could fall into her lap.

"Oh, Sebastian, what are we to do?"

"I don't know, dear," he said, quickly realising he would have to gather his patience to get to the bottom of whatever tragedy had befallen them this time. If it was anything like the last time, it was probably one of her revolting little pug dogs going missing again. "Why don't you tell me what is troubling you and I'll see what I can do?"

“Oh but it isn’t me that I’m concerned for,” his mother said, her large brown eyes full of sorrow. He gave her frail hands a gentle squeeze, hoping to encourage her to get to the point. “My poor, poor child. Oh, I knew this day would come. I just knew it! Oh your wicked, wicked father. How could he do it ... how?”

Good God, she was back onto that was she? Whatever had got her in such a pelter? He glared at the maid who shook her head, clearly disowning any portion of blame. He had long since banned any talk about his dead father or the circumstances surrounding his untimely demise as it was guaranteed to send his mother into one of her spasms. The results of this could be felt by the entire household for many weeks and he often wondered that such an apparently weak and feeble female could hold him and his entire staff to ransom when she indulged on such an emotional spree.

“What on earth has father to do with anything?” he asked, striving to keep his voice even when he was getting the strong urge to shake someone until they explained what was going on.

“Because he ruined us all with ... with that *evil* woman!”

“Mother that was almost twenty years ago now. No one speaks of it anymore. It is old news I assure you. We have weathered the storm.”

“No!” she said, with such passion that he was quite taken aback as she sat forward, gripping his hands with considerable force. Her eyes were febrile and not for the first time he feared for her sanity as she began to rage and rant. “No, we have not! It is all coming back again. *She* is coming back again! She’s come to haunt us, to ruin us, to ruin you!”

“Who’s coming back?” he demanded, wondering if she had finally descended into madness as he’d always suspected she might.

“The Siren!” she shrieked, gasping for breath and clutching at her throat.

“Agatha, get the hartshorn and mother’s vinaigrette,” he ordered.

"She's had the hartshorn already," the poor, harassed woman replied, thrusting the vinaigrette under his mother's nose. "But she's been beyond anything since she saw that wretched scandal sheet." He watched, relieved as his mother spluttered but seemed to calm a little and lay back on the couch breathing hard, but steady.

Sebastian's face darkened. "Dammit all!" he raged. "How many times do I have to tell you to keep the bloody things out of her reach? Show me, and then run and fetch Doctor Alperton. Tell him it's an emergency."

The white-faced dresser shoved a crumbled news sheet into his hands and ran for the door. With a cold feeling running down his spine like ice water he read the report that had caused his mother's breakdown.

Rumours abound that the daughter of the notorious Lady D, otherwise known as The Siren - the voluptuous red head that led the esteemed D of S to his demise, is lately in town. Chaperoned by the Earl and Lady Falmouth, it appears the young woman possesses a remarkable likeness to her beautiful and fiery mother. It only remains to be seen if she resembles her in other ways.

The new Lady D is apparently an heiress of some considerable fortune. Fortune hunters beware, who will be the hunted here?

Nausea swirled in his stomach. God no. Not now, not after all this time? For that whole sordid scandal to have to be relived all over again. He remembered being told that the woman had left her child to run off with his father, but he'd never given it another thought. Hadn't even known if it was boy or girl. It had never crossed his mind that the child would have the audacity to face the *ton.* There was a part of him that admired her pluck. After all it was her mother's sin, not hers, and if it hadn't been his own family about to suffer he could have felt sympathy for her.

Well, the bitch needn't think that he would smooth her way. He would cut her and refuse to acknowledge her, and where he led many if not all of the *ton* would follow.

Worse was the realisation that Falmouth was behind this. This was without a doubt his punishment for what he'd done to Céleste. He had read with great relief and incredulous surprise the news of their marriage last autumn. He had tried hard to take Céleste from the earl, even resorting to some underhand measures which were not at all his usual style. But he had not the slightest doubt that the bastard was enjoying every minute of his revenge. He crumpled the newspaper, throwing it across the room in disgust and putting his head in his hands.

God what a mess. For a moment the longing to run back to Georgiana was so great it was as though his heart was being crushed in his chest. He gave a snort of amusement as he considered his innocent beauty. He had never heeded Jeffries' warning about his red-headed sweetheart, but that another fiery haired woman should enter his life and turn it upside down for such different reasons seemed beyond fair.

He started as his mother laid her frail hand on his shoulder and he turned to look up at her.

"Don't go near her, my darling boy. Her mother took your father from us both. She ruined us and I have the most terrible fear that her daughter has come to finish the job."

"Mother!" He took her hands again and planted a kiss on her forehead. "You're getting yourself in a silly state over nothing. Of course I won't go near her. I shall give her the cut direct, and then see how long she'll last here. No one will receive her." He smiled at her and tried to impart a calm that he was far from feeling. The dreadful days following his father's death seemed to be parading through his mind. The fear and the terrible sorrow he'd had at the loss of his wonderful, charismatic father. The guilt that he'd felt as he realised he must hate him for what he'd done. And after that the very real anger that he *had* done it - his father had left him and mother alone for a woman, and he'd died for it. "Come now. This will blow over in no time at all, you see if it doesn't. We shall be quite comfortable again, I promise you."

***

Georgiana looked out of the window at a bright blue sky and gave a sigh of longing. At home she was used to walking miles, either to visit neighbours or just for the joy of being outside and in the fresh air. No amount of mud or cold could convince her to stay indoors, and here in the city she felt the restrictions of life chafe her. Her limbs felt heavy and dull from lack of exercise and a pitiful, heartfelt sigh from Conrad as he stared wistfully out the window beside her was the last straw.

"You're quite right, love. We both need some exercise or we'll fall into a fit of the dismals and then where shall we be?"

Conrad gave a short and joyful bark of agreement and began to jump about in circles as he realised a walk was in order.

Lord and Lady Falmouth were both out this afternoon, having been summoned by Aunt Seymour, and Georgiana had been only too pleased to cry off visiting the intimidating old woman. She had promised she was quite happy to sit at home and read by the fire, but surely a walk with her dog should be unexceptionable if she took the precaution of having a footman with her?

With the satisfaction of one still unused to wearing the latest fashions, Georgiana fastened her new holly-green merino redingote and arranged the matching silk hat with untrimmed velvet upon her bright red curls. A pale green ostrich feather curled in a becoming fashion over the brim and as she pulled on a soft pair of York tan gloves she professed herself satisfied. She turned and took Conrad's lead from her designated footman, who was in turn wearing an air of deep disapproval.

"He seems a touch excitable, my Lady," he said, looking at Conrad with dismay. "Perhaps it would be wiser if I held onto him, at least until he settles down."

"Nonsense," she said with a bright smile. "He hates men as a whole and he'll behave even worse if you take him, I assure you. He's just not used to being restrained you see." She bent down and gave Conrad a scratch behind his ears. "Are you, my poor little love? Yes, yes, we're going. Come along."

At first their walk passed off with no problem at all and Conrad even deigned to allow the footman, whose name Georgiana discovered was Thomas, to hold him while she did some small items of shopping on the way. First she stepped into Floris on Jermyn Street, ostensibly to buy a new toothbrush, but did not find herself greatly surprised when she emerged with a new bottle of perfume.

She had been called as much by the lovely blue glass bottle, engraved with butterflies as by the scent itself. But once the fragrance had been presented to her she had to have it. A light citrus with a hint of orange blossom and something spicy she couldn't quite place. Handing her carefully packaged treasure into Thomas' care, she took hold of Conrad again and they carried on until they turned the corner into Piccadilly where the lure of Hatchard's book shop was simply too much to resist. She had been itching to get her hands on the new novel by Miss Austen. Emma had been published just before Christmas and as yet she hadn't been able to buy a copy.

It was with a rather guilty conscience that she emerged from the delights of the glorious shop where she could have happily spent the entire day - a full half hour later. Both Thomas and Conrad looked very put out indeed as the footman gratefully exchanged dog for book. With a promise to herself to return another day *without Conrad* she went to walk on. Unfortunately Conrad seemed to feel that his patience deserved rather a greater reward.

They were just passing Fortnum and Mason and it would have to be admitted that the most tantalising smells issued forth from inside the elegant façade. Indeed, since they had been in London Conrad had become perfectly enamoured of Scotch eggs and would do almost anything to lay his jaws upon one. This became only too apparent as he began to pull and tug at his lead with such vigour that

Georgiana tripped and would have fallen if she hadn't been caught by a strong pair of arms. With a gasp she looked up, and then up a bit more at the vision of a golden, blue-eyed Adonis.

The two of them stared at each other for a moment, both of them startled, before Georgiana realised the impropriety of standing on a busy street in the arms of an unknown man.

"I do beg your pardon, Sir," she said, flushing and trying to straighten her bonnet. "Oh ... my dog ... *Oh!"* With a rush of horror she realised Conrad had disappeared behind the door of the elegant façade where even now, shrieks of alarm could be heard. "Oh good Lord!" Without giving the handsome man a second glance she ran into the shop in hot pursuit.

Chapter 16

"Wherein an imposter is discovered."

Georgiana surveyed the chaos laid out before her with mounting panic and clutched at her footman's arm.

"Oh, Thomas, we must get him back!"

"Yes, my Lady," the man replied with a frown before casting himself into the fray. Georgiana ran to the grand staircase and stood on tiptoe and tried to see if she could find any trace of her wretched dog. A moment later she found him, enthusiastically engaged in trying to liberate a hamper from a very red faced man who was just as enthusiastic in trying to hold on to it.

"Oh no!" she muttered in horror, before running across the room and hoping to grab hold of the idiotic creature. Too late. A moment before she arrived the clasp on the hamper ripped apart in his vigorous jaws and a multitude of cold meats, cheese, dried fruits, and, heaven help them ... Scotch eggs, went flying over the red carpeted floor.

Conrad was in heaven. As far as her misbegotten dog was concerned it was raining manna from heaven and he ran around snaffling up the goodies as fast as his fervent nose could seek them out.

"Oh dear, I'm really most desperately sorry," she said, approaching the red faced man with caution as he looked like he would suffer an apoplexy at any moment.

He turned on her with undisguised rage in his faded brown eyes. They flashed with righteous indignation beneath bristling eyebrows as he found someone on whom to unleash his wrath.

Georgiana took a breath, awaiting her fate as the short, stout fellow drew a breath and prepared to vent his spleen, when the Adonis who had caught her just moments earlier stepped up to her.

"If you would allow me," he murmured in her ear, before bestowing her with a devastating smile which he in turn brought to bear on the old man about to tear her off a strip. "General Denton," he said, holding out his hand. "Well I say, what a chance that it should be you my wretched hound has set upon. I am most dreadfully sorry. Dear, dear, what a to-do! But never fear, I will have someone replace your hamper forthwith, and what's say we pop in a nice bottle of burgundy to go with it, as an apology you understand."

Georgiana watched with astonishment as her handsome young hero deflected each furious attack from abused shoppers and turned it into something that somehow became the most charming anecdote for them to chuckle about with their friends. Standing back at a safe distance she couldn't hear what was said but indeed everyone seemed to know him. Thomas returned Conrad to her with a grimace which she had every sympathy with, but she couldn't tear her eyes from the amusing scene in front of her. By now a group of ladies who had wanted Conrad's head on a platter were laughing and flirting with the Adonis in the best of spirits.

Once every complaint had been dealt with and every ruffled feather smoothed to a nicety, Georgiana found herself standing outside the shop facing her heroic rescuer.

"Well, sir, I don't know what to say," she replied in all honesty. "I can never thank you enough for your intervention. I fear to think what might have happened if you hadn't stepped in."

"Think nothing of it," he said, once more employing that devastating smile to good purpose. "I am a great animal lover and it would have been a shame to put a period to the life of such an intrepid canine."

"Idiotic creature," she sighed, looking down at her dog with chagrin.

"Oh, come, I'm not that bad." She laughed in surprise as a pair of bright blue eyes twinkled at her with amusement. "But now," he added, with mock seriousness. "After our great adventure, will you not do me the honour of giving me your name?"

Georgiana went to open her mouth and then paused. It was only too clear that this man, whoever he was, was a member of the *ton*. He was exquisitely dressed, with everything from his carefully arranged hair to his cravat and boots, of the latest fashion. Far from being a dandy however, he was dressed with taste and restraint, a large sapphire pin winking in his perfectly tied cravat the only sign of obvious extravagance. Taking a deep breath she realised she would have to face this reaction sooner or later and reluctantly took his proffered hand.

"I am Miss Georgiana Dalton, Sir," she replied, a little breathless as she waited to see disgust flicker in those beautiful eyes. She did see something there, surprise certainly and then curiosity, but not disgust.

"Well, well, so you are the Siren," he whispered.

She stiffened immediately and tried to pull her hand free but he held it tight. "Oh, please forgive me, that was ungallant wasn't it. I did not mean to call you so, only that everyone is speculating about *The Siren.* I assure you *I* of all people would never hold your mother's sins as your own."

She unwound a little at the sincerity in his eyes. "Thank you, Sir, but I still do not have your name."

"Good Lord, where are my manners today?" he replied, shaking his head with bemusement. "The trouble is after one look at your beautiful face I have quite forgotten it I assure you."

She arched one eyebrow at him and he grinned at her.

"Too much?" he asked with a look of such innocence that she couldn't help but laugh at him.

"Certainly too much," she nodded, trying hard not to look too obviously amused. Whoever he was he was the most outrageous flirt.

He gave a heartfelt sigh and then bowed to her. "I am Charles Stafford, the Marquis of Beaumont. But you, my dear, can most certainly call me, Beau."

For a moment she just stared at him, before anger bloomed. Whoever this charming creature may be he had no right to be going around and pretending he was someone he was not.

"Oh really?" she said, her tone obviously scathing. *"You're* Beau Beaumont?"

The look on his face was one of deep consternation as he answered. "Yes, I am. Is that a problem?"

Returning a look of disgust she simply replied, "I imagine it might be, for the *real* Marquis." Not wanting to pursue a conversation with someone who was at best a loose screw and at worst, quite possibly mad she bit him a cool, *"Good day,"* and turned on her heel.

Unfortunately he wasn't about to be shaken free so easily and set off after her.

"Am I to understand," he asked, keeping stride with her quite easily. "That you do not believe I am who I purport to be?"

"You have it in a nutshell, sir," she replied with a haughty sniff.

To her surprise he gave a bark of laughter. "How intriguing," he said, showing no inclination to leave her alone.

"Please sir," she replied, stopping in her tracks. "It is most improper that you follow me about town in such a manner when I have no idea who you are. If you know of my circumstances then you must know I have the utmost need for propriety and so I must bid you good day!"

To her annoyance he ignored this piece of good sense and carried on walking beside her.

"I do see," he said, with obvious sympathy. "Probably more than you realise, but the difficulty is this." He stopped, and by gently grasping her wrist forced her to stop as well. "I really am the Marquis of Beaumont, Lady Georgiana." To her horror he reached into a pocket and removed a silver case and withdrew a calling card which he presented to her.

Georgiana looked at the elegantly engraved card and the name of the Marquis of Beaumont stared back at her, mocking her and her own foolish naivety. For the man she had fallen for *could* have been any one. He had clearly only meant to toy with her affections and had given her a false name so she would never be able to trace him. And of course who better to blame than Beau Beaumont, the most notorious rakehell in all of England.

She blinked back tears and willed herself not to cry as she heard his concerned voice filter through the shock.

"My poor dear, you look quite pale. Look at this, fortuitously we are right outside Gunter's. Won't you come in and have a cup of chocolate until you feel more the thing. Come now, it can be quite unexceptionable with your footman to chaperone us."

Blindly she allowed him to lead her from the street and for Thomas to take care of Conrad who was behaving like a meek little lamb now the devil was full of scotch eggs. She gave a little hiccupping laugh, somewhere between amusement and the depths of sorrow but could do nothing to protest as Lord Beaumont guided her to a seat and ordered her chocolate. It was with acceptance that she heard his order replied to with a brisk, "Right away, Lord Beaumont." Just in case she'd been in any doubt.

Indeed, by the time she was half way through her chocolate she felt a little more able to meet the man's eyes. Lifting her own she looked up and found him watching her with concern.

"Ah, there you are," he said, his voice quiet. "Feeling a little better?"

She nodded and tried to smile at him, though this seemed a tremendous effort. Her heart and mind were full of all the memories and dreams that had sprung up since the autumn, and now to find even her memories were constructed upon lies was almost more than she could bear.

"I can't imagine what you think of me," she murmured, looking down into her cup once more.

"Don't be foolish, child," he said, scolding her with a mild tone. "I think perhaps you have been ill used, but I strongly doubt you have anything to reproach yourself for."

She gave an unsteady huff of laughter and then covered her eyes with her hand as tears threatened again.

"You know, I am most terribly discreet when the need arises," he said, and looking up into those blue eyes, she believed him. But then she had believed another man too, she had believed every word he'd said. He sighed at her continued silence. "Am I to take it that you have encountered a man who told you he was the Marquis of Beaumont?"

She nodded, she owed him some kind of explanation for her extraordinary behaviour after all.

"And I think perhaps ... you were ... *fond* of this gentleman?"

She looked up at him but could say nothing, but it appeared he could read the answer in her eyes clearly enough.

"Oh, my poor child," he said, his eyes full of warmth and such sympathy that she felt she would dissolve into tears and tell him all. It took a great deal of effort not to do just that as she pushed what remained of her chocolate aside.

"Can you tell me anything about him?" he asked, his expression intense. "As I feel the urgent desire to have a rather short conversation with the bas-- *fellow."*

She bit her lip and shrugged, shaking her head. She didn't want to speak about it anymore and for whatever ridiculous motive, she didn't want to get him into trouble. Whoever *he* was. Though why she owed him a shred of loyalty she couldn't fathom.

"I *will* find out," the Marquis warned, the dangerous glint in his eyes only too evident.

"You have been very kind, my Lord," she said, trying to hold onto her composure and keep her dignity intact. "But I should be getting back. I will be missed if I'm away any longer."

He nodded and got to his feet, taking her back outside. "Would you like me to escort you home?" he asked.

"No, thank you. You have already been so very kind and Thomas will look after me. Besides," she added with an apologetic expression. "It probably wouldn't be wise."

"No, perhaps not," he replied with a rueful grin. "But we will meet again, Lady Georgiana, and I promise you this much, I will do *everything* in my power to make you forget there was ever another Beau Beaumont ... or ever could be." He gave her a roguish smile and bowed, before leaving her with Thomas to walk back to Mayfair.

***

It was obviously quite clear to Céleste that something was wrong the moment she got home, but to her credit she said nothing. Instead she helped her to her room and closed the curtains, instructing Georgiana to lie down upon the bed and sending her abigail off for a cloth soaked in vinegar. Georgiana didn't attempt to try and explain or make excuses. She didn't want to lie to her friend and any attempt at the truth right now would only result in tears. Though all she truly wanted was to be left alone to indulge in a really serious cry. While they waited for her abigail to return Céleste rubbed a little lavender oil onto her wrists and temples, talking silly nothings in French that Georgiana couldn't understand but found soothing.

Once the abigail had returned, the cloth laid carefully on her forehead, and Georgiana made as comfortable as Céleste could make her, her friend took her hand and gave it a squeeze

"Don't reply to me," she said, giving her a sweet smile. "I don't know what 'as happened and you don't need to tell me right now. But later, when you feel a little better ... if you want to talk to someone ..." She leaned down and kissed Georgiana's cheek. "It is a new thing for me, you see, to 'ave friends. But I promise you I am trying to be very good at it, and anything you say to me ... I will tell no one else. Not even Alex if you don't want me to. You 'ave my word."

With a last reassuring pat off her hand, Céleste got up and went to the door. "Just call if you need anything or want me to come back, *Chérie.*" And with that she closed the door quietly behind her.

Chapter 17

"Wherein plans are revealed and the fates laugh with glee."

Sebastian looked up as Beau strolled into the room unannounced and without so much as a knock. "Do come in," he drawled, tucking the sleek red curl he had been staring at with dejection into his desk drawer and out of sight.

Beau paused and looked at him, one blond eyebrow arched in surprise. "I have," he replied, before going and helping himself to Sebastian's best brandy.

"It's not even noon," he pointed out to Beau who just returned a bored look and sat down in front of his desk.

"I'm celebrating," Beau replied with a smug expression.

"Oh?" Sebastian closed the ledger that he'd been quite at a loss to make tally for the past two hours as a certain sweet country girl and her unruly red hair kept intruding on his thoughts. He was dangerously close to breaking and returning to Cornwall, for he didn't think he could bear not to see her again.

"Yes, I believe I have discovered the means to my salvation."

Sebastian blinked and tried to drag his mind away from an October day and a Titian haired beauty spread out among the autumn leaves and back to Beau's news.

"Oh?"

Beau sighed and shook his head. "You said that already."

"I did?"

"Good God, man," his friend snapped, clearly exasperated. "Will you snap out of ... of whatever *this* is!" He ran a hand through his thick blond hair and slouched back in the chair, glaring at Sebastian. "You've not been fit for man nor beast for weeks now. You can't have her! You know you can't so bloody well let it go."

"I would if I could, damn it!" he exploded in return. The unfairness of it all, the longing to see Georgiana, the pressure of the past weeks, of his mother's hysterics and her determination that they were all to be brought to ruin had worn on his last nerve. "What do you know of love?" he demanded. "You've never cared a damn for anyone but yourself. I can't forget her, I ... I can't." He stopped, appalled by his outburst. He hadn't meant to admit that to Beau, and he certainly hadn't meant to abuse his best friend for no reason. He sighed as he saw the look in his friend's eyes. His face had that guarded, shuttered-up quality that he wore for everyone but Sebastian. "Forgive me, Beau," he said, hearing the exhaustion behind his words. "I had no right to say that and ... and I know it isn't true. You have always been ... the very best of friends."

Beau snorted in disgust, though he seemed to relax a little. "No I haven't. Far from it, and you well know it. But you are and I don't expect to hear you of all people call me out for it."

Sebastian laughed, relieved that he'd been so easily forgiven. "To tell the truth, it's been the most damnably awful few weeks."

"I suppose a broken heart will do that to you?" Beau replied, curiosity lurking in his blue eyes. "You really think you love the girl?"

"I don't think it," he replied with a crooked smile. "I know it. I have never felt this way before. It's like all the air has been sucked out of the world and I can't breathe anymore."

Beau grimaced with disdain and picked a tiny piece of lint from his perfectly tailored sleeve. "How terribly uncomfortable. I must make sure I avoid it at all costs."

"You do," Sebastian replied laughing. He grew serious again as Georgiana's lovely face drifted back to mind. "I can't get her out of my head," he admitted.

"You must, unless you would offer her a *carte blanche?"*

Sebastian smiled as he imagined the look on Georgiana's face if he dared to offer to keep her as his mistress. "I don't think she'd take that offer very kindly," he said, shaking his head with amusement.

Beau gave an impatient tut of annoyance. "Well you must think of something because I can't stand all this moping about, it's revolting. Just imagine what your mother would say if you told her you intended to offer for a doctor's daughter with no name and no fortune. Good God, that would be the spasm to end all spasms. You might actually kill her!"

Sebastian buried his head in his hands. "Right at this moment she might actually welcome the idea, as it's far from my only problem."

"You're not serious? What else can have ... oh!" Beau trailed off.

He watched as Beau fell silent and thought he detected a slightly guilty air about him.

Sebastian narrowed his eyes, leaning over the desk to better scrutinise the angelic countenance in front of him. "You're up to something unspeakable!"

He was given an eye roll as Beau finished his drink and stood to pour another. "Oh very well," he replied. "But you go first. Tell me why your darling parent is having the vapours now, though I think I can guess."

"I'm damned sure you can. Fix me one of those," he added, pinching the bridge of his nose as a headache began to bloom behind his eyes. "The blasted scandal rags are full of Lady Dalton, *The Siren!* So the whole bloody scandal is going to be raked up again, just at the moment I'm out to find a wife and mother is convinced the chit is somehow going to ruin me like her mother ruined father."

"Ah," Beau handed him his glass and a sympathetic expression. "Yes I do see. But ... it may be that I can help you there."

Sebastian paused with the glass halfway to his lips. "What the devil do you mean?"

"Well," his friend said, winking and raising his glass at him. "It's an ill wind ..."

"Oh for the love of God, do stop talking in riddles. You know it drives me insane when you do that."

Beau chuckled, his blue eyes glittering with calculation. "Well it just so happens that The Honourable Miss Georgiana Dalton is an heiress and I have every intention of making her my wife."

Sebastian stared at his friend, the words seemed to circulate his brain but it was taking longer than usual to accept the meaning of them.

"You ... want to marry her?" he replied with care, wanting to be sure he'd really understood as the enormity of it hit him.

Beau pursed his lips, a thoughtful expression making him look more bloody perfect that usual. *"Want to* is perhaps giving the matter a little too much force," he replied with perfect sincerity. "I don't *want* to marry anyone. However, seeing as I am probably days away from *point non plus* and some of my creditors are really not the kind of men who take kindly to being told my pockets are to let ... then yes, I most certainly will do all in my power to marry her as fast as I may. They say she's rich enough to buy an abbey you know, and gifts like that don't fall into your hands every day."

"She would be your wife, Beau. The daughter of the woman who ruined my life, who killed my father and tore my family apart while the *ton* looked on and gossiped. You would marry *her?"* Sebastian found he'd got to his feet without somehow noticing it. His fists were clenched with rage as the ferocity of his words rang around the room.

Beau met his gaze, his expression placid but there was something in his eyes that gave him pause. "I'm sorry, Sebastian, truly I am. If I had any other choice I swear I would take it. But heiresses are thin on the ground, and please don't think I overstate the case when I tell you I am ... in trouble ..."

Sebastian sat down again as his anger fell away. He stared at Beau and for the first time he could ever remember he thought he saw fear in his eyes.

"Your father?" he queried, though he knew what the answer would be.

"For God's sake, Sebastian. When will you get it through your head that the bastard hates my guts. He would laugh himself to death if I got carted off to debtor's prison, I assure you. Though frankly I'd be lucky to get there after some of the callers I've been forced to receive recently."

"Christ, Beau!" Sebastian shouted and pulled out the desk drawer, fully intending to write his friend a banker's draft there and then.

"Don't you dare!" Beau sprang to his feet, his eyes almost feverish. "I won't take it, damn you. I made this bloody mess and I'll get myself out of it. I won't take a penny from you so don't try to give it to me or we will most certainly fall out."

"You can pay me back, you bloody fool, with interest if it will make you happy!"

"No!"

The two men stared at each other as Sebastian tried to force down the anger that was bubbling in his chest.

"So you would rather marry that ... that creature than borrow money from me?"

Beau let out a small bark of laughter and the fight seemed to go out of him. "I assure you it isn't any great sacrifice on my part," he said with a wry smile. "She is perfectly adorable and very beautiful, and I would dare to suggest - nothing like her mother."

Sebastian gave an incredulous snort, despite the fact he'd thought it quite unlikely she was cast in the same mould himself.

"I'll never be able to receive you both here."

Beau shrugged. "Not while your mother lives perhaps, no."

Shaking his head in frustration, Sebastian folded his arms, staring at Beau, trying to understand him, which was something he had never fully been able to do. "What makes you believe things would be any different when she's gone? Why should I receive her?"

Beau just met his eyes and smiled. "Because you are the fairest and most forgiving person I have ever known."

"Don't try and fob me off with Spanish coin," he replied, his tone gruff, though he was pleased by the compliment nonetheless. "You might be able to use that silver tongue to bed whomsoever you please, but don't think you'll bamboozle me into believing you marrying Lady Georgiana is anything other than a recipe for utter disaster."

"Well at least if I marry her the *ton* will stop looking so hard for gossip, especially if you can bring yourself to acknowledge her at least."

"I have every intention of giving her the cut direct," he replied, his tone brooking no argument, no possible point of discussion.

He heard Beau's sigh of disappointment. "Yes, I thought you might."

"You know ... she might not *want* to marry you, did you ever consider that?"

Beau gave him a smirk. "Of course it's *possible,"* he allowed, though the twinkle of amusement in his eyes made it clear he thought it unlikely.

Sebastian snorted, outraged if not surprised. “God, you’re an arrogant devil.”

Chapter 18

"Wherein our heroine faces the ton, and an Adonis makes his move."

"I think the white," Céleste replied, looking at the row of beautiful dresses with a critical eye. "Oui, I'm certain."

"B-but, I can't wear *white!"* Georgiana protested. It was finally the day she had been both dreading and waiting for. She would be making her come out tonight at Lady Allen's rout party.

Céleste put her hands on her hips and turned on Georgiana with such fury in her eyes that she was quite taken aback. Small and delicate she might look, but the countess was a little firebrand when her temper was up, as Georgiana had discovered.

When she had finally confessed to her new friend everything that had happened to her, Céleste's anger on her behalf had been quite spectacular. She had raged and cursed both in English and in French, to such a point that Georgiana had found herself in strange position of trying to calm her. "What if I'm just like my mother?" she'd asked, appalled. "What if ... if I'm ... *fast?"*

Céleste hooted with laughter. "But 'e was 'andsome, *non?"* she demanded, her blue eyes wide with amusement.

"Well, yes, very."

The countess just threw up her hands in a *well there you are* gesture, which didn't help at all until she sighed and shook her head at Georgiana and took her hands. *"Chérie,* just because you are a woman does not mean you do not want or desire. Oh!" she huffed with annoyance and waved one elegant hand in the air. "We are supposed to be so prim and sweet and innocent on the outside, but if you got to the bedroom and just laid there like a stick I assure you they would soon lose interest. They want it both ways these men. But I promise you, in bed they want to be wanted and desired, they want you to gasp and moan for them and call their names. You are perfectly normal, silly goose, and don't ever think otherwise."

Georgiana blushed scarlet but found herself more than relieved by her friend's blunt answer. That being the case, she wondered if Céleste could enlighten on a few other topics. Of course she'd lived her whole life in the country and wasn't totally ignorant as to the way procreation was supposed to happen but ... a few details would be appreciated.

Céleste, of course, was more than happy to fill in as many details as Georgiana wanted, some of which made complete sense alongside the conclusions she'd come to, and others ... which shocked her to her bones. Their discussion had carried on, in hushed whispers, when they went downstairs for luncheon. When Lord Falmouth walked in on them and they both fell silent, however, his frown of suspicion had them both succumbing to such hysterics they drove the poor man from the room muttering about addle brained females.

Now, however, Céleste was holding up a pure white dress with a glint of determination in her eyes that was unlikely to be talked down.

"And why, tell me, should you not wear white? Are you a fallen woman? A Cytherean? Did you give the imposter your virtue?"

"No!" Georgiana exclaimed in horror. "You know I didn't."

Céleste gave a little huff of triumph. *"Alors,* then you will wear the dress, very simple with just some pearls, I think, and you will steal every man's breath, I promise you." As though that was the end of the argument, Céleste headed for the door. "Now I must get ready too, or I will be late and Alex will be cross." She winked at Georgiana who knew as well as she did that Alex would be nothing of the sort and left her to attend to her own toilette.

Georgiana sighed as her abigail gave a light scratch at the door to announce her arrival and the preparations began.

Some time later, standing before the mirror, Georgiana had to concede that Céleste had a point. The dress was of white watered gros-de-Naples, with very rich lace around the hem surmounted by embroidered orange flower blossoms. Real orange blossoms adorned her hair which was burnished and curled around her head with the exception of one errant curl. This, at Céleste's instruction, had been left to fall over her shoulder and rest just above her breast. Georgiana had been scandalised, thinking it looked a little too daring when she was supposed to be the model of propriety.

Céleste had just given her a pitying look. "What do you want from this, *mon poussin?"* she asked. "Do you just want to please all the old gossips and the nasty bitches who will talk about you no matter what you do? Or do you want to attract an 'usband? An interesting man who you could love and respect and do the same for you in return?"

Georgiana huffed and raised her hands in surrender and Céleste nodded with approval. "Then you do as I say. If you look too dull and virginal people will think you are trying too 'ard. You 'ave dressed with perfect propriety but this." She tugged at the fiery curl with a smirk. "This is you poking your tongue out and daring them to try and squash your spirit. *Tu comprends?"*

Oh yes, Georgiana thought with a sigh, she did understand.

***

Though it was still early in the season, Lady Allen's party was a crush. Georgiana clung to Céleste like a limpet for the first hour or so, too unused to such numbers of people and too terrified by the calculating looks in their eyes whenever she caught them staring at her. She took a breath and tried not to wish she was back home, sitting by the fire and reading one of her favourite novels.

"I feel like I am caught in a dream."

She turned, startled by the soft voice that was suddenly so close at hand and found herself looking up into the blue eyes of her heroic Adonis. He was, if it were possible, even more handsome in the candlelight, but then of course this was his natural habitat. This was the hunting ground of the notorious seducer and he was clearly intent on making her his next conquest. The thought amused rather than troubled her as her heart was too damaged to allow another to hurt it any further.

"A dream you say, Lord Beaumont?" she replied, amused. "Should I pinch you to be sure?"

"Oh, no," he tsked and shook his head. "For then I might wake, and what a pity. For you see, I am remembering a summer night when I was a very small boy."

She turned a little further to face him directly, intrigued now. He smiled at her, a warm and inviting smile that she imagined had tugged at a good many hearts. "I had crept out of bed and gone to my father's orangerie. I had gone to see if any were ripe."

"And were they?" she asked, quite unable to resist returning his smile which was as infectious as it was delightful.

"Alas no," he replied with a mournful expression. "But it was warm and the scent ..." He closed his eyes and leaned a little closer to her, and when he spoke again the words seemed to shiver over her skin. "The scent was decadent, as sweet and heavy as opium and I slept the whole night there like a babe, dreaming such wonderful dreams." She looked up to see him watching her, and his eyes darkened in the most alluring manner. "The scent of you makes me want to never wake again."

She swallowed, well aware she was in the hands of a sophisticated lover and very far out of her depth. To her relief he saved her from any further form of reply.

"Shall we mingle and see who can amuse us tonight?"

"No." The deep masculine voice was implacable and Georgiana looked around to see Lord Falmouth glaring at the Marquis.

"Falmouth." The Marquis inclined his head just a little in greeting. "A pleasure to see you this evening. I was just asking Lady Georgiana to take a turn about the room with me."

"Oh, Alex, do let 'er. Beau is such fun, *hein?"*

The Marquis' lips twitched a little as Lady Falmouth came to his defence. "Lady Falmouth, may I say how very lovely you look this evening."

"You may," Céleste replied, a naughty twinkle glinting in her eyes and Georgiana realised she was only too well aware of the glowering fury of her husband's obvious jealousy. "Now then, run along, children," Céleste said, making a shooing motion as if she was some elderly dame. "And, Beau, behave yourself. I'm watching you." She pointed her fan at him in a threatening manner though there was laughter in her eyes. As they turned to walk away Georgiana heard her breathless laughter as she turned to her husband.

"Oh, darling, Alex, how can you be so silly when you know I adore only you."

Georgiana sighed and wondered if she would ever be lucky enough to be granted a wish as great as that one appeared to be, to love and be loved, with no lies, no pretences and no games.

"They are a lucky pair aren't they?" She looked up at Beau in surprise, to find his face quite open and free of what she had begun to see was his usual playful flirtatiousness. "What?" he asked her. "You think I can't see it too? You think I can't wonder what life would be like if I made such a match?"

He paused, his eyes on hers very intent.

"Do you?" she asked, genuinely curious. He didn't answer and they began to weave in and out of the crowd as he nodded to acquaintances in passing. "I used to read of you every week you know," she said, smiling as she saw him regard her with amusement.

"Ah," he said, with a sorrowful shake of his head. "My reputation precedes me."

“It does indeed,” she agreed, as she noticed two women staring at them with obvious jealousy and spite on their painted faces. “In fact, I became quite concerned after you disappeared to Scotland for such a time.”

A low masculine chuckle of amusement rumbled beside her and she couldn’t help but smile in return. There was something quite irrepressible about him and she could quite understand why women dropped at his feet. “I am honoured to have stirred such pity in your breast.”

“You did,” she said, smirking. “Though I began to fear you weren’t half the rake I’d believed you to be when you stayed away for so long. I thought perhaps you’d ... lost your nerve.”

She laughed at his expression and then shook her head, fascinated to watch how his eyes dropped from her eyes to her mouth and then to the little curl that had come to nestle in her décolletage. There was certainly hunger in his gaze and it soothed her bruised heart a little to know that she was desirable.

“Now I know how Eve felt standing beneath that apple tree,” he murmured, never taking his eyes off the curl. “I have the most desperate desire to reach out and give that little curl a tug.”

“But you won’t,” she said watching as he raised his eyes back to hers with obvious reluctance.

He pursed his lips as if giving the matter grave thought. “Not ... this time,” he replied. Settling her hand back on his arm they continued on their survey of the room. “I suppose I must relinquish you back to Falmouth. For now ...” he added with a wink. They walked a little further in silence before he paused and turned back to her. “Do you know, I had a lot of time to think when I was in Scotland.” He gave a self-deprecating smirk. “Believe me, it is usually a pastime I avoid at all costs, but ...”

She raised her eyebrows at him, a little uneasy at the look in his eyes. “But?”

"But what would you think if I said I was considering mending my ways and settling down?"

She suppressed a smile and gave him a sympathetic look. "I would say your creditors are shouting rather louder than usual, my Lord."

He gave a shout of laughter and looked back at her in delight. "Yes, you *would* say that wouldn't you." But then he covered her hand with his own and his face grew serious. "And I must marry for money, it is quite true. But it never occurred to me before tonight that ... that it could perhaps be more than that."

She caught her breath, unable to say more as Lord Falmouth's disapproving presence loomed over them. Beau raised her hand and kissed the fingers, a warm look in his eyes.

"Good evening, Lady Georgiana. It has been a great pleasure, and one I intend to repeat very soon." He nodded to Lord Falmouth, said goodbye to Céleste and left them alone.

Chapter 19

"Wherein Almack's hallowed grounds are daunting."

Sebastian strode in through the impressive doors of his home on Grosvenor Square, surrendered his hat and coat to the footman and shut himself in his study.

Good God but what a tedious and unprofitable afternoon. Two days earlier he had obliged his mother by presenting his own list of eligible females and between them they had whittled the names down to five. Five possible choices for his future duchess.

He had gone this afternoon to pay a call on the one that had risen to the top of the list. Lady Anne Scunthorpe was the granddaughter of an earl. Her family came from a distinguished and well-respected line. Whilst she was no beauty she was by no means unattractive with a sweet, round face and a pleasing figure. She was also accomplished and well used to hosting her father's impressive rout parties since her mother died some three years earlier. She would make a perfect duchess and, to make the match even more desirable, her marriage price included a vast tract of land that Sebastian had always coveted as it sat cheek by jowl to his own estate and was ripe for development.

And yet.

She had smiled at him, laughed at his - frankly appalling - jokes, and never ventured an opinion further than, "I'm sure you're right, your Grace."

She would never do anything to displease him, she would look the other way to his affairs as long as he was discreet and she would always tell him he was right.

He felt sick.

And now he had to face bloody Almack's. Dammit all if there was another place he detested more on the face of the planet, he couldn't yet bring it to mind. He'd have to stand there, like a prize bull, while mothers chivvied their daughters into smiling and batting their eyelashes at him in the hopes of casting a lure to hook a duke on.

He groaned and sat back in his chair clutching a large glass of brandy. Holding the cool glass to his temple he closed his eyes, and his thoughts immediately strayed to Georgiana.

Oh God. He couldn't bear it. Not one more day without her. He would leave, he decided. First thing tomorrow he would go back and find her and ... and ...

His brain stalled. Could he really offer her marriage?

Beau was right about one thing, his mother might fear him falling into the clutches of *The Siren,* but bringing home a country doctor's daughter as his bride might be enough to finish the old girl off for good. Ever since he was old enough to understand the concept, she above all others, had drummed into him the duty he owed his position. The privilege he had been given was great and he must make his own sacrifices to be worthy of it. But did that truly mean he could never be happy?

There was only one thing he knew with any kind of certainty. He could never be happy without Georgiana.

So he would leave tomorrow and he would find her and he would see what he felt, how she felt, when they met again. But if she loved him still, he didn't think he was strong enough to say goodbye to her a second time.

***

"Look at this one!" Céleste said with glee, waving another newspaper at her. Georgiana snatched it from her hand and poured over the relevant page.

Last night at Lady A's fabulously attended rout party, the great and the good of the ton were treated to their first glimpse of the dashing Lady D.

Dressed demurely all in white this elegant lady seemed to take all in her stride and charmed many, much to the dismay of others. Our own dashing M of B was dressed to the height of fashion and was noted to have spent much time in admiring the lady himself. We await with impatience ...

"The bloody impertinence!" Alex thundered, snatching the newspaper off the table in front of her and glowering at it. "Georgiana, you must stay away from Beaumont. I know he's an entertaining chap but he's nothing but trouble, and he certainly can't do you any good."

"Oh, Alex, don't be so stuffy," Céleste replied laughing at him and feeding her spaniel a piece of buttered toast from her fingers. "His interest has already done her a great deal of good, and besides, from what Georgiana said he's not toying with her. He means to take a wife."

Georgiana nodded. "Oh, of course it is my fortune that tempts him, my Lord. Please be easy, I have no silly ideas that he would look at me twice if not for that."

"Oh, he'd look at you twice," Alex muttered with a grim smile. He looked back to Céleste and Georgiana watched with amusement as his face softened. "So, it's Almack's tonight?"

"Yes," Céleste replied with a heavy sigh.

"What's this?" he demanded, his cool, grey eyes frowning with concern. "There have been more plots and intrigues to get these blasted vouchers than the Duke of Wellington ever employed in the entire bloody war. Don't tell me you don't want to go?"

"Oh, non," Céleste replied, reaching out and clasping his arm. "But you won't be there so it won't be any fun at all."

"Nonsense," he replied, though Georgiana could see he was more than pleased by the comment. "You'll flirt and dance with all your *cicisbei* and not give your poor old husband another thought."

At this point Georgiana felt it was prudent to leave them alone, as there was a look in Céleste's eyes that proved her husband's words wrong.

***

The ritual of readying herself for the coming evening was not quite enough to dispel the thunderous fluttering of wings, that seemed more akin to crows than butterflies, as Georgiana's stomach clenched in anxiety. She'd barely eaten a thing all day, too aware that tonight was the real test. Almack's was the holiest of holies, hallowed ground to the *ton*, and whilst Seymour might have been able to blackmail her way into gaining her vouchers, she couldn't force them to accept her.

She let out a shaky sigh as her abigail stepped back and nodded with approval.

"Oh, my Lady, you do look a picture."

She smiled at her maid in the glass. She was perhaps a year or two younger than Georgiana and had quickly formed an attachment to her mistress that boded a good relationship. "Thank you so much, Sarah. You've done a wonderful job."

Madame Lisabeth had indeed outdone herself with her wonderful design. The dress was her own version of the Saxe-Cobourg robe which had been the talk of the *ton* just a few weeks previously. It fell off the shoulder with little satin sleeves at her upper arms and she'd used the newly discovered and very sought after Chinese gauze in a pale shimmering gold. It was trimmed with tulle and ivory satin and set against Georgiana's deep russet locks the whole image presented that of something burnished by the sun. Although it was by no means the fashion, once again that single lock of hair had been allowed to tumble carelessly over her shoulder.

This time Georgiana's misgivings were even greater than before. Céleste, however, had been adamant. The curl remained.

By the time they had greeted Lady Russell outside the doors of Almack's Georgiana felt positively nauseated by the thought of having to face a ballroom full of the ton's most powerful and fashionable figures. Tonight could make her, or it could ruin her once and for all.

"Come," Céleste whispered, taking her arm and giving it an encouraging squeeze. "I am beside you and who cares what they think? They don't know the truth about either of us. They will believe the face we show them if we carry ourselves with confidence."

Georgiana returned a smile that made her face feel tight and Céleste tutted at her.

"Mon Dieu, Georgie, don't you know 'ow ravishing you look tonight? You've already got Beau 'anging on your sleeve and if you think it's your fortune alone that captured 'is attention you are much mistaken!"

She could do nothing but give a little huff of laughter in the face of Céleste's obvious indignation. Well at least her friend was confident on her behalf, and ... well that thought did actually make her feel better.

"You 'ave friends 'ere," Céleste whispered with a severe expression, and so Georgiana smiled, a little more naturally, took a deep breath, and entered the fray.

They walked through the grand entrance hall and were relieved of their cloaks before ascending the elegant stone staircase to the ballroom. Music and laughter and the soft burble of voices could be heard long before they approached the great doors and Georgiana caught her breath as she saw the famous ballroom for the first time.

The room was vast and exquisite with plasterwork medallions and swags in a classical design and a vast chandelier lit with more candles than she had ever seen in one place. The walls were white and a pale gold and the draperies a soft duck egg blue. On one side of the great room was a large balcony that ran almost a third of one wall and allowed people to watch those who were dancing and swirling below them in a dizzying flurry of silken skirts.

With a feeling close to panic closing about her throat, Georgiana realised she had never seen so many people all in one place before in her life. The place was packed full of hundreds of people, all of them dressed in the finest fabrics and most glittering jewels, if not always with the best judgement or taste.

A whisper seemed to flutter through the crowd and Georgiana became gradually aware that her arrival had been noted. The panicky feeling began to take a greater hold of her until a sleek voice whispered in her ear.

"And here is that shiny red apple again. I really don't know what you expect a poor, helpless creature to do against such temptation, my Lady. I am being drawn into dangerous waters."

She looked around and almost sighed with relief at the vision of Beau's beautiful smile.

Dipping a curtsey, she returned his greeting with one of deep gratitude. "Good evening, Lord Beaumont. I confess I am very happy to see a friendly face."

"Friendly?" he replied, one eyebrow a little quirked. "Darling, I'm not sure that's the word you're looking for. I have no intention of being your friend, I'm afraid."

She laughed and shook her head. "Very well then, I'm glad to see you even if you're not the least bit friendly."

He grinned at her and then his eyes fell to the curl once again and he sighed. "I intend to have a lock of that hair you know."

"Oh do you?" she replied, aware that Céleste was speaking to Aunt Seymour and another acquaintance that had joined them but was also keeping an eye on her protégé. "And just how do you propose to do that?"

"I couldn't possibly tell you that, now could I?" he replied, those impossibly blue eyes glittering with mischief. "But I should beware dark corners or I will be forced to take advantage of you."

Georgiana bit her lip against a grin. She knew she shouldn't really encourage him. He was very far from the kind of man she wanted to marry but it was nice to have an admirer, especially when he was undeniably the best-looking man in the room. But against her will her eyes never stopped looking for the one she had believed to be Beau. After all, he'd clearly been wealthy and from a good family. There was every chance he was here ... somewhere ...

"I thank you for the warning, though I thought it was I who was the danger to you? Not the other way around."

"Oh you are," he replied, and this time his voice was more serious. "You are a very dangerous game indeed," he murmured.

At this point Aunt Seymour and Céleste turned back to her and Beau chatted politely to them all for a little while, securing dances with both her and Céleste before leaving them alone to join some other friends.

"That's a good start for you, my girl," Seymour said with an approving nod. "Though it won't do to be seen too much in his company. Too much in the petticoat line that one, and that would do you no good at all. But his interest will spur a good many others to seek you out, mark my words."

"I'm surprised to see he's even allowed here," Georgiana said in a low voice. "I mean after everything last year and his reputation and all ..."

"Oh but he's the height of fashion, my dear," the old lady replied chuckling. "And such an amusing man, such engaging manners. Respectability isn't the only way to gain access here you see, it's a little more complicated than that." She gave Georgiana a wink before complaining that she had been standing quite long enough and went to seek out some of her cronies.

It soon became clear that Seymour's words had been perfectly correct. Although Georgiana heard many whispers about The Siren, and caught many sneers and disgusted looks that made her blush with mortification, that wasn't the only attention she caught. She even noticed one or two ladies with a familiar curl falling with great daring into their décolletage. It appeared she had started a trend. But it was certainly not just the women who had noticed her.

"Like bees around a 'oney pot," Céleste hissed in her ear at one point as Seymour was sought out time and again by various men, eager to be given an introduction to the newest and brightest diamond in the room. For that was what many were calling her, and Georgiana was torn between deep embarrassment and bemusement at some of the extravagant compliments that were cast her way. But naturally, she couldn't help but wonder ... how many of them would have been so keen if the fact she was an heiress hadn't also been dangled in front of them, and how on earth was she to tell?

Chapter 20

"Wherein the ton holds its breath."

"I've brought you a sensible man this time, Georgiana."

Looking up Georgiana found Seymour advancing on them once more and felt sorry for the old lady who'd barely had a moment's peace all evening. Georgiana had been rather hoping for a little rest herself after having been danced off her feet for the past two hours. But beside Seymour was a tall and terribly gaunt young man with spectacles. He seemed rather serious and ill at ease in his own skin, as if not quite sure what to do with his height. He bent to greet her but remained a little stooped, as if his lofty frame might offend somehow.

"He's shy but kind, and as rich as Croesus." Seymour hissed in her ear. "Lady Georgiana, may I present Lord Nibley."

Georgiana curtsied and looked up, to her amusement finding the poor man had blushed scarlet, but there was a kindly and intelligent pair of brown eyes behind the rims of his wire spectacles.

"I am very happy to meet you, my Lord," she said, smiling at him.

"The pleasure is mine," he said, and then swallowed hard.

They stood in rather awkward silence for a few minutes while Georgiana racked her brain for a topic of conversation.

"It's very ..."

"Do you ever ..."

They laughed as the two of them had finally spoke at once.

"I do beg your pardon," Georgiana said. "Please continue."

Lord Nibley shook his head in a rather shamefaced manner. "I'm not sure it would be worth the effort. I'm afraid I don't have much talent for this sort of thing."

"If you are a sensible man, as Lady Russell said, I hardly doubt it. A great deal of talk about nothing very much cannot be something you aspire to, surely?" she said, grinning at him.

He let out a breath and seemed to relax a little. "Oh but I do," he replied, his expression quite earnest. "I would give anything to be able to converse with ease at ... at these gatherings but I'm afraid the knack of it escapes me."

He seemed to prove the point by falling silent again and Georgiana cast around once more.

"What do you usually do when you're not in town?"

His face brightened perceptibly and she hoped she might have struck gold.

"Rocks," he said, with some enthusiasm.

Georgiana smothered a grin and wondered if she had a guardian angel with a twisted sense of humour. Somehow she doubted he was speaking of golden rocks.

"Yes, geology you see, fascinating subject," he said, with real passion lighting his eyes now. "Do you know anything about it?"

"Not a thing no," she admitted, wondering with some amusement if she was going to be able to keep it that way.

She began to lose the will to live sometime after he uttered the words rock strata and began a detailed explanation about the different kinds of fossils to be found in each layer.

Eventually he fell silent again, apparently having become aware he was monopolising the conversation by the look of embarrassed chagrin on his face. Taking pity on him she tried again.

"Do you have any friends here tonight, my Lord?"

He shook his head and clasped his hands behind his back with a sigh, putting her strongly in mind of a gloomy heron and then brightened as a thought occurred to him. “Oh, yes. Of course, Lord Beaumont is here. He’s a devilish fine fellow, we were at school together.”

Georgiana chuckled. “Well devilish I can believe.”

Lord Nibley gave her a rueful smile and scratched his nose. “He does have something of a reputation I suppose. Sindalton is here too of course. Usually if Beau’s around Sin’s not far behind ... been saying that since Eton, like brothers they are.”

Georgiana’s heart seemed to give a little stutter in her chest and her stomach clenched.

“S-Sindalton?” she stammered, staring up at him in horror.

“Yes of course, I saw him earlier, he ...” Lord Nibley stopped in his tracks, staring at her and mirroring the horrified look in her eyes. “Oh, good God. M-my Lady, I never even considered. I b-beg you to forgive me ... it never crossed my mind.”

She forced a smile and shook her head though her face felt flushed and rather hot and the atmosphere in the room had become oppressive at the idea that she might have to face him at any moment. “Please don’t think anything of it, my Lord. It ... it was just a shock.”

Lord Nibley stooped a little further, his voice pitched low and full of concern. “You didn’t know he was here?”

She shook her head, seeming unable to form the words.

“S-silly of me,” she murmured.

“Not at all,” he said, suddenly sounding rather forceful. “I have to say I think you’re ... you’re magnificent.”

Georgiana looked up at him in surprise and he blushed a little at his rather forward statement and pushed his spectacles further up his nose. “I can’t imagine the courage it must take to face all of these awful people, Lady Georgiana. Though I for one consider you totally blameless and anyone who thinks otherwise is nothing but a narrow minded, scandal monger," he said, with some considerable heat.

"I couldn't have said it better myself, dear Percy," drawled an amused voice and Lord Nibley turned as Beau arrived, smiling at Georgiana with a knowing look in his eyes.

"Though I don't think Lady Georgiana has anything to worry about. From everything that has been said in my hearing, she is a great success." He adopted a thoughtful expression as though he was trying to recall the comments. "Ah yes, her ladyship is perfectly charming, quite unaffected, delightful manners and quite as she ought to be ... oh, and terribly, *terribly* beautiful." There was an intense look in his eyes as he finished his little recital and Georgiana was forced to look away from him ... and straight at the tall and striking figure of a man she thought she had known very well.

She held her breath and stared.

He had his back to her but Georgiana knew, without a shadow of a doubt, that it was him. She had the strangest feeling that the world had frozen around her and her lungs had seized with it. She clutched at her throat as panic fluttered in her chest and was suddenly aware of a warm hand clasped gently around her wrist.

"What is it, love?" Beau asked, his voice quiet but urgent. "Who have you seen?"

"The m-man I thought was you. H-he's here," she stammered, knowing he was one of only two people in the world she could admit that to. Beau's head whipped around and he scanned the crowd.

"Where?" he demanded. "I swear I'll kill him."

"No." She shook her head, unable to take her eyes from him though her vision began to blur. Beau followed her gaze and caught his breath just as he turned and made his profile visible.

"That's him?" he demanded, with such rage in his voice that she caught her breath. "The tall fellow with dark hair, next to the lady in violet?"

She nodded, too miserable to deny it. Seeing him again brought his lies and betrayal rushing back to her and she was torn between wanting to cross the room and slap his face and running away as fast as she could. In the end she did neither, too frozen to react at all.

"I'll bloody kill him," Beau raged, glaring at him.

"Who is he?" she asked, her voice trembling as she looked up into his furious blue eyes.

"That, my Lady," he replied, with cold anger glittering in his eyes. "Is Sebastian Grenville, the Duke of Sindalton."

She didn't have time to react, to have the luxury of assimilating this horrifying piece of information, because at that moment the duke turned around and their eyes met.

For a moment, behind his obvious shock, she thought she saw something in his eyes, relief, happiness even ... and then he took in the fact that Beau stood beside her, and that the eyes of everyone in the room were watching them.

The moment stretched on, stretched so thin it was as though the oxygen had been sucked from the room. Overwhelmed she didn't know what to do, how to react until she heard Beau's voice.

"Look at me. Now!" His voice was low but so forceful she could do nothing but obey him and her eyes snapped to his. "Take my arm," he said, holding her gaze, his voice calm now but brooking no argument. Once her hand was settled upon his sleeve he covered it with his hand and pulled her in the opposite direction. "We shall take a little walk," he said, keeping his voice soft. "And everything will be just fine. Now look at me and laugh."

She looked up at him, blinking, too bewildered to understand what was happening. "Laugh?" she echoed, wondering if he'd run mad.

He ducked his head a little to whisper in her ear. "Everyone is watching us," he said. "They are watching your reaction. Do *not* give them the satisfaction. Now laugh."

He looked back at her and winked as though he'd just said something rather shocking and she forced a laugh that sounded a little too close to hysteria for comfort.

"Good girl," he replied, nodding with approval. "We'll get through this, don't you worry," he said, patting her hand. "And then I have every intention of killing my best friend."

***

Sebastian forced his feet to move, to take him away from the scene that had just played out. It couldn't be. It simply *couldn't* be. His head was seething, like his brain was full of writhing snakes and he just ... couldn't ... *think!* He forced his way through the crush, unheeding of gasps of disapproval, trying to block out the malicious whispers as the gossips fell upon the latest juicy morsel he'd provided for their entertainment.

He'd been determined to cut Miss Dalton, to turn his back on her and show the *ton* that the Duke of Sindalton did not approve of her arrival among their select ranks. But it had been she who had cut him. And it hadn't been the woman he'd imagined seeing here. She had been brassy and knowing and far too vulgar for anyone to wish to know. No. That hadn't been her at all. It had been his own sweet, Georgiana, the girl he'd been determined to run back to tomorrow because his heart was breaking without her. Except it couldn't be because if it was that would mean ... The facts and the dreams he'd built up around the woman he'd fallen for collided and span in his head. She couldn't be the daughter of Lady Dalton. The woman was an heiress and Georgiana was a nobody, a doctor's daughter with no name and no fortune. Unless ...

He ground to a halt, one hand leaning on the wall beside him for support because the pain of it was so fierce he could hardly draw a breath. Unless she had known who he was from the start. Unless she had planned it, as a way to avenge herself on him and his family. Perhaps she hadn't meant to, the way they'd met had been improbable after all but once she'd realised ... But he'd said he was Beau. The thought occurred to him now that Beau must know what he'd done and nausea roiled in his gut. Good God. And Beau was determined to marry her.

No. No. No! What had he done? What had *she* done? Blind with rage and shame and heartbreak he strode down the stone steps to the foyer and out into the night.

***

Beau forced her to dance with him and with Lord Nibley, who was terribly kind and gallant though he trod all over her toes and was the most dreadful dancer she had ever encountered. Between the two of them and Céleste and Seymour who had sought them out the moment they'd realised what had happened, she was sheltered as far as they could manage. They spoke to her with care, moving her from one spot to another and away from the eager chattering that seemed to follow her like a plague of locusts, chirruping in her ears so loud she thought she might lose her mind. But through it all her mind spun around the impossible truth.

He was the Duke of Sindalton. The son of the man who had shot her father and ruined her mother, ultimately leading her to her death. Had he known? But how could he have known who she was when she hadn't known herself? No. She dismissed the idea. It was too inconceivable that he should have met her by chance, guessed who she was and set out to ruin her ... wasn't it?

But then she remembered that he hadn't ruined her at all, though he could have done. He could have taken her because she'd been too wrapped up in him to refuse him anything. And yet he hadn't. He hadn't taken that from her which was irreplaceable and he'd said it was because he loved her. But why? Why had he pretended he was Beau when he was a wealthy *duke?*

The thoughts swirled in her head until finally, she was ushered into the carriage and taken away into the blessed darkness of the night. She allowed the gloom of the street to swallow her up and take her back to a place where she could go and tend her wounded heart in private, and try and consider what on earth she could do to mend it.

Chapter 21

"Wherein old lies tangle up the future."

Sebastian woke with a start and clutched at his head. It was throbbing in the most violent manner and as he forced himself to sit forward the empty decanter at his feet told its own tale. He groaned, shivering as his stomach turned, acid burning in his chest and throat. The fire had long since died in his office and the room was freezing, dark, and more unwelcoming than he'd ever known it. This had been his father's space. His sanctuary. The room where Sebastian had always felt closest to him. He looked up at the portrait of the man whose image still hung on the chimney breast. A severe-looking man with dark hair and darker eyes, but there was humour lurking behind the fierce expression and kindness too.

Mother had told him that Lady Dalton had taken his father away from them. That she'd bewitched him and driven him mad. Mad enough to kill the woman's husband and run away from his lawful wife and son. The betrayal of that had been more than he could bear. He'd hated Lady Dalton with a cold burning fury that would have consumed him whole, if Beau hadn't turned up and shown him life could still be worth the trouble of living it.

Almost as if he'd conjured him the door opened and he was confronted with Beau's furious blue gaze. He'd known, of course, that he'd have to face this. He got to his feet, a trifle unsteady but he stood, walking a few steps into the room and waiting as Beau advanced on him. The blow hit him square in the jaw and he fell backwards, sprawled across the study floor with lights exploding behind his eyes.

"You bastard!" Beau, yelled at him, the furious sound ringing through his tender brain. "I ought to damn well kill you," he raged. "Damn you for being drunk!"

Beau turned his back on him in disgust while he staggered to his feet, rubbing his jaw and testing his teeth one by one to see if they were all still intact.

"I'm sorry," he mumbled, collapsing back in the chair with a groan. He looked up, watching as Beau glowered at him. "I *am* sorry, Beau."

"What *exactly* is it you're sorry for?" Beau demanded, leaning against his desk and folding his arms across his chest. "Forgive me if I'd like a little clarity, but there appear to be a number of crimes to be laid at your door."

"All of it," he croaked, as his throat closed up. "For God's sake give me a glass of water."

Beau scowled at him and tutted but did as he was asked, pouring out a glass from a jug on his desk and putting it into his hand.

"Thank you."

"I should throw it in your face," Beau muttered. "You know you nearly ruined her last night. How could you?"

Sebastian downed the glass and tried to ignore the way his stomach clenched in protest. "I didn't mean to," he said, putting the empty glass aside and clutching at his head. "It was just ... such a shock, seeing her there."

"Not as much of a shock as she got when I introduced myself the other day, I assure you," Beau replied with a pointed expression.

"Oh God," Sebastian groaned. "I am sorry, Beau."

"So you keep saying."

He looked up and frowned, staring at his friend. "She ... She was truly shocked? She didn't know?"

"Of course she didn't know!" Beau exploded, making him wince as the sound tore through his head and slashed at his brain. "How the devil should she when *you* are apparently the Marquis of Beaumont. Came as a bit of a shock to me, I can tell you!"

"I know, I know ... I can't ..."

"Why?" Beau demanded. "Why in God's name would you do such a thing? Isn't it enough that you're a duke, that you've money enough to buy me a hundred times over without even noticing?" Sebastian dared to look up at his lifelong friend and wished to God he hadn't as he'd never seen such hurt in his eyes. "Damn it, Sebastian, all I have is this," he shouted, gesturing to that perfect face. "And the dubious honour of being the Marquis of Beaumont. Why would you want that too?"

"I just ..." He closed his eyes and sighed, wondering how on earth he could make him understand. "It was only meant to be for a day or two. It was just ... I was so tired of being hunted, of knowing these bloody women only want me for my title and my money. I just ..." He paused and shook his head, running a shaky hand through his hair. "I just wanted a bit of fun and I thought ... if she believed I was you, she'd know I was never offering anything serious. She'd know I was just playing with her and that there was no money to be had from me. If she wanted to be with me it could only be because ... she wanted to be with *me."*

He looked up again and met Beau's eyes, overcome with shame and humiliation. "I didn't mean it to go so far. I ... I never meant to fall in love with her."

Beau gave a snort of disgust. "That, at least, I do believe."

They sat in silence for awhile, until Sebastian heard the chink of a decanter and looked up as Beau offered him a small measure of brandy. He grimaced and turned away but the glass was forced into his hand.

"Hair of the dog," Beau said, his voice gruff. "Make you feel better."

He downed the measure in one go and shuddered. "Oh God."

"You have no idea how I am enjoying your suffering," Beau said, his voice dark. "But what do you intend now?"

Sebastian swallowed, the acidic taste in his mouth making him want to retch. He looked up at Beau, needing to know the answer to his question before he could reply to that. "Did ... did she truly not know who I was?"

Beau returned an incredulous look. "Of course she didn't know, you fool! You believe she could fake a reaction like that?" He got to his feet and stalked over to the chair, glowering down at him. "You'd damned well better sober up fast because I want to hit you again!" Turning on his heel he marched to the door and grabbed the handle. "And I give you fair warning, Sin. I meant what I said. I'm going to marry her, and I'll be damned if I'll let you or anyone else get in my way."

With that he slammed the door on Sebastian and left him alone.

***

They stayed at home for the next few days, a respite that Georgiana was only too relieved by, but she knew she couldn't hide forever. So tonight they were out, to a grand ball, though she couldn't find the interest or the will to discover whose or where. It would be just another sea of critical faces, all of them judging, all of them believing they knew what she was about, whether they viewed her kindly or not.

The idea that she might have to face the Duke of Sindalton on top of all that was not a thought that helped in the slightest. Sebastian Grenville. *Sebastian.* She tried to fit the new name to him but somehow it felt foreign and awkward to think of him like that.

Beau, however ... the Marquis of Beaumont lived up to his name quite perfectly. She remembered her thoughts when she'd first encountered *Sebastian.* He hadn't been what she'd expected of the notorious rake. Beau, however, Beau was exactly what she had believed him to be, just as she had imagined. Though in truth her imagination couldn't have conjured a face and figure that embodied masculine beauty to quite such a perfect degree. He was breathtakingly handsome, charming, witty, indolent, and rather kinder than she had expected.

In a last-ditch effort to cheer her up and take her mind off tonight's trial, Céleste had suggested a trip back to Hatchard's. She had told the countess all about the fabulous book shop and her friend had been just as eager to sample its delights. So a pleasant morning had been spent among its thousands of books and she did indeed feel a little lighter in spirit. Until they reached home and she saw the serious look on Lord Falmouth's face.

"Georgiana, might I have a word with you please?" he asked, and though he smiled at her his eyes remained grave.

"Of course," she replied as her stomach turned with anxiety.

Céleste went to turn away and give them privacy but she reached out and grabbed her friend's arm. "No, there's nothing that you can't hear and I think I might need the support," she said, laughing though she was only half joking.

Céleste smiled in return and squeezed her hand and they followed the earl into the masculine confines of his study. Georgiana had always liked this room. It was quite sparsely furnished compared to the rest of the house, but the dark wood panelling and shelves upon shelves of books gave it a cosy feel. Especially on a cold, damp day when spring was not yet making its presence felt. The fire crackled with a merry snap in the fireplace and the room smelt subtly of cognac and cigars. The earl took his place behind a massive oak desk and she sat and waited as Céleste settled herself in the chair beside her.

"I had a visit from your uncle this morning," he said with no preamble. The look of disgust in his eyes gave her the clear impression he had been as unimpressed by the baron as she'd been.

"Oh," she said, her heart sinking.

"Oh, indeed," Lord Falmouth replied with a grimace. "And a more ill mannered, over-stuffed piece of self-importance I've never had the misfortune to deal with."

"I'm so sorry," she muttered, blushing at the idea he'd had to deal with one of her obnoxious relations because of her.

He waved her apology aside. "You cannot be held responsible for your relations, Georgiana. Not in my mind at any rate," he added, as they all knew among the *ton* everyone could and would be held responsible. "But the man is intent on causing trouble. It appears you missed an appointment to meet your cousin, Mr Rufford?"

Georgiana shuddered and gave a brief nod. "He was supposed to propose to me and I was expected to accept him. A man I've never met before in my life," she added with such venom that Céleste reached out and grasp her hand again, squeezing the fingers.

"No one, will make you marry 'im!" Céleste cried. "I swear it. Nor anyone you don't want to."

Georgiana swallowed as a swell of emotion seemed to clog her throat. "It isn't as easy as that, Céleste. If he decides to ruin me you will be tainted by association."

She looked up and met Lord Falmouth's eye, knowing what a burden she could become to them, how badly she could hurt their reputations. They would be well shot of her no matter if they still wished they could help. But she knew the earl would be honest with her. He was a kind man under that severe exterior, but he never varnished the truth. "Do you need me to leave this house, my Lord?"

Céleste gave a cry of protest and she was more relieved than she cared to consider when she saw real shock in Lord Falmouth's eyes. "Good God, no!" he replied, looking genuinely aghast at the idea. "As if we would turn you out? Don't even think it."

She let out a breath, closing her eyes and covering her mouth with her hand as the relief washed over her. Céleste clung to her hand and a moment later she opened her eyes to see Falmouth standing over her, pressing a glass into her free hand.

“Brandy,” he said, his voice soft. “It will make you feel better.”

She accepted the glass, aware of Céleste’s hand still holding hers. It was a comfort to know she wasn’t alone in this. She had friends still, and if the worst happened, she could go back to her aunt and uncle and live quietly. An old maid. That thought had never sounded quite as bleak as it did at this moment.

“Georgiana.” She looked up again as the brandy began to heat a little puddle of warmth in her stomach. “I have dealt with the baron for the time being,” Falmouth said, something in his eyes that made her believe that the baron might not have left the house in quite the same state he arrived in. “But a man like that won’t be silenced forever. It may be that ... more severe measures are called for.”

She felt a shiver roll down her back and suddenly wondered what it was about the earl that made her believe he could be a truly dangerous man.

“I need you to tell me immediately if he approaches you again, or contacts you in another way, by letter or via a third party. I will not let him hurt you, do you understand?” His voice was implacable and she could only nod her agreement.

“I ...” she began, hearing her voice break. “I don’t know how I can ever thank you ... for everything.”

“Nonsense,” he said, brusk now and clearly uncomfortable with the possible threat of tears imminent. “And if that bastard Sindalton upsets you again you need only say the word. I’ll bloody kill him!”

“Alex!” Céleste exclaimed, glaring at him.

“I’m sorry, Céleste. But after what he did to you ...” He paused and glanced at Georgiana and away again. “The man is not to be trusted, surely you can see that?”

He stared at his wife, his usually stern face by now a mixture of regret and defiance as Georgiana felt her stomach clench. *After what he’d done to Céleste?* What else didn’t she know?

"If you'll excuse me." She looked up as he nodded to her and sent his wife an apologetic glance before leaving them alone.

"Merde!" Céleste exclaimed with a huff of annoyance. "Just like a man, cause a scene and leave me to explain it. Typical!" She turned back to Georgiana and gave a crooked smile. "It really isn't as bad as it sounds, and ... and I truly think 'e was trying to 'elp me, you see? But Alex, 'e is still very angry."

Georgiana finished the brandy and set the glass carefully down on the big oak desk.

"So the man who I believed was the Marquis of Beaumont is in fact the Duke of Sindalton. He's lied to me about who he is. He very nearly seduced me and made me fall in love with him before leaving me alone. And then he nearly ruins me by making a scene at Almack's when he must know how precarious my position is. He is the son of the man who murdered my father and ruined my mother," she continued with her voice rising steadily as hysteria threatened to overtake her, but her heart was breaking. "And now ..." she said, staring at Céleste with her eyes shining. "And now ... *what?"* she demanded. "Please just tell me and get it over with so that I can put him out of my head for good."

"Oh, ma puce," Céleste cried, and in a flurry of silken skirts she sank to the floor at the side of Georgiana's chair and pulled her into an embrace. "I don't know why he did the things he did, Georgiana. But I don't think he was trying to ruin you at Almack's. Did you not see the shock in his eyes? I think he was every bit as stunned as you were." She shook her head so that golden ringlets danced about her face. "I believe 'e is a good man, Georgiana. The truth is the duke was going to offer for me. Oh, don't look so appalled, 'e didn't love me, I promise you, nor did I care for 'im. The duke knew I was in love with Alex. But 'e also believed, as I did at the time, that Alex didn't care for me, that he would only ever make me his mistress, not a wife. I think Sindalton wanted to show me the kind of man Alex was, so he paid for one of Alex's old mistresses to come here late one night and cause a scene."

Georgiana gasped, horrified by the idea he had almost destroyed one of the happiest marriages she'd ever encountered. Céleste smiled at her and shrugged.

"I ran away because of it," she admitted. "Which I see is foolish now. One should never run away from a problem. You must face it. If I'd done that I could 'ave saved us both a lot of pain." She held Georgiana's hand to her cheek and smiled. *"Alors,* you see, that is why Alex hates the duke so much. But I truly believe that he was trying to protect me. You should talk to 'im, Georgiana. Find out the truth first. *Oui?* Before you make a decision based on things you believe ... when you 'ave no certainty."

Georgiana let out a strangled laugh, totally bewildered by now. She didn't know what she was supposed to believe.

"You must be certain," Céleste insisted, her blue eyes more serious that Georgiana had ever seen them. "People do foolish, cruel and stupid things sometimes, *Chérie*. But that does not make them monsters. It makes them *h*uman. If 'e made a mistake ... if 'e cares for you ... wouldn't you want to know that, *Oui?"*

Chapter 22

"Wherein our suitors take their places."

Sebastian scanned the ballroom and felt his heart clench as his eyes immediately settled on a burst of fiery red hair. She stood out like a beacon, a lovely blaze of glory in a sea of insipid pallor. Every other woman in the room paled beside her in his eyes. Not one could hold a candle to her beauty, she shone like a sun, dazzling him and hurting his heart all at once.

He had promised himself he would approach her. He would be calm and polite and try and arrange a time when he might call on her and explain ... explain *what?* How in the name of God could he explain the manner of madness that had come over him that fateful day?

For there was no doubt of it now. Friends of his father's, the few truly honourable and trustworthy people who had stood firm in their friendship to his family, had all agreed. She was the image of her mother. This was the face of the woman that his father had fallen in love with. The woman he had loved so desperately and passionately that he had murdered her husband when he'd discovered their affair and left Sebastian and his mother to face the outcome alone. For the first time in his life Sebastian felt he had some glimmer of understanding as to how his father had felt. For if that woman had been anything like Georgiana, he felt compelled to admit that he sensed that same madness overtaking him too. And it was utterly terrifying, the gnawing realisation ... that he might do just about anything to be with her.

Ever since his father's death, ever since he had become the Duke of Sindalton and the man of the family, he had required utter and absolute control. He knew every detail of his estate's management. He never left any decision to be made without it first going through him. Every aspect of his life had been strictly managed by him with utter discipline. Down to his decision that it was time to take a wife. Lists had been made. Pro and cons considered. Until she had come into his life ... and everything began to spiral out of control.

"Good evening, your Grace," chimed an ingratiating voice in his ear. "I do hope you are enjoying our little soiree."

Little soiree? Sebastian gave an inward snort of amusement. Lady Ashton's ballroom was packed to the very elegant rafters, there were candles blazing in such numbers the glare was giving him a headache and no conceivable extravagance had been overlooked. Little soiree indeed. Sadly, it wasn't conceit that led Sebastian to believe that a great deal of effort and an obscene amount of money had been spent on the outside chance that he might look at her daughter with an eye to marriage.

"It is a very great success by the looks of things," he replied, trying hard to force his unwilling face into some semblance of a smile. "I think half of London must be here tonight.

"Oh, your Grace!" The obnoxious woman trilled, smacking his arm playfully with her fan. "Only the better half I hope," she added, as her daughter gave an ear-splitting shriek of laughter at her mother's tasteless joke. She fell silent suddenly and an over familiar hand slid over his forearm. "Of course, I would have rejected ... *that* woman if I'd been able to, your Grace," she said, her voice dropping to an intimate whisper. "But it is so terribly awkward. One dare not insult the earl, such a terrifying man!" she said with a visible shudder. "He positively puts me in a quake. But I know you will forgive me," she crooned, her fat hand caressing the impeccable line of his sleeve. "After all, one unwelcome presence at a crush like this is really rather inevitable isn't it. And *we* are all on your side, of course."

Too late she looked up and blanched as she saw the white-hot fury that he knew must be blazing in his eyes.

But Sebastian had not been raised a duke without knowing exactly how to crush someone who had incurred his displeasure without making a scene. "If you will excuse me, Madame," he replied, every word dripping ice and disdain as he turned his back on her with a sneer and walked away. It didn't afford him the same satisfaction that wringing the blasted woman's neck might have done but he'd given the gossip mill enough fodder for the time being without murdering his hostess. No matter how appealing the idea might be.

Without his ever having consciously moved his feet in her direction, he found himself crossing the floor. The closer he got to her, the harder his heart seemed to thud and the impossibility that she would ever be his seemed to grow. Could she ever forgive him? Even if she did, would she choose him over Beau or any number of the dazzled looking suitors who were gathered around her like planets circling a sun. And if by some miracle she did want him, could he really marry her, knowing his mother would never forgive him. Could he be so cruel to her after all she had suffered after the scandal his father had wrought. She had been destroyed that day and had barely left the house ever since, too terrified to face the outside world and the varied pitying or sneering faces of the ton. Could he really bring Miss Dalton into the home that her mother, Lady Dalton had shaken to its foundations? It would surely kill her.

But he couldn't stay away.

She was wearing white, her creamy shoulders revealed by the cut of the dress, a demur single row of pearls at the slender column of her throat and pearl drops at her ears. On any other of the young women here it might have looked insipid, but against the blaze of her hair she was breathtaking. He felt a jolt of desire so overpowering that he had to pause for a moment to collect himself before he moved any closer.

She was talking to Percy Nibley and the poor bastard was as obviously in her thrall as every other man that seemed to be hovering about her. He took a step closer and suddenly she became aware of him. Her head came up, the smile falling from her lips, her shoulders growing taut. Misery washed through him at the idea his presence would take the smile from her face and put her on her guard. It had been such a short time ago she'd lain in his arms and laughed and whispered secrets to him. Why hadn't he realised how precious that had been before it was too late? Lord Nibley moved forward, shielding her from him, as though he was some kind of enemy to her.

"Your Grace?" Nibley bowed, but there was a challenge in his eyes that Sebastian had never seen before. Percy had been bullied at Eton. Too tall and gangly, bookish and useless at sports, he'd never been able to stand up to anyone and had been a target from day one. Sebastian had been too caught in his own troubles to notice for much of the time, but he'd seen Beau step in and protect him on occasion and so Sebastian had followed suit without really questioning it. Once everyone knew he was under their protection the bullying had died away. But now, here he was, challenging Sebastian, as though *he* was the bully and Georgiana in need of defence!

"Percy," he replied, keeping his voice and manner as non-threatening as he could manage, which wasn't easy as he wanted to pick the fool up and throw him over his shoulder.

"Lady Georgiana," he said, looking past her spindly protector. "It is a pleasure to see you here."

She stared back at him but he could read nothing in those tawny eyes except suspicion. She put him in mind of a fox watching out for the hounds. He had a sudden and vivid image of himself in a red coat, out to destroy her. Was that what she thought of him? Was that what she believed he wanted? The longer she stayed silent the more he believed it was.

"I hope you will forgive me for my behaviour the other night," he said, hoping she could hear the sincerity in his voice. "I ... I was surprised beyond measure and it stole my manners from me. I assure you I meant no disrespect."

She still said nothing, but had that been a slight tilt of her head, an acknowledgement of his words? He wasn't sure. He did know that everyone around them had fallen silent, that the stares of the entire ballroom were burning the back of his neck.

He lowered his voice as far as he dared and took a step closer, his heart plummeting as she flinched. "Would ..." he began, suddenly feeling as nervous as a green boy, seeking the hand of a woman far beyond his reach. "Would you do me the honour of dancing with me?"

She swallowed, her eyes darting away from him, as though looking for an escape. "The next dance is already taken, your Grace," she said, with such a cool tone that part of him wanted to slink away in shame. He took a breath, determined not to be thwarted. "Then pencil me in for another," he replied, smiling at her and willing her to give him the chance.

Her expression didn't change, a considering gaze that seemed to weigh up the sum of his parts and find him wanting in every respect. "That might be a little awkward," she replied.

"Oh?" He heard the disappointment in that simple sound as clearly as if a bell had rung but he suspected she hadn't finished yet. "How so?"

She raised one elegant eyebrow at him. "However would I know what name to write down?" she asked, the well aimed blow finding its target with deadly accuracy. For the first time since he was a small boy he felt a flush of embarrassment stain his cheeks. Before he could demand she allow him to explain, his breath caught as a smile curved over that lovely mouth and pleasure lit her eyes. But not for him.

"Lord Beaumont," she replied, holding her hand out to Beau as the smooth devil raised it to his lips. He kissed her fingers, holding her gaze. "Hello, Eve," he replied, winking at her. "Still waving that apple under my nose I see."

Her laughter seemed to wrap around Sebastian's heart and squeeze tight. Though it seemed to be a private joke, the meaning was obvious enough and the intimacy of it stole his breath. He glared at Beau, wanting nothing more than to smash his fist into that damned perfect face.

"My dance I believe," Beau said, sparing a cursory glance for him as he settled her hand in the crook of his arm. "Sindalton," he replied, nodding as they passed, the glimmer of a smile at his lips. The smug bastard.

He watched with jealousy raging through his body, his muscles taut with the desire to cross the floor and tear them apart as he saw Beau take her in his arms. Worse than anything was the picture they presented. Beau's dazzling colouring, the rakishly careless styling of his golden hair that gave him the look of a fallen angel, set against the fiery red of Georgiana and that pure white dress. They looked like ancient deities come to play for a while in the human world before returning to their perfect lives.

He couldn't let Beau have her. He wouldn't. He had to get her back.

***

"You dealt him quite a blow, sweet Eve," Beau said to her, amusement glimmering in his gorgeous blue eyes. "I shall have to guard my heart I see. If I ever dare reach for that apple I might get quite a set down."

Georgiana didn't know what to say to that. Her heart and mind were in turmoil. Seeing him there, *Sebastian,* asking for her forgiveness. It had been everything she'd wanted but she'd quickly realised it wasn't enough. She'd trusted him with so much, with her whole heart, and he'd betrayed her trust. He'd lied from the first.

How could she ever believe anything he said now, no matter how much she wanted to. But she thought she'd seen real regret in his eyes. A sincere desire to make amends, to explain. Céleste believed she should give him a chance after all and ... she did want to hear an explanation. If he'd really loved her, he wouldn't see her fall into Beau arm's and walk away, though. Not if he loved her.

And she had to admit, Beau's were very strong arms to be held in. She looked up and admired the handsome profile of the man holding her. She had fallen in love with Sebastian, but there was no denying this man made her pulse race when he got close.

He was charming and funny, he made her laugh and the time seemed to fly in his company, and the look in his eyes, that obvious desire ... that was a heady thing. He felt her eyes on him and turned towards her gaze, his eyes darkening, his hands pulling her a little closer.

He lowered his head, his warm breath fluttering over her skin and making her shiver. "I would do anything to be alone with you."

Her breath caught and she swallowed but looked back at him, refusing to look like a flustered school girl. "I'm sorry, my Lord, but that is something I cannot allow you."

"Damn these people," he cursed, though his voice remained soft. His eyes on hers intent. "The next time I intend to claim every dance on that blasted card."

She laughed and shook her head, amused by the vehemence of his words. "What is it, my Lord? Do you fear to see my bank balance slipping from your grasp."

For a moment anger lit his eyes and he looked away from her, but when he looked back she thought he looked hurt. "I never lie, Lady Georgiana. Of all my faults, and I assure you I can claim many, that has never been one of them." She felt the tension in his arms, and knew this was true. He was someone who would always tell her the truth, and she knew now, that was something of great value. "I would have never allowed myself to spend such time with you if you hadn't been an heiress. I don't set out to ruin innocents and if I marry, yes, it will be to a woman with money. But if you think that is the only thing that keeps me coming back to you, you are very much mistaken."

She flushed and looked away from him, shamefaced. He hadn't deserved that comment. He'd been nothing but kind, and honest.

"Forgive me," she murmured.

The dance came to a close but he didn't release her for a moment. She dared to look back up at him and found a bemused smile tugging at his lips.

"Crook your little finger, Eve," he whispered. "I'll come running,"

Chapter 23

"Wherein a rake reveals a heart."

It has been noted that the ton's darling M of B, that handsome devil, has been paying extraordinary attention to the dazzling new Siren in our midst. Could it be that our most delightful bachelor has marriage in mind at last? Extraordinarily, the D of S is also dancing attendance but his attentions are not received with any visible pleasure. The Siren continues to call to all the most eligible men, but who will get burned this time?

The following ten days passed in a blur. Dances and routs and shopping and picnics, and yet more shopping and more dancing. Georgiana felt giddy, as though the world was spinning too fast and she couldn't keep her grip on reality. It was like some strange dream where everything was a little too bright, a little too colourful, and too perfect to be real. But she let the colours and the attention and the compliments shower over and about her, and watched the glittering world around her without ever truly feeling a part of it.

The duke was always there, watching her with those dark eyes. He was like a storm gathered on the horizon. Everyone knew, sooner or later he would break, and the lightening would probably scorch her to the bone. She felt she would welcome it. It was hard to keep pushing him away, to keep rejecting his advances when she could still see the heat in his eyes. But she wouldn't be his plaything this time. She wasn't a toy he could pick up again, simply because another boy had decided he wanted her. If Sebastian wanted her he would have to declare his interest as Beau had. He had to make it clear to the world he was courting her. He needed to offer far more than just an affair that could ruin her and destroy all of her dreams.

She wanted him still, loved him still ... but did he love her enough to put the scandalous past aside? Did he love her at all?

"That's Lady Chartley," Beau whispered to her as they took a turn about the room. "She's been sleeping with Derby for almost a decade now, spends more time there than at her own home by all accounts."

Georgiana looked at the elegant brunette with a raised eyebrow. She would never see forty again but she was still a beauty. "But Lord Derby is a fat old goat," she hissed to him, in disgust. "If she must take a lover she could do far better."

Beau smirked and raised an eyebrow. "Oh, but I never said Lord Derby, now did I?"

Georgiana felt her mouth make a little O of surprise as Beau chuckled.

"Oh, I do love opening your eyes, darling Eve. It is such a delight to educate you."

She cast him a sideways look. "I'm not shocked," she retorted, though she knew he dearly loved to make her blush. He seemed to count it as some kind of delightful sport. He was very good at it too. "I'm just surprised, that's all I just ... never considered ..."

She trailed off, annoyed that she was blushing now. "I mean I know that men sometimes like other men, so I suppose it makes sense," she replied, shrugging as Beau went off into peals of laughter beside her.

"I do love it when you try to sound as though you are so very sophisticated and experienced of our dark world, sweet little Eve."

She huffed and glared up at him. "Well it's not as if I get a chance to discover anything about it myself, is it? All I learn, I learn from you. I never realised you were such a dreadful rattlepate."

He put a hand to his heart with a groan. "Oh, that hurt. After the lengths I have gone to keep you entertained. A rattlepate! Is that the only thing you can find to say of me after all the extravagant compliments I give you? Here I am, hanging on your sleeve as ever, your obedient lap dog, and you never so much as throw me a bone."

Now it was her turn to laugh at this wounded expression, ignoring the looks of disapproval from some of those they passed by. "Oh, you are an odious, spoilt creature. That is for certain."

"Oh, Eve," he replied sounded so dejected and giving her such puppy dog eyes that she did really feel sorry for him.

"Beau, you're a dreadful flirt and I know well your game by now, but you know I adore you so stop trying to lure me into spoiling you further. Dreadful man," she added, tutting as his eyes lit with appreciation. She couldn't help but return his smile, but then her breath caught as he paused, his eyes darkening.

He covered her hand with his and leaned towards her. "Marry me and I'll teach you everything you want to know, Eve."

She swallowed, unsettled by the look in his eyes. God, she couldn't deny the idea of bedding him didn't make her skin burn. She'd overheard whispers about him from other women, about his prowess and skill in the bedroom. Somehow she didn't doubt a word of it. But though he might be able to make her body respond, her heart was already engaged, and she wasn't so fickle that it could be taken by another with such ease.

He reached out a hand, the back of one finger touching her cheek for a bare moment.

"I'll make you forget about him, darling, I promise I can do it."

She smiled and shook her head. "And once you had taught me everything you know you would grow bored and leave me alone. Back to chasing your pretty light skirts, spending your nights with your Cythereans rather than your dull wife."

His face clouded over, a frown in those gorgeous blue eyes. "Who says I would grow bored. I can't imagine it now."

Georgiana couldn't help but laugh, he looked like a scolded boy who had been denied a treat. "That's because there is finally something you cannot have, and the more you cannot have it the more you want it."

"I do want it," he returned, his voice fierce and such fire in his voice that she caught her breath. "I want you," he said, and she could see the truth of it in his eyes. "I'll do anything you want, Eve. Command me. Make me earn your hand if you will but don't refuse me."

"Don't, Beau, please," she begged him. "Not now."

He sighed and shook his head, allowing them to move on once again. "Very well, my sweet torment. Punish me if you must. But I'm not giving in."

"I should hope not," she replied with an arch smile that made him laugh.

"Vixen."

They walked a little further until they came upon a crowd of people exclaiming and gathered around. There was something, no ... *someone*, on the floor.

"Oh, the poor woman!" Georgiana exclaimed. For there was indeed a poor creature in the throes of some kind of fit, her thin limbs jerking and twitching as people watched and exclaimed with horror.

"Get out of the way!" With no little surprise she watched as Beau scattered the crowd with fury flashing in his blue eyes. "Get away from her, you devils!" He reached down and swept the woman up as though she weighed nothing and Georgiana ran ahead of him, throwing open the door as he strode through, searching for a quiet place to set her down.

"Here!" she called to him, opening a door onto a darkened library, lit only by one oil lamp.

The woman's body was rigid with tension, her right arm twitching fiercely but Beau carefully set her down on a couch and knelt beside her. Georgiana watched, astounded as he undid the buttons on the high neck of her gown and then as he held her steady, to stop her tumbling off the side of the couch, and gently restraining the erratic movement of her arm. He spoke to her in a clear, calm voice, and began stroking her hair with his hand as the tremors began to die away.

He let out a breath of relief and she noted how pale and drawn his face was with curiosity. He waited until she was still, her breath fast and shallow but steady. "She'll be alright now," he said, sounding a little shaken as he got to his feet. "But perhaps you should loosen her stays, make her more comfortable.

"Yes, I think my uncle would say to do so," she admitted, looking up at him in wonder. "How ..." she began as Beau turned his back and she tried to make the woman more comfortable.

"Someone I knew when I was a child," he said, his voice short. "He had similar seizures."

It was clear he didn't wish to speak about it, so she returned her attention to the woman. She was desperately thin, almost emaciated, and even Georgiana found little trouble in moving the poor thing about like a limp rag doll. Her dress was worn and badly faded and Georgiana felt a jolt of pity, realising how very lucky she was.

"I wonder what caused it," she asked quietly. "I remember one of uncle's patient's having something of the sort."

"Stress or an upset used to trigger my ... my friend's attacks," he said, before adding. "Perhaps I should fetch some water?"

"Yes," she replied and smiled up at him, wondering at his intervention. Not many men, as it had been seen, would have intervened in such a way. Madness was a terrifying thing, and any sign of something that approached it was to be shunned and reviled. Though her uncle was adamant that fits and madness were not one and the same thing and neither were they contagious, not everyone shared his view by any means. "Do you know her?" she asked, wondering if that was the reason he had acted so quickly.

"No, though I have seen her around before now. I know of the man she came with by reputation though, and a bigger bastard you never did meet."

"Oh," she replied, looking back at the sleeping figure with regret. "Perhaps we shouldn't inform him then.

"No." He shook his head. "We'll stay with her until she wakes and then find a way to get her home."

She smiled at him, suddenly struck that she'd underestimated him. She'd judged him as she'd raged against those who'd judged her in turn.

"What?" he asked, obviously bewildered by the look in her eyes.

"I was just thinking ... how very kind you are."

He actually looked embarrassed for a moment before he gave a snort of derision. "Not kind," he replied, sounding almost gruff. "I just hate to see those carrion crows picking over the bones of people who can't defend themselves. It makes me sick." He strode to the door and muttered his intention of getting water for her.

By the time he got back the woman was beginning to stir. She was very plain, her thin face all angles and her dark hair scraped severely from her head in an unbecoming style. A small pair of spectacles sat on her nose and Georgiana watched as Beau removed these and sat her up, supporting her with one strong arm behind her back.

"Here," he said, his voice gentle. "Sip some water. It will make you feel better."

The woman did as she was bid, though she was clearly disorientated and it took a moment before her eyes opened properly and she was able to focus.

She blinked and Georgiana was startled by the widest pair of dark brown eyes she'd ever seen. They were too big in her gaunt face, and they widened further as they focused on Beau.

"Lord Beaumont!" she said, gasping, her face one of utter astonishment and appalled embarrassment.

"Don't look so alarmed. Lady Georgiana is here. It's quite alright. I'm afraid you had something of a turn. Is there anything we can do for you, Miss ..."

"Sparrow," she said, her voice barely audible. "Millicent Sparrow."

Georgiana thought she had never heard a more appropriate name for this little scrap of a woman. The poor thing shook her head and looked up at Beau as though he was some angel sent to save her. "You've already been so kind. I can never thank you enough."

"Think nothing of it," he replied, his smile warm and reassuring. "Miss Dalton, would you be so good as to see Miss Sparrow safely home tonight?"

"Oh yes!" Georgiana replied, smiling. "Of course I will."

"How very kind you are," Miss Sparrow murmured, still gazing at Beau, and Georgiana found she couldn't fault her for it.

"Yes," Georgiana echoed, staring at Beau herself with new eyes. "Yes, he is, isn't he."

Chapter 24

"Wherein hot air causes mischief all around."

"I can't think how you persuaded me into this," Beau remarked as they strolled in and out of picnicking families strewn about the grass in Hyde Park as they made their way towards *The Ring.* The grand circle of trees enclosed a large space where the fashionable came to see and be seen, to promenade and sometimes ride or show off a new sporting curricle or a tilbury, which was becoming quite the rage, and some flashy high steppers. Today, however, a crowd had assembled for the spectacle of a balloon ascension. The silky, blue and gold mound of fabric was billowing disconsolately in the warm spring breeze, however, and showed no immediate signs of taking to the skies.

Georgiana looked up at Beau with amusement. "Persuaded you? You wretch! You practically begged to escort me."

He shrugged and pursed his lips. "Perhaps," he admitted. "But it's rather unkind of you to remember that fact." He sighed and looked down at his dusty boots with an expression of deep distress. "My valet won't speak to me for weeks, you know."

"Mortifying," she said, tutting and shaking her head sadly as he narrowed his eyes at her.

"You can mock, sweet Eve. But it will be entirely your fault if he sends me out with my cravat askew and last season's coat on my back, I assure you." He looked pained at the amusement in her expression. "My reputation may never recover," he complained with a sad shake of his head.

"How terribly shocking," she murmured, trying not to chuckle and failing. He grinned at her, pleased as ever to have made her laugh. "Oh, come on then," she replied, taking pity on him. "Let's go to the Cake House and get an ice. It's really very hot and dusty isn't it."

Agreeing with obvious pleasure, he escorted her to a charming little white-painted house with a multitude of beams, pretty latticed windows and a gabled roof. It was an idyllic picture and a surprisingly Arcadian setting in the heart of the capital. Wild flowers and oleander bushes grew in profusion and a little stream ran directly in front of the entrance door. A rickety plank forming a rustic bridge had to be traversed to gain entrance to the building. Beau went first and reached his hand out to help Georgiana across.

Smirking at him Georgiana refused his hand and immediately regretted it as the plank tilted a little to the left and her heel slipped on the dry timber. With a squeal she righted herself and scurried forward to be hauled against Beau before her balance deserted her for a second time. She gasped and looked up, only too aware of the hard male body pressed flush against hers. For a moment his hold on her tightened and she could feel the heat of him through the fine sarsnet of her gown. Looking up she found his blue eyes full of desire and knew without a doubt that he was desperate to kiss her.

She wondered what it would be like, to be kissed by him. Could he really make her forget Sebastian?

He released his hold on her before anyone could see, but there was reluctance in his eyes.

"Careful, Eve," he whispered in her ear. "I have only so much self-control, my sweet temptress."

She huffed at him and raised an eyebrow. "Well it isn't as if I lost my balance on purpose, is it?" she muttered, smoothing out the line of her pale blue walking dress. He reached out, on the premise of picking an imaginary piece of lint from her darker blue velvet spencer but instead wound the red curl he found so tempting around his finger and gave a little tug. She looked up, startled by his boldness. Although he spoke far too freely with her, he never overstepped the bounds of propriety. In fact, he seemed to be on his best behaviour in that respect, as aware as she of the eyes on them. There was a fierce look in his eyes now though, as he tugged the little ringlet again and raised it to his lips.

"I won't be denied, Eve," he said. "You cannot keep me on a leash forever with that tempting red apple so close to my jaws. I'm not the spoilt little lap dog you'd like me to be, no matter that's how you treat me."

"I do not!" she replied, indignation staining her cheeks.

He snorted and she couldn't read the expression on his face but she wondered if she'd hurt him somehow. "You think I don't see how you watch him? Waiting to see how jealous he is when he sees us together?"

"I ..." She stopped before she began her rejection of his accusation, too aware of the truth of it. Had she really just been using him all this time? She stared back at him, stricken and unable to form a reply. For she did care for him, very much, and he would be dreadfully easy to fall in love with ... if her heart hadn't already been taken.

"I'm sorry, Beau, I ..."

He dropped the curl and waved his hand looking annoyed. "Don't you dare feel sorry for me," he snapped and she was a little taken aback by the anger in his eyes. "I give you fair warning, my lovely siren, I won't play nicely any longer. Do you understand?"

She nodded, disquieted by the look in his eyes.

"No," he murmured. "I don't think you do. But you will." He offered her his arm and they walked into the little shop. "Come now," he said, smiling at her again, his fit of temper apparently passed. "Let's cool ourselves off with an ice, and then I'll take you out in one of the boats. How does that sound?"

"Lovely," she replied, smiling back at him, relieved that he seemed to have got over whatever fit of jealousy had struck at him.

By the time they found their way to the edge of the Serpentine and rejoined Céleste and a group of her friends, the afternoon sun was growing really rather warm. The countess waved at them and they wandered over to meet her.

"Do you want anything to eat? There is so much food!" she complained with a grimace. "I am so full it's disgusting and nobody else has eaten a morsel!"

Georgiana shook her head, too consumed by the sight of the tall, dark figure making his way towards her. To her everlasting gratitude Céleste took Beau's arm, insisting that he must help her do justice to the extravagant feast that had been provided. If Beau realised he was being manipulated he was too polite to protest. He went as bid, to sit beside Céleste and her lady friends who welcomed him with beaming smiles and fluttering eyelashes.

Georgiana turned her back on the advancing figure and went to stand by the edge of the river where the air was a little cooler. There were several little jetties where the pleasure boats were tied up and after lunch they would be busy with people buying tickets and going out onto the water. But for the moment it was quiet as she stepped onto one boarded walkway, and the only sounds were the gentle hum of conversation at her back and the quack of a hopeful duck paddling around in search of a generous benefactress.

"Good afternoon, Lady Georgiana."

She turned without surprise, having had time to prepare herself on this occasion. She met those dark eyes with a placid expression, curtsying to the large presence who had provided some much needed shade by blocking out the sun.

"Your grace." She looked at him, silent, refusing to help him navigate the tension between them as he stared at her.

"Georgiana," he whispered, the longing behind her name quite taking her breath away. "Please don't keep punishing me, love. I'll run mad if you won't talk to me ... give me a chance to explain."

She stared at him, wondering if she could put any value on those words, on the desperation in his eyes.

"Please, my own dear love. Nothing has changed, can't you see that?"

Her heart felt as though it was falling from a great height, a rush of exhilaration and fear so profound she could hardly breathe. She had so longed to hear those words, but how could she place any trust in anything he said?

"You still have my heart," he pressed, taking a step closer. "Don't you ever wear the little gold one I gave you?"

She was torn between giving him a sharp *no* which he thoroughly deserved, and telling him the truth, that she slept in it and returned it to her jewellery box every morning.

"How can I?" she replied, after a pause that seemed measured out in her own heartbeats. "When I don't know who gave it to me."

"And I never knew you were Lady Dalton's daughter!" he threw back at her, dark eyes blazing. "I thought you were sweet Georgiana Bomford, the lovely, innocent girl I lost my heart to!"

She took a breath, startled by the fury in his voice and unsettled by the realisation that he was right.

"That's because I didn't know myself!" she said, flushing with anger. "I *was* Miss Bomford, the doctor's daughter. I have been all my life, until my uncle arrived on my doorstep after you had left me alone and told me the truth. He told me I was an heiress and he called my mother a whore and said I was just like her."

He stared at her, appalled shock in his eyes at her revelation.

"I never lied," she said, biting out the words and holding his gaze so he was forced to see the truth in her words. "You did, your Grace."

He was silent for a moment, clearly at a loss. "Let me explain then," he replied, his voice low and urgent and obviously frustrated.

"Very well, explain," she replied, daring him to tell her everything.

He looked around the crowded park, and she became aware of the eyes watching them conversing, whispering about how the Duke of Sindalton of all people, had searched her out *alone.* "Not here," he replied. "I'll meet you somewhere, anywhere you choose. I could come to the house?"

She knew he did have a point about them being watched and moved carefully around him, back to where the jetty met the land. She had to laugh at the idea of him coming to the earl's home to visit her though. "Good God, Falmouth would kill you if you set foot on the doorstep after what you did to destroy his relationship with Céleste."

His face darkened and she knew she'd hit home. Yes, Sebastian, I know more of your dark little secrets, she thought and then wondered how many others there were that she didn't know.

"So I'm guilty of all charges I see," he replied, and she could see the cost to his pride to keep pursuing her when he met nothing but rejection after rejection.

"Perhaps not," she replied, relenting a little. "But I have no reason to trust you and meeting you is something I cannot contemplate after the way your father has already ruined my name."

He stiffened at that, fury in his eyes. "My father was the best of men," he said, his voice harsh and implacable, his bearing suddenly showing every single generation of pride and power that came with his many titles. "He was led into vice and until very recently I've never been able to understand how a woman could ruin such a good and honourable man. But now I *do* see."

She gasped, appalled by his words and more hurt that she would have believed possible. That he of all people should use that against her. She took a step back, her eyes filling with tears.

"Then I suggest you get as far away from me as possible, your Grace," she replied, her words sharp with the pain of disappointment.

"Before I cause you any further embarrassment." She turned and found Beau right behind her. He took one look at her tear-filled eyes and drew her hand into the crook of his arm, turning to stare at the duke with fury.

"Stay away from her," he replied, his voice cold. "God help me, if you hurt her again, I'll make you pay for it."

"You're the one hurting her, Beau," Sebastian snapped in return. "You're the one damaging her chances of making a better match but you don't care about that do you? For the fewer on the field the more chance that she'll marry you and you'll get your grasping hands on her money."

Beau clenched his fists and went to take a step forward but Georgiana grabbed hold of his arm. "No, please, Beau," she begged him. "Please don't make a scene." With obvious reluctance, Beau took a step back, but the two men were still glaring at each other, the atmosphere so fraught Georgiana hardly dared breathe. "You promised to take me out in a boat, remember."

He turned to her, his face white with restrained fury but he nodded and began to lead her back down the jetty.

"You should not go alone in the boat with him, Georgiana," Sebastian said as they came closer, his voice full of anger. "Don't you see, you little fool, he wants your reputation shredded so no one else will want you. Your fortune is slender enough temptation against your tenuous position as it is."

Fury lanced through her as his words struck home. How dare he pretend to care and give advice while he slandered her in the same sentence. Slender enough temptation! Why the arrogant, top lofty ... But before she could think of a suitably cutting rejoinder the duke turned to walk away from them, his face dark with anger. As he passed however, Beau deliberately turned out one elegantly booted foot and Sebastian tripped. Too wrong footed to save himself, he plunged off the side of the jetty and ended up hip deep in the Serpentine.

"Oh I do beg your pardon, your Grace," Beau replied with a malicious glint of satisfaction in his blue eyes. For a moment Georgiana rejoiced in seeing him getting his comeuppance, but then she realised what was at stake.

"Why you ..." Sebastian began and Georgiana looked at him in appalled horror. If he caused a scene now everyone would be talking about them. They would know that she'd come between the duke and his best friend and everyone would say like mother, like daughter. She'd never live it down. She stared at him and gave the slightest shake of her head, pleading in her eyes. Please, Sebastian, *please* don't do it. For a moment all she could see in the gaze that turned to hers was righteous indignation and hurt pride. But then he stilled and the tension fell from his stance. Those dark eyes seemed to warm as he looked at her, and the rumble of laughter that came from him was throaty and delicious, and the most wonderful sound she'd ever heard.

"Beau," he said, with a wry smile. """You will be receiving a bill from my tailor and I dare you to ever face my valet again."

"By all means, Sebastian," Beau returned with a charming smile. "I will put it in a drawer with all the other bills I have been unable to pay."

They watched as he strode out of the river, the sodden material clinging to his powerful thighs in a most disconcerting manner as gasps of astonishment met him on the bank.

Although desperately relieved that he'd not made a scene she was still utterly furious about his earlier remarks. Because of it, Georgiana allowed Beau to help her into one of the boats, despite knowing Sebastian was probably right. She shouldn't go with the notorious Marquis, but if the high-handed, top-lofty duke thought so little of her ... Oh, but she was enraged and hurt and she'd do as she damned well pleased. But she couldn't take her eyes from his dripping figure as people crowded around him to discover what had occurred.

"That wasn't a very gentlemanly thing to have done, Beau," she scolded, as he handed her into the boat. Though privately she thought it was exactly what the smug devil had required.

"Oh, hush," he replied, snorting, settling himself down and picking up the oars. "You loved seeing him plunge into that cold, muddy water, and don't pretend you didn't."

She sat back in the boat with a sigh and admired the bunch and glide of his powerful shoulders under the exquisite cut of his superfine coat. The sun glinted off his golden hair and she thought she had never seen a more beautiful man. But still her eyes drifted to the bank and the large dark figure of his friend disappearing into the shadows.

Georgiana trailed her fingertips in the chilly water and wished life wasn't so complicated. Her heart still wanted Sebastian but she was so very angry and hurt at his treatment of her, and his cruel words. That he could blame her mother entirely for the affair, as though his father had possessed no will of his own, and then would compare the two of them in such a way. That had been beyond hurtful.

He'd meant to hurt her too. But then the way he'd spoken of his father, he'd clearly idolised him. In that she supposed she'd been lucky. She'd never known her parents, for good or for bad, so she'd been saved the heartbreak of losing them. Hers had been a gentler loss, though just as enduring. For although she'd never felt the lack of love through the kind attentions of her aunt and uncle, she had always wished she had known her real parents. She'd seen the loss in Sebastian's eyes though, the fury at the idea his father could have been in any way responsible. He must have been eleven or twelve, perhaps, when his father had died. An impressionable age for any young man, and devastating to lose the father he'd clearly idolised. The idea softened her heart a little as she realised how dreadfully angry and hurt he would have been, and clearly still was.

"You're very quiet, Eve."

She looked up and found Beau watching her. Shaking the water from her fingers she sat up a little straighter and turned her attention back to him.

"Just wool gathering," she replied, smiling and feeling bad for not giving him her attention.

"Ah, yes," he said, amusement pulling at the corners of that sensual mouth, a mouth made for kissing and decadent pleasures, she thought, and then scolded herself for thinking it at all. He smirked, as though well aware of her train of thought, before carrying on. "It must take a lot of thought I suppose, the question of whom to marry."

"Well of course it does," she replied, tutting at him. "Though what on earth makes you believe I was thinking about who I'm going to marry?"

"A wild guess," he replied, his tone dry.

She looked across the water, glittering in the spring sunshine as more people took to the boats and wandered up and down the banks of the river.

"Oh look!" she exclaimed, as the huge blue and gold striped balloon began to ascend into the azure skies.

They watched for a while as the balloon rose higher and higher.

"What a marvellous view they must have from up there," she said, shielding her eyes from the sun with one hand. She looked away, blinking, as Beau grimaced.

"I'd rather keep my feet on the ground," he muttered.

"Oh?" she replied, laughing at him. "Are you not very adventurous? How disappointing."

He raised one eyebrow at her, a look in his blue eyes that made her skin prickle with awareness. "Oh, but I am extremely adventurous, darling, more than you can possibly imagine," he replied, his voice all silk sheets and candlelight as a slow smile curved over his mouth.

She blushed, only too aware of what he was referring to and then gasped as small trailing branches dragged past the sides of the boat and they disappeared behind the curtain of a willow tree.

"Beau!" she exclaimed. "Take us back out immediately, people will think ..."

"People will think that I'm taking advantage of the moment to kiss you," he supplied for her, settling the oars in the rowlocks. "And they'd be quite right."

He shifted and she squealed as the boat dipped violently to one side before he settled beside her on the narrow seat and put his arms around her.

"Beau!" she said again, a warning in her voice as she pushed him back, both hands pressed against the flat of his chest. The crisp clean scent of starched linen and a warm, very male body drifted to her as she looked up at him. "Was Sebastian right? Are you hoping to spoil my chances with anyone else?"

He laughed, a warm, caressing sound that seemed to glide over her skin.

"I'd be a fool if I didn't, darling Eve," he replied. "But you're not considering anyone else except Sebastian, and he's not offered for you, has he?"

She looked away from him, her heart in turmoil. No, he hadn't, though she'd not given him much of an opportunity. But from his words earlier it sounded unlikely that he would. It sounded like he thought loving her was a kind of madness, the kind his father had suffered when he had met her mother.

"He can't, Georgiana," Beau said, and though his words were harsh they were spoken gently, as though he knew it would hurt and was sorry for it. "After everything his family suffered, and I'm blaming neither party," he added before she could take offence.

"From all I've heard about it the two of them were madly in love, and if she was anything as lovely as you, darling, I can hardly wonder at it." She swallowed and refused to look up at him but waited for him to carry on. "But the whole affair destroyed his mother. She was always a nervous sort from what I understand, prone to hysterics and the like. But since then she's been a recluse and she uses her ill health to manipulate her son. If she had the slightest inkling that he was interested in you the shock would likely kill her."

She did look up then, as her hopes, slim as they'd been, came crashing to the ground.

Beau was watching her with sympathy in his eyes.

"Come, Georgiana," he said, reaching out a hand and stroking her cheek. "I know you don't love me. But we are friends. We like each other's company and more than that ... I think you desire me."

She opened her mouth in shock, though whether to deny it was true she wasn't sure. But he just chuckled, amused by her discomfort.

"Were you going to contradict me?" he demanded, his voice soft with amusement, and then slid his hand behind her neck and pulled her closer, his lips pressing against hers.

She began to push him away but his lips were soft and warm and very tender and her heart was in turmoil. She knew he was telling the truth. She trusted him in that. Sebastian would never be able to offer her marriage. The most he would ever want from her was to make her his mistress, and that she would never do. But Beau was here, he was handsome and clever, funny and unexpectedly kind and yes, he was right, she did desire him.

There was no denying that as his kiss became more insistent, searching and she opened her mouth to him. The expression, give him an inch and he'll take a mile, came forcefully to mind as he possessed her mouth with a soul stealing kiss that made her tremble with alarm. Good God, she thought as his hands slid over her body, his arms pulling her tighter against him. How could she feel this way for a man she didn't love? The idea that she was perhaps her mother's daughter after all crept into her mind but she pushed it away. She slid her arms around him in return, pressing closer, wanting to forget another man and another place, an autumn idyll that could only ever have been a dream.

He broke the kiss and looked down at her, his eyes were pleased and heavy with wanting. "You see, sweet Eve," he murmured, dipping his head to trail his mouth along her jaw line, feathering a line of hot little kisses down her neck as his skilled fingers opened the fastenings on her spencer. She gasped as his large hand cupped her breast and his head bent further to press a kiss on the soft rise of her breast just above the neckline of her dress. Closing her eyes as desire flamed to life she felt his thumb rub the peak of her nipple beneath the soft fabric of her gown and bit back a moan.

"I can please you, Georgiana," he whispered kissing a path over one breast to the other. "I could show you such pleasure. I want to, love ... so badly."

She drew in a breath as his fingers tweaked her nipple and his head raised to nuzzle the soft skin beneath her ear. "It wouldn't be so bad would it, to be married to me? Friends who desire each other, it's more than many people begin with."

"Not so bad, no," she murmured, her body alive with sensation, her head dizzy with desire and her poor heart too bruised to allow her to think clearly.

He paused and grasped her face between his hands. "Is that a yes?" he asked, his voice rough with need.

"I--," she gasped, and then shook her head. "No, yes ... I don't know!" she exclaimed. "Please, I need time to think. Take me back now, Beau, please. I need to ..."

He pulled her into his arms once more and kissed her ruthlessly, leaving her breathless and flustered as he released her and took his place at the oars once more.

His eyes on her were intent as he rowed them out from under the tree and she quickly refastened her spencer. She didn't doubt she looked flushed and thoroughly kissed, and she raised her chin in defiance at the scandalised glances of another couple who passed close by as they rowed back to shore.

"That's it, darling," Beau whispered, his glittering gaze warm and approving. "Who gives a damn for what they think. They're all liars and hypocrites after all."

Chapter 25

"Wherein proposals are made."

"What in the name of God were you thinking?"

Georgiana blanched and stared at the toes of her satin slippers. She didn't know how to answer the earl, who was quite obviously at a loss to understand her motivation.

"Oh, Alex, do stop chastising the poor girl!" Céleste scolded him, coming to sit beside Georgiana and taking her hand. "It is perfectly obvious why she did it after what Lord Sindalton said." She squeezed Georgiana's fingers in a reassuring manner and smiled at her. "I'm so sorry, dearest, truly. But Alex is right, you must 'ave a care."

"He wants to marry me," she said, effectively stopping the conversation.

"Lord Beaumont has offered for you?" Alex said in surprise and then glanced at his wife.

"It's alright," Georgiana replied, smiling. "I'm well aware of his reputation and yes, the only reason he's suddenly desperate to marry is because his creditors are getting impatient, to say the least. He was very honest with me. But he is also very entertaining and we're good friends."

"But you're really considering it?" Céleste demanded, the surprise only too apparent in her eyes.

She gave her friend a speaking glance. "What choice do I have but to consider it?"

Céleste had already heard the whole pitiful tale last night. She'd unburdened herself of Sebastian's hateful words, the truth about his mother and why he'd never offer for her ... and Beau's kiss.

"You don't love him," Céleste said, her voice echoing the sadness visible in her eyes.

"No," Georgiana agreed. "But not all of us are as lucky as you were, Céleste."

Her friend's face fell as Lord Falmouth put his hand on his wife's shoulder and they shared a look of such intimacy that Georgiana's stomach clenched with jealousy. That was what she longed for, that unspoken connection, that deep and unbreakable tie that needed no words to prove the depth of its love and regard, and that was what she was never likely to have.

They looked up as a scratching sound was heard at the door and the butler appeared.

"My Lord, there is a Lord Nibley to see you."

Lord Falmouth nodded and left the room as Céleste and Georgiana looked at each other in surprise. She gave Georgiana a broad smile. "I think perhaps Beau isn't the only one with marriage on his mind."

***

Twenty minutes later, with a scarlet-cheeked Lord Nibley wearing a hole into the carpet, Céleste was proved right.

Lord Falmouth, judging that Georgiana was in no immediate danger from Percy Nibley, had allowed the man to attend her alone. A fact for which Georgiana wanted to throttle him. She sat demurely, outwardly calm at least, while she ran through all the possible ways of letting the man down gently.

"I'm sorry, I'm afraid this really isn't my area of expertise," he said, breaking the awkward silence that had been smothering them both for the last interminable five minutes. It had felt like hours. "If I was Beau I'd have something witty and charming to say," he added with a chagrined smile that was really rather endearing. "And if I was Sindalton ..." He shrugged. "Well a duke doesn't have to say much to be impressive does he?"

Georgiana scowled; that shouldn't be true. She certainly wasn't impressed by *his grace.* She had loved the impoverished Marquis he'd claimed to be so much more. She wished he'd been a plain Mister more than anything. Someone who didn't have generations of ancestors expecting him to make a brilliant match.

"Oh dear," he sighed and sat down in the seat beside her. "I'm making rather a mull of this aren't I?"

She gave him a smile which she hoped was kind but not too encouraging.

"The thing is, Lady Georgiana," he began, and as she looked up at him she found his eyes were serious. "I know you don't love me, I'm not so very foolish as all that," he added with a rather disarming smile. "But I thought perhaps, if I explained a little, you might consider my heartfelt, if not romantic, proposal."

She inclined her head, not having the heart to give him an immediate rejection before he'd said his piece. The least she could do was listen.

"The thing is," he said. "Is that I've become most terribly fond of you. You are a lovely young woman who I'd be overjoyed to make my wife. But I've been trying to think what could possibly induce you to marry such a dull fellow."

"Oh, my Lord!" she exclaimed, for that was too harsh. Yes, he was certainly a bookish type and yes, her eyes did glaze over when he became particularly enthused in explaining the difference between ignatius, sedimentary and metamorphic rocks. "I cannot allow that. Why, you are wonderful company."

He smiled again, deep pleasure showing in his brown eyes as he adjusted his wire framed spectacles. "Well, you're very kind, too kind perhaps," he added, looking down at his shiny boots. "I'm not about to pretend that I can claim any of the attractions of Beau or ... or your other suitors. But ..."

She waited, realising she did want to know what this curious, rather awkward gentleman thought they could find together. "But I would never embarrass you, my Lady. I would be faithful, reliable and your happiness would always be my foremost concern. I ... I think you know that I am ... well, not so badly situated," he said, obviously finding the subject of his finances distasteful. "So you need never be concerned that your fortune held any lure to me and indeed I would let you keep whatever money is yours as your own and hold no claim to it." He paused and to her astonishment slid to one knee and took hold of her hand.

"Miss Dalton ... Georgiana," he amended, his rather thin face colouring a little, though there was a sincerity in his eyes that made her throat tight. "I admire and respect you. You are the most courageous, charming and perfectly lovely woman I have ever known. I know my limitations only too well but ... if you marry me, I will show you the world. We'll travel and explore and ... and I will give you anything in my power to make you happy, if you would do me the honour of becoming my wife."

Georgiana swallowed hard. Somehow this funny, awkward fellow had made the most charming proposal and quite unsettled her. She gave her circumstances and her choices a good hard look. The man she loved could clearly never countenance the idea of a marriage between them with anything other than abhorrence. Beau was seductive and charming and kind and he'd be very easy to fall in love with if her broken heart ever recovered enough to make the attempt. But Beau would likely smash it to pieces all over again as he was the worst candidate for husband material that she could possibly consider.

He'd never be faithful to her and she'd have to accept she would never be his one and only love. Indeed love had never been something he'd even offered her and nor would he. She knew that much. Thanks to him, too, the scandal sheets were full of their shocking disappearance into the trees yesterday. Far worse than that, though, were the bets that history would repeat itself, that the two powerful men who were previously the closest friends were now rivals, and the affair would end inevitably by one murdering the other.

"I-I truly don't know what to say, my Lord," she replied, putting one hand to her cheek and finding her face hot. "I am more honoured than you can possibly imagine by your ... your quite wonderful proposal." She smiled at him, a genuine warm smile that grew as she saw the way his face lit with pleasure at seeing it. "I think you underestimate yourself, by the way. You really are terribly romantic."

He gave a startled little laugh, his eyes so full of hope that she felt very afraid. She didn't want to hurt this man by getting his hopes up but ... but he might be far better for her than any other offer she could hope to get and she did need to think about his proposal. At this point someone reliable and dependable, someone who wouldn't hurt her ... that sounded a rather wonderful thing. She looked at him again and knew she could never feel passion for him. She'd never feel the heated, desperate need to tear at his clothes and lose herself in his body, in his touch. But maybe that was all to the good. She'd experienced the destruction such furious emotions could wreak. Perhaps it was best avoided.

"Does that mean ..." he began, as if he hardly dared hope.

"I can't answer you yet, my Lord," she said, her free hand clutching the tapestry cover of the sofa she was perched on.

"P-Percy," he stammered, looking stunned beyond measure. "You may call me Percy."

She smiled at him and nodded. "Percy. You have given me such a lot to think about. But I must tell you ... the truth is ... m-my heart is ..."

"I know," he interrupted, squeezing her hand. "I know that your affections are otherwise engaged. That is ... I guessed as much. You needn't tell me anymore. But ... can I hope that you will *consider* my offer."

Georgiana took a deep breath and nodded. "I promise you. I will consider your offer with every seriousness, and I am very aware of the great honour you've done me, Percy."

He let out a breath, looking really rather overwhelmed and then, rather daringly, lifted her hand to his lips and kissed her fingers. "Thank you, Georgiana," he said, his voice very soft. "But the honour is entirely mine. I will wait until you are ready to give me your answer but ... may I call on you again?"

"Why of course, Percy," she replied, smiling at him. "I should be very put out if you didn't."

Georgiana spent the rest of the morning going round and around in circles as she considered her options. If she looked at it dispassionately, then Lord Nibley was the perfect solution to her situation. He had promised to take her travelling, something she had longed to do, and he'd said her happiness would always be his priority. She believed he meant it too. But her nature was a passionate one, something she had no doubt inherited with her red hair from the mother she had never known. But would marrying Percy mean that she would never experience the passion that she had felt with Sebastian again? That desperate need to join themselves together that had been so very overwhelming. She wanted to know how it felt, to lie with a man who loved you, or at the very least desired you as much as you did them.

"Oh God," she muttered and put her head in her hands. She looked up as her abigail scratched at the door and popped her head around.

"There's a gentleman here to see you," she hissed, her eyes alight with excitement.

"Oh? Who is it, Sarah?" Georgiana replied, though from the blush on the girl's cheeks she'd lay money that she could guess the answer.

“The Marquis of Beaumont,” she replied with a dreamy sigh that made Georgiana snort with amusement.

“Very well, I’ll come down.”

“Not like that!” Sarah exclaimed, suddenly all business. “You’re not seeing him afore you’ve changed your dress, my Lady! And you in your plainest dress. Goodness me, I should think not. Besides he’s talking to Lord Falmouth.”

“He is?” Georgiana exclaimed in astonishment.

“Yes he is,” Sarah said, wrestling her out of the modest dress that had been good enough for Lord Nibley, and turning to her wardrobe with a squeal of glee. “Two proposals in one day I reckon, my Lady! Oh what a conquest you’ve made.”

“My bank balance has made, you mean,” Georgiana said with a snort as she stepped into the fine Indian muslin gown that had been selected for her.

“Nonsense,” her indignant abigail snapped at her as she did up the laces at the back of her dress. “Lord Nibley is rich enough to buy an abbey but he runs for cover whenever women try and target him. Everyone knows that. Shy he is, but he found his courage for you, my Lady, didn’t he?” she demanded, to which Georgiana had no answer that could help.

She allowed Sarah to primp and fuss her until she caught a glimpse of herself in the glass and gave a gasp at the amount of décolletage on show in the low-cut gown. “Good heavens, Sarah! What have you put me in? Aren’t I in enough trouble already?”

“Not sure you could ever get in enough trouble with Beau Beaumont, my Lady,” her amused abigail retorted with a smirk.

“Give me that fichu this instant,” she demanded, narrowing her eyes at her maid as the girl returned a mutinous glint.

“Shan’t,” she replied, holding the gauzy scarf behind her back and standing guard in front of the drawers where such items were kept. “I’ve got a reputation to consider and you’re not going to receive a proposal from the Marquis looking like an old maid. And that's final," she added with a sniff.

"Oh, well as long as *your* reputation doesn't suffer!" Georgiana replied with a huff and allowed herself to be ushered out the door.

"Oh do hurry miss, you've kept him waiting long enough!"

"I've kept him waiting? Well I like that ..."

But by the time she was practically forced through the door of the drawing room it was clear Beau had indeed been kicking his heels for some time. He turned and smiled at her, one eyebrow raised.

"I was beginning to think you'd escaped via a back door to avoid me?" he said, the usual twinkling of warmth in his blue eyes as he looked her over with appreciation. "Though if this is what I was waiting for I heartily approve. You may give your abigail my deepest appreciation."

"I'll be sure to do that, my Lord," she replied, wondering if the wretched creature was listening outside the door.

He crossed the room and lifted her hand to his lips, kissing her fingers and then slowly sliding his hands over her skin as he turned her arm and kissed the inside of her wrist. Her heart immediately picked up speed and everything she had been considering earlier about passion came to clarity before her eyes. Percy would never, could *never,* make her feel like this.

"I've thought of nothing else but you since yesterday," he murmured, pulling her arm and hooking it about his neck as his other arm snaked around her waist. Suddenly their bodies were flush and she gasped at him.

"If Lord Falmouth comes in ..."

"Oh but he won't," he replied, smirking. "Even a bounder like myself should be allowed to make a formal offer in private, don't you think?"

She felt her breath catch. He really meant it this time. He'd proposed before, but this time he'd spoken to Falmouth, he'd come to her home. He was announcing to the *ton* that his interest was serious. He was saving her reputation.

"You've spoken to Lord Falmouth?" she replied, a trifle unsteady.

"Yes," he said, smiling at her while one hand cupped her cheek, his thumb stroking her lower lip with a soft caress. "He's not enamoured of the idea but better me than Sindalton, for obvious reasons," he said, with a shrug as his other hand slid to the small of her back and pressed her against him. "Though it appears I am not the only one in the running after all. Who'd have thought old Percy had it in him, a dark horse indeed."

"It's always the quiet ones you have to watch," she replied, dismayed by the breathless sound of her voice, but he'd pulled her very close indeed and his desire for her was only too obvious.

"You don't want Percy," he replied, ducking his head and kissing the tender skin between her neck and her shoulder. She gasped and before she could think clearly about it one hand had sunk into the thick warmth of his golden hair as the other clutched at his shoulder. "You're too much for Percy, sweet Eve," he murmured, nipping at her earlobe as he moved her until her back hit a wall. "You'd frighten him if he saw even a glimmer of everything you want."

"And what do I want?" she asked, wanting to know what it was he saw in her.

His laughter rumbled through his chest and he looked down at her with knowing in his eyes. "You want to experience life, you want to feel love and passion, desire ..." He nipped at her lower lip and then kissed it, his words breathing against her mouth. "You want to give in to lust and tear at my clothes. You want me to take you right here and now ... it burns in your eyes, darling, did you know that?"

His hands dropped to her hips and he pressed against her, the hard length of his strong thigh sliding between her legs and pressing unerringly against the delicate nub of flesh that was crying out for attention. She moaned and then buried her face against his shoulder as shame flooded her.

"Oh, Georgiana," he whispered, his mouth gliding over her skin as his hot breath fluttered over her neck. "We could set the world alight, you and I."

She shook her head, but what kind of answer she was giving she didn't know.

He stilled and held her face in his hands. "How can you decide whether you'll marry me or Percy unless you know what it means?" he said as though reading her thoughts, his eyes serious now. "You will never have passion with dear old Nibley. We both know that. Let me give you a small taste of what you'll be missing. Let me show you how I can make you feel."

"B-but we can't do this ... *here!"* she protested, but Beau just grinned at her, devilry sparkling in his eyes.

"Oh, darling, I could do this anywhere," he said, a chuckle rumbling through his chest. "But I told you, we are being given privacy for my proposal. No one will interrupt us, I promise you."

He kissed her then, a kiss that heated her skin and made her shiver at one and the same time and she knew the truth of his words. She gasped as his large hands cupped her breasts, his thumbs teasing the nipples through the chemise that covered them.

Georgiana let her head drop back against the wall as pleasure spiked through her, the heat of his mouth against her neck. Her thoughts seemed more muddled than ever. Beau was simply temptation incarnate. She couldn't deny her attraction to him, couldn't deny that she liked him, was fond of him even but ... but ...

"No more," she said, her voice unsteady, pushing him away. "You've made your point."

Beau smiled and brushed a last kiss against her lips.

"I can't pretend to have any riches to bestow on you," he said a moment later, his voice quiet, and she looked up to see he had crossed the room. He was standing looking outside at the street below, his face uncharacteristically serious. "I can't pretend that I don't need your finances, and I won't insult you by pretending that isn't so. But if you think I'm unmoved by you, if you think that any of my ... seduction is in any way forced, you are very wrong indeed."

He turned to look at her and she could see the truth of his desire still burning in those usually cool eyes. "I want you in my bed, Georgiana, and if you agree to be my wife I swear you'll not be disappointed. I can't pretend that I'm ideal husband material. We both know I'm not and I won't make any promises that are doomed to failure. But ..." He moved closer to her and held her hand, his fingers closing around hers. "But you are my friend, my very dear friend and you have my word that I will try very hard not to make you unhappy. I might even succeed in making you happy," he added with a slightly self-deprecating smile. "I promise at least, that I will try." He leaned into her and kissed her cheek, just close enough to her mouth to make her heart thud again. "Please, Georgiana, say you'll marry me."

She pulled her hand from his grasp and walked away. Oh God, what was she to do. The only man she truly wanted a proposal from wasn't even here, and the other two ... how long could she keep them waiting for?

"I don't know," she said, feeling helpless and powerless to do anything about it. "I don't know what to do for the best. Sometimes I think I'd be best to marry no one at all and just become some odd little eccentric. I could travel the world alone, or keep cats or ... or ..."

She jolted as his hand closed around hers once again.

"That would be a terrible waste, Georgiana," he whispered. "You need to live, and you need to choose how. You can be safe and probably content enough with dull, sweet Percy. You could allow Sindalton to offer you a *carte blanche* and be near the man you love without ever truly being a part of his world. Or you can marry me, and I promise you this at least, you will always have the protection of my name, and life will never, *ever* be dull."

She gave an unsteady laugh of acknowledgement. That was something she could readily believe.

"I need an answer soon, darling," he said softly. "You don't know how it grieves me to admit it, but I owe money to some people that I'd really rather not cross, and if you won't have me my options are becoming rather terrifyingly limited."

She looked up at him in alarm. "You're in real trouble?" she asked, seeing the answer in his eyes.

He nodded. "I am, so please, don't delay. If the answer is no I may need to run for the continent or spend the next five years or so in rather unpleasant circumstances." It was said with a light and jovial tone that she didn't for an instant believe. He kissed her cheek again, with warmth in his expression. "Don't keep me in an agony of suspense, sweet Eve. Say yes and put us all out of our misery."

Chapter 26

"Wherein love is given a chance to hope ..."

Lord Falmouth looked up in surprise as she entered the breakfast room.

"I know, a ridiculous time of the day to be up," she said by way of apology. "And I expect you were looking forward to a peaceful breakfast alone."

He chuckled and shook his head, folding the paper he had been reading and putting it aside. "Not at all," he replied. "You know perfectly well I usually join Céleste at a later hour, but as it happens she is feeling a trifle under the weather at the moment," he replied, concern in his grey eyes. "Just a bit of a headache I understand. She'll be up presently I'm sure." He gave her a rather searching look and she braced herself for his question.

"I take it you didn't sleep well?"

"Not a wink," she replied with a bleak smile as she poured herself a cup of chocolate. She was tired beyond measure, the whole night spent tossing and turning as variations of her possible futures paraded behind her eyelids and made sleep impossible.

"I am not the slightest bit surprised. I don't envy you the choice."

She laughed and shook her head. One of the things she had found rather intimidating about the man opposite her was his rather forthright nature, but she had come to appreciate it. You knew where you stood with a man like that. "Well if it comes to that, neither do I!" she replied with some asperity.

He chuckled again and then gave her a more concerned glance. "Seriously now, have you any idea to accept either of them?"

"Yes, no ... I don't know," she replied with a grimace. "There you see my reasoning."

"Hmmm," he replied. "I'd be bound to say, I'd rather you accept Nibley. He's a decent man, a kind one. He'd make you a good husband."

"Yes," she said, "I know that."

"But ..." he added, and there was a glimmer in his eyes that made her believe he knew exactly her dilemma. Given the passionate nature she'd come to know his wife possessed, she found that wasn't as embarrassing as it might have been.

"But," she repeated nodding her head. "You have it in a nutshell."

They ate their breakfast in companionable silence for a while, until he spoke again.

"I'm going to Hatchard's this morning," he said, surprising her. "My sister-in-law Henrietta is desperate for some new English titles, she lives in France you see. So I promised to send a parcel to her, and I rather fancied a browse myself. I find it relaxing," he added, smiling at her. "Would you like to accompany me?"

"What a wonderful idea," she replied, grateful for anything that distracted her attention from her troubles for an hour or two.

"It also has the added attraction of being practically empty at this early hour as all the fashionable people are still abed."

"Better and better, my Lord," she said, grinning at him.

He smiled and nodded at her. "My carriage will be ready in ten minutes, oh, and Georgiana?"

"Yes, my Lord?"

"I think perhaps you might call me Alex."

Georgiana spent a pleasant hour browsing the shelves and wandering around by herself. Alex had been quite correct, the place was deserted and was a wonderfully peaceful place to be. She was walking along one of the upper levels. A thin balustrade overlooked the floor below and at the end of the long room was a beautiful arched window. Leaning against the frame of the window, a book held in his hands, stood a tall, dark figure that made Georgiana's heart leap in her chest.

She carried on along the walkway, observing the look of concentration on his face. A slight frown furrowed his brow as though something didn't make sense to him, though she was just as taken by the way the sunlight glinted on his deep brown hair, showing glints of chestnut and bronze. From her lofty vantage point she could look down on him without being observed, and she leaned over the balcony a little, trying to observe what it was that was causing him such consternation. The title of the poem he was reading leapt out at her and made her catch her breath. *The Corsair.*

"I thought you didn't like that one?" The words were out before she could consider the wisdom of speaking to him after the scene the day before last.

He looked around, startled by her voice, and on seeing no one nearby, looked up. The pleasure in his eyes on seeing her chased away any doubts she'd had. They were warm and inviting, the smile that spread over his mouth quite obviously genuine.

"Georgiana!" he exclaimed, and then held the book up with a rueful smile. "I'm afraid my opinion remains the same. Am I a terrible philistine?"

"Oh yes, certainly," she replied, shaking her head at him. "Though at least you are making an effort to try," she added with her most condescending tone.

He laughed at that and nodded. "I am very trying," he said, joking with her in return.

She gave a surprised laugh, delighted by his silly joke. "But why are you reading it?" she pressed, staring into those dark eyes and praying that she had guessed the answer correctly.

He stilled and the smile fell from his face. Smoothing his hands over the sleek leather cover, he shook his head. "I don't know really, just that ... It reminded me of you, of ... our time together and I thought perhaps if I understood what you loved about it I could ..." He stopped and looked up at her, a beseeching look in his eyes that made her chest ache with longing.

"You could what?" she whispered, clutching the rail of the balustrade so hard her fingers hurt.

He took a deep breath and she could see the tension in his broad shoulders, admired the sleek fit of his waistcoat as his chest expanded. "I could find a way to make you forgive me," he said in a rush, the desperation in his voice only too audible now. "To ... to go back and find everything I lost."

She stared down at him, her chest too tight for her to breathe easily, and she felt she could hardly breathe at all.

"I've been such a fool, love," he whispered, staring up at her with anguish as she felt tears prickle in her eyes. "I was coming to you, you see. The night before Almack's. I couldn't stand it any longer. I missed you so much."

"Y--you were going to Cornwall, to see me?" she stammered as the idea sank in.

"Yes," he said, such longing in that one word that she didn't know whether to laugh or cry. "I didn't mean the things I said." She stared at him, struck by the look on his face, by the uncertainty in his bearing. "I was angry that ..." he paused and ran a hand through his thick hair, dishevelling the carefully careless arrangement he'd crafted and leaving something rather softer in its place. He looked younger suddenly, unsure of himself. "I idolised my father," he admitted. "I always wanted to remember him as this ... paragon." He gave a self deprecating laugh and shrugged his big shoulders. "It was only after ... after Beau dunked me," he said with a grin. "That I came to think about him as an ordinary man." His face grew serious and he stepped closer to the balustrade, staring up at her. "I was right about one thing though. If your mother was half as lovely as you, if he felt a fraction of what I do ... I know just how he felt. I understand now how he could be so reckless, why he risked everything. For if he was plagued by dreams of her, by endless nights and empty days where all he could do was live for the moment he might see her again ... I understand it. I do."

She gasped and felt for a moment that she was living in a dream. It seemed so impossible and unlikely that he should be declaring himself in the middle of a book shop of all places.

"You look like Juliet," he said, smiling up at her. "I only hope we have a happier ending," he added, his voice low and full of anxiety.

"Me too," she replied, her words little more than a whisper.

"May I come up?" he asked and she nodded, wiping away a tear that had fallen despite her best efforts as she watched him almost run for the stairs, and then mount them two at a time. She took a deep breath and tried to calm her leaping nerves, and then there he was, standing in front of her.

She looked up at him and wondered if she had forgotten just what an impressive sight he was, for he stole her breath all over again. His dark blue superfine coat was perfectly cut and clung to him lovingly, accentuating hard muscle and powerful arms. She remembered what it had felt like to have those arms around her, the weight of his body on hers, the touch of his hands on her skin. A flush burned over her cheeks, and she hoped he couldn't guess at her thoughts.

"I wanted to kill Beau," he said, his voice rough and yet hesitant. "When I heard ..."

She looked away, embarrassed that he should know about that. "You were right," she admitted. "I should never have gone in the boat with him."

"He kissed you?"

She looked back at him in horror, how could he stand there and ask that? Did he really expect an answer? It was clear he didn't need one further than her silence as his fists clenched and he cursed under his breath.

"He's offered for me," she said, wanting him to understand how precarious her position was. She would have to marry someone, she'd be no man's mistress, stuck in a half-life between his worlds. "So has Lord Nibley."

His eyes widened, his throat working as he seemed to struggle to find the words for his next question.

"You've ... have you ..."

"No," she replied with a sad smile. "No, I've not answered yet. I couldn't when ..."

She stared at him, unwilling to put into words what ought to be blatantly obvious.

"I can't ..." he exclaimed, holding out his hands to her, the sentence left undone, hanging in the air between them.

He can't marry you, she thought. That's what he's trying to say. Except suddenly his hands were cradling her face, his lips so close she could feel his breath on her skin.

"I can't let you marry someone else!" he rasped, his voice harsh and urgent, his eyes so wild she took a breath. "I'll run mad if you do, Georgiana. Please, please, love. Tell me you'll not accept them?"

She felt her breathing hitch, wanting so much to tell him what he wanted to hear, but *he* hadn't asked. "I ... I have to marry, your Grace. You know I must."

"Your Grace?" he bit out. "Not your Grace, dammit, Georgiana. *Sebastian.* Say my name."

"Sebastian," she whispered, and she realised she was trembling, caught in the fire in his eyes, terrified she might accept whatever indecent offer he put to her.

"Tell me you still love me," he commanded, and she felt as though he really had control of her thoughts, of her tongue, as she was powerless to refuse the need in his expression. She stared into the dark of his irises, lost again in the little universe of golden flecks that burned in his eyes.

"I love you," she whispered. "I love you, Sebastian."

She heard the catch in his breath, felt the warmth of his thumb as it caressed her cheek.

"Will you be in tomorrow morning if I call on you?" he asked, a new note of determination in his voice.

She nodded, too shocked to speak, hope blooming to life like a flame in her chest, warming the heart that had been so frozen with sorrow since he'd left her.

"I'll call on you," he said, so assured in his manner she couldn't doubt him. There was a look in his eyes that promised so much. "I have things to do, to consider ... things I must ... arrange. But I'll come, I swear it."

She nodded again, blinking as her vision blurred.

He stepped closer, their bodies touching, here in the book shop, where anyone could walk in and see. "Wait for me," he pleaded. "Wait for me, love. Promise?"

"P-promise," she stammered, half laughing, half crying as he laughed too, and pressed a kiss to her lips.

"I won't let you down, my love," he said, his smile wide and brilliant now. "Until tomorrow."

He stepped back and began to walk away, but then paused and turned back to her, as though needing to reassure himself she was really there.

"Until tomorrow," she whispered, pressing her fingers to her lips in wonder. *Until tomorrow.* She hugged the words to her heart, watching as he strode out of sight.

Chapter 27

"Wherein tempers run high and the gossips delight."

Sebastian walked the streets in a daze, seeing nothing but his future. A future that he could share with her, with Georgiana. On the one hand he was ecstatic; he had found her, the woman who would be his wife. He'd discovered that impossible creature who didn't want him for his money or his title. The girl who loved Byron and her ugly mongrel and walked for miles in all weathers. She made him feel foolish and giddy as a schoolboy, and like the most powerful man on the earth when she smiled at him.

The feeling in his chest grew and expanded until he could believe that everything he felt for her couldn't possibly be contained in the fragile confines of his body. It was too grand, too powerful, too consuming. Suddenly Byron and Keats and those overblown romantic sentiments that he'd always thought rather foolish and a little embarrassing made perfect sense. They were trying to capture the essence of something that was indeed foolish and fantastical and larger than anything else in life, with words on a page. He wanted to laugh and shout that he understood now. It all made sense now.

With a wry smile he looked around at the fashionable men and women strolling up and down as he made his way to St James' Street, blithely unaware of his turbulent thoughts as the other side of the coin presented itself to him.

What on earth would he say to his mother?

He imagined a scene where he was brave enough to tell her that he'd fallen in love with a girl who was the image of the woman who'd ruined her life. The girl was in fact the Siren's daughter, the creature who had stolen her husband, left her son without a father, and herself too ashamed and humiliated to face the world again.

How would he put into words the news that Lady Georgiana would now take the title that had once been hers? She would become the Duchess of Sindalton. Could he really be so cruel? Could he really push her past hurt aside for his own future?

His face clouded as the future became less clear, the path less obvious. He loved Georgiana and he didn't care what the gossip mill made of it. They would cause a titillating stir and be the talk of the *haut ton* for some months. But then another scandal, another poor broken heart or embarrassed cuckold would take the stage ... and their story would fade into history.

But the scandal could destroy his mother, the shock of it putting too great a strain on a nervous creature who spent so much of her time near hysteria as it was. This could really break her mind for good ... or maybe even kill her. Could he live with the guilt of that?

The impressive Palladian façade of his club came into view and he crossed the street. The white Portland stone gleamed in the sun as he entered the cool and sophisticated surroundings of White's. Moving past the empty space in the bow window reserved for the Duke of Wellington, since poor old Brummel had done a run for it, he found a table in a quiet corner and hoped to be left alone. He wondered if the other Beau of his acquaintance would share the same fate, fleeing to France to escape debtor's prison. Because he was damned if he'd let him marry Georgiana to save him. He'd happily bail him out, without ever demanding a penny in return, but even for his closest friend he'd not give up the woman he loved. He loved Beau like the brother he'd never had and would do near anything for him, but not that.

The idea that he'd kissed her made anger and jealousy burn bright and furious behind his eyes and he snatched at the decanter that had been placed quietly before him and poured a large measure. He closed his eyes and exhaled as the liquor eased through him, infiltrating his blood and creating a warm glow in his stomach. He downed the glass and filled another and sat staring at the amber liquid as he filled and refilled his glass as the day wore on. His brain ran in anxious circles, round and around the same dilemmas, the same arguments, the same results. He looked up sometime later to see little of the brandy remained in the decanter as was attested by the ache in his head. The only thing that remained clear to him throughout, the only constant that he could hold on to, was that he loved Georgiana. When that thought pierced the fog of his tangled brain it was bright and clear and irrefutable. It was the only thing.

His attention was taken as a shadow fell over the table and he forced himself to focus on his surroundings rather than the thoughts writhing in his brain.

"Oh God, not now, Beau," he growled, shaking his head. "You don't want to be near me now, I swear it."

"Perhaps not, but I think you've spent enough time with this for company," his friend remarked gesturing for a server to remove it. "Bring a pot of coffee," he added, watching Sebastian with caution in his eyes. "You're foxed," he observed with some surprise. "You must be in a foul mood."

"Oh, I am," Sebastian replied, not taking his eyes from the man looking down at him. To his dismay Beau didn't leave well alone as he'd hoped he might but sat down opposite him.

"I think you should hear it from me," he said, holding Sebastian's gaze, his blue eyes troubled. "I've offered for Miss Dalton. I know I told you I should but ... well you're my friend and I won't do anything behind your back. So it's done. I await her reply."

"I know," Sebastian said, wishing the bastard hadn't had the brandy removed because he really needed a bloody drink.

Beau narrowed his eyes, considering. "Well now, I know the gossip mills turn fair and fast, but that's quick work even for these parts. *How* do you know that, may I ask?"

Sebastian smiled at him and sat back in his chair, not caring if he looked smug. "Because she told me."

There was an almost imperceptible tightening of Beau's jaw, his eyes glinting in a way that Sebastian knew meant trouble. "She told you?" he repeated. "When?"

"This morning," Sebastian replied, holding Beau's gaze. "She also told me she didn't want you, or Nibley. She loves me still, Beau. It's me she wants."

Beau snorted and shook his head. "I know she loves you, you fool. But what exactly are you offering her? Are you actually going to face your mother and tell her you're marrying Lady Dalton? Because frankly I think that's going to take more balls than you've got."

Sebastian stiffened in fury and leaned across the table.

"Don't you dare insult me when all you want is to get your hands on her money!"

Beau glared back at him, his face white with indignation. "Oh, but that's not all I want to get my hands on," he said, his voice low. "And she may not love me, but I assure you, she doesn't find the idea in any way repulsive."

Before Sebastian could think about what he was doing, about where they were and the damage it would do, he simply reacted. The idea of Beau, the *ton's* most notorious rake, with his hands on Georgiana made rage, white hot and irresistible, flame through his drunken brain. He threw himself forward and knocked Beau out of his chair, the two of them falling to the floor as Sebastian drew back his fist to throw a punch.

There were shouts of alarm and to Sebastian's frustration he was hauled away from Beau before he could land a punch. Beau was also struggling like fury, two men holding him back as they glared at each other with the need for violence in their eyes.

"Gentlemen!" said a shocked, cultured voice to the side of them and Sebastian forced himself to look away from Beau and encountered the surprisingly angry eyes of Lord Nibley. "I think you should be ashamed of yourselves," he said in a low tone. "Now you will both sit back down and take a drink together."

They both stared at Nibley as though he'd grown an extra head, as the idea of sitting down with Beau made Sebastian want to hit him again.

"I don't see how I am to blame for this little scene," Beau replied, rearranging his cravat and still glaring at Sebastian. "I rather think I'm owed an apology."

Sebastian snorted at the likelihood of that happening and Nibley grabbed hold of his arm with surprising violence.

"You will do this and anything else required to try and limit the damage you have already done to a blameless young woman," Nibley hissed, his lanky frame taut with anger.

Sebastian took a breath as the sense of this filtered through his liquor-soaked brain. Good God, what had he been thinking? To attack Beau, *here* of all places? To his further annoyance he saw that Beau had already seated himself and was ordering a drink, looking perfectly unruffled. At least Sebastian thought he looked unruffled, until he sat down himself and looked closely into those blue eyes and saw the cool glitter of resentment still lurking there.

The three men sat together and drank, though this time Sebastian stuck to coffee, and tried to present a calm appearance. The atmosphere at the table however was far from jovial despite Nibley's best efforts.

They forced themselves to remain for a half hour at which point the three men stood, shook hands and forced a smile to their faces before going their separate ways.

***

It appears The Siren has struck again as violence erupted within the sacred walls of White's of all places! Friends since boyhood came to blows and yet another suitor was forced to intervene. It appears bets have been taken as to which of these hot-blooded lovers will win out. The ton stands agog as the scene unfolds before us. Will there be murder and bloodshed and a repeat of a previous decade's outrageous scandal? Whilst the ever charming M of B and wealthy Lord N have both publicly declared their interest in ton's newest fiery beauty, the D of S has not seemed to be received with any pleasure or to have put his hat in the ring. What exactly is the man offering and why is he so enraged by his best friend's courtship of a woman who can surely bring nothing but embarrassment to his distinguished family?

Georgiana stared at the horrid scandal sheet with her cheeks burning. How could they? How could they fight over her in a public place like dogs with a bone! She thanked goodness that Alex had been called away early this morning and Céleste was still abed. She didn't think she could face anyone for a while. How she was going to attend any of the dozens of formal functions she was committed to over the coming weeks was beyond her. The constant stares and whispers had been grating enough before, but now this! She screwed the revolting sheet up and flung it across the table before putting her head in her hands.

A scratch at the door indicated the presence of the butler before he opened it and stepped into the room.

"His grace, the Duke of Sindalton, is here to see you, my Lady."

She nodded, smiling at the anxious look in the old man's eyes. The earl was away from home and all the staff knew his feeling about the duke. Yet they all knew the gossip, just as well as the *ton*, and she had a feeling the old man didn't want to stand in the way of a love affair, if that was what this was.

"It's quite all right," she said, giving him a reassuring smile. "Please show him in."

"Should I send Miss Sarah to accompany you, my Lady."

"No, thank you. His grace is quite the gentleman I assure you."

The butler looked totally unconvinced by this statement, and she knew he was quite right. She should not allow Sebastian to be alone with her in the circumstances, but he went away and did as he'd been instructed.

She took a breath and smoothed down the silk of her Mexican blue morning dress. It was trimmed with white Peruvian lace and she had been more than pleased with the effect when Sarah had arranged her hair and added her favourite slim row of pearls around her neck. She had dressed with care, bubbling with excitement at the expectation of his call upon her. But now she was not certain whether to be furious or disappointed, or every bit as anxious and happy as she had been on waking.

She stood and dipped a curtsey as he entered and on looking up was arrested by the look in his eyes.

He gave a little surprised huff of laughter and shook his head. "I'm sorry," he said, smiling. "I am just struck every time I see you. I think each time we part that I have committed every particular of your beautiful face to my mind, and every time I see you I find you far lovelier than I remember."

"Perhaps you just have a poor memory," she replied a little sharply, though in truth she was charmed by his words. But his behaviour as reported in the scandal sheets could not be forgiven without comment. How could he have been so thoughtless?

His smile fell away and he stepped a little closer to her.

"I cannot be surprised that you're angry with me," he said, his voice quiet. "In truth you cannot be more furious than I am at myself. I ... I'm afraid I was very drunk, not that it is any defence, but Beau and I argued and ... I'm afraid I was extremely jealous. The idea of you with him ..." His voice became harsh and he shook his head, turning away from her. "I've made everything worse I know. But I am here and if you think you can forgive me for my terrible behaviour, there ... there is a question I would ask you."

Her breathing hitched and she watched as he turned around to face her again.

"Ask it," she whispered.

He smiled and crossed the room, his hands finding her waist and pulling her closer to him, their bodies almost touching.

"Georgiana," he whispered. "I have loved you since the day you scolded me so soundly in that cave. I love you to distraction, to the point where I wanted to murder my best friend for daring to consider he could make you his. You're mine, darling. We belong together." His grip on her waist tightened as she stared up into his eyes, which were grave and more serious than she had ever seen them.

"It won't be easy, my love, my ... my mother is going to make life hard for us I'm afraid but ..." He took a deep breath and sank to one knee, and he took her hands in his. "Please, Georgiana, tell me you're brave enough to face it all. Tell me we can laugh in the faces of our parent's scandal and bring something good and right out of the chaos they threw us into. I love you with all my heart. Please, love, marry me and make me the happiest of men."

He looked up at her, anxiety and expectation in his dark eyes as she gave a little choked laugh and nodded as her eyes blurred.

"Yes," she said, her voice thick. "Yes, yes, of course yes!"

He laughed and got to his feet, pulling her into an embrace and kissing her. His lips were tender and she felt the smile against her mouth as she heard him laughing again.

"Thank God," he whispered. "I was so afraid I'd ruined everything."

She clung to him, her head on his shoulder as the enormity of what they faced filtered through to her. "Will your mother be very angry?"

He was silent for a moment and she knew then that Beau had been right. He was afraid of what the news would do to her.

"Yes," he said, his voice full of regret. "Though I'm not sure anger is the right word." He looked down at her, his handsome face troubled. "She's not a strong woman, Georgiana, and ... I'm afraid to tell her."

"Would it help her to meet me, do you think?"

"My God, no!" he exclaimed, letting go of her and turning away.

"She'll have to, sooner or later," she said, dismayed by the vehemence of his reaction.

"Yes, of course she will," he agreed. "But I need time to talk to her, to ... to try and make her understand."

There was such anxiety, such obvious doubt in his voice that she knew just how unlikely he believed the possibility of her ever understanding was.

"Can you really do it, Sebastian?" she asked, terrified that he would change his mind even now. Her hands clutched at each other, the fingers twisting together as she began to fear he couldn't face hurting his mother so badly. "Can you really tell her you'd make Lady Dalton's daughter your duchess?"

He swung around then, and any doubts fled as he closed the distance between them and kissed her. His kiss heated her skin and set her senses on fire as desire blazed to life. She had longed for this for so long. This was what she needed to know. Nibley had offered her security and friendship, Beau a sensual world of physical pleasure devoid of love, but this ... this was everything. Sebastian was everything they offered and more. She liked him as fully as she loved him. She felt safe in his arms and wanted to tear the clothes from his back with a passion even Beau couldn't have aroused, because there was nothing headier than friendship between them.

Her awareness in Sebastian's arms seemed heightened and dulled at one and the same time. She was acutely aware of him, of the heat of his mouth, the insistent slide of his tongue as he wrapped his arms around her body and pulled her as tight as was possible without squeezing the air from her lungs. She was aware of the weight of him, the disparity of his harder, larger body crushing her own softer frame and the urgency of his hands as they slid over her. Yet everything beyond him and his touch fell away. The sound of the world beyond the walls of this room, the ticking of the clock on the mantle, the impropriety of kissing him with such passion in Falmouth's home ... all of that was gone.

He released her with obvious reluctance, his breathing as harsh as her own.

"My God, Georgiana, we must marry as soon as it can be arranged," he said, the frustration in his eyes almost comical and indeed she struggled not to laugh.

He huffed out a chagrined chuckle of his own, as she'd patently failed to disguise her amusement.

"Did I answer your question fully enough, love?" he whispered. "Do you see that we cannot be parted? I'll face anything for this, anything at all. Wouldn't you?"

"Yes!" she exclaimed and then stilled as an awful thought occurred to her and she felt the colour drain from her face.

"What is it?" he demanded, taking her in his arms again, clearly shocked by her sudden pallor. "What are you thinking?"

"This is how they felt," she whispered. "Your father, my mother ... this is what drove them."

"No," he said, his voice implacable, his strong face full of surety. "It won't happen to us. We are both free agents. We are hurting no one save my mother, and I will do everything in my power to make it easier for her, as will you I know. It isn't the same, love. You know it isn't."

She nodded and smiled at him, trying to feel reassured by his words, but the sense of unease lingered and only grew once he had left her alone.

Chapter 28

"Wherein madness is inevitable."

As Sebastian headed up the steps of the house in Grosvenor Square, his harassed looking footman, powdered wig askew, emerged from the front doors. Forcing on his hat as he closed the doors and shrugging into his coat as he ran, he was clearly on some errand of urgency. His face cleared in an almost comical manner as it landed on his Master.

"Oh, your grace!" he said, with such obvious relief that Sebastian was struck with an immediate sense of foreboding. His staff never exclaimed nor expressed curiosity or any emotion unbecoming in a member of his household. So the footman's lack of propriety could only mean something of a very grave nature had occurred. "I was just on my way to find you."

"What is it, Benson?" he demanded, ushering the shaken looking fellow back inside the house before anything could be made of it by anyone else.

Once the door had closed Benson seemed to remember his position and straightened himself.

"It is the dowager duchess, your Grace. But I assure you we had no idea she would ever ... I mean to say, your Grace ... As you know it is her habit to stay in her rooms until noon so the staff, none of us expected ... that is to say ..."

"Say what? Are you half-witted man? I never heard anyone say so much and tell me so little!" he exploded, fearing the worst.

His fears seemed to be confirmed by the grave look in his servant's eyes. "We were unaware that her Ladyship meant to visit the breakfast parlour, your Grace. If we had known we would of course have taken pains to have removed ..."

"She saw the morning papers," Sebastian supplied for him with a grim expression.

The footman nodded, his face one of terrified pallor. "I-I must take full responsibility, you grace ... I should have ..."

"Nonsense," Sebastian replied. "I may be exacting, Benson, but I don't believe I have ever demanded my staff to have second sight."

The relief of the man in front of him was palpable and marked. "Thank you, your Grace," the man replied, with deep sincerity.

"Don't thank me yet," Sebastian said his face grim as he put his coat and hat into the care of the second footman. "It means you're still a member of this household and in a situation which may yet be our undoing. How is my mother now?"

Benson blanched a little as a crash of china came from above stairs.

"Never mind," Sebastian said, his heart sinking to his boots where he had no doubt it was likely to remain for the rest of the day at least. He began to run upstairs, calling back to Benson. "And call Doctor Alperton. Tell him it's an emergency." He had just reached the top when there was a scream and Lady Rush, his mother's companion, flew through the doors as though pursued by the devil. She ran helter skelter down the corridor to her own rooms, wailing hysterically all the while as Sebastian cursed and ran to his mother's door.

She was pacing and muttering, her long grey hair loose and dishevelled about her shoulders, her black bombazine skirts crumpled. Seeing him enter the room, her febrile gaze turned to one of fury and she ran for the mantelpiece and snatched up a Staffordshire china dog, one of a pair that had been in his family for generations. Not for much longer though as she lanced it with considerable force for a woman of her meagre frame. With surprising accuracy too, as Sebastian was forced to duck as the vacant-faced canine missed his head by a hair's breadth and exploded against the wall.

"Devil!" she screamed, running to snatch up its china companion and throw it in the same manner. "How dare you!" The china dog shattered at his feet this time as she looked for another missile. "How dare you come from your whore to me? You'd ruin us for that red-haired witch, that slut ..." To his astonishment she gave up her search for a weapon and flew at him instead, scratching at his face, trying to claw at his eyes as he was forced to hold her off.

"Mother!" he shouted. "Stop this!"

"Wicked, wicked man ... oh, Sindalton, Sindalton, how can you ... with that evil ... evil creature! Do you not care for your own son?"

With growing horror Sebastian realised that it wasn't him she was seeing but his dead father all those years before. She subsided as he held her wrists in his strong grip and she crumpled to the floor. Sobbing and raving, she cursed his red-headed whore with vicious and crude words that he had never believed his mother even knew.

By the time doctor Alperton was shown into his study some hours later, Sebastian had managed to find a measure of tolerable calm. His mother's behaviour had become increasingly erratic and volatile as the years passed, but this had truly shocked him. By now though, he was composed enough to face the man who had delivered him into this world and knew as much of their family scandal as there was to know. A short and rather portly man with a terrible and frivolous taste in waistcoats for a doctor, Sebastian had always thought him a rather frippery fellow. But he was always very solicitous and if Sebastian felt he rather indulged his mother's fits of anxiety, he was grateful beyond measure for his discretion and the quiet dignity with which he now spoke. There was real sorrow in his eyes as he went to shake Sebastian's hand.

"Your grace," he said, his expression serious. "I cannot tell you how sorry I am to find your mother in this state. I have sedated her of course and I'll return first thing in the morning."

"Will ... will she recover?" he asked, hardly daring to hear the answer.

The doctor sighed and gave him a crooked smile. "You know I cannot give you a certain answer to that, my Lord, much as I wish I could."

"Then what is your feeling on the matter?" Sebastian demanded in obvious bad temper, knowing he was being unfair; the man wasn't God after all. "Because if she doesn't I fear I have done far worse than kill her with my own hands!" He stopped and went to pour himself a drink and another for the doctor. "It's my fault you see. I ... I have offered for Miss Dalton ... I needn't ask for your discretion in this, I know, after all these years, but Mother saw the wicked gossip in one of those damned rags this morning ..."

He broke off and downed his drink in one large swallow before handing the other glass to the doctor.

"May I speak frankly, your Grace?" the doctor asked, his voice gentle and a surprising amount of sympathy in his eyes.

"Of course," Sebastian replied, taking a seat beside the fire and gesturing for Alperton to do the same. "You've known me all my life, and you knew my parents before. There's hardly anyone I'd trust more."

The doctor smiled at him. "You have no idea how much that honours me, your Grace, and so I'll take advantage of that familiarity if I may." He smoothed a hand over his rather plump belly, which was covered by a truly garish waistcoat, as he gathered his thoughts. "I knew your parents before they married, as you know, and to be frank, a worse match it would have been hard to countenance." He broke off, his smile for Sebastian warm and genuine.

"Your father was a fine man, but he was betrothed to your mother when they were little more than children. As they grew it became clear that your mother was perhaps ... rather high strung to say the least. She was never in the most robust of health and she was spoilt by over indulgent parents. She was prone to fits of temper and ... and irrationality. She was, however, quite a beauty in her young days and, well to be frank, your father was too good natured to cry off."

Sebastian felt a knot of tension begin to unravel a little at the doctor's words.

"I didn't drive her to madness?" he asked, his voice rough.

"No!" the doctor exclaimed, shaking his head with vigour. "The truth is that your mother has always been of a nervous and rather unstable temperament. In all honesty, she drove your father away. He was lonely, especially after you were born. The experience of childbirth ... well it did not sit well with your mother. She doted on you, but she would never let your father touch her again."

They were quiet for a while as the doctor allowed him to digest this new and revealing piece of information.

"He was a good man," Sebastian said, his voice quiet.

"He was indeed," the doctor replied smiling. "And he was so very proud of you. Prouder than you perhaps realise."

Sebastian felt a lump form in his throat and had to look away, staring into the fire as the smiling face of his father came to mind.

"He loved you," the older man said. "And he loved Lady Dalton."

Sebastian looked up, and he found the man's kindly eyes on him. "He would never have done it if he'd have realised what it would mean for you, of that much I'm sure. But he loved her, that I do know. And she loved him."

Sebastian closed his eyes and let out a breath. "Thank you," he said.

"There is nothing to thank me for," Alperton replied. "They are only the reminiscences of an old man after all. But none of this is your fault, nor is it any of your young lady's. I can't tell you if your mother will recover her mind or not, your Grace, but I will say this much. Don't let their tragedy be yours. Don't let history repeat itself. Your mother has lived her life as she saw fit and this is the result. Don't change your life to try and create another generation of misery, not to appease someone who can never be truly happy, no matter what you do."

Chapter 29

"Wherein farce and violence are the order of the day."

Georgiana flung her needlework aside as howls and barks came from below stairs. Alex and Céleste had gone to lunch with his Aunt Seymour, but the old lady had been taken ill while they were there and they had sent a message to let her know they wouldn't be returning until the next day. It was nothing serious, but Alex wanted to wait to see the doctor and reassure himself his aunt was in good hands. They had been due to attend a masked ball tonight, but Alex had arranged that Lord Nibley and his sister should take her, a fact that made her smile.

She wondered if Alex believed he was match making, though it did give her an opportunity to tell poor Percy that she had reached her decision. But her hosts' absence meant she'd been left alone, which suited her well. She'd barely managed to set a stitch that wasn't crooked but, she didn't care a jot. Sebastian had asked her to marry him. The delicious words of his proposal, the passionate manner in which he had kissed her, all of it was examined and replayed in detail in her mind's eye, to the detriment of her stitching. She had hoped to hear from him today, if not see him in person, but she knew he must be spending time with his mother, trying to help her come to terms with his impending nuptials to a woman she couldn't help but despise. She would see him tonight though, at the ball, and the idea made anticipation burn with pleasant warmth through her veins.

The barking and yapping became ever more raucous, and her curiosity now peaked, Georgiana decided to investigate. Opening the door she looked out into the hallway to see the butler hurrying downstairs and the barking getting ever more intense. Wondering what manner of devilry her dreadful canine had embarked upon now she decided she'd best follow, and then picked up her skirts and ran down the stairs to the kitchens as a scream of horror trembled the walls.

The scene that awaited her as she entered the hallowed territory that belonged solely to the dictatorship of the chef, Alphonse, was one that only Bruegel could have done justice to. In fact, it put her forcibly in mind of The Fight Between Carnival and Lent, a painting that had struck her with amusement when she was very young.

Standing on the kitchen table in all of his stately majesty was Alphonse. In one hand he wielded a ladle and in the other a shockingly expensive Westphalian ham, around one end of which was clamped the jaws of a determined looking spaniel.

"Oh thank heavens," Georgiana muttered, relieved beyond measure Céleste's wicked Bandit was to blame and not Conrad. Her reprieve was short lived, however, as a squirrel ran across a shelf of the dresser, sending china crashing to the floor in its wake as Conrad barked with wild abandon and chased it towards the larder.

"Good gracious," she exclaimed as the housekeeper shrieked when the squirrel suddenly diverted and leapt across the room, tail whisking, a bare inch from her face. In her shock the beleaguered woman dropped a full jar of cornichons. The glass shattered sending the pickling liquid over the hem of Georgiana's skirts and filling the kitchen with the pungent aroma of vinegar. The squirrel leapt again and swung from the oil lamp over their heads, chattering with fury as Conrad leapt up on the table beside Alphonse to get closer. This was too much for Alphonse who took a swipe at Conrad with the ladle, missed and lost his footing. To give the elderly butler his due, he moved pretty fast to intercept the rather weighty chef before he hit the ground, but only succeeded in breaking his fall.

With a sinking heart as the scene descended further into chaos, Georgiana decided enough was enough. She helped the winded butler to his feet as Alphonse rolled off him, and then ran down the passage that led to the scullery. Here she found two trembling housemaids lurking. Scolding them soundly for being so chicken-hearted, she sent them out into the fray armed with brooms and baskets.

After a fair amount of squealing, shrieking and running about, the squirrel - who was sadly Conrad's responsibility after having brought the wretched thing in and letting it go - was safely confined in a picnic basket. This was given into the care of the second footman to remove to Hyde Park without delay. Georgiana was hard pressed to decide which of the haughty creatures was more disgusted by this arrangement. The furious squirrel had taken to growling with unsettling ferocity from the confines of its prison, while the second footman gave a revolted sniff of disdain and picked up the basket as though it contained a bloody head rather than a small, disgruntled rodent.

With one problem less, Georgiana removed the ham from Alphonse's hands with a stern demand to know who exactly he thought would want to eat the wretched thing now? Alphonse, who had been sitting in a heap on the kitchen floor and keeping a continually yapping Bandit at bay with the ladle, finally saw the sense in this. He relinquished the ham, if not the ladle, and Georgiana threw it into the garden. It was an easy matter then to remove the two reprobates who had caused all the trouble as they followed the ham as an unjust reward for their roguery.

With a sigh Georgiana returned her attention to the kitchen. The housekeeper sat in the corner sobbing into her apron, Alphonse was helping himself to the earl's best brandy and threatening to hand in his notice in passionate if broken English, and a scene of devastation lay before her whichever way she turned.

An hour later she had sent the butler, Alphonse and the housekeeper to have tea and cake in the back kitchen whilst the housemaids returned the kitchen to rights. She had promised Alphonse two Westphalian hams to be delivered from Fortnum and Masons' the very next day at her own expense, and a bottle of that fine establishment's best brandy for each of them to settle their nerves. Thus leaving them suitably mollified, she returned to the kitchen to find the maids putting everything in its place and climbed the stairs with a sigh, wondering if she would ever get the stench of vinegar out of her favourite sprigged muslin. The sight that next greeted her was not, therefore, one she could meet with any equanimity. Baron Dalton, clearly finding the door unlocked and no footman or butler to deny him, had entered the house and was awaiting her.

She paused in the hallway, staring at him with disfavour.

"I'm sorry no one was here to receive you, Uncle," she replied, keeping her tone polite if icy. "There was a commotion in the kitchens which needed our attention. I'm afraid Lord Falmouth cannot speak to you at present. If you would like to return later perhaps ..."

"I know damn well Falmouth isn't here, girl," he replied with a sneer, his thin lips just as cruel and malicious as she remembered them. "I waited until your guard dog had left the premises, though I never expected to have such luck as to evade the butler and his minions too." He gave her a callous grin and gestured towards the drawing room. "Shall we ..."

"I have no wish to further my acquaintance with you, Sir," Georgiana replied, her heart hammering with unease. "So I would ask that you leave now."

The baron snorted and to her horror crossed the hall, grasped her by the wrist and hauled her behind him into the drawing room where he slammed the door shut.

"If you haven't realised by now that I don't give a damn what you want then you have even less brain than I credited you for," he said, his face full of hatred as she snatched her hand from his grasp and staggered away.

"Say your piece, you brute, and then get out before Falmouth returns. He doesn't like bullies," she said, sneering at him in return. Before she had time to even consider that her words were not well placed before a man she knew inclined to violence, his hand snapped out and struck her face, a stinging blow that had her staggering backwards. She fell onto the sofa behind her, tears of shock and pain blurring her eyes, but before she could scream or cry for help he had her by the throat, his large hand squeezing just enough to make breathing very hard indeed.

"Listen to me, you little whore. I've seen the way you've got the men running after you like you're a bitch on heat, and if you think I'm vacating my home for a tart with no more class than a threepenny upright you're sadly out on your reckoning." He squeezed a little tighter as Georgiana clawed at his hand to no avail. "This is the thing you're going to do. I will send you a message in two days, telling you where and when, and then you will come along like a good girl and marry Mr Rufford."

He released her and she fell to her knees, gasping as tears fell from her eyes. She hauled in a breath and moved away from him, watching as he stared at her as though she was less than nothing.

"And if I don't?" she demanded, pulling herself back up onto the sofa, determined that he shouldn't see her tremble before him, even if her knees were unlikely to carry her from the room if she tried to run from him.

He reached into his pocket and for an appalled and horrifying second she saw the glint of a knife and thought he meant to kill her. Instead he grasped hold of her hair, pulling her head cruelly backwards, and cut off one thick ringlet, holding it up in front of her face with triumph in his eyes.

"If you don't, I'll make sure every man of the town is given a share of this little token and a fair price to illustrate to anyone who'll listen about how they spent their nights availing themselves of your pleasures."

Georgiana gasped and shook her head. "Please, no! You can keep the house, and the money, I don't want it. Just leave me be, I beg of you."

"No," he replied. "You're not the kind of woman who leaves well enough alone. Oh, you're cowed enough for now with my fist in your sights," he said, his face bearing such malice for her she felt truly afraid. "But I wouldn't want you getting the idea you can get the better of me and get back what you believe is yours. No, you'll do as I say now or I'll finish the job of ruining you that your slattern of a mother began." He strode to the door, before pausing and turning back. "You'll receive my message and you'll do as you're bid or face the consequences."

"I'll never do as you want," she exploded, rage overcoming fear as the unfairness of it took a hold of her and put fire in her blood. "You come here, accusing me of being worthless when you're nothing but a vile bully who uses his fists to force himself on those who can't fight back. I'll never put myself further into your power, *never!"*

He didn't even blink, his serpentine eyes staring at her with cool disgust. "Then I'll ruin you," he replied, before closing the door in her face.

Georgiana sat trembling, unsure of what to do, of who to turn to. Her first thought was to run to Lord Falmouth, but he had been to so much trouble on her behalf already and with his Aunt Seymour taken ill too ... She would have to wait until tomorrow to speak with him. But Sebastian would surely know what to do. In any case she must tell him before such dreadful stories could come to his ears by another means.

But it would be quite improper of her to arrive on his doorstep alone; she would have to send a message to ask him to call immediately. But looking at the mantel clock, however, she saw how very late it had grown. It was almost time to get ready for the masquerade ball where she would see him anyway. She would have to contrive to speak to him privately there and they would think of something. They had to.

Chapter 30

"Wherein ... the plot thickens."

Lord Nibley and his sister, much to Georgiana's delight and surprise, were dressed as a pair of Spanish dancers. She exclaimed in delight, having unjustly supposed Percy would look down on such rowdy amusements. He coloured a little at her exclamation and then grinned.

"I admit I had grave misgivings about this evening," he said, looking a trifle sheepish. "Hen-hearted I know, but you get such *odd* and varied sorts as these affairs. I always feel it's not quite the thing for young ladies, but Florrie was determined to come and well ... do you know it's rather liberating to be someone else for an evening and everyone none the wiser."

Georgiana laughed, though her own thoughts were too tangled to enter into his amusement as fully as she might have done. Privately she also thought anyone acquainted with Lord Nibley would never be deceived no matter the amount of garish colours he clad his long limbs with. His sister, Florence, was also tall and lean, though thankfully not to the extent of her brother. She had his kind brown eyes though and was a cheerful companion, much inclined to enjoy herself and see everything there was to be seen.

"But I have not yet told you how very lovely you look," Nibley added boldly, colouring a little but saved by his sister who nodded vigorously.

"Oh, yes," she breathed, looking flatteringly awestruck as she took in Georgiana's attire. "The very image of a goddess. You really are very beautiful, and Artemis with her silver bow and arrow is just the thing for your lovely figure."

"The very image of a goddess indeed," Nibley said softly, this time causing Georgiana to blush.

Looking suitably awkward Florence settled back against the squabs and they enjoyed a pleasant conversation as the carriage took them via the less fashionable but drier route over Westminster Bridge rather than chartering a boat to Kennington.

They reached Vauxhall Gardens in Lambeth within the half hour, and it looked like an enchanted fairyland glittering in the darkness. Thousands of glass Chinese lanterns were hung all about the wide, sweeping avenues, glowing gold, and the ornamental lake was lit with floating candles. The grand rococo rotunda too was all aglow, and everywhere the eyes were assaulted by colourful costumes and the swirl of domino cloaks as masked figures laughed louder and more boldly than usual. For the first hour Georgiana despaired of ever finding Sebastian in the crush, but she had been right about Lord Nibley's singularly lanky frame. Beyond relieved, a familiar voice slid over her skin, sending shivers of anticipation down her spine.

"Good evening, lovely Artemis," he whispered against her ear and she turned, confronted with a black silk domino, lined with scarlet and a black mask. She knew the dark eyes that glittered behind the mask, however, and felt her tension ease a little. Sebastian would surely know what to do. "I would be afraid such a powerful goddess would steal my heart away," he said, his voice still low and serious. "But alas you must find another for mine is already claimed."

"Oh?" she replied, smiling up at him, despite the fear in her heart that trouble awaited them. "You do not find me to your liking, your Grace?"

"Oh how could I not?" he exclaimed, shaking his head. "But I have lost my heart to a mortal woman and have promised to have no other."

"I should think not!" she said, with an arch look, making him laugh.

"You look so very beautiful, love," he whispered and then stepped back a little as Lord Nibley and his sister joined them.

"Your grace," Nibley said, nodding, though Georgiana thought she detected a cool look in Percy's face that surprised her.

They walked on along the gravelled avenue as the strains of music tangled on the evening air. In every grove, temple and lodge they passed, music was heard and the scent of food and chink of glasses as every variety of refreshment and entertainment was offered and the crowds grew ever livelier. They passed small, brightly coloured tents where gypsies offered to read cards and tell fortunes and the structures of the large Turkish tents glowed with golden light. The music grew louder as they approached the umbrella of the music room, as dancing was the entertainment within, and Georgiana thought her chance of speaking to Sebastian privately was only to be found here.

She gave a little urgent tug on his arm and gestured towards the rotunda. His mouth quirked into a smile and he paused to bow to her with a very formal air.

"Would you do me the honour, Lady Dalton, of dancing with me."

"Why, your Grace, what a charming idea."

With a promise to meet Lord Nibley and Florence at the box he had reserved for supper in a quarter of an hour, Sebastian led her onto the floor.

The enormous and extravagantly painted domed ceiling was hung with a vast chandelier over eleven foot wide, and the noise of music and laughter rose and echoed around them. An infectious atmosphere swept among the dancers who moved with more than usual effervescence, as colourful silks of skirts and cloaks swirled like intoxicated butterflies. For a moment Georgiana allowed herself to be swept along with them in her partner's strong arms, but her uncle's ugly promise could not be banished from her mind for more than a few moments. She looked up to see Sebastian's eyes on hers, his expression troubled.

"We both have much on our minds I see."

She nodded, and gave him a beseeching look. "Oh, Sebastian, I must talk to you alone. I am in so much trouble."

"Trouble?" he repeated, his voice sharp. "How is this?"

His voice was indistinct with the volume of noise around them and she shook her head.

"We can't discuss it here. I can hardly hear myself think."

With skilled ease, he guided them through the throng to the edge of the dancing and led her back out onto the paths.

"We'd best make our way back to Nibley," he said, his voice low. "Neither of us can afford a scandal right now. I've had the very devil of a day, persuading my mother's companion not to go babbling to her family about how ill-used she's been. Not to mention how my mother recently lost her mind and tried to kill her!"

"What?" Georgiana exclaimed. "You're not serious?"

"Deadly serious, love," he replied, his face grim.

"Oh! This is all my fault isn't it?"

He stopped and grasped hold of her hands. "No! Never think it!" He squeezed her fingers, his eyes warm behind the mask. "I have blamed myself for much of her ... illness. But I spoke to her doctor and ... and he explained a great deal that I hadn't understood. Georgiana, none of this is of our making. You were but a babe at the time it began and I'll not allow our futures to become mired in their mistakes."

"B-but she knows ...about us?"

He sighed and placed her hand back on his arm. "I don't know if she does or not, truth be told, Georgiana. She's ... she's lost her mind. She attacked me too, though she thought I was my father. She'd been reading the scandal rags and ... I think it was too much. It brought the past too much to her mind and ..." He shrugged and gave a crooked smile in response to her horrified expression. "Do you think you can really bear it, love? It is such a lot to ask of you, to face the scandal all over again and to be married into such a family."

"Oh, how can you think I would change my mind over such a thing!" she cried, shaking her head. "Only," she paused, hearing her voice tremble as the violent encounter with her uncle came to mind again. "It may be that you ... you'll have to, when I've told you ..."

"Impossible," he replied, interrupting her, the word sure and stern. "Nothing will stand between us, not now. But you'd best tell me and we'll see what's to be done."

The moment was lost, however, as Lord Nibley approached them.

"I saw you wandering off in the wrong direction," he said, his voice light, though he cast Sebastian a very dark look. "So I thought I'd best come and rescue you before you became hopelessly lost. They're about to serve supper, you see."

Georgiana murmured that he was very kind and they followed in his wake back to the private box he'd booked for the evening.

"I'll find a way to speak to you," Sebastian whispered. "I must return to my own guests now but I'll think of something. Until later, love."

She nodded, looking up at him and praying he'd think of something. A whole sleepless night without the comfort of knowing her troubles were shared with him was not something she could face easily.

The meal was pleasant and Lord Nibley and his sister amiable company, but Georgiana's appetite had deserted her. Vauxhall's famous muslin thin ham and a vast array of cheeses and salads were presented and would usually have pleased her greatly. But she could hardly do it justice, though she tried her best to cover her distress. It was a sore trial to have to smile and pretend to be amused when her thoughts were snarled around her wicked uncle and his despicable plans to control or ruin her.

After supper they returned to the paths to wander back to the Chinese Pavilion to await the fireworks. Florence paused for a moment with her brother at one of the stalls to look over some pretty silk fans, but too lost in her own thoughts to stand still, Georgiana continued on, albeit at a slow enough pace that they could catch her up with ease. She was startled then to be approached by a tall, well build man of older years. He was dressed as a Harlequin but the eyes behind the colourful mask were knowing. He had the look of a libertine, once handsome and charming, but now rather jaded and a trifle shabby.

"My Lady Georgina," he said, bowing and giving her a smile that she did not find reassuring in the least.

"I do not know you, Sir," she replied, and made to return to Lord Nibley and his sister but her way was blocked as the man moved to stop her.

"Oh but I know you, my Lady, and I bear you a message from your uncle, the baron."

He raised his hand, and between his finger and thumb he held a lock of red hair. "Just a little reminder for you," he said with a sneer. "And you may be sure, I remember every particular of our *intimate* rendezvous, as I have always been blessed with a remarkable imagination."

Georgiana gasped and took a hurried step backward. "Get away from me, you vile creature."

She was given the benefit of a theatrical bow and the man stepped away. "Until we meet again, Lady Georgina," he said, his voice loud as he melded back into the crowd.

Georgiana stood trembling. Oh God, oh what was she to do? She looked around, alarmed as she felt a cold hand touch her arm. A scruffy looking street boy of perhaps eleven stood staring at her, his brown eyes frank.

"You Lady Georgina?" he demanded, scratching at his thick dirty hair with one hand.

"Y--es," she replied, her tone cautious.

"This is for you then." He thrust a small white card into her hand and ran away before she could ask him anything further.

Her tension left her all at once as she read, *His Grace, The Duke of Sindalton,* embossed on the fine white card. She turned it over to read the words, *my carriage awaits you on Kennington Lane. I will make all good with Nibley. Hurry. S x*

Sparing a last, backwards glance towards Lord Nibley and his sister and hoping Sebastian could find a way that they would forgive her rudeness, she ran down the gravelled path towards Kennington Lane.

Chapter 31

"Wherein desperation plays its hand."

Her relief was overwhelming when she saw the tall figure in the black silk domino and mask. One of the footmen wearing the familiar Sindalton black and gold livery stood by the open door of the carriage and she wasted no time in accepting a black gloved hand to help her in.

Once inside the plush confines of the town carriage she let out a sigh of relief as Sebastian climbed in after her and wasted no time in pulling her into a passionate kiss.

Georgiana melted into him, for although her mind was all at sixes and sevens the chance to be in his arms again was not to be overlooked lightly. Yet as his skilled hands skimmed her sides and pulled her closer, she felt a frisson of unease. His lips were warm and soft, tender and yet passionate but ...

She pulled away from him, looking up into a face all in shadows.

"Sebastian?" she said, not knowing why she had voiced his name as a question, only that something was wrong.

"Come, darling Eve," said a silky and familiar voice. "Surely you can tell the difference between his kiss and mine."

A sudden slant of moonlight lit the carriage and fell upon a pair of glittering blue eyes behind the mask.

"Beau!" His name burst from her in horror as she gave a little shriek of alarm and pushed him away. "What is this?" she demanded.

"This is desperation, my sweet temptress," he replied, a note of apology in his voice. "I'm at *point non-plus* and I've nowhere left to run but France, and I never did learn the blasted language well enough for that."

"You've run mad!" she gasped, reaching over and trying the carriage door and finding it secured. "What ridiculous plan have you formed, you wretch? I demand that you rethink before this goes too far. I'm in the devil of a fix already without you adding to it you ... you black-hearted fiend!"

"Oh, come now, Eve," he said, his voice soothing. "It's not so very black as that. I promise I won't be a cruel husband. You'll need never fear me or think I'd be a tyrant, for I would have you be happy."

"Happy? Good God! Beau, you don't understand. Sebastian has offered for me and I've accepted. If you do this now, he'll never forgive you. Neither will I, come to that!" She raged, as her mind ran in circles, wondering what on earth she could do. She didn't believe Beau would ever hurt her, but as he removed the masquerade mask there was indeed a glint of desperation in those usually cool eyes.

He had stilled at the news of Sebastian's proposal though.

"Well, I've wronged him then. He loves you more than he fears his mother's death or madness. I'm surprised, I'll admit. But it changes nothing," he replied, dashing all the hopes that Georgiana had clung to as he'd begun to speak.

"It changes everything!" she cried, begging him to understand. "Beau, he's your best friend, and I love him - with all my heart. I will only make you miserable if we marry, for I will hate you for this until the day I die."

Beau sat back against the plush interior of what she assumed must be his carriage. The door had been opened ready as she approached and so she had never noticed that the door bore the crest of the Marquis of Beaumont, not the Duke of Sindalton. She assumed the acquisition of a footman's uniform was hardly beyond his scheming either.

"You won't hate me, Eve," he said, his voice bleak. "Oh, I've no doubt you'll despise me for a good while, and perhaps you'll never love me. But your heart is too kind and too open for so black an emotion. Hatred takes a deal of energy and the single-minded kind of devotion that takes more devilry than this to nurture for any length of time. Believe me, I know. You don't have it in you. You'll grow used to me in time, and I promise you I'll do my best to make it sooner. I can be very charming you see, when I put my mind to the task."

"He'll kill you," she said, her voice now trembling with rage, but Beau just shook his head again, his long fingers untying the deceptive black and scarlet domino as he cast the silky material aside. "What and throw you headlong into another scandal. I think not."

"He'll certainly never forgive you!" she shouted, thumping the thick carriage cushions in fury. "How can you, Beau? He's your friend!"

He gave a bitter laugh and fixed her with his blue eyes. "He was my friend. Until he attacked me at White's. I knew then things had gone too far. He wanted to kill me then, sure enough. But I'd told him my intentions. I'd been clear from the outset and he'd not had the balls to make his move. Too caught up in the sorrows and shame of people long dead to move forward and take what he wanted. To do what *you* needed him to!" he returned, his voice equally angry now. "Well I'm done playing fair. It's this or I run. I know now I'd never live long enough to see the inside of the Marshalsea even if I chose to bear the shame of it, and I've never run from anything in my life. I don't intend to start now."

"How much do you owe?" she said suddenly. "What amount would clear your debts?"

"Twenty thousand pounds," he replied without flinching. "A pretty penny, don't you think? Enough that five very unpleasant fellows bundled me into a back alley yesterday and held a knife to my throat. They made themselves very clear, I assure you. I could pay up within the next fourteen days or I could die."

"Oh, Beau!" she exclaimed, moved to pity him despite the situation. "I'll give you the money. Stop this nonsense now. Take me back to Vauxhall and I'll never breathe a word of this to Sebastian. I swear he'll never know. I'll get the money to you."

Beau laughed and shook his head. "You don't get control of the money until you marry, love."

"But I'm under age!" she shouted, suddenly aware that she held a trump card. "You need my uncle's permission, and bearing in mind he's blackmailing me into marrying his brother-in-law, I doubt he'd agree!"

"What's this?" he demanded, sitting up straighter.

"I'm under age ..." she repeated.

"Not that!" he exclaimed, waving the words away as if they were of no consequence whatsoever. "You said he's blackmailing you?"

She nodded and her hand crept to her throat, an involuntary gesture that obviously betrayed her fear as the next moment, Beau was close beside her again and had taken her hand.

"Georgiana, love," he said, his voice suddenly full of concern. "What did the bastard do? Tell me."

She blinked away tears, the drama and the fear of the past day was becoming exhausting, her head ached and she wanted to wish it all away, but that wasn't going to happen. "Baron Dalton, my uncle and my guardian. He wants control of my money and to keep the home he's made his own. The home that I will inherit when I come of age, or I marry."

"So he wants you to marry a man who's under his sway?" he replied, his voice dark with anger.

"Yes." She nodded. "And yesterday he came to the house and Falmouth was gone and the servants were all occupied. I was alone and ..." to her horror she found tears springing to her eyes and covered her mouth with her hands.

"Oh, Georgiana. Love, I'm so sorry." He tried to pull her to him but she pushed him away, angry all over again.

"Well, you're not helping!" she snapped. "He's going to ruin me unless I do as he says. He attacked me and cut my hair and he's given a piece of it to every libertine he can share it with to spread the story that I'm a slut. And you know people will believe it because of the dreadful scandal of my mother and ... Oh!" she shouted, by now thoroughly enraged. "And I was going to tell Sebastian and now you've ruined everything."

Beau snorted. "I assure you I'd have more luck in dealing with this than Sebastian. He's too thoroughly decent to know the kind of people who could end a situation like this, given the right encouragement of course."

She sniffed and looked up at him. "You think you could?"

He nodded, smiling at her. "I know I could. If I had the funds to finance such a scheme."

Georgiana cursed and shook her head. They were back to square one. Unless ... "Sebastian would give you the money you owe, you know he would."

"I'd rather die."

His voice was harsh, and when she looked up she saw his face was troubled, beyond anything she had seen before.

"This isn't just about the money is it, Beau?"

He stared out of the window, not looking at her, and not answering. She took a deep breath.

"You're alone."

He shrugged, a negligent gesture that betrayed the fact that it was anything but. "I've always been alone. Nothing new there."

"You had Sebastian before. Before this began."

"Yes," he agreed, turning to face her. "He's the only one who ever saw past the façade. The only one who realised it *was* a façade. I hadn't even realised it myself," he said softly. "But he made me see I wasn't irredeemable. I even believed him for a while."

"Beau, you're not irredeemable. I can see that."

He laughed and shook his head. "Nice try, sweet Eve. But you're right. I'm tired of being alone and Sebastian will never forgive me. But we are friends, you and I, and you *will* forgive me, in time."

Georgiana swallowed, she felt really afraid now. There was a determined note to his voice. He wasn't going to change his mind.

"Where are you taking me?"

"Where do you think?" he asked, one eyebrow raised. "Not very original I'm afraid, but needs must when the devil drives."

"Good God," she replied in disgust. "An anvil wedding at Gretna Green. Of all the clichés to endure."

He laughed at her indignation. "I know, Eve, I feel it just as you do. But I promise the wedding night will make up for it."

"I'll kill you first," she hissed at him, but his eyes just glittered with amusement.

"We'll see," he replied, so obviously amused that she wanted to strike him.

"But surely we can't go all the way to Gretna like this," she replied, realising that there had been no valises or anything that might be required for such a long journey.

"We'll stop off at Ware. I have arranged another carriage to await us there with such supplies as we'll require."

"Ware?" she repeated, as the name sounded familiar. "In Hertfordshire? But that's your father's seat! You'd dare?"

Beau laughed, his tone mocking. "My darling girl, it's the least of the dark deeds that have been witnessed under that roof, I assure you. Besides, I happen to know my esteemed father is in Brighton for the next six weeks and he'll have shut the house up and taken most of the staff with him. So you see, you need not fear meeting your dastardly father-in-law. I'm afraid he's far blacker at heart than you could ever accuse me of being, so if you were hoping for a heroic saviour you're far off the mark. This might actually be the one time in my life I do something that pleases him."

There was such bitterness and disgust in his tone Georgiana didn't have to puzzle any longer over who it was that he had hated for such a long time. Despite everything Beau was right, he was hard to hate. But if he found a way to force her to marry him, she'd give it a damned good try.

"I'll not do it," she said, her voice quiet but determined. "You can take me to Gretna and stand me before the blasted anvil, but I won't say yes."

"Yes, you will," he replied, sounding weary and just as revolted as she felt. He turned and stared at her, those bright blue eyes glinting with sorrow in the moonlight. "You'll have to, love. For what choice will you have? You'll be beyond Sindalton's reach. Even if he would bear the damage to his own name, I doubt you'd let him ruin himself and any offspring you may have. You're too noble and brave a creature to do that to someone you love. So you see ... I'll be your only option."

Chapter 32

"Wherein our hero discovers a betrayal."

Sebastian strode up to Lord Nibley to find the man white-faced against his ridiculous costume.

"Where is Lady Dalton?" he demanded.

"How the devil should I know?" Nibley threw back at him with surprising violence in his voice. "The last I saw she was stepping into your carriage, you rogue."

"What?" Sebastian exclaimed, too alarmed to refute the accusation.

"I never thought you, of all people, would treat a lady so!"

"Nibley, talk sense man! If I'd taken her somewhere what the devil would I be doing here, demanding where she was?"

Nibley paused and took a breath, giving Sindalton a hard look. "You swear you've not seen her since before supper?" he demanded.

"Upon my honour!" he raged, grasping Nibley by the arm and barely restraining himself from the need to shake him. "Where is she?"

"I don't know, but there's some havey-cavey business going on here and no mistake," he replied, his voice dark with foreboding.

"You said she got into my carriage?"

The tall man nodded, his brow furrowed as he remembered. "Yes, not more than a half hour ago. I thought it was damned odd, but she didn't look to be being forced away. There was a footman in your livery and the man beside her had your build," he said, staring at Sebastian as though he doubted he was being entirely honest.

"And he was wearing that black domino mask - though the hood was up," he added, as an afterthought.

Sebastian clenched his fists and cursed. "She was desperate to speak to me," he said in a low voice, knowing he could depend on Nibley's discretion. "She said she was in trouble."

Nibley frowned harder and nodded. "She wasn't herself tonight, I could tell. I admit I assumed ..." He sighed and looked directly at Sebastian. "I assumed she'd decided not to accept my offer and was wondering how to let me down gently."

Sebastian paused, knowing this was hardly the time but he owed the man the truth. "I've offered for her too, Percy."

Nibley gave him a crooked smile. "Ah," he said, nodding. "Well I can't pretend I'm not sorry on my own account but ... well, I'm glad you've come up to scratch at last. It was clear she was in love with you."

Nibley held out his hand and Sebastian shook it warmly, but his face was grave. "But I don't think that was what was troubling her, Percy. I think it was something very serious, and if you believed she was stepping into my carriage, then there is every chance that she believed it too."

"Good heavens!" Nibley exclaimed, and then lowered his voice, drawing Sebastian further away from the crowds. "You mean you think she's been kidnapped, but who on earth ..."

"Wait," Sebastian said as a cold feeling ran through his blood. "You said the man was built like me but his hood was up ... to cover his hair."

"Yes, that's right but ..." Nibley's words ground to a halt as his eyes widened.

"Beau!" they said together.

They took off running as Sebastian headed for his carriage.

"I'll go to his place in town," Nibley shouted. "I've left my sister with friends so she'll be taken home. If he's not there I'll go and shake up Falmouth, he seems to know every cut-throat in London from what I hear. He'll have a trick or two to play I'm sure. What about you?"

"He'll head for Gretna," Sebastian said, hollering to his coachman to get moving as they approached. "But he might change at Ware and I may at least get news from his servants."

They both went their separate ways and Sebastian promised himself the pleasure of beating Beau's pretty face black and blue when he got his hands on him.

***

Georgiana could see little of the outside of the vast building that was the seat of the Duke of Ware. It appeared to be a sprawling Tudor mansion and looked very ancient and rather terrifying as the moon slid behind a cloud and plunged them into darkness. She hoped it was less frightening inside, but when she set foot over the threshold, she found it cold and stark and extremely unwelcoming. There was an uncomfortable air about the place and she could well believe Beau's claims that dark deeds had been enacted under this roof. There had been no staff to greet them, save the scandalised looking housekeeper who had peered around the door, taken one look at her and Beau and slammed the door again, something which had made Beau laugh.

Though fanciful, she imagined there to be malevolence forged into the very fabric of the walls. It made her shiver as rows of dark-eyed ancestors glared down at her. She pulled her white silk cloak closer around her and shivered. The costume she wore suddenly felt stupid and frivolous and certainly not warm enough to withstand the chill that seemed to be creeping into her bones.

"Lovely, isn't it?" Beau chuckled, his voice echoing across the cavernous space as he made an expansive gesture around him. "Home sweet home," he said, his tone clearly mocking. "And all my kith and kin here to welcome us, lovely Eve." He stared up at the gilt-framed paintings, his blue eyes almost feverish with loathing. "Half of them were mad, the other half murdering bastards. We come from a long line of wicked lunatics. So you see, I didn't turn out so very badly. I've not actually killed anyone yet." He paused, his eyes taking on a darker look that made her skin prickle. "Not intentionally anyway," he murmured.

He led her up the stairs to a large bedroom where she hesitated outside the open door.

"Don't fret, love," he said, and she was relieved to see the glitter had fallen away from his eyes and he was in control of himself again. "I'll not lay a hand on you before we're married. Go on, you'll find a change of clothes in there. I think I guessed right," he added with a smirk.

She walked in and then gasped, struck by a painting of a beautiful blond woman. She was a more fragile, feminine version of the blue eyed man beside her, but the likeness was marked and unmistakable.

"Your mother?" she asked, unsurprised when he nodded. "She was very lovely."

He shrugged, frowning, but she noticed he didn't look up at the painting, but turned away from it. "If the painting is anything to go on, certainly. I wouldn't know." She looked back at him, waiting for an explanation. "She died having me," he said, and then walked to the door. "Don't dawdle, Eve, we need to make haste." Pausing, he grasped the handle before he fully closed the door. "And don't think to take too long, for I'm not beyond carrying you out in your chemise if I have to."

The door closed and she was left alone. She ran to the windows but the countryside was dark and expansive and there was no obvious escape route. Besides, the grand house had appeared to be miles from the village and she had lost any sense of which direction it was in.

Changing out of this ridiculous outfit had to be her priority and with relief she saw that the items Beau had provided were perfectly respectable. A pretty, white carriage dress with a small green motif, and admittedly more décolletage showing than she was comfortable with in the circumstances, were hastily pulled on. It was awkward without an abigail to help her with the fastenings, but she would have rather cut her tongue out than ask him for help.

She felt a little less furious over the low cut gown when she found the matching green silk spencer, trimmed with dark green satin and a cashmere shawl. The spencer was hastily buttoned to her neck and she pulled the shawl about her shoulders with relief. It had been a warm evening for May, but now she felt chilled to the very marrow of her bones. Her mind spun as her trembling fingers fumbled with the laces on the satin half boots he'd provided. Sebastian must know by now that something had happened to her. She'd told him she was in trouble and he knew she desperately wanted to speak to him alone. One blessing was that he didn't yet know about the baron's threats so there was only one likely reason for her disappearance.

Two, she thought with a sinking heart. What if he thought she'd gone willingly? The idea made her nauseated. No. Surely he knew how she felt about him. After everything that had been said ... She took a deep breath. No, he trusted her now, and she trusted him. They'd endured too many false starts and revelations, she wouldn't lose faith now. He'd come after her, she was sure of it. Which meant she had to try and delay Beau for as long as possible.

She looked up at the painting of his mother. There was a terrible sadness in the woman's eyes, and as she looked again she realised she was little more than a girl in the painting. She gave a little scream of surprise as the door opened and Beau strode in.

"You could knock," she said, glaring at him.

He grinned at her, unabashed. "Oh, come now, Eve. I knew you'd heed my threat. If I'd wanted to see you in your chemise that desperately I'd have insisted on staying here whilst you changed."

"Oh, you odious creature!" she exclaimed. Taking a breath she tried to set aside her anger. She doubted losing her temper would get her anywhere. She had to think how to deal with him. Beau wasn't a cruel man. She knew he hated seeing the weak taken advantage of. He'd shown that clearly enough when he'd cared for Miss Sparrow. Lowering her voice, the words were beseeching. "Beau, how can you treat me so? You said yourself we were friends. How can you make me so unhappy?"

He had glanced up at the painting of his mother and when he turned back to speak, he hurriedly averted his eyes. She wondered how often he'd looked at it. There was an expression on his face that made her believe it wasn't often.

"Perhaps it's in my blood," he said, his voice dark and angrier than she'd ever heard it. She swallowed a sudden tremor of fear.

"What do you mean by that?"

"Nothing," he said, sullen all at once. "Come on, we should go ..."

Panic rose in her chest. No, no. She needed to give Sebastian more time. "She was very young, when this was painted," she said, hoping her bid to delay wasn't too obvious. But once more his unwilling eyes seemed to be dragged back to his mother's.

"That was after my father had abducted and raped her," he said, his voice cold and emotionless. "She didn't want to marry him. Didn't want him at all. So he took her." He turned and stared at Georgiana and she felt her blood run cold. "He forced himself upon a girl barely out of the school room and you see the result of that happy union standing before you. Bearing in mind she died in childbed I think the pitiful look in her eyes is rather well captured. Don't you?"

"Oh, my God, Beau," she whispered. "I'm so very sorry."

"Not as sorry as she was, I'd wager." His tone was light, as though he was discussing a far different topic, of little consequence.

But Georgiana didn't believe his nonchalance was anything of the sort.

"She would have loved you, Beau. If she'd been given the chance."

"Good God, Georgiana!" he exploded, making her take an involuntary step backwards. "Don't turn me into some tortured hero when I'm nothing of the sort. I'm in debt and I've already burnt my boats with Sindalton. You're the only hope I have of getting out of this without getting my throat cut and my body thrown in the Thames." He advanced on her, anger glinting in the blue of his eyes. "I'm not a rapist, love," he said, as he grabbed hold of her wrists and pinned her to the wall. Georgiana felt her breathing catch, her chest heaving as her heart thundered behind her ribs. "I'll not follow my father's footsteps that close I swear it. I would never take you by force, you have my word on that. But you *will* have me."

He backed off abruptly, but kept hold of one wrist, pulling her behind him and out along the landing. "Now stop this pathetic bid to delay us and get down to the carriage."

"No!"

He was standing at the top of the stairs and with her free hand Georgiana shoved him hard and pulled on the wrist he held. He cursed and stumbled down the first two steps before righting himself but lost a hold on her in the process. With a gasp, Georgiana stepped a little away from him, her eyes glancing around the dark wood panelled walls for escape, and then picked up her skirts and ran.

She hadn't the faintest notion of where she was going but even if she locked herself in a room, it would take some considerable time to get to her. The thin soles of her satin boots slipped on the parquet as she heard his heavier footfalls close behind her. With a shriek she dived down a dark corridor. A small oak console table sat against the wall at the end of it and she spared a second to stop and tip it over. She heard the crash of china as whatever sat on it shattered and then ran as Beau's curses echoed around the eerie gloom of the mansion. A small spiral stone staircase appeared, barely lit by a glimmer of moonlight through the tiny lattice panes of a window and she flew down them two at a time. Misjudging the final steps as the stairs took an erratic turn to the right at the bottom, she stumbled and fell hard on her knees on the cold stone floor.

"Georgiana, stop this ridiculous charade!" Beau, yelled from behind her as she yelped and scrambled to her feet. Flinging herself forward into the pitch black she ran down another wider corridor, once more the walls were panelled and lined with doors. Choosing one at random she yanked it open, slamming it behind her and praying there was a lock. The huge iron key turned with a shriek of complaint, but turn it did and she stepped away, panting as Beau hammered on the heavy oak door.

"Open the damn door, Georgiana!"

"No," she said, gasping for breath. "Sebastian will come for me, you know he will, Beau. I'm staying right here."

He fell silent and she strained to listen for him, as all she could hear was her own heart thudding and blood rushing in her ears.

"So you'd see me dead then." His voice was bleak and despite everything she felt desperately sorry for him. He seemed terribly alone.

"Of course I wouldn't!" she shouted, exasperated. "I would help you; Sebastian would help you. I know he would."

There was a snort of amusement. "Sebastian will kill me himself," he replied through the door. "Still, better to die at the hands of a furious lover, than an ignominious murder in a back alley for something as sordid as unpaid debts."

"Oh, God, Beau!" She slammed her hand against the door in frustration. "You must let us pay the debts for you."

"No."

"You can pay us back!" she yelled, beyond furious now. "We'll even charge you interest if it will make you feel better."

"Oh, much," he replied, his tone ironic. "And bearing in mind my father is as hale and hearty now as a man half his age, by the time your children have grown I'll be so utterly beholden to you that you'll own the shirt on my back!" he shouted. "I'll put a gun to my own head before that happens, love."

He fell silent again and she hoped he had given up on this outrageous scheme to carry her to Gretna. Leaning against the door she put her ear to the wood and listened, but heard nothing, until a floorboard creaked close behind her.

She screamed as she realised someone was in the room with her.

"Oh good, God, you frightened me," she exclaimed, seeing him standing half way across the room and holding her hand over her still thudding heart.

He laughed, though not unkindly. "I'm not surprised. This part of the house is very old, and very haunted. The family was Roman Catholic, back before we ... lapsed," he said with a smirk. "The place is riddled with secret passages and priest holes. We were a fanatical lot back then, went to a lot of trouble to hide people from the priest-hunters during the reformation."

"How long has your family been here?" Her voice quavered as she backed away from his approach.

He chuckled, knowing well that she was stalling him. He took her hand, though he was gentler this time, and unlocked the door, meeting her eyes with meaning.

"This was built in the early sixteenth century, but we've been here a deal longer than that. One of the oldest families in England," he said, but she heard that now familiar mocking tone again instead of pride in the fact. If Sebastian spoke about his father there was such fierce pride in his eyes. All she could see in Beau's was disgust. "Perhaps it's time we died out," he added, turning and grinning at her.

"Don't say that, Beau," she pleaded, tightening her hand on his.

"Why not? Sebastian will be here soon, I've no doubt. The timing was always going to be my undoing, but I had so little time to prepare, you see." He drew her down yet another corridor and she wondered at his ability to find his way in the dark. "It's my first abduction, so you'll have to forgive me," he added.

"Oh, stop it, Beau!" she cried, wishing with all her heart there was something she could do to untangle the mess they were in.

"Hush, Georgiana," he said, turning back to smile at her. "You've played your part well, love," he added, his voice full of admiration. She paused, tugging at his hand.

"Let me speak to him, let me explain ..."

He laughed and shook his head. "Sweet, lovely, Eve. You are such a temptation. But no. I've been villain enough for one night. I'll not compound it by hiding behind your skirts."

They both turned to the window as the sound of horses moving fast over gravel came to their ears. In the glimmer of moonlight that glinted behind a thin grey cloud, a carriage and four grey horses could be seen, thundering towards the house.

"And here comes our hero," he said softly. "Right on time."

Chapter 33

"Wherein the past catches up."

Sebastian wasn't sure if it was simply relief he felt as he saw Beau's carriage and horses, loaded and ready for a long journey. That she really was here and he'd found her in time was his first concern and the overwhelming relief that he could stop them marrying was beyond anything. But Beau had betrayed him so utterly ... Anger, cold and dark and ugly spread through his veins. He reached down and grabbed hold of the coachman's pistol, always kept close by in case of highwaymen. There was no need to check it was loaded and primed. His staff would never overlook such a consideration. The gun felt heavy and cold and reassuring in his grasp as he leapt down from the carriage and ran towards the doors of the glowering mansion.

It was strange to think, in all his years of friendship with Beau, he'd never been here before. He knew Beau hated the place, and in truth it surprised him that he'd come here at all. It was only a gut feeling that made him think it likely. He could never be more thankful that he'd been right.

Slamming through the heavy oak doors of the entrance with a crash, he stilled and tightened his grip on the gun as Beau appeared, his hand wrapped around Georgiana's wrist.

"Well, what a surprise," his friend exclaimed, sounding jovial and relaxed, though there was a febrile glint in his eyes that betrayed him. "Have you come to felicitate us on our impending nuptials, Sindalton?"

"Let her go," Sebastian shouted in fury, as he fully locked the hammer on the pistol and raised it, levelling it at his friend.

Beau dropped Georgiana's hand but to his surprise she exclaimed and ran to stand in front of him.

"No! Sebastian, don't! You'd never forgive yourself." He watched in fury as Beau gave her a hard shove, sending her stumbling forward, almost losing her footing.

"Bastard!" he shouted, relieved to see Georgiana catch her balance but never taking his eyes off Beau as he stepped closer. His friend just laughed at him.

"I knew I shouldn't have dallied," he said, his eyes mocking. "But she was so very sweet, so very innocent ... I just had to have a taste ..."

He didn't think about it, didn't have time as rage, pure and cold and furious swept over him and his finger squeezed the trigger.

"No!" Georgiana screamed and the sound of the gun firing rang in his head. It magnified in the cavernous space and echoed around the gloomy walls of the old house as the judging eyes of generations of Ware's glared down at him. He took a breath, aware that Georgiana had pushed him, but before or after he'd fired? Suddenly praying he'd missed he held his breath. But Beau staggered backwards and crumpled to the floor.

"No!" Georgiana screamed, running towards his fallen friend. "My God, Sebastian, what have you done?"

"He hurt you!" he raged, too frozen to take a step closer and see what exactly he had done.

"He didn't!" she cried, falling beside Beau, her face white with horror. "He never touched me, Sebastian. He wanted to provoke you into killing him!"

"Oh God."

Sebastian dropped the gun, numb with shock and abhorrence. He'd relived the past, just as his mother had predicted. But his actions were worse than his father's ... he'd killed an unarmed man, his closest friend, and now the scandal sheets would lay it all at Georgiana's feet, just as they'd condemned her mother.

"He's not dead!" Georgiana exclaimed. "But we need a doctor. He's bleeding badly."

They both looked up at a commotion at the front door as Falmouth, Lord Nibley and the most ill-assorted looking bunch of men Sebastian had ever laid eyes on filed into the hall.

"Damn it, Sindalton!" Falmouth said in disgust, striding over to inspect the bleeding figure on the floor. "What the devil have you done?" He turned to a giant of a man who looked just like an image of a cut-throat in a favourite book about pirates Sebastian had treasured as a boy. "Mousy, fetch the doctor," he ordered. "Thank God we stopped to pick him up."

Sebastian steeled himself and walked over to look down at Beau who was white faced, his breathing harsh.

"You always were a wretched shot, Sin," he rasped and then bit his lip as Falmouth tore his shirt open. The wound was high in his shoulder and bleeding profusely.

"You bastard," Sebastian said, his voice quiet. "How could you do it, Beau? You knew I loved her."

Beau just stared back at him. "I'd burnt my last boat," he said with a twisted smile, adding only, "You should have killed me." Before turning his head away.

With relief Sebastian saw that the doctor was none other than Alperton. At least they could rely on him to keep his mouth shut. Georgiana moved from Beau's side to let the doctor get to him, and after a moment's hesitation, ran into his arms, sobbing.

"Oh, Sebastian, whatever are we to do?"

He drew his arms around her, holding her tight. "I don't know, love. I ..." he began and then stopped, clutching her tightly. "God forgive me but I wanted him dead. If he had taken you from me ..."

Georgiana clung to him, shaking her head. "I'm here. I'll never be anywhere else, but I don't want him to die. Sebastian, he was desperate." She looked up at him, her lovely face stained with tears. "The men he owes money to, they'll kill him. That's why he said he'd ..." She stopped and swallowed, clutching at his waistcoat. "He said he'd rather you killed him than ..."

He held her as she sobbed against his chest. Their attention was taken, though, by the men lifting Beau and taking him upstairs. Alperton turned and came to them, his face grave.

"Will he live?" Sebastian asked, feeling as though his voice came from a great distance away.

The doctor nodded. "For now, certainly. The wound of itself is not serious. It's missed bone and organs, but it's the infection that may follow that will be the devil of it. I swear to you I'll do my best though, your Grace."

"Please," Sebastian said. "Please do everything."

Alperton grasped his arm and squeezed. "I'll do everything I can to keep him alive and you out of another scandal."

Sebastian nodded, too exhausted to explain it wasn't only the scandal he feared. Beau had been like the brother he'd never had. He knew he could never forgive him for what he'd done in taking Georgiana, but the idea that he might be responsible for killing him pulled at his heart.

"Come." Falmouth strode over to them and steered them into a room that proved to be a library. Somehow the earl had taken over and a fire had been lit and he forced a glass of brandy into each their hands.

"We need to get you both back to London," he said as Lord Nibley entered the room, looking as ashen faced as Sebastian felt. "Nibley here will swear you were both in his company all evening if it comes to it. The doctor has also agreed that ... if the worst happens, Beau contracted an illness of some description and it aggravated a heart condition no one knew about. There will be *no* scandal. Do you hear?"

"Oh, God," Sebastian said, rubbing his hand over his face. "I pray it doesn't come to that."

"Don't we all," Falmouth snapped. "You've plunged us all into the deuce of a tangle, Sindalton!"

It was too much. Sebastian threw his glass at the wall and lunged at the earl, shoving him hard against the wall. "He abducted her, Falmouth. He was going to force her to marry him!" he yelled. "I wanted the bastard dead! What would you have done, if it had been Céleste?"

To his credit the earl didn't so much as flinch and waved away the men who came bursting through the door as Georgiana exclaimed in horror.

"I wouldn't have missed," the earl said with a grim smile, breaking the tension. Sebastian snorted and let out a breath before allowing his hands to fall from Falmouth's neck.

The earl readjusted his cravat and sent his men out of the room again.

"I do understand," he added, giving Sebastian another glass and a sympathetic look. "More than you might imagine."

"That's not all though," Georgiana said, her voice little more than a whisper.

The three men turned around to look at her. Her arms were clutched around her shivering frame, the elegant white muslin dress stained red with Beau's blood. She looked over at Sebastian, her pretty eyes so full of fear that he hated himself for having dragged her into this mess. He crossed the floor and took her hands, steering her to sit down beside the fire.

"I-I told you I was in trouble," she said, looking wretched as tears ran down her face.

"It wasn't Beau threatening you?" he demanded, wondering what the hell else could stand between them. Hadn't the fates had enough? Did every generation of their family have to suffer for their parent's unhappy marriages?

She shook her head. "Beau would never have hurt me, Sebastian, you know that. B-but my uncle, he would. He did."

"What?"

With horror they listened as she revealed in a halting voice her terrifying encounter with the baron.

"I'll kill him," Sebastian raged. "How dare he lay his hands on you, the bastard!"

"No," Falmouth said, his eyes dark. "You'll not kill him. We've already got the possibility of one body to account for. I'll not willingly add another."

"Then you think we should let him get away with it?" Sebastian demanded. His fists clenched with impotent fury. What in the name of God did he have to do to keep this woman safe?

"Of course not, and you will be free to beat him to a pulp I assure you. Just don't kill him," Falmouth said with a touch of impatience. "But you're right about one thing, Sindalton. I think it's time we paid the baron a little visit."

"Sebastian!" He looked around to see Georgiana looking terrified and wide-eyed with shock. "He's my guardian, we can't marry without his consent."

"Oh don't worry, love," he said with a grim smile. "He'll give his consent."

The moonlit journey back to London was long and relieved only by the fact of having Georgiana safe in his arms. She was quiet and still, too shocked to sleep, and too weary to do anything but gaze out of the window at the silvered landscape with eyes that saw nothing at all.

If she was seeing anything he suspected the scene was the same as he was replaying: That dreadful moment when the gun had fired and his childhood friend had staggered back as the bullet drove into his flesh. Sebastian screwed his eyes shut and pinched the bridge of his nose. He didn't want Beau dead, though he hated him for what he'd done. But he knew too, if he stood there again in that moment, he'd do exactly the same thing.

Chapter 34

"Wherein revenge is served with cool satisfaction."

They returned Lord Nibley home and then Georgiana, with as little noise and attention as was possible. Céleste had sent all the servants to bed as she'd been told to and took Georgiana up to bed herself, nodding at her husband's instruction to burn the bloody clothes she wore without so much as a blink.

Sindalton climbed back into the carriage with Falmouth after promising Georgiana that he would come to no harm and would call on her as soon as he was able.

He faced Falmouth across the carriage and wondered how it had come to pass that in the same night he'd shot his best friend, he found himself allied with a man who considered him an enemy.

"I've never had the chance to apologise," he said, his voice uncomfortably loud in the confines of the dark carriage. Falmouth's cold grey eyes glinted, his face devoid of emotion. "For what happened with ..."

"When you sent my ex-mistress to my house to cause a scene and the woman I loved to flee, you mean?" the earl said with a smile that looked like he wanted to rip his throat out, with his teeth.

Sebastian cleared his throat. "Yes. For that."

"Then please do."

God he was a cold bastard, Sebastian thought, though not without a grudging admiration.

"I thought you were using her," he admitted. "I had no idea you were offering marriage. Your reputation was not the kind that made the thought enter my head."

He saw something in the man's posture shift a little, the taut line of his jaw perhaps a little less rigid.

"I'd never been in love before," he said, his tone gruff.

Sebastian laughed, nodding. "I know just what you mean ... with Georgiana!" he added, seeing the murderous glint return to the earl's expression. "Anyway, I am sorry for it. I had no idea of the mischief the woman would cause, but she clearly had her own agenda."

Falmouth grunted. "That she did," he replied, his tone dry as he stretched his long legs out in the confines of the carriage.

They were quiet for a moment, the rumble of the carriage through the dark streets of the capital the only sound.

"Thank you," Sebastian said, needing to make him understand that he was only too aware how deeply he stood in the man's debt. "For tonight, and for everything you did in ... in giving Georgiana her come out. She's told me how very kind and generous you've been."

"I only did it to annoy you," Falmouth replied, and this time the smile was genuine.

Sebastian laughed. "Well that I do believe." He frowned, suddenly more than curious about the enigmatic earl. His reputation was that of a dark and violent character, and judging from the motley crew that had turned up with him tonight, Sebastian was only too willing to believe it. "Who are those men?" he demanded. "And why does the word *pirate* spring to mind whenever I look at them?"

The earl just gave him an inscrutable smile and shrugged. "I have no idea what you mean, your Grace."

***

The Baron Dalton's town residence was an elegant, stuccoed house on Upper Wimpole Street. Whilst not an address of the *haut ton,* it was home to the wealthiest on the fringes of that exclusive world, and the nouveau riche. The carriage took them some way past the house, stopping quietly and moving swiftly on as Sebastian, the earl and those of his men who had ridden on the outside, jumped down.

Another carriage, some distance farther back, also disgorged a number of rather terrifying looking occupants who, at a gesture from the earl, disappeared to the rear of the house.

Moving quickly and with surprising stealth, the earl motioned for Mousy, the unlikely name of the largest man Sebastian had ever seen in his life, to go to the front door. This the big man did and crouched down, with some small iron pins in his hand. To Sebastian's surprise the front door sprang open, without the faintest sign of protest, and he and Falmouth stepped inside with Mousy and two other armed men at their backs. There was a quiet scuffling sound from below stairs which was quickly subdued, and then a large, barrel-shaped man stuck his tattooed arm around the door signalling them to enter with a rather devilish grin.

"Well done, Harry," Falmouth said, nodding his approval. The men spread out, opening doors and checking the downstairs rooms were empty before they made their way up the stairs.

They halted behind a door, the only one of which showed a glimmer of light at the threshold.

"We've dealt with 'is missus," Mousy whispered as he came striding out of one of the other rooms and then gave Sebastian a reproachful look at his horrified expression. "Keep yer 'air on, yer grace, we didn't ruffle 'er none. Just tied her up and tol' 'er to keep mum, is all."

From this Sebastian deduced with some difficulty that the woman was alive but restrained and gagged, and he turned back to the baron's door.

"After you," Falmouth said, with a polite gesture.

Sebastian snorted and went to move forward but the earl's arm checked him. "Don't kill the bastard," he warned. "I quite sympathise, but London will be waking soon and it's a bloody difficult time to dispose of a baron."

Sebastian opened his mouth to demand how he knew that and then closed it abruptly. He didn't want to know.

The baron sat up in bed with a start as Sebastian strode through into his bedroom.

"What the devil is the meaning of this?" he barked, his face reddening with fury as the Duke of Sindalton and the Earl of Falmouth sidled into the room as if they owned the place.

Sebastian lost no time in grabbing the man by his night shirt and hauling him to his feet. He pushed him into the room a little and the baron stumbled back, looking around at the two men with growing rage. "My God, I'll have your heads for this!" he shouted. Sebastian didn't wait to hear more but drew back his fist and punched the man full in the face. There was a rather satisfying crunch as the man's nose broke and a howl of rage as he went down.

"That was for laying your filthy hands on Lady Georgina, you bastard," he growled and hauled the man to his feet to repeat the process. The baron slammed back against the wall, blood pouring from his nose.

"Don't think your titles will protect you," he spluttered, the words somewhat distorted through the blood. "I'm a powerful man ... I have friends ..."

Falmouth took an exaggerated look around the room. "Where?" he demanded, one black eyebrow raised. "I see no friends, do you, your Grace?"

Sebastian put his hand to the baron's throat and began to squeeze as the man clawed at his wrist. "I don't see a soul, Falmouth. I think the man must be delirious."

"Probably lack of oxygen," the earl remarked, watching with a placid expression as Sebastian put his mind to throttling the life out of the despicable creature who had terrorised his beloved. "Best put him down now, your Grace," Falmouth said, with obvious amusement. "You don't know where he's been."

With great reluctance, Sebastian let go and watched as the man slid to the floor, the baron's slightly blue-tinged face turning a deep purple with rage and humiliation.

"I-I'll get you ... for ... this ..."

"No," Sebastian replied, his tone even. "You won't. The only reason you're still breathing at all is because Falmouth there thinks disposing of you would be more trouble than you're worth." He crouched down and put his face level with the baron's. "You're a cowardly brute who likes to inflict pain, just because he can. Well, you bastard, now it's our turn, and we mean to have our pound of flesh."

The man blanched, perhaps finally realising the threat for what it was.

"What is it you want?"

Sebastian snorted. "What I want is you dead at my hands, but as that has been denied me," he said, sending a chagrined look at the earl. "Then I'll have to be satisfied with being rid of you."

"I hear America is ... pleasant at this time of the year," Falmouth replied, making a show of inspecting his fingernails.

"You can't make me disappear!" the baron exploded, apoplectic with rage. Falmouth reached out his hand and gave a quiet tap on the door, stepping back as it flew open and the room filled with men. Suddenly silent, the baron looked around with wide eyes at the disreputable looking crew assembled in his elegant bedroom. He stared at Falmouth.

"Who the devil are you, really?" he demanded.

"It's really best you don't know," the earl replied, his eyes cold and hard. "Help him pack Mousy, there's a good fellow."

"Aye, aye, capt'n," the big man said with a nasty grin as the earl left the room.

Sebastian stayed for a moment, staring down at the despised and now terrified creature at his feet.

“What will happen to the good baron if any rumours should begin about Lady Georgina, Mousy?” he asked, never taking his eyes from the baron.

“Oh, don’t you be worrit about that, yer grace,” the big man said, a chuckle rumbling through his big frame. “We’ll explain all about it to ‘im once yer safe away. An also what might ‘appen, should ‘e go gettin’ a fancy to come back to England, I reckon.” He rubbed his hands together, looking more piratical than Sebastian could credit. “Seems the crew o’ The Redemption are on a trip to America, an they’ll ‘ave plenty o’ time to see the baron understands jus what’s in store for ‘im, should that maggot ever enter ‘is brain, like.”

Sebastian laughed and slapped Mousy on the shoulder. “Well then, if I can just find some paper and ink, I have one last little job for the man before he sets off on his travels.”

Chapter 35

"Wherein forgiveness is withheld, but a joyous day begins."

With all the attendant scandal of their pasts, Sebastian rejected the idea of a special licence.

Georgiana had pouted and wheedled, but to no avail.

"Well if you don't want to marry me," she said with a huff, and not for the first time, as they strolled a little behind Céleste and Alex through Hyde Park. It was a glorious day. The spring flowers were out in profusion and everything looked green and fresh in the sunshine.

Sebastian chuckled and covered her hand with his own.

"Only another five days, love," he murmured, looking down at her with warmth in his dark eyes.

"Oh!" Georgiana said wrathfully, as she put up her chin and gave a sniff of disgust. "I don't believe you love me at all, you wretch! How can you sound so nonchalant? Five whole days!" she wailed. "It's an eternity."

He paused then, and drew her as close as was possible considering the very public setting, but the need in his eyes was raw enough and only too visible. "If you think this is easy for me, then you are very, very wrong," he said, his voice low. "I'm going slowly out of my damned mind. But after the scandals we've had to grow up with, we're doing this properly. So that no one can ever point the finger and say there was anything the least bit shady about it." He swallowed and raised her hand to his lips, kissing her fingers with a soft brush of his lips. "But I admit, it's killing me too, love. I can't sleep. I can't think of anything but you."

Georgiana gave a contented little sigh and leaned her head on his shoulder as they walked on. “Well, that’s alright then. Just as long as you’re suffering as much as I am.”

He gave a little bark of laughter. “More, you heartless hussy!”

She chuckled, stopping for a moment to remonstrate with Conrad, who was looking at the ducks on the Serpentine with a considering expression. Chastised, her adventurous hound loped off after Bandit, and Georgiana decided not to wonder about what chaos the two idiotic dogs would bring down on them next.

“Well I think it’s too bad that the Duke of Sindalton can’t get an earlier date for the wedding,” she said, deciding she hadn’t teased him quite enough yet, after all. “I mean, what’s the good in being a duchess if I can’t always have my own way?”

“Oh, it’s like that is it?” Sebastian looked down at her, one eyebrow raised and his haughtiest ducal expression in place. “I’ll have you know that if I wasn’t a duke, you’d have to wait another two months before there was an available space at St George’s! I had no idea the place was so overrun.”

“No, really? I thought you must always get your own way in everything ... I mean, I thought that would explain it at least.” She had the utmost difficulty in looking at his outraged expression and not allowing her lips to twitch.

“Explain what?” he demanded.

“Oh, you know,” she said, waving her hand in an airy fashion and holding back her amusement with difficulty. “Your high-handed manner.” She was unable to tease him further as mirth got the better of her. “Your face,” she exclaimed laughing as he huffed at her. “Oh, dear, you did look affronted.” Leaning into him, she looked up and batted her eyelashes. “I’m sorry, Sebastian, but you are so deliciously easy to tease.”

He narrowed his eyes at her, an expression in them that made her shiver with anticipation. “Indeed, madam? Well just you remember those words on our wedding night.”

She felt the flush rise up over her neck and suffuse her cheeks as her fiancé gave a satisfied chuckle, content that his remark had hit home.

They walked a little farther in companionable silence until Georgiana was brave enough to ask for the information she'd been hoping he'd volunteer.

"Have you had news about Beau?" she asked, knowing it was a sore subject but not wanting it to be something they couldn't discuss.

She saw his face darken. "I had a letter from Alperton, this morning," he admitted. "The fever's broken. He'll be weak for a while but ... he's going to recover."

"Oh thank God," she whispered, closing her eyes as the relief hit her.

Sebastian looked down at her, his eyes troubled. "You care about him." It wasn't a question and Georgiana rolled her eyes at him.

"Of course I do, as do you!" She squeezed his arm and sighed. "He's my friend and I know what he did was despicable and I'm still furious with him for it but ... Oh, Sebastian, he's so very alone and in a deal of trouble."

She could feel the tension singing through his body, the arm she held taut beneath her fingers.

"I tried to help him, but he was too damn proud to take it. No, he must go and steal the woman I love instead!"

Georgiana sighed, knowing it was useless. "I know," she said. "But I can't help but feel sorry for him, and for you. You'll miss him."

Sebastian made no reply, and they continued their walk in silence.

***

Despite Georgiana's protestations the five days did pass, though slowly. The morning of the wedding was bright and sunny, a perfect early summer's day.

Céleste, looking quite stunning in a peach blossom, satin dress with cypress gauze, wiped at her eyes and waved her lace handkerchief in agitation.

"Mon Dieu!" she exclaimed, shaking her head. "Oh you look so very beautiful, Georgiana, but I wish that you did not, for now I'm going to cry and I shall look perfectly dreadful for the wedding."

Georgiana laughed and held out her hands to Céleste who ran up to claim them, lovely blue eyes sparkling with tears.

"Oh, dearest, Georgie," she said, holding one hand to her cheek. "I am so very 'appy for you."

Georgiana beamed, but the lump in her throat seemed too heavy to speak around, so she just nodded and laughed and prayed she wouldn't cry herself.

Madam Lisabeth's design was, in its creator's own words, a masterpiece. The body of the gown was a white satin slip, ornamented at the hem with a flounce of broad lace and surmounted by satin lilies. The stalks of the lilies were contrived in silk cord and disposed in waves around the border. Georgiana smiled as she took in the intricate details and smoothed down the gown of spotted British net that overlaid the satin in an open train that met just below her bust and fell in a gentle curve to the ground.

A delicate wreath of roses and lilies trimmed the slip and one perfect white lily was pinned in her hair against an elegant background of fern leaves. It looked pristine and delightful against her shining red hair. As ever, she had left one long ringlet to trail over her shoulder and if she was well pleased with the effect, she was only echoing the thoughts of her abigail and her dearest friend.

A slightly harassed demand, as it was by far from the first time of asking, came from the landing as Lord Falmouth enquired, "Are you ready *now?"*

"Oui!" Céleste called, and ran to the door, hurrying through it to her husband. "Oh, Alex! Just wait until you see 'er, I fear you shan't look at me again all day."

"Never, *mignonne,"* his Lordship replied with more obvious honesty than gallantry.

Feeling suddenly a little shy and overwhelmed, Georgiana left the room and was gratified by the look of appreciation in Lord Falmouth's usually cool grey eyes.

"Well indeed," he said, smiling at her. "Céleste has the right of it as ever. Georgiana, you *do* look a picture."

"Thank you, my Lord," she said, grinning at him.

"Oh, and just think, in such a short while, she'll be a duchess!"

"Not at this rate she won't!" Falmouth exclaimed with a snort. "Now will you hurry, or Sindalton will think he's been jilted, and much as that might amuse me, it won't him."

"Oh do stop fretting, Alex," Céleste said, taking her husband's arm and allowing him to escort her down the sweeping staircase of his home. "And you know you said you'd quite forgiven 'im and that 'e was really a decent fellow."

"I'm sure I couldn't have said any such thing," Falmouth said, winking at Georgiana over Céleste's head.

"You did and you know it," Céleste insisted, taping his arm with her fan in a scolding manner.

"I must have been foxed," the earl said mildly, and escorted the ladies to his carriage.

***

Sindalton frowned as Lord Nibley enquired if he had remembered everything necessary for the smooth running of the wedding.

"Well, I'm here," he replied with a grin, believing that everything was well in hand for the wedding breakfast, which Lord Falmouth had graciously undertaken to give at his home. Sebastian's mother was still not in her right mind and confined to her own wing of the house. The idea of holding the wedding breakfast under her nose, even if she was unaware of it, had made both him and Georgiana acutely uncomfortable and put them in a quandary. Alex had settled the matter, however, in his usual high-handed way. The wedding breakfast would be held by Lord and Lady Falmouth and no argument would be heard.

"What about the ring?" Percy asked. His friend's eyes rolled as Sebastian felt a jolt of panic and banged on the carriage roof.

"Halt!" he yelled. "Dammit, Percy, you couldn't have remembered that before we left the house?"

Leaping down from the carriage, he sprinted back the short distance to his home on Grosvenor Square, earning himself the disapprobation of some stern looking dowagers in passing.

He took the stairs to his front door two at a time and hurtled through, grinding to a halt as he found a white-faced Beau standing in the entrance hall speaking with his butler. Biddle, aware that his services were suddenly not required, made a tactical withdrawal.

The two men stared at each other in mute shock and Sebastian had to bite back an exclamation of surprise at the sight of his former friend. Beau looked drawn and pale, his usually angelic countenance grey and his eyes heavy. He'd clearly lost a great deal of weight, one arm held securely against his chest with a sling. Sebastian couldn't help but feel a pang of sorrow at seeing him so unlike himself.

"I-I thought you'd gone," Beau said, looking awkward. "I would never have come otherwise."

"Forgot the ring," Sebastian said, his sorrow deepening as he knew that Beau would never have let him do such a thing if he'd been here.

Beau gave a soft laugh and shook his head. "Why doesn't that surprise me." The two men stood together, both only too aware that the closeness of their friendship was dead and gone. "I just came to bring you this. A wedding present," he said with an uneasy smile. "I leave tomorrow but ... well I thought perhaps Georgiana might like it."

He handed over a small parcel and Sebastian took it from him. He untied the string and opened the brown paper to reveal a painting. It was a delicate landscape painting, beautifully executed by a master painter. An idyllic scene of a thatched cottage in the autumn, and a family going about their day in the countryside.

"This was your mother's," Sebastian said, looking up in shock. He had seen it hanging in the study of Beau's town house. It was one of the few personal items of hers that he possessed. "We can't possibly take this," he said, feeling out of his depth. He knew Beau was trying to apologise, yet he wasn't ready to forgive him. But ... he didn't want to reject such an obvious show of remorse out of hand, nor yet take something of such huge personal value.

Beau shrugged, looking uncomfortable. "Well I can't take everything with me and I expect the bailiffs will clear the place out once I'm gone." Sebastian heard the familiar nonchalant tone but he didn't for a moment believe it. The painting was small enough to be easily packed. "I'd rather you had it," Beau said, pleading in his eyes.

Sebastian stared back at him and didn't know what to say. The anger at what Beau had done was still too raw, too fresh, but this was one of the only items he knew meant anything to his friend, and he knew what it meant to him to give it up.

"You're going to France then?"

Beau nodded. "At least the weather is better there than Scotland, and if it's good enough for Brummel," he quipped, trying to make light of it, but Sebastian could tell his heart wasn't in it. "Anyway, I leave in the morning, assuming I make it to the boat in one piece," he added with a lopsided grin. "Maybe you'll get lucky and someone will finish the job."

Sebastian felt his throat tighten. "Don't," he said, too confused to know what it was he wanted to say, but knowing he couldn't leave things like this. "I don't want you dead," he said, hearing his voice so harsh and gruff it was as though he didn't mean any such thing.

Beau smiled at him, but there was such pain in his eyes Sebastian had to look away. "I know that, Sin. To be honest I wish you did. It would be easier, but then ... well, you always were so much more honourable than I."

Sebastian didn't stop him as he headed for the door, but Beau paused on the threshold. He didn't turn around but Sebastian didn't need to see his face to see the sincerity in his eyes as he spoke.

"I'm so sorry, Sebastian. Truly. I know you'll never forgive me and ... well of course I understand that. But I wish you every happiness. You're a very lucky man."

Sebastian didn't stop him as he left, though there was a part of him that wished he had. He took a deep breath and put the painting away in his office with care, before rushing up to his room and getting the ring, which he'd left on the mantelpiece in his haste to get to Hanover Square in time. By the time he got back downstairs the carriage was waiting for him once more and he got in, yelling at the driver to make haste.

"Was that Beau I just saw?" Nibley demanded as Sebastian settled himself against the squabs once more.

He nodded and passed the small ring box to Percy to keep safe until it was required.

"Did you speak to him?"

"Yes," Sebastian replied, hoping Percy would leave it at that. He'd not known who to ask to accompany him this morning. The idea that Beau wasn't invited to his wedding seemed impossible.

He'd thought Percy would refuse too, as it was hardly appropriate as he'd offered for Georgiana as well. But Percy had seemed genuinely pleased to be asked and Sebastian had been grateful for it. He tried to put the unhappy face of his friend far from his mind. There was no use dwelling on it. Beau had made his own bed.

Georgiana loved him, not Beau. That he knew with no question or doubt in his mind and the thought eased away the tension that had made his shoulders tight as the carriage drew up outside the grand portico of the St George's church in Hanover Square. The church's tower stood proud against an azure summer sky as they walked into the cool gloom cast by the six massive Corinthian columns and made their way inside. It was a rather plain, if impressive structure with a wide nave, and gave the impression of light and space. With relief Sebastian noted that they had made good time and took a moment to gather himself before the day he had been waiting for with such anticipation began in earnest.

He smiled and greeted Georgiana's aunt and uncle, who looked rather daunted at first meeting him. They had been unable to come before the wedding, as a sudden outbreak of scarlet fever had kept the good doctor with his hands full until that very morning. Happily they soon relaxed as Sebastian took pains to make clear that he really wasn't as high in the instep as Georgiana had teased him about being.

For the fiftieth time Sebastian reached for his watch chain to check the time, just as Percy elbowed him in the side. Doctor Bomford had slipped discreetly away to meet his niece and now Lord and Lady Falmouth entered the church. Céleste looked ravishing in a pale peach colour which set off her golden hair beautifully, and Falmouth, looking unbearably smug, gave Sebastian a wink of encouragement.

And then, there she was. Sebastian caught his breath and held it as she made her way down the aisle on her uncle's arm. Doctor Bomford looked proud enough to burst something and Sebastian was quite taken aback by the force of emotion that came over him at seeing his lovely bride make her way to the altar.

Her glorious red hair shone copper and gold in the sun light and was no less dazzling than her smile and the light in her eyes. She carried a simple bouquet of three white lilies surrounded by fern leaves and if she was in any way as nervous as Sebastian suddenly felt, the bouquet hid any noticeable trembling of her hands. The exquisite dress she wore clung to her curvaceous frame in such a way that he wanted nothing more than to dispense with the ceremony and the blasted wedding breakfast with all haste and get his bride alone so that he could divest her of it in short measure.

At least some of his impatience must have been visible in his eyes as his irrepressible bride chuckled in a very unmaidenly fashion and had the temerity to wink at him.

Sebastian snorted and promised himself the delight of extracting retribution in the very near future as the ceremony began and everyone fell quiet.

Chapter 36

"Wherein .... a wedding! And a loving retribution is joyfully given."

The wedding breakfast was an intimate affair with just Georgiana's aunt and uncle, Lord and Lady Falmouth and Lord Nibley and his sister, Florence. The audacious Conrad was also in attendance with his partner in crime, Bandit. The two irredeemable rogues surveyed the floor and cast hopeful gazes upon the assembled company. Unshakeable in their belief that someone would give them one of the scotch eggs which they were well aware were somewhere among the lavish spread supplied by Fortnum and Mason's, they continued to wag eager tails. Sebastian had, however, been adamant that Conrad would *not* be going with them on honeymoon to Paris, despite Georgiana's protestations that he would pine for her. On applying to Lord Falmouth to ask if he would keep him for the duration, so that at least his dearest companion Bandit might be close at hand to keep him company, Lord Falmouth had simply replied, "Good God, no!"

So Conrad would return to Cornwall with Aunt Jane and Uncle Jo, where Georgiana was assured he would be walked daily and allowed to chase rabbits to his heart's content.

If Georgiana felt that her new husband's pleasure in the day was lessened by the absence of his best friend, it was a thought she kept to herself, though she resolved to do everything in her power to remedy the rift as soon as she was able.

The wedding breakfast finally came to an end after much toasting and the congratulations of their nearest and dearest. A tearful farewell was indulged in by the ladies and Aunt Jane was obliged to cling hard to her husband's arm while that heartless individual laughed, though not unkindly and implored her not to be such a silly goose. Georgiana just smiled and decided it would be churlish to point out that she'd noticed Uncle Joseph surreptitiously wiping his eyes just moments earlier.

The journey to Claridge's was ridiculously short and Georgiana teased her new husband for being too terribly proud and top-lofty to walk the short distance from Grosvenor Square to Brook Street.

Sebastian just snorted and told her to mind her manners for retribution was due, before kissing her with a ruthlessness that left her still flustered and red-cheeked as she entered the hotel.

If the staff thought it odd that his grace would spend his wedding night a few doors down from his own home, they gave no cause for either of them to suspect it. For her part Georgiana was delighted with the sumptuous hotel, and more than relieved not to be entering the domain of the dowager duchess of Sindalton, the mere idea of which had put her in a quake. Sebastian had quickly laid to rest her fears admitting that he felt entirely the same way. So a night at Claridge's had been decided upon before setting off on honeymoon to Paris and then down through France and on to Italy. Lord Falmouth had insisted that they stop off at his brother's home close to Bordeaux as he was sure Georgiana and his sister-in-law, Henri, would hit it off wonderfully well. Céleste had agreed with this, only adding with a mischievous grin that Sebastian would also like Lawrence far better than he did Alex.

Finally alone with her new husband in a large and elegant bedroom which held the slightly daunting focus of a huge double bed, Georgiana found herself unaccountably nervous. Especially as there was a challenging light in his eyes which she knew she had put there with her teasing over the past days. Refusing to look too much the blushing bride, she put up her chin and met his gaze head on.

"It's been such a lovely day, Sebastian, and thank you so much for being so kind to my aunt and uncle. They adored you of course."

"Of course," he said with a smirk, divesting himself with some difficulty of his skin tight coat.

"Here, let me help you." Georgiana helped him ease the exquisitely tailored article over his broad shoulders without creasing the art of the peerless Mr Weston too severely. "Oh, dear, your valet would have kittens to see me doing this, wouldn't he?"

"Oh good heavens, don't," Sebastian said, snorting with amusement. "He'll be sulking for weeks as it is for being given the evening off. I'll no doubt be told apocryphal tales about half a dozen young bloods who would merrily stab me in the back just to get their hands on him as revenge."

"Well it was your idea to get rid of all the servants until tomorrow. Most improper according to Aunt Jane, though you won Céleste's approval at any rate," Georgiana said chuckling, though she was aware it was a rather nervous sound as Sebastian's hands went to his waistcoat buttons. She swallowed, watching the progress of those strong fingers as they made their way down the extravagantly embroidered silk of this impressive garment. Sebastian cast it with negligent care onto the floor and stepped closer to his bride with a decidedly feral grin.

"Now then, your Grace," he said in a low voice.

"Oh!" Georgiana said in surprise, interrupting him. "That's me now, isn't it?" She gave a little laugh of surprise. "Your grace! How strange it sounds."

"Yes it is," Sebastian said, sounding rather impatient. "Now do be quiet, love. I want to seduce you."

"Oh," she said again, trying and failing to smother a laugh. "I do beg your pardon."

"I should think so," he replied, shaking his head at her and then frowning at the dress as he turned her and discovered the thirty-three tiny pearl buttons that ran down her back. "Good God!" he exclaimed. "What manner of sadist went and put all those blasted buttons on the wretched thing!"

"Sebastian!" Georgiana exclaimed, smothering her laughter with a trembling hand.

"Well, damn it, love. I'll be here all night!"

Shaking with silent mirth, Georgiana waited as Sebastian undid one fiddly button at a time, all the while complaining and cursing bitterly about confounded dressmakers. Finally reaching the end of the buttons and his patience, she heard an audible exhale as the heavy satin slithered to the ground. Shivering with anticipation, she stepped out of the gown and kept her back to him as she removed the final items of her underclothes. She cast her stays and chemise aside, with rather less nonchalance than he'd managed with his waistcoat, and turned to look at him wearing just her stockings and garters. For a moment she struggled to look at him, feeling her skin hot with mingled embarrassment and anticipation. But on meeting his gaze all qualms were cast aside more easily than any garment on seeing the love and desire blazing in his dark eyes.

Without further hesitation he swept her into an embrace, his mouth claiming hers with an impatient urgency that she was only too happy to imitate. He stopped suddenly and took a deep and rather shaky breath as he turned his attention to removing the pins from her hair.

"I've been desperate to see this all loose about your shoulders," he said, his voice low as his fingers slid through the thick copper of her hair. He watched with obvious fascination as the shiny locks glinted against his large palm and fell against her pale skin. "So very lovely," he said, his voice reverent and husky with need.

She watched with interest as his face grew a little guarded and his brow furrowed.

"Love, I know we ..." He cleared his throat and looked strangely ill at ease before he continued. "Er ... dallied a little, together in Cornwall but ..." Another pause in which he frowned a little harder. "Do you ... do you know what to expect? I mean ..."

Georgiana gave a little gurgle of laughter, delighted to discover that her husband was just as nervous as she was. His reputation for being a shocking flirt and a ladies' man notwithstanding.

"Oh yes, darling. After all I am a country girl. One does see *things* in the country you know, and after that Céleste filled in the bits I was missing."

"Oh thank God," he said, with obvious relief. He smiled down at her, so much tenderness in his expression that her heart seemed to squeeze in her chest. "So you're not nervous then."

"Only very little," she said, returning his smile. "I know you'll take care of me." She bit her lip and then added with rather more daring than she was truly feeling, "I'm really just terribly impatient. Do get on with it, darling."

"Why you little wretch!" he exclaimed wrathfully, sweeping her up and throwing her on the bed, where she bounced a little and tipped her head back laughing as he prowled over her. "Get on with it!" he repeated, mirth glittering in his dark eyes. "Of all the unmaidenly, improper, *wicked* things to say to me!"

He grabbed hold of her hands and pinned them to the bed above her shoulders as he insinuated his large body between her legs. She gasped, surprised again at the weight and size of him, relishing the feel of his much heavier frame against her own. He leaned down and nipped at her earlobe, trailing his tongue over the very edge of her ear, nuzzling the tender flesh beneath and painting kisses along her jaw and neck. Georgiana sighed and squirmed, arching against his body. He allowed her to press against him for a moment, his eyes darkening as she gasped and flushed with mounting desire.

He chuckled, the sound low and intimate as he moved away from her.

"Where are you going?" she demanded, sitting up on her elbows. He sat back and undid his cravat with obvious and painstaking care, a smug grin hovering over his mouth. With a huff she laid back, glaring at him as he carefully folded the long length of pristine white silk and returned to his buttons. Each one was undone with great care and growing amusement on his part as Georgiana narrowed her eyes at him.

"You are a very unkind, husband," she said, with a sniff, but was quite unable to tear her fascinated gaze away as he removed his shirt to reveal a hard, muscular frame. The more of his finely tailored and sophisticated clothes that were removed, the more she was struck by the contrast of the virile masculinity that had been hidden beneath it. He seemed all at once a great deal less civilised and far more rugged. The thought made her heart thud harder. She continued to watch, knowing he was well aware of her scrutiny as her eyes took in a broad chest, lightly dusted with dark hair that led in a tantalising trail beneath the band of his trousers. She caught her breath, and the sound at least had the result of making him hurry. Putting all pretence at a studied nonchalance aside, Sebastian cast his boots into the far corners of the room and removed the remaining items of clothing as fast as he was able.

She blinked as he prowled back to the bed once again, more than slightly daunted as Céleste's encouraging words returned to her and were put in the light of the impressive figure of her husband.

"What, nothing to say, love?" he teased, his mouth slightly quirked as one hand slid up the back of her leg and tugged at her garter. She watched, her mouth dry as he drew first one silk stocking and then the other from her legs as his hands continued to stroke and caress her.

"Good Lord, don't tell me I've finally rendered you speechless?"

"O-only ... momentarily," she gasped as his naked form finally pressed down upon her. The feeling of his hot skin so close to hers was enough for any further thought at proving him wrong to be banished from her mind. Yes, yes indeed she was speechless. Entirely robbed of any coherent thought or grasp on the English language as she was reduced to a incoherent bundle of nerves that could do nothing more complex than gasp and murmur with delight as his lips and hands began to explore her.

"Oh!" was the most rational sound she was capable of as he kissed a path to her breasts and drew one aching nipple into the warm heat of his mouth. She whimpered and arched into him, sinking her hands into his dark hair and grasping at the thick locks. She allowed her hands to slide down his neck, exploring the great expanse of silky skin that covered his broad back and shoulders.

Grasping at the heavy muscle of his arms, she moved restlessly beneath him, aware of a growing sense of emptiness, a need to be joined with him that made her impatient. He chuckled against her skin, clearly more aware than she was of what it was she needed as he worked his way down her stomach, painting her skin with his tongue as he descended lower. She shivered, too intrigued to be embarrassed by the intimate path he was set upon. With delicate fingers, he parted the curls at the apex of her thighs and with a last, lingering look of challenge in his eyes, lowered his mouth to her most delicate skin.

Momentarily startled, she hauled in a breath and then gave a perfectly shocking moan as pleasure radiated through her body. Georgiana had never felt so completely exposed, and not just physically. There was such trust in this, such pleasure in knowing that he wanted to love and please her. She was lost in the feel of his tongue, sliding over her, at times teasing, at others demanding as he alternately lapped and tormented her. Any sense of embarrassment that she might have felt in looking down and seeing that dark head bent between her thighs dissipated with the knowledge that she was loved.

This was very different from the only other time they had been intimate. Then she had been so dreadfully afraid, certain that he was toying with her and unable to relinquish herself fully to the joy of his touch. Now she allowed herself to be overwhelmed by it, rushing with greedy abandon to the pinnacle of pleasure as he continued to tease and indulge her tender flesh with his mouth and tongue.

She sucked in a breath as she felt the intimate touch of his fingers as they slid inside her, first one, then another, caressing and stroking in unison with his tongue as his mouth closed over her once again. Her thighs fell further apart with wanton sensuality as her hips rose towards him, encouraging him as she cried out and clutched at the bed clothes as the climax shook her and she fell into a voluptuous sea of bliss.

Chapter 37

"Wherein our hero and heroine discover the future is wonderful place."

It took more than a few minutes before Sebastian could coax his wife to open her eyes again. There was a satisfied smile lingering over her lips that he couldn't help but feel a little smug about, however, so he allowed her a few moments to recover. He couldn't help but think this a heroic, possibly even saintly gesture, as his own body was screaming for release and his lovely Georgiana temptation incarnate.

Stroking his fingers over the satin skin of her belly, he lingered at the soft curve of her breast and cupped his hand around the warm, inviting mound. She gave a deep sigh of contentment and stretched, arching further into his hand with a luxurious gesture that made his body taut, and his own needs refused be ignored a moment longer. Moving over her he pushed her legs open and settled himself between them, sliding his aching shaft over the slick, swollen skin he had so recently pleasured. She gasped, her eyes flying open as he smiled down at her.

"I hoped that might get your attention."

Her eyes grew hazy again as he continued to slide against her and he felt a possessive surge of desire as she let out a soft moan and raised her hips to meet him.

"Oh, love," he whispered against her skin as he dropped his head to claim her mouth. She met him with her own, their tongues sliding together in rhythm with their bodies as Sebastian moved to enter her. She was everywhere perfection, and he was beyond desperate to be inside of her. That she was here at all seemed at once too impossibly wonderful to be true and startlingly real. That after so many obstacles had been set in their way, after he had made so very many idiotic decisions, that she should be here, *his wife*, seemed nothing short of miraculous.

He groaned as her tight heat encompassed him and he slid a little further into the decadent pleasure of her body. Aware of her hands clutching at him, at the sudden tension in her body, he forced himself to still, though it took every ounce of self control not to simply plunge into her and find the release he had longed for, for such an eternity.

"Am I hurting you?" he asked, his voice rough, hating that he had forgotten himself to the extent that he hadn't asked her sooner.

To his surprise she gave a little laugh and shook her head. "No, no ..." she whispered. "It's just so ..."

He moved, just a fraction deeper inside of her and she caught her breath, her eyes going wide as her head tipped back, exposing her throat to his searching lips. He kissed every inch of skin that he could reach as he moved deeper, in excruciatingly small increments designed to drive him out of his mind. Every muscle in his body was rigid, locked down with the need to keep control as he tried desperately not to hurt her.

But then he felt her hands slid down his back to the taut muscle of his buttocks and she pulled at him, raising her hips at the same time, encouraging him deeper. Any lingering shred of self-control fled in the face of such wanton need and he sheathed himself inside her with one deep thrust. She gave a startled cry of surprise but to his everlasting relief he felt her relax beneath him as he continued to move, her body meeting his as her breathing became faster and harsher. He allowed his weight to fall upon her, gathering her body in his arms and abandoning any pretence that he had any control over this at all. He was lost, beyond anything but the pleasure to be found in the woman he loved, in the need to be with her, a part of her.

"Oh, God," he whispered, the words full of surprise and wonder that anything could feel like this, so much more than he had ever expected. The idea that he had almost lost this, that if the fates had conspired harder against him she could even now be in Beau's arms not his, made emotion claw at his heart. "I love you," he said, the words harsh and true as he thrust into her and pleasure stole any last reserve he may have had. "Oh, my sweet girl, I love you so."

He heard the soft words of her reply but they became lost in the raw cry of his climax. Shuddering as the force of his release tore through him, he believed nothing could be more perfect until he felt her clutching at him with desperate hands. He moaned against her hot skin as her body tightened around him, sending him hurtling into the white light of rapture as her cries of elation took them both further than they had ever been.

They lay together, a tangled mesh of sated, sweaty skin and limbs as their breathing slowed and the languid stupor of satisfaction made their bones feel too heavy to move.

"Am I crushing you?" Sebastian asked, wondering if he could find enough energy to move away from the delicious pillow of her body.

"Yes," she sighed, rubbing her face against his neck. "It's quite wonderful."

A chuckle rumbled through his body and she began to laugh too. "Oh stop, that ... that tickles," he said.

With a supreme effort he moved just a little, easing out of her body and regretting the little wince he saw tighten her eyes.

"I've hurt you?" he asked, looking down at her and feeling like a brute for not having taken more care.

"Oh, no!" she exclaimed, her eyes wide as she reached her hand up and touched his face, such love in her eyes that something close to pain bloomed in his chest at the wonder he felt. He could never lose this. "It was ..." She stopped, her mouth still open, but the words had apparently deserted her.

"It was?" he asked, feeling just a little anxious after all.

"I don't have the words," she said, laughing, a surprising amount of reticence in her eyes until she found what she wanted to say. "It was perfect."

Sebastian let out a breath of relief and pressed his mouth to hers. *"You* are perfect," he murmured, with absolute sincerity.

She gave a delightful gurgle of laughter that made happiness jolt through him. "If you think that, your Grace," she said with mischief dancing in her eyes. "Then I can assure you, you're in for the most shocking surprise of your life."

He smiled at her, cupping her lovely face with his hands. "As long as I am the only one in your heart or your bed, I think I can handle it."

"Oh, you say that now ..." she replied, the mischievous look growing brighter. "But just you wait until the Siren gets to Paris. Can you imagine what damage I can do to your ducal reputation in such a decadent place?"

He allowed her to push him onto his back as she climbed over him and sat astride his hips. He felt his body grow hard again at the closeness of her and put his hands to her waist.

"Oh, I think I know how to keep you in line, little minx," he said, grinning and raising his hips to nudge his hardening body against her soft flesh. She gave a little gasp of surprise and stroked one hand over his chest, her face growing suddenly serious.

"I don't need anything or anyone but you. Just love me, Sebastian. That's all you need do."

"I have every intention of it, darling."

She smiled at him, suddenly looking a little shy as she leaned down and kissed his forehead, his eyelids, his cheeks, nose and finally his mouth. "I love you," she breathed against his lips. "I'm so happy I don't know whether to laugh or cry or ... quite what to do with myself."

He chuckled at that and tumbled her onto her back as her body opened to welcome him with enthusiasm. "Well, love, in that case it's a good thing that your stuffy, top-lofty husband has a very definite idea."

"Yes," she murmured, laughing against his skin. "A very good thing indeed."

The End

Keep reading for a sneak peek of Book 4, Beau's story.

The Devil May Care

Rogues & Gentlemen Book 4

Dishonoured and ashamed, the ton's scandalous darling, 'Beau' the Marquis of Beaumont, is forced to flee England to escape debtor's prison after his callous father refuses to help him.

After a chance encounter, it appears his only remaining friend is to be found in the unlikely person of Miss Millicent Sparrow.

Miss Sparrow lives up to her name. Damaged and terrified by her cousin's violent abuse, Milly is used to being overlooked and prefers it that way, until the desperation of her bleak world is gilded by rakishly handsome Beau's extraordinary friendship.

When his father dies suddenly and Beau inherits the Dukedom, he seeks out Miss Sparrow, the author of the lively letters that helped him through his banishment. To his shock he finds a woman in despair and moved by pity, offers her the protection of his name.

But Milly becomes impossible to overlook, and the more Beau needs his wife, the less interested she seems in her gorgeous husband.

For this rake, getting a woman's attention has never been so hard.

Chapter 1

"Wherein the past is reviewed with regret, but a new friend is made."

2nd June 1817

Beau watched as his boyhood friend, Sebastian Grenville, the Duke of Sindalton, ran down the stairs from his grand home on Grosvenor Square. The tall, imposing figure leapt into the waiting carriage and the glossy black conveyance, drawn by four equally glossy bay horses, drew him away. The gold leaf of the duke's coat of arms glinted with the perfection of true quality in the early summer sun on the carriage doors, and Beau tried hard not to feel envious of his friend's secure position: a wealthy man, setting out to marry an equally wealthy and beautiful lady who loved him to distraction. Such lives as most people could only dream about. Struck by a forceful pang of sorrow as the carriage turned the corner and out of sight, he drew in a breath and told himself not to be so hen-hearted. He had no right to feel sorry for himself. He had his own notoriety as Charles Stafford, the Marquess of Beaumont, though all knew him as simply *Beau*. But he had brought this sorrow upon himself. That much was clear.

Beau shifted his arm in the sling as his shoulder throbbed as though reminding him of his own black-hearted folly. Raising his hand he rubbed at it with a grimace. It was healing well now, but it still hurt like the devil. Still, that's what you got when your best friend put a bullet in you. He could only be grateful Sebastian had never been such a good shot as he was himself. For both their sakes. He doubted Sebastian would take the idea of fleeing to France in disgrace with any more enthusiasm than he had himself. But there was no other choice for him now.

He turned and nodded to the two burly and disreputable-looking men who were lingering on the corner of the road. They were temporary guards courtesy of the Earl of Falmouth, who was just as eager for him to leave the country, for Beau owed some very ruthless men a great deal of money, and they'd take their payment in blood and bone if nothing else was forthcoming.

Lost in his malady, he found himself walking towards Hyde Park, the streets still quiet and deserted at this unfashionably early hour of the morning. He should go home. There were still so many things to arrange before he caught the packet boat in the morning. The idea of going back made his throat disconcertingly tight though. Best put it off for a while.

He wandered through the pretty gardens at a leisurely pace. The grass and trees still wore the fresh acid green of a damp spring, with vivid swathes of colourful planting drawing the eye as the new summer colours vied for attention. For once Beau found no pleasure in it though, his thoughts too mired in his past and the gloom of his immediate future. What the devil was he to do?

He sat down on a bench, casting a sympathetic eye to the two men who were still shadowing him. He waved them off with an impatient air and they obliged with begrudging distrust.

Beau wasn't sure how long he sat there, staring at the water of the Serpentine and considering all of the ill-conceived, idiotic things he'd done in the past year alone. It wasn't a pleasant thing, to realise that you were wasting your life, that you'd done nothing that you could feel pride in. He had spent his time indulging his baser instincts and not giving a damn who he hurt in the process. He was tired of emotional scenes, of women he didn't care about weeping and begging him to stay. He was tired of gambling at all hours to try to keep himself afloat. Rubbing his hand over his face in irritation he cursed himself. He was better than this, surely? But his father's laughter still rang in his ears.

It had almost killed him to turn to his father for help. He'd been far from surprised that the evil old bastard had delighted in telling him he was a failure and a disgrace and he'd not lift a finger to help him. No change there then. So he'd swallowed his pride for no good reason.

Beau swore he'd show him, one day. One day he'd make a success of his life and he'd look his father in the eyes and tell him he was wrong. Beau wasn't the failure, he was. The Duke of Ware was the failure, for he'd set out to break his own son and he'd not yet succeeded.

He frowned, broken from his thoughts by a soft voice and looked around him. At first he saw no one, but then the voice came again and he turned to his right a little farther to see a woman looking at him.

"Hello," she said, her voice tight with anxiety. "I-I'm so sorry, my lord. I-I h-hope I'm not disturbing you?"

He smiled politely at the woman, wondering what the devil she was about speaking to a man she didn't know in the middle of the park. But then he realised there was something familiar about her.

She was not a glamorous specimen. Indeed Beau would have walked past without giving her a second glance, so how he knew her he couldn't fathom. Shabbily dressed in a worn brown pelisse, her equally brown hair was drawn severely back from her face into a tight bun. Thin to the point of looking emaciated, Beau thought a strong gust of wind would likely knock her off her feet.

She flushed, the two points of colour vivid against the pallor of her complexion.

"No, you're not disturbing me," he said, looking at her with curiosity. If she'd been better dressed and rather more attractive he'd have not been so surprised. He was not unaccustomed to women acting badly to get close to him. "Is there something I can do for you, Miss ..."

"Oh, Miss Sparrow," she said in a rush, taking a hesitant couple of steps closer. "No, nothing at all, my Lord, in fact I would never have dared approach you, only ..."

She ground to a halt and Beau was struck by the fear in her dark eyes. It was a look he recognised.

"Only?" he asked, keeping his voice warm and reassuring. She wore the look of a woman who was afraid of her own shadow and he felt the instinctive need to put her at ease. She wore a dainty pair of spectacles that made her look rather older than she perhaps was and pushed them up her nose a little before she spoke again.

"Only, I wanted so much to thank you."

He raised his eyebrows, wondering what on earth he could have done to have earned her thanks. "Sparrow?" he repeated, frowning as he realised the name was familiar. "Oh, Lady Derby's ball?"

She smiled and let out a breath. "Yes, that's right. I'm afraid I caused the most dreadful stir." The high points of colour on her cheeks seemed to brighten further and he felt a wave of pity for her embarrassment.

"Not at all," he said, smiling at her. "And there is not the least need to thank me. It was no more than anyone would have done."

Her smile fell away and a haunted look returned to those wide brown eyes. "No," she said, shaking her head. "We both know that isn't true. They would have stood and watched as I had a ... *a fit.* They would have watched and felt appalled and done nothing. No one else would have helped me," she said, her voice barely audible. "But you did."

It appeared to be Beau's turn to feel embarrassed. He was certainly undeserving of the look of slavish devotion in her eyes. "Well, I was only too happy to," he said, dismissing it with a wave of his hand.

"I know," she said, her voice full of wonder. "And I simply can't imagine why."

He frowned, turning to her with a little annoyance. "It shouldn't be so remarkable that I can find some common decency for a fellow creature. Surely my reputation is not so black as all that." The words were sharp and she gave an audible gasp of shock and he was appalled to see that look of terror in her eyes again as she clutched at the little plain brown reticule in her hands.

"N-no! I-I didn't mean. I n-never meant that *you* ... Only p-people aren't kind you see. N-not usually."

He felt a wave of pity for this poor, shabby, brown creature and wondered what her life was. He knew of her cousin, Spencer Brownlow. He'd been at Eton, a year or two older than Beau, and a nastier piece of work it would be hard to come across.

"Forgive me, Miss Sparrow," he said, truly disquieted by how frightened she seemed to be. "I had no call to speak to you so. Indeed it is only my own guilty conscience that made me think you were accusing me of being usually cold-hearted."

"Oh, I would *never* believe such a thing of you!" she said, and with such heat that Beau was startled into laughter.

"My word, a champion," he said. "Well I must say I have need of one of those right now as I'm feeling devilish sorry for myself."

"Oh?"

He looked up, amused by the curiosity in her eyes. Looking around, he wondered if she was in the park alone as the impropriety of her situation was very clear to him. She should not be speaking with him without a chaperone. She ought not to speak to him at all as they'd never been formally introduced, despite the bizarre nature of their acquaintance. Though how anyone could believe she was in danger of him making amorous advances to her was frankly ludicrous.

"Are you alone, Miss Sparrow?"

The two high spots of colour flamed once more and she shook her head. "My companion, Mrs Goodly, is with me, and indeed we have come with my cousin Mr Brownlow's son Hugo and his nanny. They are further along the park, but Mrs Goodly is sitting on that bench there." She gestured to another identical bench a little distance from them and Beau saw an older lady sitting and reading a book.

"Well then, as we have propriety in hand, would you do me the honour of sitting with me a moment?" he asked and was rewarded with a look of real pleasure.

"Oh, yes. Indeed I should like that, my Lord. That is ... if you are sure you want me to?" She dithered on the spot, her thin fingers clutching at her reticule and looking anxious lest he'd changed his mind.

"I wouldn't have asked you if I didn't want your company, Miss Sparrow," he replied with a gentle smile, and he watched with amusement as she settled herself on the very edge of the bench. She was much like a little brown sparrow, he thought, his mouth twitching slightly at the idea. She was so very skittish, as though the slightest disturbance would make her fly away in terror, and yet there was intelligence and humour in those deep brown eyes.

"What did you mean before?" she asked, looking up at him. "When you said you were feeling sorry for yourself? Is it because you are hurt?" She gestured to the sling he wore and he hesitated, wondering what to tell her. The story put about was that he'd suffered a fencing injury. He was well known to be an enthusiast, and whilst it rankled that people should think someone had gotten the better of him, it was obviously best that the truth remain hidden.

He nodded. "Yes, in part," he replied, wondering if he could trust her. He felt the sudden need to unburden himself. To tell someone that he'd been a damned fool but that he was sorry for it. That he wanted to be better than that. "The story ... is that I was injured whilst fencing."

"Oh no!" she exclaimed, tutting with irritation.

He laughed, surprised by her reaction. "No?" he repeated.

"Oh, dear me no," she said again, shaking her head and looking really rather annoyed. "You're far too clever with a blade for such a slip. Who on earth is supposed to have done it? No, no. I would never have believed such a tale even if you had stuck to it."

He gaped at her, astonished. "But ... How on earth ...?" It was true he had a reputation with a blade, and those involved in the sport would know it. But that a lady should know not simply that he fenced ...

She opened her mouth and then closed it suddenly, a guarded look in her eyes.

"Oh, come now. I shan't say a word, and I'm too curious to leave it at that, I can tell you!" he said with a laugh.

He watched, intrigued by the battle going on behind those frightened eyes. He wished he knew what it was that made her so very afraid.

"Well, it was perhaps twelve years ago," she admitted. "I was just a little girl and out with my cousin. He had to meet someone at Angelo's, some business connection. He said it would only take a moment and that I was to sit quietly on the chair in the foyer and wait for him."

"But you didn't, I collect?" Beau asked, watching her.

She shook her head and glanced up at him, a shy smile in her eyes. "There was a great deal of noise and I was curious so I went to see. It was a fencing match. You were fighting ..." she frowned as she tried to remember, her thin face turned away from him. "Oh, Lord Reece!" she exclaimed and then said with relish, "It was the most spectacular thing I'd ever seen! You were truly magnificent."

She sighed and looked up at him and then blushed with fury as she apparently recalled her words and the manner with which she'd said them.

"I did give him a trouncing," Beau replied, unable to stop himself smiling at her.

"Yes," she replied, her eyes alight. "You certainly did. You made him look like an amateur. And since then, well sometimes my cousin has business to attend to and leaves myself and Mrs Goodly to wait in the foyer, and sometimes the door is a little open and ... I get lucky."

He chuckled, imagining her peeking round the door to watch the men fighting. What a funny little creature she was. He wondered how old she was. At first sight he had thought her much older, perhaps in her thirties. But now he realised that was just the outmoded dress and the dreadfully severe hairstyle and glasses. At closer inspection he doubted she was much more than twenty. She said she'd seen the match with Reece as a child and he'd been eighteen the year he'd beaten the reigning champion, Lord Reece.

"So it wasn't a fencing accident then?" she asked, and he saw a worried frown in her eyes. "It ... it wasn't ... a duel, was it?"

He shook his head and snorted. "No. Not a duel. At least, only one of us was armed."

She gasped in shock and clutched at his wrist. "But who? Who did this to you?" He frowned at her, taken aback by her concern. She withdrew her hand from his arm immediately. "I beg your pardon, my Lord," she said, staring at her feet and looking mortified.

"Please don't be foolish. I am most grateful for your concern. But I am afraid I don't deserve your pity. I got off lightly in truth. I deserved what was coming to me and if my fate had been blessed with a better shot, I would have undoubtedly been well served."

"I don't believe that." She sounded really quite mutinous and he looked at her with growing affection. The strange little drab had obviously formed a tendre for him. It was by no means the first time Beau had been afflicted with females fancying themselves in love with him, believing they knew him simply because they'd fallen for his beautiful face. Usually he extricated himself from their presence with all haste, but he found the girl amused him. Perhaps it was merely because his ego was bruised.

"Why were you shot?"

He looked down at her, seeing no judgement in her eyes. He hesitated, finding he wanted to tell her.

"Can I trust you, Miss Sparrow?" he asked, his voice quiet.

With more boldness than he would have credited her for, she placed her hand on his for a moment. "Anything you tell me I would take to my grave, my Lord," she said, with the utmost sincerity. Then, a little glimmer of humour warmed her eyes and she added. "Besides, who on earth would I tell? No one talks to me!"

She gave him a little mischievous smile which was terribly endearing. But that was more because she didn't hear the appalling loneliness behind the words than because she'd made a joke. Beau found he couldn't smile with her, too full of pity for her predicament. What a life for a single female with neither fortune nor beauty. Cast upon the charity of her relatives to be used or abused as those individuals deemed fit. And Beau felt very strongly that someone was abusing Miss Sparrow.

"Then the world is a very cruel and foolish place, Miss Sparrow. For I can think of no one I would rather speak with."

It was prettily said and he was pleased with the glow of pleasure that lit her eyes at his words. More than that, he realised it was true. He was surrounded by acquaintances, he had replaced Beau Brummel as the most fashionable man of the *ton,* and yet ... he was utterly alone. Sebastian had been his closest, and his only true friend. It would have been him he'd run to if he was in trouble, but now that friendship was over. And it was entirely Beau's fault.

He gave a sigh and sat back on the bench, wincing as his shoulder pained him at the movement. "The truth is I was shot by my best friend because I abducted his fiancée. I planned to take her to Gretna Green and force her to marry me."

He looked back at her, expecting to see condemnation and disgust in those frightened eyes, but instead she nodded, her expression placid.

"Yes, I thought perhaps that was it," she mused, apparently unperturbed. "Lady Dalton was an heiress of course and you're up to your neck in the river tick and desperately need funds, so I suppose it was the only thing you *could* do."

He stared at her, blinking as she gasped and clapped her hand to her mouth. "Oh, curse my wretched tongue. I never could keep it between my teeth. I do beg your pardon!" she said, looking mortified.

Beau laughed, quite perplexed by this funny young woman. At one moment she was stuttering and looked as though she was terrified he would strike her, and at the next she said something perfectly outrageous.

"Not at all, Miss Sparrow. You have it in a nutshell but ..." He turned a little and stared at her, fixing her with his undivided attention. It was a look that was guaranteed to make most women tell him anything he liked, providing he kissed them in payment. "But why aren't you disgusted with me, Miss Sparrow? Because I can see that you aren't. You ought to be, you know. *I'm* disgusted by me! So it is most unnatural that *you* ... are not."

She flushed a little again, but didn't seem unduly agitated by his observation. Instead she just shrugged, the movement highlighting her bony shoulders. Beau wondered when she last ate.

"I think perhaps you're right," she said, a slight frown in her eyes. "I never seem to do or say the things I ought to. And of course I see that you simply cannot go around abducting unwilling females. Not that it would be an abduction of course if they *were* willing ..." she added with a thoughtful expression. "And you should never have done it of course, I know that but ..." She paused, apparently thinking it over.

"But?" he prompted, feeling absurdly entertained by her words and the serious little frown that crinkled her brow.

"But I do see why you felt you must," she said, shaking her head and looking up at him with such sorrow in her eyes that he was really quite touched. "Are ... Are things so very bad?"

He smiled at her, not wanting her to worry on his account. He had a feeling she had troubles enough of her own. "Oh, not so very bad. After all, if it's good enough for Brummel, I dare say it's good enough for me."

"France!" she exclaimed, her face the picture of horror. "Oh no! Don't say you're leaving?"

He was at a loss for a reply for a moment, too taken aback by the real disappointment in her eyes. Well at least someone would miss him, he thought with a wry smile.

"Sadly, yes. Miss Sparrow. Circumstances are such that ... well France should prove a little more comfortable than debtor's prison at all accounts. But I promise you I'll be back. I shall come about, sooner or later."

"Oh."

He watched as she looked away from him, blinking rapidly.

"Please don't upset yourself on my account, Miss Sparrow. I will be quite all right, I promise you."

"I'm afraid it isn't on your account at all," she said, disconcerting him once again. "It's on my own."

"Oh?" he replied, wondering what on earth she would say next. She looked back at him and laughed, apparently amused by the expression on his face. It was a surprisingly deep sound from such a tiny frame, and he couldn't help but smile in response.

"I've done it again haven't I?" she said with a rueful expression. "My dreadful tongue. Only ... well I have been following your exploits for such a long time and now to meet you, and speak with you ... Oh, Lord Beaumont, England will be such a very dull place without you in it. Indeed it will."

He stared at the woman in front of him. She was everything that was drab and brown and unremarkable, and yet she had such spirit once she had cast away her fears.

"Well now, that will never do," he said, his voice soft. He wondered what on earth he was doing but ... if he could at least make one person happy, perhaps it would go some small way towards wiping his slate clean. "I cannot have you bored to tears without my scandalous affairs to entertain you, now can I? What kind of gentleman would that make me?"

"My Lord?" she replied, looking perplexed.

"Miss Sparrow, would you allow me to write to you, and perhaps do me the honour of writing in return. I should be glad to know of everything that is happening over here, and I fear there is no one else who will trouble to do so."

He was gratified by the look in her eyes. "The honour would be mine entirely, my Lord," she said, sounding quite breathless. "I-I would be delighted to, if ... If you are sure it is what you would like?"

"I promise you it is," Beau replied, finding he was perfectly sincere. "And I know that ... perhaps I shouldn't ask you. In fact I know I ought not to. Unmarried as you are and writing to me of all people ..."

"Please think nothing of it!" she said in a rush, shaking her head, obviously desperate to reassure him. "I am quite able to post the letters with no one any the wiser and ... And if you would perhaps address the letters to Mrs Goodly? She has an elderly aunt who lives close by, you could send the letters to her address and no one would be any the wiser."

She scrabbled in her reticule and withdrew a small notebook and pencil, jotting the address down for him.

Beau grinned at her, shaking his head. "Miss Sparrow, I feel your talents have been quite wasted. You should have worked for Wellington during the war. You have a mind that bends easily to intrigue and I feel you would have made the most accomplished spy."

She gave that deep little chuckle again as she handed him the address and he couldn't help but grin in return.

"Well, sadly I must leave you now. I'm so sorry that we shan't meet again for a while. But I do look forward to hearing from you soon."

He got to his feet and held out his hand to her.

"Are you sure?" she said, her face suddenly grave as she took his hand and held it between hers. They were tiny and cold against his larger, warmer hand. "You're sure you're ... not just being kind to me?"

"I can assure you I am being entirely selfish," he said, squeezing her fingers a little before he released her hand. "You see, I am relying on you to entertain me, for my French is appalling and I have no idea how I shall go on."

She cast him a mischievous look from under her eyelashes. "Oh, come, my Lord. *You* don't need words to find entertainment. I'm quite sure of that!"

Startled once more into giving a bark of outraged laughter, Beau shook his head.

"Watch that tongue of yours unless you're writing to me, Miss Sparrow. I feel it will lead you into trouble!"

Want more Emma?

If you enjoyed this book, please support this indie author and take a moment to leave a few words in a review. *Thank you!*

To be kept informed of special offers and free deals (which I do regularly) follow me on *https://www.bookbub.com/authors/emma-v-leech*

To find out more and to get news and sneak peeks of the first chapter of upcoming works, go to my website and sign up for the newsletter.

http://www.emmavleech.com/

Come and join the fans in my Facebook group for news, info and exciting discussion...

Emmas Book Club

Or Follow me here......

Emma's Amazon Author page

Emma's Amazon UK Author page

Emma's Twitter page

About Me!

I started this incredible journey way back in 2010 with The Key to Erebus but didn't summon the courage to hit publish until October 2012. For anyone who's done it, you'll know publishing your first title is a terribly scary thing! I still get butterflies on the morning a new title releases but the terror has subsided at least. Now I just live in dread of the day my daughters are old enough to read them.

The horror! (On both sides I suspect.)

2017 marked the year that I made my first foray into Historical Romance and the world of the Regency Romance, and my word what a year! I was delighted by the response to this series and can't wait to add more titles. Paranormal Romance readers need not despair however as there is much more to come there too. Writing has become an addiction and as soon as one book is over I'm hugely excited to start the next so you can expect plenty more in the future.

As many of my works reflect I am greatly influenced by the beautiful French countryside in which I live. I've been here in the South West for the past twenty years though I was born and raised in England. My three gorgeous girls are all bilingual and the youngest who is only six, is showing signs of following in my footsteps after producing *The Lonely Princess* all by herself.

I'm told book two is coming soon ...

She's keeping me on my toes, so I'd better get cracking!

KEEP READING TO DISCOVER MY OTHER BOOKS!

Other Works by Emma V. Leech

(For those of you who have read The French Fae Legend series, please remember that chronologically The Heart of Arima precedes The Dark Prince)

Rogues & Gentlemen

The Rogue

The Earl's Temptation

Scandal's Daughter

The Devil May Care

Nearly Ruining Mr. Russell

One Wicked Winter

To Tame a Savage Heart (March 23, 2018)

The Regency Romance Mysteries

[Dying for a Duke]

[A Dog in a Doublet] (January 26, 2018)

[The Rum and the Fox]

The French Vampire Legend

[The Key to Erebus]

[The Heart of Arima]

[The Fires of Tartarus]

[The Boxset] (The Key to Erebus, The Heart of Arima, The Fires of Tartarus)

The Son of Darkness (2018)

The French Fae Legend

[The Dark Prince]

The Dark Heart

The Dark Deceit

The Darkest Night (May 12, 2018)

Short Stories: A Dark Collection.

Stand Alone

The Book Lover (a paranormal novella)

Interested in a Regency Romance with a twist ?

Dying for a Duke

The Regency Romance Mysteries Book 1

Straight-laced, imperious and morally rigid, Benedict Rutland - the darkly handsome Earl of Rothay - gained his title too young. Responsible for a large family of younger siblings that his frivolous parents have brought to bankruptcy, his youth was spent clawing back the family fortunes.

Now a man in his prime and financially secure he is betrothed to a strict, sensible and cool-headed woman who will never upset the balance of his life or disturb his emotions ...

But then Miss Skeffington-Fox arrives.

Brought up solely by her rake of a step-father, Benedict is scandalised by everything about the dashing Miss.

But as family members in line for the dukedom begin to die at an alarming rate, all fingers point at Benedict, and Miss Skeffington-Fox may be the only one who can save him.

FREE to read on Amazon Kindle Unlimited..Dying for a Duke

Lose yourself in Emma's paranormal world with The French Vampire Legend series..... Book 1 is a FREE download on Amazon….

The Key to Erebus

The French Vampire Legend Book 1

The truth can kill you.

Taken away as a small child, from a life where vampires, the Fae, and other mythical creatures are real and treacherous, the beautiful young witch, Jéhenne Corbeaux is totally unprepared when she returns to rural France to live with her eccentric Grandmother.

Thrown headlong into a world she knows nothing about she seeks to learn the truth about herself, uncovering secrets more shocking than anything she could ever have imagined and finding that she is by no means powerless to protect the ones she loves.

Despite her Gran's dire warnings, she is inexorably drawn to the dark and terrifying figure of Corvus, an ancient vampire and master of the vast Albinus family.

Jéhenne is about to find her answers and discover that, not only is Corvus far more dangerous than she could ever imagine, but that he holds much more than the key to her heart …

FREE download

The Key to Erebus

Check out Emma's exciting fantasy series with hailed by Kirkus Reviews as "An enchanting fantasy with a likable heroine, romantic intrigue, and clever narrative flourishes."

The Dark Prince

The French Fae Legend Book 1

Two Fae Princes
One Human Woman
And a world ready to tear them all apart

Laen Braed is Prince of the Dark fae, with a temper and reputation to match his black eyes, and a heart that despises the human race. When he is sent back through the forbidden gates between realms to retrieve an ancient fae artifact, he returns home with far more than he bargained for.

Corin Albrecht, the most powerful Elven Prince ever born. His golden eyes are rumoured to be a gift from the gods, and destiny is calling him. With a love for the human world that runs deep, his friendship with Laen is being torn apart by his prejudices.

Océane DeBeauvoir is an artist and bookbinder who has always relied on her lively imagination to get her through an unhappy and uneventful life. A jewelled dagger put on display at a nearby museum hits the headlines with speculation of another race, the Fae. But the discovery also inspires Océane to create an extraordinary piece of art that cannot be confined to the pages of a book.

With two powerful men vying for her attention and their friendship stretched to the breaking point, the only question that remains...who is truly The Dark Prince.

The man of your dreams is coming...or is it your nightmares he visits? Find out in Book One of The French Fae Legend.

Available now to read for FREE on Kindle Unlimited.

The Dark Prince

Acknowledgements

Thanks as always to my wonderful editor for being patient and loving my characters as much as I do. Gemma you're the best!

To Victoria Cooper for all your hard work, amazing artwork and above all your unending patience !!! Thank you so much. You are amazing !

To my BFF, PA, personal cheerleader and bringer of chocolate, Varsi Appel, for moral support, confidence boosting and for reading my work more times than I have. I love you loads!

To the betas! Varsi, Alejandra Avila, Varsha Shurpali, Veronique Glotin Phillips. Thank you so much for all your help and advice.

I'm always so happy to hear from you so do email or message me :)

emmavleech@orange.fr

To my husband Pat and my family ... For always being proud of me.

Made in the USA
Middletown, DE
03 June 2021